Wanderer Springs

Wanderer Springs

a novel by

ROBERT FLYNN

Texas Christian University Press
Fort Worth

Library of Congress Cataloging-in-Publication Data
Flynn, Robert, 1932–
Wanderer Springs.
I. Title.
PS3556.L9W3   1987   813'.54   86-30014
ISBN 0-87565-071-6

Design by Whitehead & Whitehead

This book is printed on and bound with acid-free materials.

CONTENTS

In memory of Brigid Erin Flynn, 1959–1971

Wanderer Springs

COUNTY NAMES

The Ranchers

LANCE:

  Ma Lance, who brought her cattle to the county, and her three sons:

    Wilbur, who broke his back in a fall from a horse

    Earl, who shot Oscar Spruill, and probably Wilbur

    Delmer, "Earl's brother?"

  Cristobel, Delmer's wife, who dug up chickens and bore Delmer four children:

    Mattie, who discovered two strange children:

      Bobby Penn, who spoke Latin until cured by Sister Druscilla Majors

      Shirley, who had "turtle eyes," could not speak at all, and may have been the woman with the black cat.

    Etta, who eloped with an Indian

    Selena, who escaped her own wedding

    Lucy, everyone's favorite Lance, who played the organ at more than 200 funerals, and married

    Clifford Huff, veterinarian.

SPIVEY:

  Eli, who ate Rough on Rats to pay his debts, and his wife,

  Una Bea, who saved dishwater for chickens. Their son,

  Junior, who helped his father cut down trees to feed his cattle. His wife,

  Helen, who claimed her name was Helene. Their children:

1

Bubba, who gave his life to his country

Duane, who gave five years of his life to his country.

SPRUILL:

Oscar, who was shot in the barber's chair, and his wife,

Ruby, who went deaf like all the Spruill women, and their son,

> **Elmer,** who is remembered as a hunter although the only thing he ever killed was the last buffalo in the county.

KINCHELOE:

Josh, who saw an animal no one else ever saw, and went right on having children. One of his daughters,

> **Persia,** married Elmer Spruill. Their daughter,
>
> > **Jessie,** married J. C. Tooley. A grandson,
> >
> > > **Joel,** was sentenced to life in prison for murder and robbery.

BRYANT:

Monte, who almost lost his ranch to swindlers. His son,

Buster, who saved the ranch by an extraordinary ride. His son,

> **Boots,** who never made a ride like his father but was lord of the range.

The Farmers

CALLAGHAN:

Will, an Irish immigrant, who came to Texas to build a railroad, bringing his wife,

Carrie, who traveled to California unchaperoned, and their two sons:

> **Emmett,** a Texas bad man
>
> **Will II,** who died in antiseptic isolation. His wife,
>
> **Lettie,** who died on the front porch. Their son,

Will III, one of the great howevers, who spent his
entire life trying to become a human being.

McCARROLL:

Harmon, who became superstitious. His wife,

Mary, who lost the cows, her mind, and her daughter,

> **Beth**, who escaped her mother's clutches by marrying
> **Babe English** (who was shot at his trial), and escaped
> that tragedy by marrying
> **Ferguson the Fiddler** (who would drop a plow or milk
> pail to fiddle at a dance), and bearing him a son,
>
> > **Ira**, who spent his life trying to escape his Grand-
> > mother McCarroll's disease.

BALLARD:

Limp, who would rather fish than farm. His wife,
Ida, who had sixteen fences to cross going home. Their
nine children, one of whom,

> **John**, helped make the county what it was.

TOOLEY:

Horace, who bled to death unheard by his wife,
Jessie, who was addicted to silence, and their daughter,

> **Roma Dean**, whose naked body was found in Turtle
> Hole.

DRIESCHNER:

Emil, a skilled carpenter, and the best farmer in the
county, but Emil married a young woman who gave him
three daughters and then died, causing everyone to feel
superior to him. However, Emil raised his daughters right;
they worked like men and were yelled at like women.

> **Genevieve** married Guy Shipman and made a success
> of him.
>
> **Amanda** married Albert Slocum. When Emil took sick,
> Amanda went home to look after him, and Albert and
> the children moved in too. Albert let the farm run down,
> sold or lost Emil's tools, repaired the pig pen by tearing
> planks off the barn, and accidentally burned down the

house. Folks said Emil had to burn down the house to get Albert out of it. It was a Wanderer Springs joke. Albert was trying to start a fire in the wood stove by throwing coal oil on the wood. Then he absent-mindedly set the can of coal oil on the stove while lighting the fire.

SLOCUM:

Albert, who married Amanda Drieschner and led her to ruin. Their children,

> **George,** who died in the front yard during a norther
> **Walter,** who hid in the broom closet at the school
> **Emma Slocum Harkness,** who was rescued from her home and turned into a teacher by Hulda Codd.

TURRILL:

Grover, who married

Edna, at the request of both families. Their children,

> **Grover, Junior,** who was buried by cowboys
> **Billo,** who died of burns
> **Polly,** who was bumped to death in her mother's arms.

HIGHTS:

Virgil, killed by Joe Whatley. His wife,

Minnie, who refused to go farther. Their children,

> **Buford,** who picked up road-killed animals for dinner
> **Homer,** who took in five hippies.

COX-TURKETT:

Luster Cox, blacksmith for the Prod, who died in a fever epidemic and was plowed up every year. His daughter,

> **Zollie,** the county's first black child—a crime that had no penalty limited by law—who married
> **Tomoliver Turkett,** who died outside the fence. They had ten children, two of whom died in their country's wars, and
> **Haiti,** who died exercising her right to vote. Haiti had two children,
>> **Tom,** who died in Korea, and

Madeline, who worked as a maid, but whose son,
Tommy Waters, fled the acceptance his parents
never found.

Wanderer Springs Townspeople

DODSON:

Roy, who ran a trading post at the springs, and his son,
Fred, who ran away when his father sent him to cut
timber for a store and who saw gold when he died.

WORLEY:

Denver, a Confederate veteran. His daughter,
Augusta, who spent her life taking care of others.

PERKINS:

Millard, the barber, who went to a revival and lost his
wife,
Millie, who received a healing miracle.

HOPKINS:

Otis, the saint of Wanderer Springs. His daughter,
Rebel, who was addicted to innocence.

SHIPMAN:

Guy, whose wife, Genevieve, put him in the hardware
business. Their son,
Herschell, who waited at the window. Children sometimes called him "Anteater" because you could see up his
flared nostril. His wife,
Maisell, who was born in a dugout and couldn't endure
dirt. Their daughter,
Wanda, who ran away from home. Her daughter,
Dixie Davenport, who went in search of her
mother.

MURDOCK:

Reverend Malcolm, circuit riding preacher who organized

a Methodist congregation in every community in the county. His wife,

Trudy, who idolized her son,

   Wesley, who drove Eva Wiley out of retirement before marrying

   Fat Sue, who gave him an unexpected surprise,

      Marshall, who tried to save the world by improving it.

WHATLEY:

   Joe, who was hanged by the Methodists. His wife,

   Ozelle, who died in the boarding house fire when no one tried to save her. Their children escaped the fire and the town, except

      Benny, who owned the Live and Let Live Grocery. Benny married

      Fat Faye, who died in the store after giving Benny two children,

         Fat Sue, who married Wesley Murdock

         Maurice, who prowled. In a neighboring county, a farmer was burning an old haystack when he heard screams. Not knowing what to do, he went to the house and consulted the almanac. When he returned, he found a badly charred body in the ashes. The body was never identified, but since Maurice was known to sleep in haystacks and since he was never seen again, a lot of folks thought it was him. Before he disappeared, Maurice brought to the store a wife, **Nadine,** the only Whatley woman who wasn't fat. Nadine and Maurice had two children,

           Vivian, who married Otis Hopkins's daughter and spent his life trying to look good

           Biddy, who sold people what she thought they wanted.

BYARS:

Lowell, a farmer who married

Lulu, who died of frivolity. Lowell moved to town and married
Hulda Codd, who saved Lowell from ruin. Their grandson,

> **Hooper,** was known as a winner but carefully picked his opponents. Hooper returned as school superintendent with his wife,
> **Branda,** who let the water run while she was washing dishes.

McELROY:

> **Ed,** the postmaster who shot Bud Tabor and who was driven from the county by the unforgiving spirit of his daughter,

> > **Sherry,** who had been impregnated by Bud Tabor. For years "playing post office" was forbidden at school parties because folks thought it was a euphemism for what Bud and Sherry were doing. Sherry married
> > **J. C. McKinney,** who lost an arm in Lowell Byars's gin, and helped rear Bud Tabor's daughter. J. C. had been a bugler in World War I. Folks used to say, "Maybe he wasn't no hero over there, but it took a brave man to do what he did back here." During World War II, J. C. spoke in bond drives and everyone pretended he had lost his arm as a doughboy.

HESLAR:

> **Dr. Robert,** who came to Wanderer Springs to bring healing, his wife,
> **Debbie,** who shopped in Dallas and socialized in Center Point.

Center Point Townspeople

ARP:

> **Chris,** founder of the Center Point newspaper, who wrote

that folks in Wanderer Springs killed bullsnakes because
they believed the snakes sucked their milkcows dry. Some
folks did believe that, not because they had seen such a
thing, but because it confirmed their opinion of snakes.
His son,

    Clement, who published the news of Turtle Hole. His
son,

    Harley, who gave the public what they wanted.

Brassfield, the sheriff who was given power because he
looked like he had power.

Assorted politicians, officials, clerks and businessmen whose
only contribution to county history was stealing the
courthouse.

Those Without Known Family

Larissa Bell, who is believed to have had a husband although no one knows anything about him. Larissa was the
only person in the county who had enough faith in newspapers to die.

Dr. Vestal, whose profession permitted neither family nor retirement in the county.

Buck Fowler, who escaped the lures of Vernell Finch and
died in Augusta Worley's nursing home.

Wink Bailey, who was given power because he was believed
incapable of using it.

One-Eyed Finch, an oil smeller who had pretensions. In the
days of auto air-conditioning, folks thought Finch was putting on the dog pretending he had a cooler when he didn't.
He wasn't. He had driven with his windows up ever since
he had a wreck because a wasp blew in the car and when
he slapped at it, he knocked it between his crotch and the
car seat.

Vernell Finch. Someone once said that Vernell Finch was "old Wanderer Springs." Biddy Whatley said, "Vernell Finch ain't old Wanderer Springs. Vernell Finch is old Elma Dell."

Eva Wiley, prostitute, who found it difficult to retire.

The woman with the black cat, who may have been Shirley, one of the children found by Mattie Lance. Some thirty years after the disappearance of the woman with the black cat, a car broke down near Wink Bailey's Big Pile Up. In the car was a woman with three small children. Haskell Cheek stopped to offer assistance. His wife, Opalee, stayed with the children while Haskell took the woman to Center Point. Neither Haskell nor the woman have been seen since. Opalee said the woman had "turtle eyes." Some folks say the woman had a black cat but Opalee said it was a poodle.

Outsiders

Dr. R. B. (or **Arby,** no one knew for sure) **Binion,** a small, dapper man who traveled up and down the railroad with a folding chair, foot motor, and chest of dental tools. He got off the train at every stop and set up practice for the day— in the barber shop for men, in the depot for ladies. One day, Dr. Binion crumpled over his chair and died. His patients paid for his funeral out of what they owed him, but his grave was unmarked. They didn't think they owed him that much.

Sister Druscilla Majors, who brought her husband and her spiritual healing campaign to Center Point.

Papa Hinojosa, who promised his wife,

Mama, that she would never have to do stoop labor again. Their children,

Rosa, who expected her children to break her heart and her husband to break her face

Delores, who married Will Callaghan and lost her story
Her two daughters,

    Rebecca, who was a butterfly

    Margaret, who was a stray dog

Manuel, who invested in his country.

Odeen Sitz, who found God in horseflesh.

Dr. Roosevelt Hopkins, who believed there was something to be learned from those lives.

SAN ANTONIO

where history runs as deep as the river

GOING back was a mistake but it was one of those mistakes I had to make. Not to go back would have been bigger than a mistake, it would have been a sin. A mistake is something you do to yourself, like shooting yourself in the foot. A sin is something you do to others, like forgetting a friend. Like not going back for Jessie Tooley's funeral. Wanderer Springs taught me that.

That was one of the quaint values the Institute wanted me to write about. I was writing booklets about the Germans in Texas, the Wends in Texas, the Poles, the Chinese, so that schoolchildren named Hinojosa or Drieschner or Chinn could read about their heritage and know that they were the descendants of Abraham and Moses Austin, Luther and Carry Nation, George Washington and Samuel Colt. I outlined Texas history for them—the longhorn, the fence, the plow, the railroad, the windmill, the oil field, the highway, and the military installation.

"Write about Wanderer Springs," the director said. The Director of the Texas Institute for Cultural Research is from Chicago. He is also young and a member of a minority—those being unwritten requirements to give him a broad perspective on Texas. By its own rules the Director of the Institute cannot be from Texas, the South, or Southwest. Something about "political disinterest." Every effort was made to assure that the director's opinions were not colored by experience. In terms of political disinterest, a black ghetto in Chicago was considered somewhere east of Pennsylvania.

I am the token Texan at the Institute, my fifty years in Texas treated with amusement and awe. I am everything a black from a Chicago ghetto could expect a Texan to be. I am tall, lanky, talk with a drawl, and say ma'am. I have ridden horses, herded cattle, played football, and owned guns. I am a walking exhibit of Texas culture, brought out to demonstrate authenticity to natives who view Dr. Roosevelt Hopkins with suspicion. "This is Will Callaghan, the third," the director says. "A real Texan. His grandfather, uncle, and mother were all shot in gunfights." A benchmark of Texan machismo.

Roo, as the director likes intimates to call him, saw more stabbings, shootings, and beatings before he was eight than I have seen in a lifetime. But those were family, gang, and barroom fights with not a corral or showdown in sight. They were sudden, senseless, bloody killings, and guns were associated with crimes and cowardice, not heroism and romance. He imagined shootings in Texas were different.

With wise men from the East bearing grants, I portray a different kind of Texan. "This is Will Callaghan," the director says. "His grandfather was an Irish immigrant who came to Texas to build the railroad. His grandmother was from Vermont. Will spent most of his life in a small Texas town. How small was it, Will?"

"Wanderer Springs was so small there was only one Baptist Church. It was so small you had to go to Center Point to have a coincidence."

"Tell them about love in a small town."

"The only great lover we had was Bud Tabor." I remembered to drawl. "Bud was a married man, and Sherry McElroy's father shot him through Box 287. Ed McElroy was the postmaster and when Bud came in to get his mail, Ed stuck a pistol in the open end of the box and shot Bud in the eye. Ed was a conscientious man and he waited until Bud opened the box and looked inside so as not to deface government property.

"They never found Bud Tabor's eye; buried him without it. They fixed him up with a glass eye for the funeral, but afterwards Sherry and Bud's wife got in an argument over who got to keep it for a souvenir. Sherry won. She put it on a chain and wore it hanging down between her breasts. Folks used to say Bud may have gone to hell, but his eye went to heaven. Some folks' idea of heaven is mighty small." That's a Wanderer Springs joke.

"Were you a great lover, Will?" Roo is black, short, and cheerful enough for a "black is cheerful" poster. He loves playing straight man.

"The only time I came close, I was nuzzling Roma Dean Tooley's ear and I lost my chewing gum in her hair. It was Fleers bubble gum and it still had some of the sweet in it. I spent the next hour and forty-five minutes alternating between kissing her eyes and frisking her scalp, and holding my hands over her eyes while chewing her hair. Her mother called her three times before my jaws came unstuck.

"The only sex education we had in my day was Delmer Lance's pet heifer, Snuggles. Snuggles was raised on a bottle and was as friendly as you'd want a heifer to be. Until Delmer locked her in the barn with Earl's range bull. The next morning Snuggles was gone. Also the barn door. The top rail off the fence.

"Delmer chased the cow all over the county but Snuggles went wild as a new rope. One night Delmer was driving down the highway and ran over Snuggles. Delmer said he recognized her when she passed over the windshield by the puzzled look on her face. I spent half my life thinking I could recognize a bad girl by the puzzled look on her face."

I didn't mind playing Texas bumpkin. I have always been good at roles. I played "victory-or-death" Travis on the football field that was our Alamo. Like Bonham, who had returned to the Alamo knowing it was doomed, I had escaped Wanderer Springs and then returned there to teach school, out of loyalty. Or friendship. Or maybe to exact the retribution I thought I wanted to escape. Once I was back in Wanderer Springs, like Fannin, I vacillated between being a hero and a fool. It isn't easy to measure up in Texas.

Finally, I followed Deaf Smith to San Antonio de Bexar playing John Wayne playing David Crockett playing Coonskin Davy. We all have our skinning and grinning to do. The grant money made it possible for me to live in San Antonio and to send my children to the university, and it permitted the Institute to produce books and information for public schools and libraries in Texas, and for national and governmental demographics and social research.

I liked the job. It was similar to teaching but without the fawning on superiors; similar to writing the column of county history for the Center Point paper, but without the truckling to important people. And I believed I was helping the young people of Texas to understand the forces in their lives. But when Roo said, "Write about Wanderer Springs so that kids today will know what growing up in a small town was like," I balked. Texas is one of the most urban states in the union, but no one knows it yet. Certainly Texans don't. Even those living in Dallas and Houston think they're cowboys. They may have sold their saddles, but they're hanging on to their boots and guns. And every one of them takes the freeway in pursuit of the riches and pleasure at the end of the trail, believing that nothing can stop a salesman who keeps on coming, and that a contract nails coonskin to the wall.

Wanderer Springs goes back only three, at most four, generations. No one important lived there, nothing of importance transpired nearby, and the town was powerless to influence the times, even to shape its own destiny. Its history could be written in one sentence—born beside the railroad track, died beside the Interstate.

The new interstate highway bypassed the town, cutting it off from its last lifeline, turning it into an asphalt-age ghost town. There are still buildings there and a business—The Wanderer's Rest—which houses most of the people of the town, the old and infirm, most of them strangers to each other and to the town. They sit under shade trees or walk down streets they never knew, past houses they never visited, where rusting stop signs still guard once-dangerous crossings. Delivered to Wanderer Springs to die.

As a community, as a place where people live rather than die, Wanderer Springs is defunct, although its name still appears on county maps and although the cemetery continues to grow in Ira Ferguson's wheat field. But we were not the kind of Texans Roo was looking for—the Texans of legend and song who died at the Alamo, drove cattle to Kansas, fought Indians, and killed each other in gun duels. We were not oil barons or cattle kings. We were the kind of Texans who were on our way to someplace else and who for some reason got stuck in Texas and who for some reason breathed the Texas myth.

Roo had no understanding of rural Texas. Sometimes he imagined it as a modern Eden where we went skinny-dipping in sky-clear water, lounged in glades, frolicked in the grass.

I explained. "The reason you go skinny-dipping is because the only water is in dirt tanks and holes in creeks and it is red with mud and stains your clothes. The grass is about as inviting as bob wire. Haven't you ever heard of cactus, mesquite, grassburs, cockleburs, goatheads, bull nettle, or chiggers? And when it comes to glades a cow will get ahead of you every time. That's what makes the grass so green."

On the other hand, Roo believed Wanderer Springs was a Saharan wasteland with miles of nothing but sand and barbed wire fences. I suppose I was responsible for both misconceptions. It was the land of the mirage, the land of false hope, heartbreak, disillusion. The country was rich enough to draw those hungry for land, eager for isolated exemption, desperate for another chance, ripe for dreams. The railroad lured settlers and left a string of little towns it had platted, sold, and then abandoned.

The land was good enough to hold those who believed in hard work and predestination, but it was not fertile enough to reward them with more than sustenance for a lifetime of toil. Those who prospered were those who were rewarded for the work of others, like Otis Hopkins who shot his Aunt Velma, Dr. Heslar who discovered a gold mine in the infirmity of the old, and Ira Ferguson who was bound by loyalty to nothing but profit. Nevertheless, those who left the land were regarded as deserters, unable or unwilling to bear the burden of belonging.

It was not an ugly land, but it was plain, its best features of the utilitarian kind like a new cottonsack or gooseneck hoe. And like a cottonsack or hoe, the joy of it was quickly forgotten.

The country alternated between flood and drought. "The average rainfall is twenty inches," I told Roo. "But I've never seen an average year." It was a Wanderer Springs joke. In times of drought the wells went dry, cattle died, crops withered in the fields. In times of flood, the rivers washed away crops, soil, houses, bridges, roads, and livestock. The record high for the county was 120 degrees; the record low was twenty below zero.

One year Red River froze so solid it could be crossed by wagon. One year it was so dry the ground cracked open and swallowed Delmer Lance's chickens. One year the grasshoppers ate the crops so that the only thing the farmers had to eat was eggs. Dad said the hens ate so many grasshoppers the eggs had blood in them.

Every year high winds damaged crops and rooftops. Before the farmhouse was built a high wind blew away all the bedding that Grandmother had brought out of the dugout to air. She chased it across the prairie but what she recovered was so full of prickly pear it had to be burned. One year a high wind grounded a French air show and turned Otis Hopkins into a conscientious objector.

Roo, who remembered the noise, smells, and teeming humanity of the ghetto, found San Antonio about as isolated as he wanted to get. He shuddered at the spaces and "the awful silence of the plains," which he imagined as some post-holocaust still. The plains were never silent. The first sound a child heard was the wind outside the door. The wind whispered, whistled, shrilled, and howled. Insects droned, cattle lowed, dogs barked, passing their messages of alarm across the countryside, farm machinery clanked and roared. The first thing a child saw beyond his mother's face was the sky extending to the horizon. His first step was into the limitless land.

The terrible silence folks talked of was the absence of human sounds: laughing together, telling stories, making plans, expressing feelings and ideas. On the plains silence was not golden, silence was death. To withhold speech, to refuse to share feelings and plans was a fearful punishment, a powerful weapon, the only weapon some had.

When the Rural Electric Association brought electricity to the county, the first thing most folks bought was a radio. Avidly they listened to the weather, the market prices for cotton and slaughter hogs. The news elicited nothing but complaints but there was magic in the human voice, and some men and women talked more to the radio than to each other.

Roo paled at the emptiness of our lives. There was no television and for most no radio until after World War II, but our lives were not as barren as Roo imagined. Families worked together. Grandmother, who had been a school teacher in Vermont, taught Irish songs to Dad and Uncle Emmett as they worked in the fields and taught them the alphabet and multiplication tables by coal oil lamp when the work was done. There were no schools for blacks but Zollie Cox taught all her children the Bible and to read and write as she worked beside them in the field.

Folks got together for a dance played by Ferguson the Fiddler, who wasn't much of a farmer. He was long, gaunt, with a sad face, and all he liked to do was play his fiddle at dances, get drunk, and shoot at dogs that gathered to howl.

Until Joe Whatley bit off his thumb. After that he wasn't much of a fiddler.

Folks got together for the Mollie Bailey show or Sister Druscilla Majors's camp meeting. They went on picnics at Turtle Hole or Medicine Hill. They got together to worship, led by Brother Malcolm Murdock who had a voice that could be heard in Sand.

And they talked. At the gin, the barber shop, the grocery store. The men sat on the high curb in front of The Corner Drug and the women sat in cars between the depot and the Live and Let Live Grocery Store so they could watch the train come in, and see what farm wives were buying. They talked of their friends and enemies, polishing rumor into myth.

But the most exciting thing they talked about was DOOM. It was going to hail, or blow, or rain the bottom out. Or Otis Hopkins was going to foreclose. People loved the talk of doom and every successful preacher and politician knew it. Chris Arp built his newspaper around it, scoring his first triumphs by successfully predicting a yellow fever epidemic and a lynching. If the grasshoppers didn't get us, then the integration, or the Day of Judgment would. If we had been there at Wink Bailey's Big Pile Up probably half the town would have believed along with Wink that the end had come.

Some like Buster Bryant and Clifford Huff found fulfillment working with animals. Others followed obsessions, like Elmer Spruill spending his life searching for an animal that no one but Josh Kincheloe ever saw, or Mattie Lance looking for two strange children who weren't even hers.

There were women who found fulfillment in taking care of the needs of their families. Augusta Worley gave up her dream of husband and children to care for her ungrateful father and, after his death, gave her home and life to those who needed her care. Opal Drieschner became a son to her son-less father. "If I'm going to work like a man I want to be talked to like a man," she said. "I don't want to be yelled at like a woman."

Her sister, Amanda Drieschner Slocum, wasted her life caring for her good-for-nothing husband, Albert Slocum, and died of his imaginary heart attack.

Ida Ballard came to the county as a bride of sixteen and lived with her husband, Limp, in a dugout on the Mobeetie River, south of what would become Bull Valley. Limp, one of the first farmers in the county, had selected some worthless land near the river because Limp loved to fish. Folks didn't call him Limp because he was crippled, but because he lacked the ambition that was a commodity among the early settlers.

Ida charged groceries at Dodson's trading post until Limp made his first crop, and when the bill came to nine dollars and forty-two cents, Limp threatened to send Ida back to Iowa because he didn't want to be married to a spendthrift woman. "When I married Limp, my mama told me, 'That man will keep you at the wash tub the rest of your life and don't expect nothing better,'" Ida told me when I interviewed her for the column I was writing for the Center Point paper. "I couldn't go home and tell her she was right so I got down on my knees and promised that man that if he'd let me stay, I'd never ask for another nickle. More than a dollar of that bill was for his Tinsley chewing tobacco, but I never said nothing about that."

Limp let her stay but he refused to speak to her. For two weeks Ida heard nothing but the wind and the lobos sniffing and howling outside the dugout. When she ran out of flour, Ida was afraid to charge at the store, so she ground up redtop maize for bread. "Damn woman don't know how to make biscuits," Limp grumbled to no one in particular. Ida was happy just to hear a human voice.

Ida bore their first child unassisted—Limp was off fishing—while a lobo prowled outside the doorless dugout and killed a calf. "I've heard folks say them lobos won't eat a body," Ida said, "but it was folks that lived in houses that said it."

For two years Ida didn't go back to the store and at the end of those years, Limp bought her a hemp carpet for the dirt floor of the dugout. "I sat down on the ground and held it and cried," she said. "It was the first time in my married life that my feet had been clean. I wrote Mama, first time since I married, and told her where I was and that she could come see me now because I had a carpet on the floor."

Her mother never came, and Ida never went back to Iowa, never saw her family from the day she married. She bore Limp nine children, most of them born in a dugout. "He may be slack but he ain't limp," folks said. It was a Wanderer Springs joke. All the children left home as soon as they were able.

"Almost left home myself," Ida said. Limp told her to take the wagon and get him some chewing tobacco. He told her to go to Dodson's trading post at Wanderer Springs instead of the closer Bull Valley store because he hadn't paid his bill at Bull Valley. It was after fences had come to the county and Ida had sixteen fences to cross, having to climb out of the wagon sixteen times to open wire gaps that could be closed only by straining and pushing.

Ida got to Dodson's trading post, got Limp his tobacco, some flour and coffee for herself, some horehound candy for the kids, and started back toward a dugout, a shiftless husband, and six sore-eyed kids. Sixteen gates to close. "'How many gates back to Mama?' I asked myself," Ida told me. "But I went back to Limp and the kids. Maybe it wasn't what I thought my life would be, but it was what my life was."

How could I convince school children, or anyone else, that Ida Ballard and Amanda Slocum were not spineless victims of low esteem and abusive men? We hadn't seen it that way. Amanda Slocum following her husband, Albert, on his way to ruin was our example of what love was. Albert Slocum and her sons were Amanda's burden, and she bore it as faithfully and bravely as any saint.

Amanda's daughter, Emma Slocum Harkness, escaped that burden and took up one of her own, educating the children of the county. Others might think Emma a career woman, but in Wanderer Springs Emma was not liked or respected because her brother George got drunk on moonshine their father had made, lay in the yard amid coffee grounds, egg shells and rusty cans during a blue norther and died of exposure. It was Emma's job to save him. No matter how unfair our opinion, not to have picked up her mother's burden made Emma less of a woman in our eyes. If the children couldn't understand that, they couldn't understand anything about us.

I tried to explain to Roo. "It's easier to write the history of a state than it is the history of a small town. There aren't any major movements or events, just families and relationships. You can't understand us without understanding them. Amanda Slocum, and Earl and Delmer Lance, and Grover and Edna Turrill had as much to say about what we were like as Washington, and Jefferson, and Lincoln.

"And it can't be written chronologically, precedent and antecedent, cause and effect." Time for us was not a continuous line on which events were strung like beads, not a chart or graph outlining expenditures, expansion, or growth. The reality of our lives was not where we had been or what we had done but where we came from; not just the geographical locale, but the historical womb. We were born into a web of identity that reached to the geographical and historical limits of Wanderer Springs County.

Time was a web that tied us together, so that Earl Lance's life, and Eli Spivey's death, and Grover Turrill's dream of California were woven into my life. They had come to the county as young men, or like Denver Worley they had lived so long that I knew most of them not just by name and myth. I knew their faces, their voices, their frailty.

"That's why you should write it," Roo said. Roo imagined that writing history was like Ida Ballard making certain sixteen wire gaps were securely closed behind her. But it was more like the Hights deciding which parts of road-killed game to discard and which to put in the stew.

"That's why I can't." It's not easy to write whether Houston intended to fight or run at San Jacinto, whether Fannin was tragic or inept, whether Crockett's death at the Alamo saved him from ridicule as a tiresome old yarnspinner who had out-lived his audience. Nevertheless, that was easier than writing about Denver Worley, one of those gallant men in Confederate gray who had ridden with Terry's Texas Rangers, but who in Wanderer Springs tyrannized his daughter and sat on the porch shaking a purse full of coins to entice girls close enough to fondle. Or Buster Bryant who had made the greatest ride in the county but had roped his own horse. Or Bud Tabor who was shot through Box 287. In any objective light of history their lives were absurd. It was only in Wanderer Springs that their story merited more than a chuckle.

"Can't you write about small town values?" Roo asked.

"What values? 'Small Town' is where it's okay to spend a lifetime but not a weekend. Where repetition is the spice of life. Where when there's nothing to do, there's also no place you've never been." I was slipping into my country bumpkin role because I didn't know how to answer his question.

"'Small Town' is where you can't pick your friends, you can't choose your neighbors, and your ancestors have already decided your enemies. Small town is where you use family to explain fault or flaw, where reputation is the coin of the realm. You can't start over. You're always who you used to be, and who your parents were, and who the town says you are."

"Who were you?"

"I was Roma Dean Tooley's sweetheart."

"Is that the girl who drowned?"

The girl who drowned clung more tightly to my neck dead than she ever had alive. "I was supposed to be a hero and the only way you could be a hero was to beat Center Point. If you were a boy. If you were a girl you were supposed to be loved for being lovable, and of course for being a virgin."

I sounded more bitter than I had intended. "I'm sorry,

Roo. They're just stories and I don't want to write them." There is dead pain and live pain. History deals with dead pain and I wanted Roma Dean Tooley to rest in peace.

Roo was surprised. "It's what you talk about."

When you live in San Antonio with San Fernando Cathedral, the Spanish Governor's Palace, the Menger Hotel, the Alamo and other missions you could talk about history. San Antonio prided itself on being unique. Wanderer Springs was identical to a thousand other prairie eyesores that met their deaths at the hands of the automobile. All that was left were the stories.

"It's dead," I said. "Wanderer Springs is dead."

I had thought I was free of Wanderer Springs, free of that kind of belonging, free of the Will Callaghan they knew—until Boots Bryant called. I had known Boots most of my life and much of that time we had been best friends. When I had left Wanderer Springs ten years earlier, Boots had promised to keep in touch. Keeping in touch meant calling to tell me who had died. In Wanderer Springs, death was the only visitor.

"Will, Jessie Tooley died today," Boots said. "I thought you'd want to know."

I did want to know but I preferred a letter mailed after her funeral. I made a note to send flowers, expensive but not elaborate, with a simple but sincere message. "Sympathy." Death lends felicity to clichés, as though compared to the deceased, even an old saw seems lively.

"I called Hooper and Marshall, and talked to Rebel," Boots said. "Rebel said she and Vivian were coming, and Marshall's coming. Hooper said he wouldn't try to come. He's in California, you know. Never was one of us. I don't reckon there'll be many there." Although I hadn't seen Boots in years, I imagined him looking as though he had just thumbed back his Stetson to better examine his cards. "Jessie don't have any kin. Just us." His voice sounded like his back was up.

Boots, who had always been slight but tough, would be

standing beside the telephone in that straight-backed, square-shouldered way caused by old rodeo injuries. Boots did not pamper himself; I couldn't expect him to indulge me. "Just us" meant "just you." Jessie's only daughter, Roma Dean, had been my high school sweetheart and because she drowned, Jessie became my liability, my family.

"I just don't see how I can get away at this time."

"I think you'd better come, Will." That circumlocution was a way of telling me that I was not free of Wanderer Springs until Jessie Tooley was laid to rest.

"I'll try, Boots. I just don't see how I can do it, but I'll try"—my circumlocution for "you've got me by the balls but I'm going to pretend the decision is mine."

Texans love gestures. Like the Alamo. Like Captain Mc-Nelly threatening to attack Mexico with his band of thirty Rangers. Like Elmer Spruill shooting at the first airplane in the county. Some folks said he thought it was a mysterious bird, but he didn't. He shot at it because it was the biggest thing he'd ever seen. Going back was my gesture that I was burning the mortgage, thumbing my nose at Wanderer Springs. I didn't need their approval. I had an identity beyond their ken.

I told Roo that I had to take a few days off to attend a funeral of a friend. "Small town is where you go home only when someone dies," I said.

"Where will you stay?" Roo imagined that I would throw a bedroll beside a small campfire on the prairie.

"I'll stay with Boots Bryant, an old friend. He has a new oldtime house." Roo loved the expression. Having grown up on jive he now collected what he imagined were westernisms.

I called the girls. They were only a hundred miles away, attending a university best known for its defensive tackles, but we did most of our visiting by telephone. We no longer seemed comfortable with each other. When they visited me they were restless in their old rooms, unhappy that nothing was the same. When we talked they were uneasy that I made plans, a life without them.

The girls had an apartment off-campus, to save money they said, and when I visited they were guarded and self-conscious, the way they had been when they were children and I sat in their imaginary playhouse and let them serve me invisible cake. As though our habitations were still that far apart.

I didn't like who they were when they were with their friends and I didn't like the kind of people I was required to associate with in order to visit my children. Rebecca, the oldest and in her third year of college, was always surrounded by football players who thought spitting was an indoor sport and law students who believed cross-examination was a parlor game. When with them, Becky was brassy, argumentative, assertive, and self-assured.

Maggie attracted effeminate radicals who drank cheap wine, mumbled obscenities, and practiced loathing, and emotional cripples who drank cheap wine, mumbled obscenities, and practiced self-pity. Margaret adapted to them, subduing her intelligence, her personality, to play nurse to their wounds. Blessed is the father whose daughters are wise toward men.

Rebecca answered when I called. "Hi, Dad, just a minute," she said. "Hello, Dad," Maggie said, picking up the other telephone. "Can you hold on a second?" I waited while Rebecca got her nail file and Maggie got a soft drink from the refrigerator. If you do not like waiting, you should not have children.

I told the girls I was going to Wanderer Springs for a few days and asked if they could go with me. Neither could. Maggie had a paper that was due, and Rebecca had a date to a football game and the most important party of the year after the game. Had the arrangements been reversed they both would have gone. Rebecca would have put off a paper as quickly as Maggie would have broken a date.

"I don't want to go and I'd really like someone to go with me," I pleaded.

"Why do you have to go if you don't want to go?" Rebecca asked. Rebecca, who had spent ten of her twenty years in Wanderer Springs, could not imagine that kind of belonging. Rebecca was whoever she wanted to be and if she belonged any place it was on the campus. When she came to San Antonio she tried to see everyone she knew, told delightful tales about weird professors, wild parties, and all the strange and bewildering people she knew, and she was gone. Rebecca was a butterfly, giving beauty and joy wherever she went but never lighting for long.

Maggie was a stray dog, radiating affection, saying little, happy to be with people she loved. She stood beside her grandmother in the kitchen listening to Mama talk of the mysteries of cooking and old age. She helped Rosa set the table and listened to the heartaches of husband and children. She sat on the porch with Gilbert who said nothing. She talked to Manuel about the hurt and anger of broken dreams.

Rebecca ran through life tasting everything. Maggie absorbed. Rebecca was half past tomorrow; Maggie was half past yesterday. Although Maggie had spent fewer years in Wanderer Springs, she had not cut her ties to any place. "Why do you have to go?" she asked, recognizing the irrelevance of Becky's conditional clause—if you don't want to.

Not for Jessie Tooley's funeral. That was a gesture, acknowledgment that I was not yet free of their opinions. I was going back for the reason man always returns—to find something he has lost. "Jessie Tooley died."

"Is that the woman who didn't hear her husband die in the yard?" Rebecca asked. With her lawyer's mind, Rebecca went for the jugular. Maggie would have asked if that was the woman who went deaf.

Jessie was a Spruill and like the other Spruill women, occasionally deaf. Her husband, Horace, had caught his arm in the haybaler and unable to free himself, had amputated his arm with his Case knife, walked to the house, and bled to death not twenty feet from the kitchen door, his cries for help unheard.

"Did I know her?" Maggie asked, unwilling to give up anything from her past.

"I don't think so," I lied. Once when I had taken the girls to see Augusta Worley in The Wanderer's Rest, we had suddenly come upon Jessie Tooley in the corridor. I didn't speak because Jessie had been permanently deaf since Roma Dean drowned. After years of exile in silence her face had taken on a bemused look, her eyebrows and one corner of her mouth pulled up as she sat gluing two water glasses together at the mouths after putting a plastic rose inside. Out of deference to Jessie, everyone in Wanderer Springs had bought at least one. When I moved to San Antonio, I had discarded three of them.

Jessie dropped the glasses in her lap and caught Maggie by the arm, pulling her close. With her other hand she felt Maggie's long hair uncut—like Roma Dean's—since birth. Jessie's face broke apart with expression. "Off came her hair," Jessie said, her voice creaky from disuse. "Got on the bus, went over the hill and off came her hair," snatching at some memory of Roma Dean cutting her hair for me. Maggie had cried and I had gently pulled her out of Jessie's grasp. I didn't want Maggie to remember that ancient hand fumbling for memories in that place where memories were disposed.

"Why did you say you had to go?" Rebecca asked. Maggie would never repeat a question I had avoided answering. Rebecca, like her mother, liked precision. Maggie took after me, believing that not everything had to be underlined.

"It's just something I have to do," I said. A mistake I had to make.

"How long are you going to be gone?" Maggie asked.

"Just a few days. I'll see you on the way back."

"How is Abuela?" asked Maggie, who insisted on being recognized as part Mexican. Rebecca seemed not to care either way.

"Your grandmother seems okay, but Rosa is worried about her."

"What else is new?" Rebecca asked. Although they lived in the same house, Rosa called her mother from work every day. Mama had given life to Rosa. It was a debt for which there was no forgiveness.

We talked about Rosa, who spent every day cleaning houses in Alamo Heights and Olmos Park, and her husband, Gilbert, who was embarrassed that his wife worked as a maid. Especially when he was drinking. After Papa died, Gilbert should have been the head of the family and he tried, but Manuel was a talker. Manuel, Papa's youngest child, owned three or four cars, all of them sporting University of Texas decals and NOWHERE BUT SAN ANTONIO bumper stickers. Manuel never traded in a car, he gave it to a relative. Almost everyone in the family had one of Manuel's cars.

"Tio Manuel was here yesterday," Maggie said. Rebecca would not have mentioned it. Manuel had been arrested on drug charges when he lived in Wanderer Springs. The charges had been dropped and Manuel had become a successful and powerful man without seeming to work. "He took us to dinner." Manuel had given them stereos and color television sets and had offered them a car which I would not permit them to accept.

"What's Manuel doing these days?" I had reached the age where I had to ask my children to interpret for me the behavior of others, but I was not so much out of touch as out of patience.

Rebecca said nothing because she was a future lawyer. Maggie said nothing because she was protective towards her uncle, and because Manuel and I were no longer friends. "How is he doing?" I amended the question.

"Okay," Maggie said. "He said Gloria was already reading and she isn't six yet. She's going to be a doctor. Mario is still going to be an astronaut."

"Isn't anyone going to be a school teacher?"

"Poor Dad. How did you get in this family?" Rebecca asked.

"Your mother invited me," I said.

Having laughed together, it was a good time to say our goodbyes. I hung up the phone and sat in silence, paralyzed with the fear known only to parents. My children were living in a world filled with ordinary people who had extraordinary power to harm. Manuel, whom Delores loved most, was one of those people.

Manuel was ambitious for his children, years before he had children. "There ain't no Mexican kid going to crawl out of a Crystal City spinach patch or Edgewood school and become president. The only chance my kids have is if I have the bread to buy them the best education, the best clubs, the best people. My kids are going to be able to buy anything they want.

"Only thing bigger than the law is money," Manuel said. "Money is God. And for a poor Mexican the only way to God is through drugs. Coke is Jesus, Mary, and Joseph. Marijuana is the Holy Ghost."

Rebecca would sample drugs for recreation. That was not my fear. My fear was that quiet, sensitive Maggie, who sheltered strays and romanticized the poor, would sample Manuel's ideas that were more addictive than his drugs. "The government has always decided who can be rich, and they're never going to be let it be someone like Papa who worked himself to death and never had a dime. They don't want to stop drugs; they just want to decide who gets the money. If they wanted to stop drugs they would have arrested Dr. Heslar. They didn't stop anything by arresting me."

Manuel said that he no longer sold drugs but was "into

investments and land speculation." Manuel invested only in what he believed were unethical enterprises—those that legally destroyed the environment, endangered life or public health, or plundered the public treasuries. It had made him wealthy. It had also given him revenge on a country that did not reward honesty and hard work.

"I tried being good," he said. He had been arrested and beaten by Rangers while participating in a migrant workers' strike. "Looking good is a hell of a lot more fun."

I hadn't argued with him. I remembered too well the rewards of looking good.

Rebecca would find acceptance and success as a lawyer, perhaps, with Manuel's money behind her, even a politician, addicted to power. I was afraid that Maggie would be addicted to innocence like Rebel Whatley. Or, like Manuel, to vindication.

THE ROAD TO RED RIVER

a map, a wedding, and a brief history of Wanderer Springs County

I LEFT San Antonio early in the morning to catch the sunrise on the hill country. It was at best an eight-hour drive to Wanderer Springs, and after the hill country there was a lot of distance between scenery. Like most roads in Texas, it was a good one. The Texas Highway Department believes that life is transition and its job is to pave the conjunctions. Texans believe the Constitution guarantees the pursuit of happiness in a private automobile.

The journey was less through space than through time— the time of the railroad and the windmill, the time of the unshuttered window and the unlocked door, milking time and the small prairie town, where hats and gloves were not for show and broken fingernails were honorable, where weather forged character and face, and determined the pace and purpose of the day.

In San Antonio I had forgotten to look out the window each morning for the threat of sandstorm or the promise of rain. In Wanderer Springs life was in the sun, the rain, the wind, the soil, and we lived because God ordained it. In San Antonio life was slow and indoors. Only the poor toiled in solitude and the sun. No one else wanted to get that far from entertainment. In San Antonio the wind sounded lovely in the trees.

The farther I got from San Antonio the farther I got from

trade unions, JCs, debutantes, the arrogance of Washington, the fads of New York, the idolization of the useless; specialty shops, French style apartments, Swiss Chalet condominiums, and homes in the English manner with Old English lampposts and security personnel in Old English guardhouses; where consumption was an end in itself and food, books, entertainment, everything, was to be devoured and forgotten. Nothing was to last, even in memory.

I was driving into the land of generalities—general store, general delivery, general practitioner, general business, general concerns, and as a general rule, generally known. It was the land of the long haul, of root hog or die, of hunker down. It was a land of waiting for the mail, for the children to come home, waiting for rain, for spring, for milking, planting, harvest, waiting to die, and waiting for the second coming. The land of the ubiquitous thermometer, rain gauge, and rocking chair.

When I had attended the one-room Bull Valley School, Hulda Codd Byars had required us to learn about Wanderer Springs by drawing a map of Texas, roughly the reverse of learning about biology by drawing an amoeba. Once we had drawn, or traced, the map, Miss Codd helped us fill in the topography. "Imagine that you start at the top with a too-hot iron, scorching the panhandle flat, pressing in the caprock, making wrinkles across the middle, putting deep creases from El Paso to the Big Bend that merge with the ripples in the hill country, and pushing all the moisture to East Texas and the Gulf Coast."

Miss Codd extolled ironing as an example of the pioneer virtue of self-reliance. She told a story of Jim Bowie dying in the Alamo in a linen shirt ironed by the same hand that wielded the Bowie knife. It was likely as true as most of the stories about Bowie, and, like most inspirational stories, it succeeded best with those who had already discovered the virtue. Unlike most inspirational stories it did not require the death of a single Mexican, Indian, or Yankee, those being the most likely candidates for killing by heroes.

"Now tack it down with Houston, Dallas, and San Antonio," Miss Codd instructed, "and without looking at your book, locate the capital in Austin, and way up on Red River but not quite in the Panhandle, Wanderer Springs County, and right in the middle of the county, Wanderer Springs."

Despite the many times I told the girls the way Hulda Codd described the state, they never quite got the picture. Maybe it was their unfamiliarity with the iron. Maybe it was because Wanderer Springs was already disappearing from the maps, and the idea of pinpointing it along with Houston, Dallas, and San Antonio offended their sense of proportion.

Although I hadn't been to Wanderer Springs in ten years, at one time the road had been the strongest cord in our lives, connecting us to Papa's illness, Rosa and Gilbert's fights, Manuel's anger. We had driven the road often, Delores and I, taking the children to visit their grandparents—going to San Antonio for Christmas with the car loaded with presents and Delores and the girls singing carols, returning home, the car filled with the things Delores could not get in Wanderer Springs. Masa, corn shucks, a hog's head.

Except for Manuel, Delores's family did not visit us in Wanderer Springs. So that Delores would have some help when Rebecca was born, I had gone to San Antonio to get Rosa, who cleaned houses in Alamo Heights but refused to work in the far north suburbs of Castle Hills and Shavano Park. It was too far from the heart of San Antonio. There was too much space, too much room between houses; it was too far from stores and crowds. On the road to Delores in Wanderer Springs Rosa was troubled by the distance, the emptiness. "How do you know where you are?" she had asked. I had laughed. We did not identify with ice houses, or bus stops, or street corners. We identified with the land: the Tooley Place, Earl's Lake.

Rosa was homesick before we got to Wanderer Springs.

She cried for Mama, Gilbert, her children, for crowds and noise. "Mama needs me," she said. After two days I put her on the bus that would return her to San Antonio.

After I got out of the army I had enrolled at a small state college near San Antonio because it had a reputation for being easy—I wasn't looking for a challenge—and because it was small, in a small town, and a long way from Wanderer Springs. I had always known I would go to college. It was one of those things I understood without being told.

Delores said she had never thought of going to college until a high school teacher said, "Of course you're going to college. What excuse do you have for not going to college?" When Delores explained that her family had no money, the teacher said, "Let's get you a scholarship."

Even with her scholarship Delores had to convince her family. She was going to be the first in her family to graduate from high school and the thought of college was terrifying. Every one of them had told me the story of the day Delores came home and said she wanted to go to college.

"College," Mama said, as though she was saying the word for the first time. Mama had an enormous capacity for sharing the pains and joys of her children, smothering their tears and giggles in her ample bosom. What she clutched to her bosom now was emptiness. She had been part of every laugh, every sniffle, every heartbreak. College was beyond her understanding, beyond her sharing. Mama's broad, sensitive face was clouded with uncertainty and fear. "You should help your brother. Manuel should go to college and make a teacher." She said "teeshur" in a soft, reverential way. Next to priest, teacher was the holiest word she knew.

"What do you want to go to college for?" Rosa asked. Everyone thought Rosa, with the long aristocratic face, light skin, and proud Spanish mouth, was the pretty one, the one who was meant to get married and have babies. In high school Rosa had worn a freshly ironed dress every day. She had dropped out of school to marry Gilbert, a war hero, and now she had two children, and a job cleaning and ironing in Alamo Heights. "Do you think college will teach you how to have kids?"

Gilbert, a big man whose dark handsome face was marred with scars on his eyebrow, his mouth, and his chin from fighting in ice houses when he was drunk, was so shy when sober as to be inarticulate. "Delores," he began, his face darkening with embarrassment, his eyes darting about as he searched for words. "Delores is smart."

"You going to be a nun?" Manuel asked. Manuel was a serious child who made As in school and read books at home until his mother told him to go outside and play.

"What do you know about it?" Rosa said to Gilbert. "You didn't even go to high school."

"I got a—a" Gilbert stuttered. Gilbert had passed the high school G.E.D. while in the Marines.

"You got a head for fighting, that's what you got," Rosa said. During the week Gilbert's slow tongue brought him scorn, but alcohol freed Gilbert from the anger and hurt and on the weekends he was the terror of the ice houses, and he took no abuse from Rosa.

"Delores thinks she is too good to get married and have babies," Rosa said.

"Delores wants babies," Mama said, horrified, as though Rosa had said Delores was lesbian.

"Delores wants—" Gilbert began tentatively.

"You don't know nothing about it," Rosa said.

"No fighting," Papa said. Papa was not as tall as Gilbert but he was strong. He had been the strongest man in Crystal City when he took his young bride and left the stoop labor of the fields to lift bags of cement and concrete forms in San Antonio. He sought the hardest jobs because they were the easiest to get, spoke English at work to get ahead, and English at home so that his children would have an advantage at school. Every year he found it more difficult to compete for jobs with younger men.

Papa was beginning to stoop and nagging pain had weakened his confidence and enthusiasm, but Papa was a proud man, too proud to admit that sometimes his muscles ached so that he had to drink alcohol in order to sleep. In his home Papa was boss. "College is expensive," he said. Papa, who had once promised his bride that their children could do anything, had learned to be cautious.

"I have a scholarship," Delores said. "I can get a campus job. I can pay my own way."

Papa studied the strong hands that were beginning to knot with arthritis. "Delores can go to college now, and when Manuel is ready, she can help him," he declared.

Mama cried and hugged Manuel and kissed his forehead as though he were leaving for college that day. Manuel beamed at Delores. Manuel wanted to go to college and now Delores could go, too. Gilbert patted Delores on the back, struggling for words. Rosa hugged Papa. "I won't leave you, Papa," she said.

Delores got a job in the college library and was in one of my classes, but I didn't speak to her. It wasn't that I was prejudiced against Mexicans; I was fearful of anything that was strange. Not only was she Mexican, she was from the city.

I listened to others talk about her. "Hot tamale," the frat men said, "and she doesn't wear too much makeup." "Mexican, but she doesn't overdress," said the sorority sisters. I sat behind her in class. I studied in the library so I could watch her shelve books or smile at those who needed help.

There was a hint of the elegant savage about her—proud, graceful carriage, and when she stood on tiptoe to reach the top shelves, something caught in my throat. She was in the freedom of her youth before the knowledge of her sex laid its burden upon her. She had brown skin, and large dark eyes that flashed. Sometimes her eyes turned to me and I turned my attention to my books.

One day in Texas history class she said, "Unless you're Mexican you can't understand what it's like to have a Ranger knock open your door and say, 'You that Meskin that's causing trouble?'"

I think the other students had been as astounded as I. Even the professor was shocked. The Rangers were more than just historical heroes, they were religious giants of the Old Testament order with a pistol-pointing "Thou art the man" righteousness. At the height of their glory they weren't law enforcement officers, they were dispensers of justice.

It was one of those things that I, along with the class and the professor, knew without knowing that we knew, until Delores brought it to our attention. No one in the class thanked her for it. Some defended the Rangers; some attacked the Mexicans. A young woman from Louisiana yelled, "If you don't like the way we do things go back where you came from." Someone asked, "Why is she taking Texas history?" Mexicans, no matter where they were born, were outsiders; why would they be interested in our history?

Delores might have forever remained a stranger had she not been attacked by the class. At that moment she became flesh and blood to me. One of "us." I knew what it was like to go from tacit acceptance to personal rejection. I apologized to her for the class's behavior, for not coming to her defense. I expected her to be humiliated.

"I'm Mexican so they say 'dumb Mexican,'" she said, finding the incident amusing. "If I weren't they'd say 'dumb broad.'" She was four years younger than I, had never been out of the state of Texas, knew little of what life had to offer but much of what it might require. All my life I had sought approval; Delores didn't expect it. Delores feared no one. I wanted her on my side.

I don't know at what point wanting her friendship, wanting her acceptance turned to wanting her love. As I had never known a Mexican-American, I was forced to use the popular media as my guide to dating a chicana at a time when misrepresentation had become an art form. Every night for a week I took Delores to a bar that featured Lone Star and loud guitars, and then parked outside her dorm. I wasn't trying to seduce her; I didn't think that possible. I wanted to be as close to her, to touch as much of her, to know as much of her as I could. It resembled wrestling. Delores said she wasn't going to see me any more.

"I thought you liked this."

"I hate this. I hate beer. I hate loud music. I hate it when people can't talk, when people aren't who they say they are."

I didn't know what she was talking about. "Who do you want me to be?"

"Be yourself. Is this what you do with your friends?"

I wasn't trying to impress my friends, and none was from the city. My friends sat under a tree and threw rocks in the river. We lay under the stars. We walked along country roads. Sometimes we talked.

"Do that with me," Delores said.

I took her to the cemetery; I'm not sure why. We walked among the graves and talked about the stories on the tombstones—those who had died young, those born in another state, another country, those whose lives were so entwined they shared a common stone. "You're fun to be with," she said. I was pleased and surprised. I had always been a sidekick.

We went swimming in the Guadalupe River and had a picnic on a small gravel island. I told her about Wanderer Springs and Dad living alone, hoping I would return, and how I wasn't sure I wanted to go back, and how I wanted to be a hero and the only way was football and war. I told her that nothing I did could change the way the town felt about me.

Delores talked about Papa's pride and pain, about Mama's

love and fear, about Rosa who wanted to be spoiled by love, and Gilbert who had failed her by not being the hero she thought she had married. In Korea he had been a Marine; in San Antonio he was a Mexican. Gilbert could not admit his failure, could not ask Rosa's forgiveness and punished her for not understanding. She talked about Manuel who was told in school that any boy could be president of the United States and was told out of school they did not mean him.

As she talked I listened to the music of her voice. Her words were soft with a strange tinkly intonation. Her lips slid effortlessly, wonderously over her teeth, and her silky eyelids slowly closed. I loved her. Sometimes I wonder if any human being knows what love is. Sometimes I think I recognize love only in retrospect, but at that moment I knew. And when I tried to get close to her, to touch her, to know her, to take her unto myself, it was not like wrestling, it was like sliding into myself and discovering who I was meant to be.

How does a man dare ask a woman to give up everything for him? That's what I asked Delores, not knowing what I was asking, not realizing how much I was asking her to give up. Her everything didn't seem like much to me. "Marry me," I said.

She shook her head and closed her eyes. "We're too differ-ent." I thought she meant our complexions, and I laughed at her, I teased her, I enumerated my prospects. She smiled. She kissed me. "I love you," she said, "but we are too different."

I went to San Antonio to meet Delores's family and prove that I was not prejudiced. Mama met us on the porch, crying into her apron. Gilbert sat on the porch drinking a beer which he lifted in greeting. Rosa, her children hiding in her skirt, stood beside Mama, arms spread, waiting to hug and kiss us both. Manuel stood at one side, waiting to be noticed. Papa waited at the door with dignity, and everyone crowded around to see him welcome me into his house.

I stayed with them, crowded as we were, in the house on

Buena Vista. It wasn't just the house that was crowded—the street was filled with people, the neighborhood, the corner grocery store. When Mama cooked, everyone crowded into the kitchen. When Papa went into the living room, everyone crowded into the living room. When Delores and I went into the back yard to talk, everyone followed.

The Hinojosas were courteous, friendly, generous. I was an honored guest but I was not one of them. When I looked at Delores I could see it in her eyes. I was not family. I thought it was the color of my eyes, the inflection of my words, the differences that made us charming or dull. It was years before I realized it was the odor of strange practices, of unfamiliar places.

"Are you going to take Delores away?" Manuel asked.

He was so serious I laughed. I thought Delores would be embarrassed, that she would change the subject. She waited with the others for my answer. Behind their eyes I could see fear nibbling like mice behind a glass window. "Delores will always be your sister no matter who she marries or where she lives," I said.

Not even Delores thought I had answered the question.

I thought I had performed splendidly in my role of winsome suitor. I had showed surprise and delight at Mama's cooking, teased Delores about her tortillas, complimented Rosa on her house cleaning, helped Manuel with a school paper, gone to the ice house where I persuaded Gilbert to ignore a slight and come home for supper, and added just the right touch of modesty when telling Papa that I would soon graduate from college, that I could always get a job teaching, and that I would someday inherit a farm in northwest Texas. When we got back to school Delores told me she couldn't see me any more. "You are so funny," she said. "I will want you too much and I can't have you."

I promised to change. I promised to live in San Antonio, on Buena Vista Street, in the same house with Mama and Papa, Gilbert and Rosa, and Manuel. Delores closed her eyes and shook her head as though I was deliberately stupid. I was running out of time; I was going to graduate in a few months. I didn't have a trump so I played a wild card. I persuaded Delores to meet my family although I was afraid meeting Dad would convince her how different we really were.

The trip to meet Dad went badly from the beginning. Delores's knowledge of small towns came from books and movies and she saw the open country as menace, the small towns as pockets of prejudice, superstition, and suspicion.

Delores had never been so far north and as we neared the county she said, "Where are all the people?" I stopped at the top of the railroad overpass. "There it is," I said. Spread before us, a mile square, was Grandfather's land—the unbroken prairie, the buffalo wallow where for years buffalo had rolled until they made a permanent depression in the land, the draw where salt cedars grew and butterflies tumbled in search of each other, the shinnery of cottonwoods, oaks, and tangles of blackberry vines where lobos, bobcats, even panthers had hidden while Elmer Spruill hunted an animal that no one but Josh Kincheloe ever saw. "Don't you have any neighbors?" Delores asked.

When we stopped in the farmyard under the cottonwood trees, she said, "Farms look a lot like junk yards, don't they?" Delores sat for a moment listening to the engine cool. Her eyes grew big as she heard the silence of the plains. The wind rustled in the cottonwoods, and the windmill rattled and thumped, but there were no cries of playing children, no mothers calling their sons, no women talking over a fence, no honking horns, racing engines, screeching brakes, no snatches of music from passing cars, no pleading voices from television sets. "God," Delores said. "Where are we?" I took heart that she did not say, "Where am I?"

"Come on to the house," I said, dragging Delores out of the car. Dad, who knew we were coming, lurked warily in the doorway. Dad, who had stood up to Sheriff Brassfield, was a quail before women.

Delores tried to kiss Dad, and Dad, who believed hellos and goodbyes were like shots in the arm—to be dispensed with quickly if not entirely—stuck out his hand, punching her in the stomach. Delores gave Dad a present and he was so touched he had to escape to his workshop behind the barn to open it. I knew it was a radio and I knew how long Delores had to work to pay for it. Delores's mother had kissed me and wept over the cheap handkerchiefs I had taken her. Dad didn't know how to receive gifts and was afraid to show emotion. He never mentioned the radio, but the next morning it was in an honored spot on the kitchen table.

Delores talked at the table although I tried to signal she shouldn't. She called Dad an "anglo." Grandfather had left Ireland because of the English, and calling Dad an anglo was the emotional equivalent of calling a Jew a Nazi.

To my surprise they liked each other. "She's a Texan," said Dad. "That speaks well of her. Her father grew up on a farm. You know, a lot of good Irishmen went to Mexico."

"He's so much like Papa," Delores said. "Proud. Stubborn. Ashamed to admit he based his life on a dream that failed."

"What failed?" I asked.

"Hard work. Pride in personal integrity. Now they're old and weak, tossed aside like something useless. Goodness, kindness, courage, being a husband and father mean nothing," she said, her eyes hard with anger.

I didn't want to talk about their dream but my dream. "A lot of good Irishmen went to Mexico," I said. "Dad thinks you're one of us."

"We're too different," Delores said. "In my family we kiss each other. We give presents. We talk at the table. We all talk at the same time. We use recipes." (Dad had done the cooking.) "We know where we belong. I can't marry a man without a family. Family is too important. If you don't understand family

you don't understand loyalty. You don't understand pulling together when times are hard. You don't understand how sometimes you must give up what you want for someone else."

I told Delores I had a family, and I did. Although most of
them were dead, they were important to me and I clung to
them, to their pictures, their memories, their names. "Look at
this house. My grandfather built this house. He put the bedroom on the east side so they would wake up at the first light
of day. He put the kitchen on the west side so Grandmother
would have the last light to work by."

That didn't sound appealing so I switched to Grandmother.
Grandmother taught Dad and Uncle Emmett to read and write
in the kitchen after she had worked all day with them in the
field. When she sent them to buy cottonseed and there was
none to buy, they stole seed because they were afraid to come
home empty-handed. When she became too old and sick to
work, neither son would leave her. I led Delores into the yard
so that she stood on everything my grandmother owned. When
Grandmother died, Uncle Emmett took her belongings, put
them in the dugout and caved in the dugout. Uncle Emmett
died trying to kill the man who killed his father. Dad stood up
to Sheriff Brassfield for me and would have killed him if he had
to. I knew about family.

Delores didn't say anything but she stared at me so intently I knew she was almost convinced. "What would I do if I
married you?" she asked.

"You'd be my wife."

She shook her head. "What do you want, Will?"

"I want to take care of you. I want to show you off. I
want—"

She put her hand over my lips. "What do *you* want?"

"I want to be somebody different," I said, and knew that I
had failed the test.

When it came time to leave, Dad, who was afraid of goodbyes, escaped on the tractor while we were loading the car. I

walked out to the field where he was plowing to tell him we were leaving; Delores waited at the house to wave goodbye. Suddenly Dad slumped a little on the tractor, plowed through a fence, and into another field before I could jump on the tractor and stop it.

Dad had blacked out. Had it happened before? Yes. Had he seen a doctor? No. I was frightened. Not just for Dad, I was frightened for myself. If I had to come home and take care of Dad I would never see Delores again. Besides, I didn't want to go back to Wanderer Springs.

"What happened?" Delores asked.

"Nothing," I said. "It's okay."

I drove back to school, and without explaining why, I told Delores I might not see her for a couple of days. I rushed back home and took Dad to the doctor in Center Point.

"Arteriosclerosis," the doctor said. He was a gray man with grave eyes and white, polished hands, wearing a frayed smock over expensive flannel trousers and sharkskin shoes. His practiced voice expressed professional exemption. "There's nothing we can do," he said. His hands washed themselves while we talked. "He will get progressively worse. Blackouts, confusion. You're going to have to take his car away from him and you're going to have to watch him all the time."

I went to Center Point to lease the farm to Ira Ferguson who was without attachments or allegiances. Upon the death of his father, Ferguson the Fiddler, Ira had sold his family farm. Such a thing was scandalous, almost criminal, and everyone assumed Ira would leave the county. Instead he bought farm equipment and started thrashing wheat or baling hay for farmers who found it faster and cheaper than doing it themselves.

Ira accumulated equipment and when farmers started leaving the land, he leased the farms and hired men to operate the machinery. He had no wife and after his mother died, no family. Ira didn't even own the house he lived in. If he felt possessive towards anything it was the Ford pickup he drove. We sat in the truck while we worked out the details of the lease.

"Having strangers driving over his fields and farming his place is not going to be easy for Dad. He gets confused sometimes. He may order your hands off the place, or tell them what to do."

Ira didn't look at me like I was someone he had known all his life, he didn't look at the fields like a farmer, he looked at the lease agreement as though it were Holy Writ. "It's the equipment that's assigned, not the men. I have no idea who or how many will be operating the equipment."

"If you could tell them to treat him kindly, just ask them to listen and be polite. They don't have to do what he says."

Ira was small like his mother, gaunt like his father, his ears crisp, his skin thin and pink with sun and age. He studied the lease, head bowed like a priest. "None of the equipment will be more than five years old," he read.

"Just for a couple of months until I'm out of college." Ira's lips moved slowly as though he were reading the lease to himself. I took that as a hopeful sign. "I'll be home every weekend to see about him."

"Arteriosclerosis," I said to Delores. "I leased the farm. Maybe if he doesn't have that to worry about—" I couldn't bring myself to tell her that I was going to have to move to the farm as soon as I graduated; that I might not see her again.

"But he's all alone," she said.

"I'll go home on the weekends to see about him. Dad's tough. He'll be okay."

Ira Ferguson called to say that his hands had been working the place and they had not seen Dad in three or four days. By the time I got home, Sheriff Brassfield had found Dad sitting in the Center Point depot waiting for the train to Borger, although only the freight trains stopped any more.

"You got to put him in the state hospital before he gets hit by a car or somebody kills and robs him," Brassfield said.

I took Dad to Augusta Worley. After Dr. Vestal had been

driven away by the town's never-ending misfortune and fecundity, Wanderer Springs had been without medical care except for Augusta Worley who took soup and home remedies to the sick, supervised the birth of over a dozen babies, and, after her father died, took in the old and infirm.

Augusta had come to Wanderer Springs with her father, Denver, a thin-faced crank of a Confederate veteran who had gone to war in his shirttail. In Wanderer Springs he had been received as a gallant hero of the glorious South, and to keep that romance alive, Augusta, the youngest child of his third wife, had devoted her life to caring for the selfish old man. Augusta had been courted by every bachelor who dared the wrath of her father. "'y God, there ain't no need for you to come sniffing around here, you sons of bitches." Uncle Emmett had won Augusta's heart but she would not leave her father to marry him.

Once Uncle Emmett had persuaded her to elope and had loaded her and her bag into the wagon when her father caught them. "Yankee," he screamed. "No more sense of duty than a Yankee. No southern woman would leave her ailing father and run after a man like a bitch in heat."

Sobbing, Augusta had run to her father without a backward glance. Uncle Emmett had carried her bag to the porch while Denver cursed and tried to spit on him.

When I knew her, Augusta was coarse and mannish with a moustache on her upper lip. I had never seen her when she looked young, or had a shape, or wore a dress that hung straight, or looked like something a man might desire. All Augusta knew of love was to serve.

When her father died, Augusta took in the old and sick, feeding and nursing them for whatever they could pay out of their old-age benefits or Social Security checks. Augusta would have thought it immoral to make a profit out of the old and sick. She was happy to see Dad. He gave her a reason for living.

"Dad's okay," I told Delores. "I found a place for him to stay."

Two weeks later Augusta called. Dad had run away. I found him in the farmhouse and he grabbed the skillet and started making coffee as though everything was in its place. "Emmett came to see me the other day. He said for me not to look for Willie Thomas," Dad said. Willie Thomas had murdered Grandfather. "He said Willie Thomas is an old man."

After coffee I took Dad back to Wanderer Springs. Dad was lucid and we talked about how he should stay with Augusta until I could complete my work at school and move to the farm to take care of him. Augusta ran to greet him like he was a lost child. She put her arms around his neck and cried. "I try to watch him every minute," she said, "but when I turn my back he's gone. One night I asked him where he was going and he said he had to take Mary McCarroll home."

Augusta agreed to try to keep Dad until I could work things out at school. I arranged with my professors to take finals early and went to tell Delores goodbye. I took her to the Pedernales River and we waded and splashed water and laughed. We sat on rocks and dangled our feet in the water, and I begged her again to marry me. "How are we so different?" I asked.

"You don't know who you are, you don't know what you want, you don't know where you belong."

"I know where I'm going to be," I said, bitterly. "I'm going to be teaching in Wanderer Springs. I have to go home and take care of Dad."

"Oh Will, I couldn't love you if you didn't care for your father."

"It means I'll never see you again, Delores."

"I can't give up my scholarship, Will. I can't quit now. I'll write to you."

"I'll be four hundred miles away. Teaching school and taking care of Dad. We might as well say goodbye right now."

"Will, please—"

"Is that what you want? Just walk away and forget you?

Forget this ever happened?"

"Can't you wait a little while?"

"I don't know how long it will take," I said. "Please. I can't go back alone. I can't care for him by myself."

"I have to be a part," she said. "I can give up school. I can give up anything, but I have to be a part."

"You won't be just a part, you'll be everything. You'll be my whole life, my whole family."

I'd like to remember that we clung to each other and talked of love, but we were overwhelmed with practical matters.

"Can we get married in San Antonio? My family—"

"I'll go home and take care of Dad until you finish this semester. You plan the wedding and I'll meet you in San Antonio."

"No. We don't know what will happen. We will go to San Antonio and get married now. You go be with your father, and when school is out, I will come."

"No honeymoon?"

"You are my honeymoon."

We were married in the Bexar County Courthouse with Delores's family as witnesses, along with Albert Duderstatt, Albert's attorney, and the jury that was hearing his trial for drunken driving. There was no church, no priest, no reception, but there was a drunk at the wedding. And there were kisses and tears for everyone. I thought the tears were because there was no priest to bless the union.

Maybe I wouldn't have minded going home for a funeral if it had been someone besides Jessie Tooley. If it hadn't been so far.

Crossing Texas is like crossing a big lake with little islands of houses and stores called Blanco, Marble Falls, Lampasas, Evant, Morgan Mill, Mineral Wells. It was still two hours to Wanderer Springs but Jacksboro was the beginning of home, the beginning of familiar things. On either side of the car the land was empty as a dream. The only breaks in the regular patterns of field and pasture were occasional clumps of trees,

or rusting piles of broken farm machinery, or flashing windmills to show where once a house had been, or a school, or a
community. The fields were empty of human life except for an
occasional tractor lost in the horizon, or a cloud of dust left by
a distant, invisible automobile. After Jacksboro, everyone who
passed, waved. Another car was a surprise, sometimes a gift,
and the wave was the salute of a neighbor.

Arriving in Jacksboro was a return to a familiar time when
it still mattered that Josh Kincheloe had seen an animal that no
one else ever saw, that Elmer Spruill killed the last buffalo. In
San Antonio, Vietnam no longer mattered and Watergate was a
curiosity. In Wanderer Springs time was more abiding and our
fathers still comforted us.

Wanderer Springs County, and several others, had waited
beyond a string of forts—Phantom Hill, Griffin, Belknap, and
Richardson in Jacksboro—while Congress debated the end of
Reconstruction and the papers gossiped about Credit Mobilier.
The land was occupied only by buffalo hunters, Indian hunting
parties, cavalry patrols, and cattle drovers on their way to Kansas when Roy Dodson built a dugout at Wanderer Springs, the
only unfailing source of water between the Mobeetie and Red
rivers.

Dodson sold supplies—some said whiskey—to buffalo
hunters, drovers and Indians on their way to the sacred ground
at Medicine Hill. After the buffalo were exterminated and the
hunters and Indians sought their fortunes elsewhere, Dodson,
the first settler in the county, operated a stage stand and sold
supplies to drovers, wagon trains, and to the Lances, who were
the first family in the county. Roy had a son, Fred, but Fred ran
away, and the Dodsons were not considered a family.

The Lances were considered a family although the father
had been killed in a cattle feud in Palo Pinto County. Ma Lance,
fearing the Indians less than her neighbors, moved her cattle
and three teenage sons to Wanderer Springs. The Lances had
no trouble with the Indians, to whom they gave cattle as trib-

ute, but did have a running gunfight with a group of drovers. Some said that the drovers had added a few Lance cattle to the herd they were driving north. Some said the herd had stampeded crossing Red River and the Lances had rounded up the strays. Some detractors, from Center Point, claimed that the Lances got their entire herd by stampeding cattle drives and rounding up the strays.

The Lances were followed by other cattlemen—the Spruills, Kincheloes, Spiveys, Bryants. There were so few people in the county that when Ma Lance died, Larissa Bell rode forty solitary miles so that Ma wouldn't have to die without another woman present. When Wilbur Lance's horse stepped in a prairie dog hole, breaking its leg and Wilbur's back, Wilbur would have died undiscovered had it not been for surveyors laying out the path of the railroad across the county.

Ahead of the railroad came the railroad gangs—paddies mostly, like Grandfather—and those who catered to the laborers' vices, like Joe Whatley who operated a saloon out of a buffalo-hide tent. Grandfather, who was foreman of the grading crews, lived with Grandmother and Uncle Emmett in a tent, a quarter of a mile from Roy Dodson's trading post.

Grandmother did not like life with the railroad. Buffalo hunters had stacked hides near the surveying stakes waiting for the trains to come, but rain set in, ruining the hides, and their rotting stench clung to the tent. Locomotives pushing rails or crossties to the crews rumbled past filling the tent with coal smoke. Drunken gandy dancers brawled outside.

Grandfather arranged for a boxcar set on a siding and moved Grandmother into it. Dad was born in the boxcar, the first child born in Wanderer Springs. Grandfather was bossing a grading crew far down the unlaid track, and Grandmother had only five-year-old Uncle Emmett to help her in the stifling August heat. The boxcar had no windows and Grandmother had closed the sliding door because curious Indians climbed on the boxcar—drawn not by the ordinary, her birthing wails, but by the extraordinary, a house on wheels.

When I told Delores's mother that story, she took my hand and patted it. Mama had been born in a boxcar crowded with migrant workers and set in a spinach field. Her people were also pioneers. Papa had taken her away from all that.

Grandmother, like Dad, was small—scarcely five feet tall—and she spent her life as a grain of salt. Born in a family of devout and dutiful Catholics, she had become Methodist and headstrong. When other women her age were seeking beaus, she was seeking scholars to enroll in the school she taught in her parents' house. When others her age were getting married and having babies, she was crossing the continent in a wagon to teach school in California. When others were settling into rocking chairs, admiring their children and grandchildren and enjoying the fruits of their labors, Grandmother was marrying an Irish immigrant eight years her junior and following him to the end of the track on the Texas frontier. Grandmother was forty-five years old when Dad was born but she had not lost her savor.

The promise of the railroad brought farmers. Grandfather quit the railroad, probably at Grandmother's suggestion, to become one of them. He bought a section of land close enough to the tracks to set his railroad watch by the passing trains, far enough away to save Grandmother's wash from coal smoke and cinders. They lived in a wagon until Grandfather built a house, and Grandmother cooked under a cottonwood tree. Grandmother demanded that a canvas be hung under the tree, not to protect her from sun or rain, but to protect the food from bird droppings. Farm wives were a demanding lot. The ranchers spent most of their lives on horseback escaping their wives, but farmers, tied to the plow, could rarely get out of earshot.

The farmers were stolid, God-fearing men. Except for

Ferguson the Fiddler who would drop a plow or milk bucket to fiddle for a dance, or Limp Ballard who would rather fish than farm, their passions were reserved for the hard land and the fickle weather that provided them with killing freezes, ice storms, dust storms, hail storms, northers, floods, droughts, heat waves, high winds, tornados, and insects.

The women endured a season in a tent or wagon or dugout but if the crops weren't rained out, hailed out, killed by drought, blown away, or eaten by grasshoppers, there would soon be a two-room dirt-floor house with one room for cooking, eating, and entertaining, and one room for sleeping, bearing children, and being sick. They put the houses as close together as possible, sometimes no more than a mile apart. Where there were three or four houses in sight of each other there was soon a school, and then Reverend Malcolm Murdock would hold services, under a shade tree if there was one and if not wherever they could get out of the sun and wind. Next would be a general store-post office, and a gin and blacksmith shop.

Not content with settlement, the women demanded civilization. For a time cowboys, railroad gangs, and bone men who picked up buffalo bones to sell for fertilizer spent their idle hours at Whatley's tent saloon. Fights, cuttings, and shootings were frequent. When a twelve-year-old girl was found raped and murdered behind the saloon, the women forced Whatley to Sand, forced alcohol out of the town, and after Whatley's religious conversion, out of the county.

They gave the communities quaint names. Bull Valley because the land was spotted with buffalo wallows, and in the spring rains the bull frogs kept the children awake with their croaking. Lank because it had been a Lance pasture and was so far from headquarters that the cowboys always returned "a mite lank." Elma Dell because Buck Fowler said he needed the post office worse than anybody because his sweetheart, Alma Deel, had promised to marry him when he got settled in a steady community, and a settlement that had a post office had to be called steady. The first postmaster misspelled the town into Elma Dell.

Red Top because one year the only crop that didn't fail was red top maize. The women made bread of the maize and used the heads for fuel as it was cheaper than coal. They used the stalks to make a brush arbor for Reverend Murdock's service. When Murdock invited Earl Lance to come see what God had wrought, Earl, who could remember when it was nothing but grass, said he didn't see God, all he saw was red top.

Sand because the citizens of Elma Dell allowed no saloon or horseplay in the town and Buck Fowler and the other rowdies who wanted to "raise sand" had to cross the river to Joe Whatley's saloon. St. Joe's Crossing because Reverend Malcolm Murdock, a stout, slung-jawed bulldog of a circuit rider claimed he couldn't get to Elma Dell to preach because the Mobeetie River was up. "It'd take a saint to cross that river," Murdock said. "Then you can call me Saint Joe," said Whatley who was headed for his saloon. "I just come across it with a load of whiskey." The Methodists lynched Whatley but the name of the crossing remained.

The spot where buffalo hides rotted into the ground remained Hide City when the only buffalos were on nickles, when the bare ground was used for medicine shows and carnivals; remained Hide City even after it was turned into a runway for Dr. Heslar's airplane.

The Lance boys had designed a brand that resembled an Indian lance and had tried to name the brand and the ranch, The Lance. Cowboys, however, said the brand looked like a cattle prod, and the brand and the ranch became known as The Prod. Delmer Lance tried to start a little settlement of his own. Although he built the only buildings and he and his family were the only residents, it became known as Prod. The only thing permanent about the community was the name.

It was the railroad that named Center Point, that marked off a spot halfway between Fort Worth and Amarillo and decreed it would be a town when there was no need for a town to be there. No one believed that Center Point was a real name, that the railroad had a right to name anything, or that the town would last. Reverend Murdock called it an "unnatural town."

Delores could never understand our animosity towards Center Point. Nor could the girls. To them it was a place to go to a restaurant, to a movie, to shop. To us Center Point was the usurper, the bastard prince who had stolen our kingdom, our throne.

As Reverend Malcolm Murdock said, it was discernible even to fools that God intended Wanderer Springs to be county seat because: Number One, it was a natural and historical location and had a natural and historical name, whereas Center Point was the invention of thieves, scoundrels, and layabouts; Number Two, Wanderer Springs was at the heart of the county whereas Center Point was at a remote corner; and Number Three, Wanderer Springs had a natural and unfailing source of water, whereas in Center Point, water had to be hauled four miles from the muddy Mobeetie River until the railroad completed the town well.

The first county seat election was won—some say bought—by Center Point on the votes of beefed-up railroad crews and the boosterism of newspaper editor Chris Arp. The railroad hired Arp to extol the virtues of Center Point and to excoriate Wanderer Springs. Arp got his chance when the Methodists, led by Grandmother, expelled Joe Whatley from the church and Whatley got into a fight with a deacon, Virgil Hight.

"Virgil Hight was killed today by Joe Whatley. If the Methodists catch Whatley they will lynch him," wrote Chris Arp who had left Fort Worth after Longhair Jim Courtright had rearranged his face with a pistol barrel for a story that Courtright considered if not untrue, at least unnecessary. Whatley was arrested and placed in the post oak log jail that was also the Wanderer Springs school.

The following day, Arp wrote, "Folks in Wanderer Springs are in such an uproar over the killing of Virgil Hight that the prisoner was spirited out of town to a safe place. This paper has learned that Whatley is being hidden in the Medicine Hill depot, there being no jail in Medicine Hill."

Guided by Arp's paper, the Methodists lynched Whatley. Folks took religion seriously in those days. Joe's last official act was to bite off the thumb of Ferguson the Fiddler who, although he was not a Methodist, never missed a party.

"A mob of lawless men who call themselves citizens overpowered the exhausted sheriff yesterday, seized Joe Whatley, and hanged him from the spout of the railroad tank, there being no trees in Medicine Hill," Arp wrote. "Acts such as this prove again how far removed is that town from civilized society and how unfit to be the seat of county government."

Citizens were upset at being called "lawless" when they were only doing what good men did everywhere—setting straight what God had let slide. Nevertheless, it cost Wanderer Springs the election. Lacking political power, Wanderer Springs set out to prove its moral superiority. We were honest, hardworking pioneers, dedicated to the good of the county. They were opportunistic railroad followers, motivated by greed, and had won by cunning and chicanery. Murdock preached that Center Point was an unnatural town and citizens boycotted the "railroad" stores in Center Point and traded with Roy Dodson, to whom expediency had lent approval.

To counter Reverend Murdock—who was a power with a Bible and a voice that even Ruby Spruill could hear—Center Point invited Sister Druscilla Majors to set up her tent at the edge of town.

Chris Arp, a stout, balding man who sported a top hat to cover the scars that Courtright had put on his head, a handlebar moustache to mask the scar on his upper lip, and a brass-knobbed cane to prevent reinjury, reported in the Center Point paper that Sister Majors was a handsome woman with long, red hair and wore a white dress that "flowed like water." She spoke with "a voice that could break men's hearts." Arp's reports of Majors's personal and spiritual beauty drew citizens from unforgiving Wanderer Springs. They camped in wagons, watched the construction of the courthouse, shopped in the two stores and at night watched Sister Druscilla Majors bring salvation and healing.

Buck Fowler was cured of boils. Mary McCarroll regained her senses. Mattie Lance took her two strange children and although the sister was unable to make the girl talk, she did cure the boy of Latin. Millie Perkins, who had been carried to the meeting on a cot, was able to get up and walk, and Ruby Spruill had her hearing restored.

"Attended the meeting," Grandmother wrote, "where I supposed the multitude had come to transact business with God. But O, how altered my opinion. Instead of that meek and humble look that should decorate a woman's brow, there was pride and haughtiness and an abundance of red hair, and her rich dress must now be at the height of the gay and fashionable."

The meeting ended when Texas Rangers arrested Sister Majors and her husband, a notorious cattle rustler. While Sister Majors preached, her husband had stolen the cattle of those at the meeting. Chris Arp's paper loudly proclaimed Sister Majors's innocence. At the trial Millie Perkins demonstrated how she was able to walk, Ruby Spruill answered questions to prove she could hear, Mary McCarroll demonstrated her sanity by smiling while her little girl, Beth, cried outside the courtroom.

Sister Majors was found innocent and her husband guilty. Perhaps it was a coincidence that the jury was composed entirely of citizens of Center Point while those who lost cattle were from Wanderer Springs, but citizens demanded another election and narrowly lost on a second counting. The screams were heard as far away as Austin.

The governor promised an investigation but his enthusiasm was modulated when half of Wanderer Springs burned to the ground. Earl Lance found one of his cows wearing a brand that had been altered into Oscar Spruill's 4F. Earl shot the cow and left the hide in the Wanderer Springs livery barn-hardware store for the sheriff to examine.

Folks had never taken to Oscar Spruill. Oscar was a stump of a man, mean-tempered, mean-mouthed, who never spoke in less than a shout. Some said he shouted because his wife, Ruby, was deaf. Some said Ruby was deaf because Oscar shouted. He left his cattle and kids for everyone else to fence out, and a lot of folks thought that every roundup Oscar branded more calves than he had cows. Still, folks would have looked the other way if Oscar had moved on or stolen the cowhide. Instead, the livery barn caught fire and burned down half the town.

The next time Oscar Spruill came to town for a haircut, he was shot through the window of Millard Perkins's barber shop in broad daylight without a single witness. Everyone gave Earl Lance credit for the killing, and no one deplored the method. It wasn't Hollywood but it was the way things were done.

Chris Arp declared that the streets of Wanderer Springs were not safe for honest men and predicted a Lance-Spruill feud. "The Spruills will punish the perpetrator of this evil deed or leave the county in dishonor." Chris was smart enough not to name Earl Lance although everyone knew he was the perpetrator.

Elmer Spruill was a teenager but being the oldest Spruill male and having killed the last buffalo in the county, he was obliged to kill or be killed by Earl Lance. He was saved from the honor when Josh Kincheloe was attacked by a mysterious animal that was as big as a yearling, wooly like a sheep, had teeth like a bear, and screamed like a panther. Chasing the animal was a manly thing to do and Elmer decided to kill the animal rather than killing Earl Lance. It was unorthodox but folks expected that kind of behavior from the Spruills.

Failing to provoke Wanderer Springs to violence, Arp accused the town of being ignorant and mean-spirited when Millie Perkins, her health restored and her marriage destroyed by a miracle, was forced to move to Center Point and take in washing. Arp wrote that she had been divorced by her husband, Millard the barber, because she had been made to walk by Sister Majors, and because she had traded in Center Point. Everyone knew he had divorced her because she had laid in bed for five years pretending she was sick when she could have been doing his washing and cooking.

When Mary McCarroll relost her senses, Chris wrote, "That good woman testified at the trial of Sister Druscilla Majors that she had been cured of nervousness, poor memory, feelings of dread, and a sense of goneness. However, the efforts of Sister Majors have been undermined by the hateful and ignorant citizens of Wanderer Springs who refuse all evidence of Sister Majors's innocence. If Sister Majors does not return, as we have requested, Mary McCarroll will be placed in the insane cell of the Center Point jail."

Sister Majors did not return and Mary McCarroll was not placed in jail. Her daughter, Beth, fled from the unhappy home at the age of sixteen and married Babe English, a genial Wanderer Springs cowboy. They had been married two years when Babe was accused of stealing a gold watch the railroad had presented to the Center Point mayor. During Babe's trial, the prosecutor and the defense attorney got into a fist fight. A deputy in the sheriff's office heard the commotion, thought Babe was trying to escape, ran into the courtroom, and shot Babe where he was sitting in the witness chair.

In Wanderer Springs it was the final outrage. Everyone liked Babe and believed him innocent. His wife, Beth, had cried outside the courtroom to prove her mother sane during Sister Majors's trial, but no one held that against Babe. A vigilante committee was formed, including Dad and Uncle Emmett, to seize the courthouse and remove all records, furniture, and officials to what Wanderer Springs had intended as a courthouse. The courthouse had already been planned when the usurpers stole the county seat. Undaunted, the citizens erected the grandiose building of three towering floors and a dome-like bell tower, using it as a school until such time as it was needed. The records and officials would be held there until Center Point admitted Wanderer Springs's God-given right to be county seat.

They were stopped by Wink Bailey, Wanderer Springs's constable, who begged them to petition for an election instead. The town had been rebuilt since the fire, there had been no recent killings, and the fact that a divorced woman like Millie Perkins would move to Center Point while her honest barber husband remained in the town was proof of the town's moral superiority.

Wink's argument seemed so reasonable and the return of the county seat to Wanderer Springs so likely that the committee agreed to give the law a chance. However, the double advantage of railroad money and an advocate newspaper was impossible to overcome. Center Point remained county seat. In Wanderer Springs there was anger and despair. Some stores talked of moving out of the county, not daring to talk of moving to Center Point. Once again, God showed his preference for Wanderer Springs.

A daredevil pilot, attempting the first interstate flight between Oklahoma City and Fort Worth, followed the wrong railroad tracks out of Wichita Falls. Frantically word was sent down the telegraph wires to head him off. In Center Point the citizens gawked as the airplane circled the crackerbox courthouse and the pilot tried to read the name on the depot. In Wanderer Springs men, women, and children strung out across the tracks, waving hats, aprons, and school books, and calling him down. The bell in the schoolhouse dome was rung so loud and long that it cracked and was used only once more, on Armistice Day.

Miracles still happened in Wanderer Springs. The pilot

landed on the bare ground of Hide City, got his bearings and a lot of advice, and bought a can of gasoline from Benny What-ley, who had opened a store closer to the railroad tracks than Dodson's dugout and who delivered. The pilot took off again while the women held their skirts, men chased their hats across the field and Elmer Spruill took aim at the biggest thing he'd ever gotten in his gunsight.

They watched the airplane until it was but a speck in the sky, seeing it rise and fall, feebly yet majestically, like a kite in the air currents, with darkness but a few hours away. And those who watched believed they had seen a portent of the future. Center Point had the railroad, but Wanderer Springs had the airplane.

Chris Arp reported that an airplane had landed in the county but neglected to mention where. No matter. From all over the county folks traveled to Wanderer Springs to see where the airplane had landed, to talk to those who had seen it, and to buy something from Benny Whatley whose gasoline had taken the pilot to Fort Worth.

Wanderer Springs had God on its side, but Center Point had money. When Brother Malcolm Murdock preached in Elma Dell, such was the power of the man—and such was the strength of his voice—that Joe Whatley and three of his patrons were converted in Whatley's saloon, which was across the river in Sand. That should have convinced the blind that when Murdock said Center Point was an unnatural town, he was speaking God's truth. Unbelieving Center Point merchants had hired the Sister Majors show where Millie Perkins pranced to prove she was not crippled and Mary McCarroll regained her senses.

When God sent an airplane to signify his approval of Wanderer Springs, Center Point merchants hired a French air show to prove that money was mightier. Or at least more popular. Some folks traveled two or three days by wagon to see the air show. Others camped out all night in a weedy field beside the tracks at the edge of town. Three French aviators arrived on the train and uncrated their airplanes. They strutted over the field and flew kites to test what the Center Point paper reported as a straight wind. In Wanderer Springs County "straight wind" was used to describe a wind that did not go round and round like a tornado but was strong enough to suck the bucket out of the well.

While the sheriff and mayor pledged that the Frenchmen would fly as soon as the wind moderated, the aviators escaped on the train, leaving the airplanes to be shipped after them. The audience was displeased. If they could have found the sheriff and mayor they would have tarred and feathered them. If they could have gotten their hands on the airmen, the French would have joined Joe Whatley in county history.

Anti-French feelings persisted for a long time. In the county schools Lafayette was ignored in American history classes, and in Texas history, Jean Lafitte was treated as a Galveston pirate. "Hell, I've climbed windmills in winds higher than that," claimed Buck Fowler. During World War I, Otis Hopkins, the county's only conscientious objector, said he did not wish to fight with the French because they would not fly in a high wind.

There was another county seat election which Center Point won by two votes. There were cries of fraud. There were threats to burn down the courthouse. Every incumbent county official was defeated in the next election, and no one born in Center Point was again elected county sheriff.

Clement Arp, Chris's son, came to the newspaper fresh from Harvard. Clement had been shocked by the hostility and rivalry between the two towns. Clement conceived the idea of channeling the rivalry into a ritualistic warfare he had observed at Harvard—football.

Clement organized the Center Point football team composed largely of railroad hands augmented by a butcher, carpenter, and two men not known for honest work. When Wanderer Springs heard of Clement's plan, they raised a football team of cowboys and farmers. It required two fist fights and the flip of a coin to establish that the first game would be played in Center Point, would be played at night, and that cars would be placed along the sidelines to light the field.

No one but Clement had seen a football game. There was no equipment but what the players had fashioned for themselves, and no cheerleaders. For inspiration Center Point had Millie Perkins who paraded along the sidelines to prove that she had been healed by Sister Majors. Wanderer Springs countered with Beth McCarroll, recent widow of innocent Babe English and recent bride of Ferguson the Fiddler.

The contest, played by whatever rules Clement could remember and explain before kickoff, was more a test of courage than of skill and was interrupted by a brawl that involved the players as well as the spectators. The brawl was won by Wanderer Springs, the game by Center Point. No one had told Wanderer Springs that the ball could be thrown downfield and caught by a player on the same team. "They stole that game just like they stole the courthouse," screamed Wanderer Springs fans.

That game was disputed until the next game, also won by Center Point. All the games were won by Center Point, even after the players became high school boys instead of grown men. We were the best, tricked out of our birthright, cheated of victory. We absorbed that with our mother's milk, shouldered it like a hoe or saddle. Armed with nothing but our own sense of honor and the town's pledge that courage and will were enough, we went forth to avenge ancient wrongs, and played on equal terms. Except for one fumble, one penalty, one mistake that inevitably decided the game.

Center Point never won because they were better, they won because some Wanderer Springs boy lost his courage or lacked the will to win. Such failures were never forgotten. The only thing we ever won was respect. The payment for that respect was a sense of dread that came with the first Christmas-wrapped football. To be a male meant that some day one must come face to face with Center Point across the line, with every play an opportunity for disgrace.

I played twice against Center Point. In my junior year I was pushed around the field by an opponent twenty pounds heavier than I but spared humiliation because a senior, Sonny Dismuke, was caught holding, nullifying what would have been a game-winning touchdown by Vivian Whatley. My senior year I failed to catch a pass that could have won the game.

Of that last game I remember almost nothing. The wet, torn grass. The ache in my thigh where I had been blindsided. The taste of blood from a cut lip and smashed nose. The clacking of our cleats on the road as we trotted back to the gym after the game, demonstrating our fitness and willingness to carry on the fight if only the referees would permit.

I remember the relief. It was over. I would never have to play Center Point again. Whatever tests life might still have for me, I had passed this one—no fumbles, no penalties, no missed tackles. I had looked good. It wasn't until we reached the locker room that I realized Vivian was crying. "It was my last chance," he said. "My last chance to beat Center Point and you dropped the ball."

"It was high," I said. I didn't blame him for a bad pass.

"It was right on your fingertips and you dropped it," he said. I looked at the others, expecting their support. What I saw in their eyes was relief that it was me and not them.

"You could have walked into the end zone and you dropped it," Vivian said. "All my life I wanted to beat Center Point and you dropped the ball."

From the safety of San Antonio and fifty years, I can

laugh at the importance we gave a game that was less significant than the style of lettering on a road sign. But sometimes
at night in my dreams I can see the glittering, dew-dampened
ball spinning in the floodlights, coming closer and closer and I
awake to relive the terror. I had been found out.

CENTER POINT

where Larissa Bell died of reading and Buster Bryant roped his own horse

I KNEW I was in Wanderer Springs County when I crossed Starvation Creek. Larissa Bell had lived on Starvation Creek. Her husband had died of some unknown ailment and Larissa had stayed on. Indian braves had tried to steal chickens from her, and Larissa had not only stopped them and lectured them on the eighth commandment, she ordered them to go back across the river and get themselves baptized. Larissa believed the only good Indian was a Baptist deacon.

Larissa held liberal views, brought on by reading, and was held in contempt by the Lances although Larissa had ridden forty solitary miles so that Ma Lance would not die without a woman present. The Lances' opinion was confirmed when Chris Arp caused a county-wide panic with headlines predicting a yellow fever epidemic caused by a wet summer followed by an early fall. "People will die like sheep with the rot," he reported.

Dr. Vestal, who was overworked, seldom paid, and finally driven out of the county by the people's need, made a hurried trip to Center Point to assure the editor that it was a far less serious fever and that no one should die of it. "It may not look like a yellow fever epidemic to a doctor but it looks like a yellow fever epidemic to me," Chris declared. "And it's my paper."

Dr. Vestal spent several sleepless nights traveling about

the county, reassuring folks that they didn't have to die. When he got to Larissa Bell, he found her beyond solace, the first person in the county to die of misinformation.

Elma Dell was gone, along with Sand. Lank had blown away in a tornado and not been rebuilt; Red Top failed to survive the Depression, and Bull Valley had succumbed to the prosperity of World War II. The gin, the store, and the Methodist Church in Medicine Hill had lasted until mid-century. Of all the county names only Center Point and Wanderer Springs still existed on any map. Only the asphalt seemed to grow. A welfare government had subsidized out-of-work engineers and contractors by paving over whatever was not plowed or used by cattle.

Off to the west, along the Mobeetie River, was where Elmer Spruill killed the last buffalo. Elmer was just a kid, riding for his father, when he found a buffalo cow and calf. Buffalo hadn't been seen in the county for a few years and Elmer knew no one would believe he had seen one. He tried to drive the buffalo to the wagon, but the cow wouldn't drive. Elmer didn't have a gun, so he roped the buffalo, snubbed her close to a hackberry tree, and rode for the wagon.

His father, Oscar, didn't believe him and refused to look until the next morning. They found the buffalo cow still tied to the tree and half eaten by lobos. They also found a buffalo calf that, left unprotected, had also been killed by the wolves. Folks deplored Elmer's methods but they gave him credit for the kill. The Spruills had a reputation for being unorthodox.

It was that reputation that permitted Elmer to chase Josh Kincheloe's mysterious animal rather than killing Earl Lance. Elmer never saw the animal he chased, but when his eyesight began to fail, Elmer married Josh Kincheloe's youngest daughter. Kincheloe went right on having children as though an animal no one else ever saw hadn't marked them, even the girls being cockeyed and dogeared. Persia, the one Elmer married, always looked like she was about to spit.

Elmer fathered four children, including a girl named Jessie who married Horace Tooley. Jessie looked like a Spruill instead of a Kincheloe. Like the other Spruill women, Jessie sometimes went deaf.

Ahead I could see the skyline of Center Point although I was still some miles away. It wasn't much of a skyline, just grain elevators. Not even a grandiose courthouse in the Texas tradition. Practical-minded Center Point had built a courthouse that looked like a bread box. "They can't see no higher than a dollar bill," folks said in Wanderer Springs, and for years talked of burning it down.

Houses built along highways seem in a state of disrepair—boards missing from fences, paint peeling from houses, weeds growing in yards, the trees scabrous and sullen as though poisoned by car exhaust. At least it was so in Center Point. The stately homes with trim yards and luxurious trees were all tucked away on cul-de-sacs or hidden on out-of-the-way streets, as though the town camouflaged its prosperity from random motorists and traveling salesmen.

To the right of the highway, above the shingles curling on rooftops, I could see the football stadium. Not the one I had played in but a newer one. Even this one, scarcely fifteen years old, held painful memories. Our last and best chance to beat Center Point came in that stadium.

The Wanderer Springs school had been integrated because of Tommy Waters and Doll McFrazier. Tommy was fast, quick, and strong, a better athlete than Vivian Whatley, some said. A team with Tommy Waters and Doll McFrazier, a huge black lineman, could beat Center Point.

Doll, who had a chance at a college scholarship, injured a knee and said he couldn't play against Center Point without a doctor's okay. Dr. Heslar said it was okay for him to play, if he didn't reinjure his knee. Doll thought the doctor said no. The coach, Vivian Whatley, thought the doctor said yes. When Doll refused to play, Vivian kicked him off the team, and Tommy

Waters and the other blacks quit. Without them Wanderer Springs received the humiliation they had fought all those years to avoid. It was more than just defeat. It was the end of the rivalry, the end of a tradition, the final admission that Center Point had won. Not because they were better, but because blacks refused to play the game.

Center Point had been located on the railroad track, built around a town square, and had expanded along the roads to the other towns in the county. Then the Interstate was built on the north side of town and the courthouse square had been deserted by all but the forlorn gray soldier who looked forever into the past although he had lost the hand that had once shielded his eyes.

Clement Arp told me that the two biggest mistakes he had made were promoting football and promoting the Confederate statue. Clement had been reared by his mother, of whom little was known. In Center Point they said she was a beautiful but frail woman who had no heart for the hardship and danger of a free press in Fort Worth. In Wanderer Springs they said she was a "Fort Worth frail."

Clement came to Center Point to help Chris with the paper. Clement was large; his father was robust. He was forbearing; Chris was forthright. Careful where Chris was clumsy; exacting where Chris was exciting; plodding where Chris was prophetic. Chris was feared: Clement was liked.

Clement's first idea was to raze a block of firetrap slum houses owned by the railroad and turn the area into a park. The idea lay dormant until the doughboys came home as voters and the politicians conceived the idea of a park complete with a doughboy statue. Their efforts to raise funds fell short, and rather than admit defeat, they purchased a surplus Confederate statue, which was all they could afford. The plans for the park were abandoned, and the statue was placed on the courthouse square where the county would be responsible for it.

A lot of Texas towns sported Confederate statues, but Wanderer Springs County hadn't existed at the time of the Civil War, there had never been a slave in the county, and most of the settlers came from free states. Clement Arp thought the statue a mistake, but it was appropriate. The statue didn't represent identification with slavery or the Confederacy but with an idealized past of gallant men and gentle women defying foreign interference and an idealized present of self-reliant men and self-denying women stubbornly resisting change.

The statue represented distrust of anything that came from Washington. Austin was as far from common sense as anyone wanted to get. True, the legislature there was composed of fools and knaves, but they were our fools and knaves, and in Austin even the dumbest knew you couldn't bale hay when it was raining. Washington knew no such reason.

Wanderer Springs identified even more personally with the statue. At that first football game, before there was a statue, the Center Point team called itself The Gandy Dancers, Wanderer Springs chose The Rebels. When football became the province of high school students, the team kept the soubriquet, and all school events were attended by a Confederate flag, a troop of girls in gray uniforms called "The Rebel Raiders," and the singing of "Dixie." It had nothing to do with slavery or states' rights, and until Marshall Murdock, nothing to do with the Confederate statue.

Marshall Murdock, the grandson of Reverend Malcolm Murdock, was the only one I knew in high school who could think of anything to do. Marshall was a Baptist, and thinking of things to do was his way of keeping us out of trouble. "We're going to Center Point to claim the Confederate statue," Marshall said. He told Rebel and Roma Dean to make a wreath.

The girls fashioned a wreath out of branches cut from a schoolyard shrub and tied with a ribbon from Roma Dean's hair. We drove to Center Point, and Marshall made a speech about never admitting defeat and forever claimed that sacred spot of ground in the name of Wanderer Springs. Rebel laid the wreath at the foot of the statue.

A car crept slowly down the street, its spotlight flashing around the statue, and then shining in our faces, blinding us. It was Sheriff Brassfield who never walked anywhere but cruised the county in his patrol car. "Get off the grass and take that crap off that statue," Brassfield growled.

Brassfield was a big man with thick silver hair that he brushed straight back and jammed under his Stetson—elected more for his looks than his ability. And reelected as long as he remained unflinchingly faithful to what the majority had decided was not only law but right. "You kids get back to Wanderer Springs where you belong."

"The courthouse and the statue belong to the county. We got as much right here as anybody else," Marshall said. Marshall, like his grandfather, was not afraid when he believed he was right. "We're here to claim the statue in the name of Wanderer Springs."

Brassfield got ponderously out of the car. Brassfield had never looked young. Wearing a gun does that to a man. It makes him serious before his time. And predisposed. Brassfield clapped a hand on Marshall's shoulder, squeezing it, intending to hurt, holding Marshall in place and standing too close to intimidate. "You kids want me telling your daddies that you are trespassing, littering, and disobeying a lawful order?" He looked at Rebel. "You want me to call Mr. Otis Hopkins, the almighty, and tell him I got his daughter in the jail?"

What had started as a lark became, over the years, an embarrassment. Because of the first foolish gesture, every year the football team, the cheerleaders, the school officials and fans, gathered before the monument for a speech, the singing of "Dixie," and the laying of a wreath while Confederate flags waved. It was emotional enough to touch the hearts of football players and high school girls. Until the first black cheerleader,

Melinda Schuman, refused to lay a wreath. What began as fun became a test of loyalty.

As I turned the corner where Buster Bryant had roped his own horse, I saw Brassfield leaning against one of the pipes that had once supported a parking meter, talking to One-Eyed Finch who was now wearing dark glasses over both eyes. Brassfield had been retired almost as long as the meters had been gone from the square, but I did not wave. I regarded Brassfield the way I regarded snakes, not so much afraid of them as re- pelled by their nature.

Brassfield, recognizing an unfamiliar car, straightened into his hands-on-hips, head cocked, sheriff's posture and stud- ied the car as it passed. Old suspicions never die. One-Eyed Finch, with dark glasses like a blindfold, emulated justice. Un- like Wink Bailey, who had lost an eye helping Grandfather, Finch had two eyes, but one of them was cock-eyed and he wore a smoked lens over it so that when he talked people wouldn't follow the wrong eye.

Finch had been a doodlebug, an oil smeller, until he lost his reputation. It was Finch who had discovered oil on the land that Otis Hopkins had inherited by shooting his Aunt Velma. Finch's picture was in the paper and for a while he lorded it over people, driving around in a car, and flying off to smell oil in Palestine. "Finch has recently returned from the Holy Land," reported the Center Point paper. "He says things are very dry over there."

Finch never discovered oil again and soon even wildcat- ters publicly acknowledged their faith in geology. Finch turned to Cheap John peddling, driving from farmhouse to farm- house, selling vanilla, scissors, packets of needles, and laxa- tives. No one would buy from him. Folks did not easily forgive a crime against the community, and failing after putting on airs was a crime.

Finch had to move in with his unmarried sister, Vernell, until he was elected Justice of the Peace. Folks liked to believe there was some mystery to the ballot and that elections indicated the will of the people and the purpose of God. They were contemptuous of anyone who volunteered for the dirty business, and they were suspicious of anyone who was trained for the job.

Vernell placed Finch's name on the ballot and Finch was smart enough not to campaign. No one liked Justices of the Peace, no one liked One-Eyed Finch, and no one was less qualified. It was an arrangement made in heaven.

The old red bricks showed through bare spaces in the asphalt and derelict buildings stood on what had once been the busiest street in Center Point. Business had moved to the Interstate, hostage to transportation. Only the newspaper remained.

Chris, the founder and first editor, had died of a stroke while waiting for the Mobeetie River bridge to wash out the way he had predicted for years. Folks were never happy with the bridge—they believed it had been put in the wrong place—until a Greyhound bus ran off the side and fell eighteen feet into four inches of water. No one was killed but there were enough bodies and luggage strewn around to make up for years of disappointment. Clement's paper had three pages of photographs.

Even after Clement came, the paper still got a laugh out of Wanderer Springs. "Wanderer Springs man ropes his own horse," Clement wrote when Buster Bryant, the greatest rider in the county, maybe the state, chased runaway cows across the courthouse square. Buster was not remembered for his courage and endurance in riding to save his father's ranch, or for his efforts to regain past glory, but because his horse slipped on wet bricks and skidded through the loop Buster had just thrown.

Nevertheless, Clement, a gentler man than his father, believed the purpose of a newspaper was to serve the community. It was Clement who asked me to write a column on county history, after I had returned to Wanderer Springs to teach. "Center Point history?" I asked. "County history," he said, aware as I that most county history centered around Wanderer Springs. Clement wanted to create a friendly feeling between the two towns and atone for the excesses of his father and for his own part in the scandal of Turtle Hole.

John Ballard had asked me to write about his parents, Limp and Ida. John was a county success story. He had left his father's home when he was fourteen, gone to Center Point where he swept floors and washed bodies in the mortuary for room and board, and studied at night. Eventually he became a mortician, married the undertaker's plain but pliant daughter, built the two-story, turreted Ballard house, and after his father-in-law died, changed the name of the mortuary from Sunset Funeral Parlor to Ballard Funeral Home.

John's face had gone to flesh as though there were not a bone in it. The fringe of hair around the dome of his head was too neat, the back of his neck too cleanly shaved. His hand was cool and slick with hand lotion when he invited me into the house.

John wanted to show me his acquisitions before taking me to his mother in the back yard. Ida was in a wheelchair, her left arm hung useless, and the left side of her face was drawn so that only a gleam could be seen in her left eye. But she remembered her early days in the county.

"Limp told me to take the wagon and go to Bull Valley and get him some chewing tobacco, and there was sixteen fences to cross," Ida said. "It took me all day to open and close them wire gaps, and when I got back home, I said, 'I hope you get sick ever time you put that tobacco in your mouth,' and you know, he done it. Before he died he said, 'Well, Ida, you got your wish.' He couldn't put nothing in his stomach without getting sick. His stomach was just eat up with that old cancer. That was the last thing he ever said to me. Never did talk much."

I tempered the story as best I could without lying—most of the folks who read the column remembered Limp Ballard—but the story Ida told me about bearing and raising children in

WANDERER SPRINGS

a dugout with no one to help but lazy, selfish Limp was not the story John had in mind. All the Ballard children had fled the poverty of their father's farm. Only John had not fled the county and the weight of his father's name. John was so offended by the story he went to the editor, Harley Arp.

Clement's son, Harley, was college trained with a degree in marketing. He was young, bright, wore his hair long and stringy and his eyeglasses oversized and yellow-tinted. Harley believed the business of a paper was to give the public what they wanted. If Chris Arp had been alive he would have said, "I say he was a slack son-of-a-bitch, and it's my paper." If Clement had been editor he would have told me to write a column about John Ballard studying at night, taking over the business and turning it into the modern funeral parlor that was a credit to the community. Harley didn't say anything; he replaced my column with a weekly summary of what was happening in the soap operas so that those who missed their favorite programs would not have to endure the suspense.

Maybe it wasn't because the Ballard Funeral Home was one of the paper's biggest advertisers. Maybe it was because life in soap operas was more interesting than life on the frontier. The paper ran an editorial extolling the funeral home for their years of community service. And Sheriff Brassfield pulled me over, cited me for speeding, changing lanes without a signal, and for having a burned-out taillight.

I did have a burned-out taillight, but ordinarily Brassfield would have warned me and let me go. Once he had stopped me for reckless driving after I had interviewed Zollie Cox, the first black woman in the county. "You're stupid, Will," he had said. "You are supposed to be a history teacher and you don't even know what you just done. You'll start something you won't be able to stop, giving them people a history." This time he hauled me before One-Eyed Finch who assessed a fine. When I left Finch's office, Brassfield massaged my shoulder in the overbearing way he had. "You're stupid, Will, making the Ballards look bad. People like the Ballards made this county what it is."

That was no doubt true. John turned the finest house in Center Point into a funeral parlor. He built a cottage on two acres of the worthless land his father had homesteaded. Roses grew on the fence around his cottage. Peach trees bloomed in the garden, orchids grew in the hothouse. Peacocks strutted on the lawn, with miniature donkeys, and Irish wolfhounds that— if he could have shot one—would have fulfilled Elmer Spruill's life. It was also true that John Ballard, who paid Brassfield to lead funeral processions and Finch to notarize papers, and who contributed to their reelection funds, also made Finch and Brassfield what they were. And the paper what it was. Right.

THE FARM

*The Big Pile Up, the death of a bad man,
the drowning at Turtle Hole
and the opiate of the people*

AHEAD of me, larger in my mind than in my eyes, had loomed the old bridge of disappointment, that had been built in the wrong place, that had broken Chris Arp's heart, where Delores had died.

I turned onto the county road that led over Paymore Hill. In the early days of the county a locomotive had killed one of Emil Drieschner's hogs and the railroad had refused to pay what Emil thought was fair value. Every night Emil and his daughters went out and greased the tracks so that the steam engines had trouble pulling the grade after crossing the Mobeetie. The railroad had reconsidered, and the grade became known as Paymore Hill. "Old Emil raised them girls right," folks said.

To the left was the McCarroll place. Mary McCarroll came from Ohio with her husband, Harmon. They had a baby girl, Beth, who was so small when she was born they put her in a shoe box. One day Harmon left on a haying trip, warning Mary that he might not return until the next day, and asking her to bring in the cows and milk before dark.

Mary either forgot about the cows or waited until the last minute hoping that Harmon would return. Not wishing to leave Beth alone, Mary put the child in the wagon her father had made her, and pulling the wagon, started after the cows. Something, perhaps the wagon, startled the cows. The cows ran and Mary left Beth in the wagon and ran after them. It was completely dark when Mary realized that she was lost and did not know where she had left her child. Mary imagined lobos sniffing her baby.

Grandmother found Mary the next morning, stumbling across the prairie, calling for Elizabeth, out of her senses with fear and exhaustion. Grandmother got the distracted woman into the house and leaving Dad and Uncle Emmett to watch over her, harnessed a mule and rode off bareback in search of the child. Grandmother found Beth playing on the ground before the wagon. The cows had come to the house to be milked. Grandmother knew that Mary was waiting for some news of her child, but she milked the cows and fed Beth before starting for home. Milk cows and children were meant to be pampered; mothers were not.

Mary never recovered from that night of terror. Sometimes Harmon would come in from the field to find Mary holding the weeping child, unable to let her go. Sometimes Dad was awakened in the night by Mary calling for Beth. Grandmother would get up, light the lantern, and with Dad and Uncle Emmett, search for the deranged woman. Sometimes they could bring her to the house and sometimes they couldn't. When they could not lead Mary to the house, Grandmother gave Dad the lantern to follow Mary until morning. Dad was still a child himself, too young to be much help in the field, and he stumbled after Mary until dawn, as frightened as she, crying and calling with her, "Bethie, Bethie."

Mary recovered her senses in the Sister Druscilla Majors meeting, and at the sister's trial Mary was required to sit before the jury unmoved while Beth cried for her outside the courtroom. But Mary had always been sane in the daytime. It was only at night that she thought she had lost her child. Until Beth married Babe English and left home.

Mary could not reconcile herself to Beth's absence although Grandmother talked to her sternly and sat with her many times. "No sooner did she see me than she saluted me," Grandmother wrote to relatives in Vermont. "'O, Carrie, I have been all day trying to reconcile my mind and I believe it is reconciled.' I visited her often but she continued rather stupid at times."

When there was no one to stay with Mary, Harmon locked her in the house while he worked in the fields. At such times Grandmother, Dad, and Uncle Emmett avoided the field nearest the McCarroll house because they could hear Mary beating on the door and crying for her child. One day the house caught fire and Mary burned to death before Harmon could unlock the door to let her out.

Harmon moved to Arkansas where, it was said, he became superstitious. After Babe English was killed in court, Beth married Ferguson the Fiddler although he was no longer invited to parties because he wasn't much of a fiddler any more and had never been much of a farmer. They lived in relative obscurity except for Beth's appearances with the football team. They had one son, Ira, who sold both the Ferguson and McCarroll places and used the money to buy farm equipment. Ira, who leases the land where his grandmother searched for his mother, has title to nothing but machinery.

A few folks claim that at night you can hear Mary calling "Bethie" and see the flickering light of her lantern. For a good ghost story you have to go to the pines of East Texas or the brush of South Texas. West Texas does have ghost stories but none are satisfactory because there are not enough trees. Wanderer Springs had barely enough trees to account for the two strange children that Mattie Lance found.

I stopped at the overpass where Wink Bailey had seen The Rapture. Not long after the end of World War II, Wink, the Wanderer Springs constable, had been given a radio-equipped

car so he could call Sheriff Brassfield because no one believed
Wink could handle an emergency. One night Wink came over
the railroad overpass and saw before him several cars, smashed
beyond belief and strewn along the highway.

Grabbing the microphone, Wink called for help. "There's
a big pile up at the overpass," he shouted. "Send the sheriff.
Call the highway patrol. Send ambulances." Half paralyzed by
fear of what he would see, he stumbled towards the smashed
cars to aid the injured. The cars were empty. There was not a
human being in any of them.

Another man might have thought of flying saucers, but
Wink was religious and it occurred to him that The Rapture
had come and true believers had been bodily snatched from
earth to heaven, leaving their cars to smash. Because of some
unknown sin, he had been left behind.

Sheriff Brassfield, two highway patrol cars, and three ambulances arrived to find Wink sitting on the ground contem-
plating his soul. It was some hours before he fully understood
that a truck carrying wrecked cars had snapped a cable coming over the overpass and had unknowingly scattered its load.

Clement Arp could not resist a laugh at Wanderer Springs.
His story on Wink Bailey and The Big Pile Up was carried by
the wire services, and all over the country folks laughed at a
hick town that could turn junk into a miracle. Otis Hopkins,
"the saint of Wanderer Springs" and a member of Wink's church,
forced Wink to resign as constable. There was no one to replace him and Wink was rehired, but first he had to apologize
to Otis for any loss of business he might have caused the bank.
Otis was sensitive when it came to money.

I had stopped on the overpass countless times before,
looking over the little valley Grandfather had chosen, looking
for something that reminded him of Ireland. I never found it. I
suspect Grandfather first saw it in the spring. A spring rain

turned everything except the sky into shades of green, a veritable paradise—a deception no less painful than Wink Bailey's Big Pile Up.

Texas was a distant and dubious republic when Grandmother was born in Vermont, the daughter of a shopkeeper. She would defy her family, cross the continent unchaperoned, marry beneath her station, bear two sons after she was forty, be instrumental in the killing of one man and the lynching of another, and hang on to the farm, and her sons, with a grasp that reached beyond the grave.

After we were married, Delores and I went to Vermont to find traces of Grandmother who had died, at the age of ninety, the year I was born. We found strangers who clung to brittle letters, a fragile photograph, anecdotes that seemed to have outlived their cautionary purpose. And Grandmother's first sight of my birthplace.

"It being a very pleasant day and I had seen but little of the country, he proposed riding and viewing the country during the remainder of the day," Grandmother had written. "The traveling was very rough, we were at a loss whether to persevere but he wanted to show me a little valley and I thought I was willing to make some sacrifices if I could see it."

Grandmother's rare letters had been passed from relative to relative and read with amusement and amazement. Many letters had been lost or had fallen apart, the others had been cherished, along with the anecdotes, as mementos of an eccentric relative, far enough removed to have lost all trace of taint.

She had gone to California to teach school when there was a school right down the road, they said, their voices rich in marvel. She traveled unchaperoned. Their tones and eyebrows still bore vestiges of disapproval.

There had been a breach in the family; Grandmother had become a Protestant and a Democrat. They were made shy by those words, not knowing whether the contamination had reached to her grandchild. During the Civil War Grandmother had played the piano at patriotic rallies where her father had exhorted young men to enlist in the Union's noble cause. According to the story, which perhaps became more romantic with the passage of time, Grandmother's fiance, Noble, had been recruited by her father for the heroic cause that maimed him. Noble lost both legs at Kennesaw Mountain. Rather than be a burden on his family, too honorable to claim the heart that had been pledged to him, young Noble took his own life. Grandmother sought solace, and perhaps revenge, in Methodism and teaching.

It is a good story, but there is considerable evidence that Grandmother became a Protestant before the war—braving the displeasure of her family—and became a teacher to establish her independence. Propriety required that she remain in her father's house despite what was sometimes open hostility.

"After the meeting, I selected Brother and Mrs. Cook and a young man from a distance to go home with me, which invitation they readily accepted. After arriving at home, my mother, not thinking that I would desire to bring anyone there, began to be fretful, which destroyed our enjoyment in her presence. Mother said she would not entertain Mr. Cook and his lady (as she termed them), and that I must not touch anything that belonged to her to entertain them with."

Some of the family believe that Noble was the young man from a distance, that Grandmother became a Methodist to please him, and that he enlisted in the army to appease her father.

Grandmother remained in her father's house, engaging and teaching her scholars, for ten years after Noble's death. She didn't go to California until after her father died. She was forty, perhaps still pining for Noble, certain that love, family, children had been stolen from her when she met Grandfather, a homesick Irishman eight years her junior, come to California to work on the railroad.

"Attended prayer meeting and enjoyed much," she wrote her sister. "There being some rude young people outside, I invited them in, and after some hesitation one of them came in with countenance sad. After the meeting he expressed himself in such a simple and plain manner that I was much embarrassed among the idle lookers on."

His simple and plain manner must have touched Grandmother, because she married him and followed him to Texas where they lived in a tent beside the tracks. The tent city boasted of dog fights, horseback billiards, saloons, gambling tents, and dancing tents, but water was so scarce that when one man finished eating, his plate was wiped with a cloth and filled for the next man. When there were non-Irish, the Irish fought them. When there were not, they fought each other.

"We were in a tent by ourselves," Grandmother wrote, "rejoicing that we were so favorably situated as to be alone. But how soon was our attention attracted by the wicked and profane people about the camp. I thought I had never heard such wickedness proceeding from humanity. They were subjects for the lowest hell. I could have wept for them if it would have benefited their souls. I had rather go to joys on high alone than sink to ruin with such a profane and trifling multitude. I think it will be impossible for us to remain upon the terms of such company."

Grandmother's kin gave me a photograph of Grandmother and Grandfather, taken in Sacramento. It is the only known photograph of Grandfather. If there were others, they were destroyed by Uncle Emmett. In the picture, Grandfather sits stiffly erect, Grandmother stands beside him. Grandfather looks like what Grandmother's relatives claimed him to be, a sentimental brawler, who had fled Cork because of some indiscretion. He is tall and even in his suit and vest he has the shoulders, arms, and waist of a man who spends his days in heavy work, and the sparkling eyes, thick, curling moustache, and sensitive mouth of a man who spends his nights singing, dancing, and fighting.

Grandmother looks like a school teacher in the days when teachers directed pupils, not like an orchestra but like traffic.

There is not a hint of humor on her face, not a rumor of a past laugh on this, the happiest day of her life. Her eyes are looking not at the camera but at the photographer; it is a look demanding that he do his job properly. She has a straight mouth that does not want for words. Her hand on Grandfather's shoulder is sure, the hand of a teacher on a pupil, not to reprimand or punish but to caution.

Perhaps it was that cautionary hand on his shoulder that caused Grandfather to show Grandmother a little valley, and with her approval and no doubt her money, buy it. Or perhaps it was because Joe Whatley had closed his Sand saloon, become a Methodist, and opened a boarding house not a hundred yards from the boxcar where Grandmother cared for her two sons.

"We have been much tried by one family," Grandmother wrote, "but neglected to act until from their continued dishonesty we concluded they were bitter enemies of the Christian religion. I was solicited to write a few words of our dissatisfaction with them and a desire of their expellment, together with the names of the interested members, and carry it to the family.

"I hesitated going on account of their accustomed misusage by a misgoverned temper but seeing my duty, I entered their house and delivered the billet, desiring that they do righteously. They replied that they were as righteous as we, making many threats. I arose to leave on which the head of the family, using the most vulgar and profane language, declared that Brother Hight could remain in his dugout no longer, Brother Hight's name being upon the paper."

A few months after Hight's death and Whatley's hanging, Grandmother moved to the farm, living in a wagon with her two sons, and hauling water from the McCarroll well. Grandfather still worked on the railroad. He came home whenever he could, dropping off a work train or handcar. Breaking and planting the land, digging a well, and building a house waited upon spare time and money.

A ten-year-old boy, Arlen Bailey, came to Grandfather begging for a job on the railroad. It was a time when railroads were protected and children were not. Grandfather took the boy home and hired him to help Uncle Emmett dig the well. One day Bailey and Uncle Emmett reached a hardpan that neither could dig through. Bailey found some dynamite that Grandfather used on the railroad, put it in the well to blast a hole, and lighted a fuse. The charge failed to go off. Bailey lay down beside the well and peeked one eye over the hole. The dynamite went off knocking out his right eye.

Grandmother sent Uncle Emmett on a mule to get Dr. Vestal but there was little the doctor could do. Bailey continued at the farm, helping Grandfather finish the well and build the house, but he was self-conscious about his appearance. Apparently Dad and Uncle Emmett teased him about it. Grandfather bought him an artificial eye made of celluloid as it had a good appearance and was cheaper than glass, but Bailey complained of headaches caused by the celluloid and he developed a tic that tempted Uncle Emmett to call him "Wink."

Grandfather took Wink to Fort Worth for a glass eye. There Grandfather met a young man, Willie Thomas, he had fired from the railroad. Thomas invited Grandfather to have a drink. As they walked across the street, Thomas shot Grandfather in the back and robbed him. They caught him two days later. He was tried, sentenced to hang; his sentence was commuted to life, and he was later paroled. Uncle Emmett kept up with his whereabouts.

Wink, still a child, caught the train back to Wanderer Springs and walked to the farm to tell Grandmother the news. Grandfather was buried in a pauper's grave in Fort Worth. Grandmother had no time to attend the funeral; there was barely time to weep. There was plowing and planting to be done, cows to milk, hogs to slaughter, boys to raise.

Grandmother worked in the fields, ruining her hands so that she could no longer play the piano she had brought from

Sacramento. After it was too dark to work, she cooked supper, and while they ate, she taught her sons, and Wink Bailey, to read, write, and do sums, thumping them on the temple with a gnarled finger when they fell asleep from exhaustion. After they dragged themselves to bed, she washed and mended their clothes.

Although the work was hard and Grandmother could not pay him, Wink stayed until constant bickering with Uncle Emmett forced him to fight or leave. Wink left and became constable of Wanderer Springs because he didn't want the job and seemed unsuited for it.

One year floods washed out the cotton three times. It was late in the season and Dad, Uncle Emmett, and Grandmother plowed as long as there was light, getting the ground ready for planting. Another failure meant loss of the farm. One day Grandmother fainted from exhaustion and the mules dragged her to the house. She was painfully scraped and bruised, and after Dad and Uncle Emmett carried her to bed, she caught them by the hands and told them they had to take the wagon to Otis Hopkins and get seed for planting. Otis had the only cottonseed left in the county because after the first washout he had not bothered to replant.

"Where's the money?" Uncle Emmett asked.

"There is no money. You must ask him for the seed."

"I'll sell the piano," Uncle Emmett said. It was the only thing they had they could sell.

"No." Grandmother had given up church, books, music, association with other women in order to hang on to the land, but she would not give up the piano. "You must ask him. You must beg him, Emmett. We must have seed."

When Uncle Emmett refused, Grandmother asked Dad to help her out of bed. Stiff with arthritis, sore from her scrapes and bruises, Grandmother dressed and, with Dad's help, walked outside. Only the fact that she was unable to climb into the wagon induced Uncle Emmett to go.

They helped Grandmother back to bed and drove to the farm Otis had inherited by shooting his Aunt Velma. Uncle Emmett asked for seed. He pledged Dad and himself for the seed. Otis refused unless Grandmother went to Center Point and signed a mortgage to the farm. Uncle Emmett explained in vain that Grandmother could not get in the wagon. He begged Otis for the seed and when Otis said Christians did not accept charity, Uncle Emmett knocked him down. He would have beaten him more severely if Dad had not intervened.

They got back in the wagon, drove out of sight, and Uncle Emmett stopped the wagon. "We'll wait for dark," he said.

"What are we going to do?" Dad asked.

"We're going to go back and get that seed."

"What if Otis tries to stop us?"

"I'll kill him," Uncle Emmett said.

Wink Bailey, the constable, came out to the field where Dad and Uncle Emmett were planting. "You boys are going to have to return that seed or I'll have to arrest you," he said. "But since it's already in the ground I reckon you can wait until fall." Dad said when they went back in darkness to return the seed, they had to wait in line. Limp and Ida Ballard, and however many kids they had at the time, were furtively shoveling cottonseed into Otis's barn.

Grandmother never fully recovered from being dragged by mules. Her will remained strong but her body betrayed her. She slowly collapsed like a weathered barn, her mind departing like shingles from the roof, followed by the inexorable caving in of her exhausted bones. Only her will remained strong and that will kept Dad and Uncle Emmett on the farm, at her side.

Dad was drafted during World War I. He was thirty years old, Grandmother was seventy-five, and he never expected to see her again. After the horror, the Armistice, the parades, he came home to find Grandmother with Uncle Emmett firmly in her grasp. "I will not have a fractious boy in my house, Emmett. Come now and do your sums."

At such times Uncle Emmett, big like Grandfather, dark like Grandmother, would add, do equations, recite the multiplication table. Dad wanted to hire a woman to take care of Grandmother. Uncle Emmett angrily dismissed the idea.

More of the farm was turned to cultivation to make a living until even with tractors, there was more work than the two of them could do. There were plenty of men looking for work, sharecroppers most of them, forced off the land and with no other skills.

Dad and Uncle Emmett built a house behind the barn and hired a widower with three strong grown sons and a young daughter. The men worked in the field, and the girl cooked and cleaned house for Dad and Uncle Emmett as well as her own family. When Grandmother's body failed, first her eyes, then her bladder, last of all her heart, the girl took care of her also.

The hands decided to move to California where jobs were better. Dad asked the girl to stay and she agreed. Her father and brothers came to the house to get her. Dad, who was close to thirty years older than she, said he would marry her. It made no difference; they insisted she go with them. There was a fight, Dad fighting alone until Uncle Emmett arrived.

Dad did marry the girl, a tall, willowy brunette who, Wink Bailey said, always seemed puzzled by the two old men who shared the house with her. Uncle Emmett was as opposed to the marriage as her family was and would have moved into the tenant house had Dad not hired a black couple, Zollie and Tomoliver Turkett, to help with the farm. Zollie was the first black child born in the county. Her father, Luster Cox, a blacksmith and cowboy for the Prod, had died during a fever epidemic and had been buried behind the Tabor house.

Hiring blacks was a surprising thing to do. Everyone knew hunger made blacks, who were naturally lazy, both industrious and cheerful. Blacks worked in the county but only at jobs that whites would not take, and there were plenty of white men who would have moved into the tenant house. Uncle Emmett brooded, speaking to no one.

During Grandmother's last days when only her heart lived and her dying body filled the house with its sickly perfume, Uncle Emmett sat on the porch, refusing to eat or speak. When Grandmother died, Dad went to Center Point for a doctor to pronounce the final earthly judgment. While he was gone, Uncle Emmett's rage exploded. He took Grandmother's things from the house, her clothes, bedding, mementoes from Vermont, Sacramento, the days beside the railroad track, her books, letters, pictures, threw them in the old dugout-storm cellar, caved it in, then drove a tractor back and forth across it to seal it. He dragged Grandmother's piano into the yard and chopped it to bits with an axe in a frenzy of destruction.

Dad returned with a doctor, calmed his brother and got him to eat a little. Uncle Emmett spoke to no one at the funeral but allowed folks to shake his hand and offer condolences. Afterwards he posed for a photograph, then announced that Willie Thomas was in Borger and he was going to kill him.

In the photograph Uncle Emmett, tall, balding, a little stooped by his near fifty years of hard work, stares at the ground. Dark face, dark eyes, dark thoughts. Dad glowers at the photographer; the photograph is not his idea. Dad is fair, shorter, and stouter than Uncle Emmett. He stands stiffly beside his wife who looks like a high school girl posing with two bachelor uncles. She looks into the future, her arms crossed protectively over the lump that is me.

In Borger, Uncle Emmett stayed in a boarding house where Thomas was last seen. One day he found a man named Clint Hargen beating a young woman. Uncle Emmett hit him over the head with the pistol Grandfather had brought to Texas. The next day while Uncle Emmett was putting air in a tire, Hargen walked up behind him and shot him five times in the back. As

Uncle Emmett slumped dead against the car, Grandfather's pistol fell from his coat.

At his trial, Hargen said that Uncle Emmett had taken his girlfriend, and when he tried to win her back, Emmett had beaten him and threatened to kill him. Seeing Uncle Emmett across the street the following day, he had walked over to straighten things out. When he spoke to Callaghan, Callaghan reached in his coat as though he were reaching for his six-shooter and Hargen shot him in self-defense.

Hargen, who had found religion and poetry while in jail, was acquitted. He went to California where he became a guitar-playing evangelist who told and sang of the wicked life he had left behind. "I had my fill of whiskey while with the girls I ran, I killed a Texas badman named Emmett Callaghan."

I don't remember much of Mother. The smell of her powder. The touch of her hand. Sometimes I can recall the way she laughed, behind her hand, trying not to laugh too loud. She sang to me, I think not very well. I did not know that she was nearer my age than Dad's.

I remember that she cried because Dad would not take me to Center Point for a haircut. In Melvin Perkins's palsied hands the clippers beat a tattoo against my skull and the scissors pulled my hair. Even Dad paled when Melvin got close to his ears with the razor. "We have to go to Melvin," Dad said. "He can't do any better."

I used to ask Dad what Mother was like, but he was not helpful. "She grew up in a family of boys . . . she worked hard . . . she was very good with Mother . . . strong . . . she could move Mother by herself . . . she didn't understand Emmett. It was like she was afraid of him."

What I liked best were the stories, maybe as an antidote to the one story I had of my own. The only clear memory I have of Mother is of her showing me her family album, trying to acquaint me with grandparents, aunts and uncles, cousins I had never seen. I was sitting on her lap, happy to be held, talked to. "Who's that?" I asked, pointing at a stiffly handsome young man posed in front of a screen with a rose arbor painted on it.

"That was almost your father," she said. "If Papa hadn't locked me in the house I would have run off and married him."

I could have been anyone, born any place. I had burst into tears. "Who would I be?" I wailed.

Mother tried to tease away my tears. "You'd be my special boy," she said. "That's who you are. That's who you'll always be. My special boy."

Dad's stories were more reassuring. "Your mother always wanted to be doing something, going some place when there was more than I could get done right here. We drove to Center Point once because they had tutti-frutti ice cream and she wanted to know what it tasted like." Dad did not eat ice cream. "You were just a tiny thing, but you sucked at it until you got the hiccups."

"She liked dressing up in Mother's old hats and dresses. I let her wear them when Emmett wasn't around. I gave her Mother's jewelry. She had a broach with pearls all the way around it."

"What happened to it?"

"Emmett put everything in the dugout."

"Didn't you ever dig them up?"

"After Emmett died I just didn't feel like it, and then—"

Then it was too late. Mother was dead too. Dad had been awakened by the rattling of the barn doors. Fearing someone was trying to steal the truck that was kept in the barn, he had gotten Grandfather's pistol, the bone handle cracked from where it had fallen from Uncle Emmett's pocket. He crawled out a back window and came around the side of the house. Keeping the house between him and the barn, he yelled, "Come out with your hands up."

Mother had been awakened by his exit through the window, and, not understanding what was happening, stepped out on the porch just as Dad called. "Will," she cried in surprise. Shots were fired from the barn and she fell dead.

I no longer know what is memory, what is information, and what is imagination. In my mind Mother was wearing a flowing white gown and when she was shot, she collapsed, as though whatever substance had been in the gown had dissolved. She fell like a gown falls, or a coat that has missed the hook on the wall.

Dad said that when he came to check on me, I was asleep. Tomoliver, the black man who lived in the tenant house, came to see what the shooting was, and Dad gave him the pistol and told him to stay with Mother and me. Tomoliver was old but agile—he reminded me of a spider, with long bony arms that worked like magic in the cottonfield. He had a small, bald head, a thin white moustache, and eyes made wise by injustice. Where some grew hard, Tomoliver grew gentle.

Tomoliver sat on the porch with his back to Mother, not because she was dead, but because she was white and because she was not properly dressed to be with black folks. For the same reason he did not enter a white man's house, even to comfort his son. Tomoliver sat on the porch holding the pistol and saying, "Ise here. Ain't nobody gonna harm you longs Ise here."

Dad had killed one of the robbers and had wounded the other. Leaving Tomoliver to guard me, he had hunted the wounded man. That's the story they tell in Wanderer Springs. That is what saved us from a reputation of weakness. Grandfather, Uncle Emmett, Mother had all been killed. No matter that Grandfather and Uncle Emmett were shot in the back and Mother was unarmed. There were no innocent victims in Wanderer Springs. To be a victim indicated weakness, and to be weak was to deserve whatever happened to you. Dad had killed one man and tried to kill the other.

Wink Bailey told a different story. Dad had left the pistol with Tomoliver to protect me. Not knowing whether or not the wounded man was armed, Dad had taken a lantern and searched all night for him, fearing he would bleed to death untended. "That was the bravest thing I ever heard of," Wink told me the night he drove me home from Brassfield's interrogation. But that story was never told in Wanderer Springs. Better that Dad was the implacable avenger.

The two robbers were young men who had been unable to get any kind of work. One of them, Joel Kincheloe, a cousin of Roma Dean Tooley, had a wife and baby and was desperate for money. His brother-in-law, a cousin to Bud Tabor, arranged with Limp Ballard to pick a truck load of melons and take them to Center Point to sell.

On the way to Center Point they ruined a truck tire and had no money for another one. Knowing that the melons would ruin if they did not get them to market, they walked to the farm to steal a tire off Dad's truck. Kincheloe was carrying an old pistol that belonged to Oscar Spruill. They were afraid someone would try to steal the money from the sale of the melons, Kincheloe testified at the trial.

Dad had startled them when he yelled. Tabor, fearing that Dad would recognize them, fired a shot at the house to prevent him from coming outside. They did not know Mother was on the porch. Dad fired at the gunflash, killing Tabor, and fired again when he saw Kincheloe run.

Kincheloe, only slightly wounded, turned himself in to Wink Bailey. His mother and father, his wife carrying the baby, came to beg Dad to spare his life. Although he had not pulled the trigger, under the law he was equally responsible for Mother's death. The mother and wife sobbed uncontrollably and at one point the mother fell to the ground. The wife, unable to fall because of the baby, sank to her knees.

The father, left to do the talking, earnestly sought Dad's eyes. "He never hurt nobody," he said. "Never been no trouble. We'll do anything you ask. You ask it. His wife here has agreed." The poor woman stopped in midsob to hear her fate.

"I'm sorry," Dad said, over and over. "I'm sorry." Dad blamed himself for Mother's death. If he had awakened Mother and told her to get under the bed before he went outside. If he had gone to the barn to confront the robbers. If he had done nothing. I think in Tabor and Kincheloe, Dad saw two young men stealing cotton from Otis Hopkins. "I'll do what I can," he said.

Dad's words produced more wails, more promises. "We'll do anything." They were poor, destroyed by grief, every dream shattered, every nightmare come true, but they didn't know how to accept a favor. They were trying to find a way to pay. Dad came in the house and left them wailing in the front yard.

Dad did ask the judge for leniency, and Kincheloe was sentenced to life imprisonment. Later he was paroled but his parents were dead, his wife remarried, his daughter, who had been told that he was dead, had a family of her own. He worked at a few jobs, stole a car, and was sent back to prison.

Dealing with Kincheloe's family could hardly have been more difficult for Dad than dealing with Mother's family, come for her funeral. I remember the faces—faces I had seen only in Mother's album. The faces were set, more mask-like than in the photographs. They stood awkwardly, not facing Dad, not looking at him, not looking at anything. Their hands agitated the hats they held.

All three brothers had married in California—young round-faced women in city dresses. They clung tightly to the men and every time one of the men said "the boy" they smiled frightened little smiles at me.

"You can come inside," Dad said.

"We'll talk here," one of them said. He was tall, thin, sharp-nosed, his mouth as sharp as his words.

"Pa wants to see the boy." This was Uncle Rufus, mother's oldest brother, and his patience was studied. "Pa ain't well. He can't come this far. You took her from us, you got no right to keep the boy."

"He's my son."

"It ain't right."

"She'd still be alive if she'd come with us," said the tall

one, jerking away from his wife. She jumped in front of him and put her arms around his waist.

"What are we going to tell Pa?" asked Uncle Rufus, deliberately, as though he were speaking to a child.

"Tell him he's welcome. You all are. You can come here without trouble unless you bring it with you." Dad kept a hand on me, claiming me, rooting me to him. I looked at him. I was not to see that look again until he faced Brassfield.

The women tugged at the men until they walked away, came back, talked some more, still not facing Dad, walked away again. Then Uncle Rufus came and kneeled beside me. He promised on my twelfth birthday he would send a train ticket to California so I could visit them. "Stay as long as you like," he said, looking at Dad.

That was the last I saw of Mother's family, except for the funeral. What I remember most was the strange faces on the people I knew. And being patted, kissed, squeezed by once friendly people who were cold and peculiar, stiff in black and white, with the church-going smells of soap, powder, and oil. They talked in low, solemn voices and seemed embarrassed when I caught them looking at me.

Uncle Rufus never sent me a train ticket; he sent me a crate of oranges instead. I was left with Mother's album of frozen faces, few of whom I recognized. In Asia the poorest peasant knows his ancestors for a hundred years. In America, richness of life means a recreational vehicle and a condominium away from it all.

Mother's death broke not only a link with her family but with Dad's as well. On Dad's side we had skipped two generations, one between Grandmother and Dad, another between Dad and me. Genes don't travel that far. Or instinct. Or tradition. Not without an interpreter. Mother was from my century. She could have told me stories about Dad, Grandmother, Uncle Emmett.

My link to the past was Wink Bailey who huffed and

puffed on his rounds through town, winking over his glass eye. Wink's uniform was red suspenders, khaki shirt and pants, brown belt and boots. Except for his funeral I don't remember seeing him in anything else. Wink was liked but not feared because he didn't wear a gun. Boys taunted him because they didn't think he was tough enough with blacks, Walter Slocum, or themselves.

I liked Wink because he told me how he came back from Fort Worth with the news of Grandfather's death. Grandmother, already stooped and arthritic, was on her knees in the field, picking cotton in one of the long black dresses she always wore and teaching spelling to the boys who picked behind her.

"She knew what had happened when I came back alone. I started crying when I looked at her. I couldn't help it. Because of my eye and all. Emmett, he come over right away. 'We are engaged in picking cotton until dark,' your grandmother said. 'Please pick with me as we converse.' She didn't cry in front of the boys, ever. Your dad cried a little but if Emmett cried it was when he was by himself. Your grandmother told us not to tell nobody. There were some who would have tried to help and some who would have tried to run us off the place—a woman and three boys. It wasn't no place to be weak."

"Me and Emmett didn't get along," he said on another occasion. "Your pa tried to have fun with everything but Emmett was different. He lit into me once because I talked back to his ma. Nobody respected that woman more than I did, but I knew then it was time for me to go. I sure hated to do it. I didn't have no folks."

"It was me that had to tell your dad his brother had been shot. Then I had to talk him out of going to Borger himself. 'You got a wife and child,' I told him. 'I ain't done no killing like you did in France, but I done seen all the dying I ever want to see. I'm asking you to spare me this. I don't never want to have to deliver another death message.'"

It was Wink who showed Jessie Tooley her daughter's dead body.

Wink walked around town checking the buildings, some of them already vacant. Sometimes after school I walked with him and he told me about Dad, and the farm, and Wanderer Springs. Until the Big Pile Up. After that the school kids made so much fun of Wink that I didn't want to be seen with him. That left no one to tell me who I had been born.

Dad and I lived with silence, especially after Mother died. It wasn't the awkward silence of strangers unsure of each other's feelings, but the warm silence of men who know what is expected of them. We rarely talked to communicate feelings the way women seem to do. Dad had lived most of his life with his mother and brother, their only privacy their secret lives. Dad was not trained to disclose his private thoughts. I was raised not to pry.

When we spoke, it was of practical matters. "Bacon?" Dad asked in the morning. I'd nod and he'd slice the bacon in thick slabs and drop it into the skillet. "Eggs?" I'd nod again and he'd push the bacon over and fry eggs and thick slices of bread beside it, divide it equally into two plates, and wipe out the skillet with a towel. "Coffee?" he'd ask, scooping grounds into the skillet. Dad was as sparing of dishes as he was of words.

In Grandmother's house, eating was a necessary break in a long and arduous day. Dad did not talk at the table, something Delores continually forgot. He ate quickly, his thoughts on the future. While we did the dishes—he washing, I drying—he told me of his plans. "I want to get after that corn." Or, "You'd better start plowing the cotton." "We need to dehorn the bull . . . creosote the hen house . . . sharpen the plow points . . . bale alfalfa . . . clean the corn crib . . . prune the fruit trees," or a hundred other chores that waited to be done.

We rarely discussed purposes or ambitions, but certain things were understood. I would go to college. I would hang on to the farm the way Grandmother had done. I would be proud the way Grandmother was proud, the way Uncle Emmett was proud, but I would do right the way Wink Bailey did right—without destroying those whom need had made wrong. There was the unstated fear that like Grandmother I might stand too intently for what was right, like Uncle Emmett harbor too implacably a wrong.

Often Dad and I did not speak from breakfast until after supper. If it was during the school year I walked home from the two-room Bull Valley School and set about my chores, gathering the eggs, and milking the cows. After a silent meal, Dad would read at the table one of the several magazines and newspapers we received.

If I had homework, Dad checked it. Grandmother had done a good job teaching him reading, spelling, and math. Where we had trouble was over history and geography. Grandmother knew the country from the inside of a school house, the backside of a mule, and the end of the railroad track. She was not impressed with the scenic glories of Texas, the moral fibre of its citizens, or its importance as a state. Dad had never seen Vermont or California, but had been to Germany and France, and from a troopship had caught a glimpse of the green glory of Ireland. Dad was kinder regarding both the local scenery and the natives but lightly regarded the heroes. My assignment was to write about a hero, and I was thinking James Bowie or William Barret Travis.

"Take away their guns and what do you have?" Dad asked. In the Meuse-Argonne he had learned to disdain glorious death.

"Tell Hulda Codd the best man this county ever had was Wink Bailey." It was an idea I neglected to communicate. Years before The Big Pile Up, Wink Bailey was sometimes the subject of ridicule. Like most everyone else in the county, I thought our heroes were Earl Lance who shot Oscar Spruill and maybe his own brother, Eli Spivey who had lost a leg at Belleau Wood, and Elmer Spruill who killed the last buffalo.

"This is supposed to be about somebody who is dead," I said, supposing that all heroes were dead. "Miss Codd said it should be about somebody who was brave." How could Wink Bailey be brave? He didn't even carry a gun.

"Why don't you write about your grandmother?" Dad said. His voice was thick, like somebody had him by the throat. It always scared me when he spoke like that.

"Was—" I didn't know what to call a woman I had never seen. "Grandmother" seemed presumptuous, "Mrs. Callaghan" callous. "Was your mother brave?" I asked.

Dad gave me a glimpse of Grandmother I had not seen before. Grandmother had seen the Turrills pass, Grover walking beside the tired mules, Edna standing in the wagon holding Polly in her arms. Grandmother knew what that meant, and she called Dad to her. Uncle Emmett was working in another part of the farm. Grandmother stood behind Dad, her arms around his chest, as they watched the wagon pass, hearing Polly's screams and the shriek of the wagon wheels.

"There wasn't much time for coddling children," Dad said, trying to explain the acuteness of his memory of those work-ruined hands holding him.

"You are not mine, son," Grandmother said, and he could feel tears falling on top of his head. "Not mine to keep. I must not hold you too tightly." Her arms were like bands around his chest, so tight that he began to cry too.

I didn't know whether that was brave or not. I didn't know what the story meant. Mostly I was embarrassed. We sat in the house together, neither of us looking at the other. Dad and I often seemed to be together, not looking at each other. The feelings between fathers and sons are too charged to pass directly and we had no wife and mother to transform the voltage of our affection. We sat locked in our own magnetic field.

Dad was an experienced non-looker. He and Uncle Emmett had avoided looking at each other when Grandmother tried to play the out-of-tune piano with work-stiffened hands or dozed while her boys recited their lessons. They avoided looking at her when she cried in frustration because her body betrayed her will. They had one neighbor, one relative, one friend. They protected her.

Dad turned pale in the presence of a gift. A present had to

be forced into his hands. He had to be instructed to open it. He unwrapped it as though he expected it to blow up in his face. He took it out and placed it on the table as carefully as if it were a bomb. He left the room like a criminal and shied from the gift for three or four days before he could bring himself to use it. It would be months before he could bring himself to say he liked it.

He was scarcely better at giving gifts. Selecting a present was as difficult and mysterious as charting the stars. For my birthday Dad took me to town and gave me money so that I could buy myself a present and take myself to a movie. After the movie I waited for him at the car and we drove home in silence. Dad was no more able to ask, "What did you get for your birthday?" than I was able to say, "Thank you for the toy six-shooter." Instead the six-shooter lay on the seat between us as though it were invisible.

Christmas was more awkward. Dad brought home a tree and I got out the decorations that Mother had brought into the house—faded green and red velvet ropes, a bent tinsel star, glass balls with hair pins or bits of baling wire stuck through the broken necks, a faded paper accordion bell. While I tangled the rope around the tree, Dad made snow out of water and soap and splattered it on the tree. By the time we finished we both hated the tree and after we had opened our presents Christmas morning, I threw it out while Dad fried bacon, eggs, bread, and coffee in the skillet.

Decorating the tree on Christmas Eve was not as painful as opening presents on Christmas morning. Before Mother died I got a stuffed animal and a toy pistol for Christmas. Dad continued the practice as though the gifts were frankincense and myrrh. I knew there was no Santa Claus. Dad knew that I knew, but Santa Claus was useful. Dad could ask, "What do you want Santa to bring you?" and I could be disappointed with Santa for bringing me a stuffed animal and toy pistol instead of a football, so I suffered the humiliation of going to bed early on Christmas Eve and saying, "Look what Santa brought me," over a stuffed animal on Christmas morning. I remain convinced that Santa was invented so folks would have someone to blame for the disappointments of Christmas.

When Dad and I reached the time we could no longer hold Santa responsible, we met in the kitchen on Christmas morning, shoved presents at each other, turned away to open them, muttered thanks, and escaped into our chores—Dad frying breakfast and I milking the cows. We usually didn't speak until after Christmas dinner. It took us that long to get our feelings under control.

It must have been worse for Dad. Every year Hulda Codd required us to make a Christmas present for our parents. Miss Codd had a deserved reputation for being a stern and uncompromising disciplinarian, but I always thought the meanest thing she ever did was to require me to give my father a dainty handkerchief, in the corner of which I had stitched his initials, entwined with a climbing rose. While Dad opened his present, I pretended to talk to my new teddy bear.

Dad must have dropped the handkerchief in the drawer with his neatly folded socks, shorts, and bandannas, because I didn't see it for a long time. Then one day I sat on the steps at the high curb in front of The Corner Drug with Dad, Buster Bryant, and Eli Spivey. Dad didn't always let me sit with him at the curb because that's where the farmers and ranchers met to discuss their wives and the government, and sometimes they forgot I was there.

This day Dad let me remain because there were only three of them, all heroes to me: Eli, with the pegleg that made it possible for him to sit a horse and drive a car; Buster Bryant who had made the greatest ride in the county; and Dad who was my favorite hero of all.

Buster's reputation had been tarnished a little because the Center Point paper had printed a story about him roping his own horse, and because Buster had no hips. A favorite prank in Wanderer Springs was to jerk on Buster's pants leg because his Levis would fall around his ankles, revealing the shorts his wife made out of her old dresses. "Buster's wearing blue polky dots," folks would say. It was always good for a laugh, but it made me sad because Buster, who had been the best, looked foolish in his cowboy boots and calico shorts, with his Stetson covering his fly.

When Dad reached in his pocket to pull out his bandanna and pulled out the handkerchief with the climbing rose, Eli and Buster burst into laughter, Buster said, "Will's got him a lady friend," I said, "Miss Codd made me do it," and burst into tears.

It took me a long time to get over that. Dad was embarrassed, not because his friends had laughed, but because I had cried and because he didn't know what to do when I acted like that. I didn't know what to do either; I was too ashamed to get up and walk away. I sat sobbing helplessly while my three heroes tried to pretend I wasn't there.

Dad never mentioned the incident but I swore I would never embarrass him again and never cry before him. And I didn't until Turtle Hole.

"You panicked, didn't you?" Brassfield asked. He put his hand on my forehead and pushed my head back until I had to look at him through slitted eyes. "She choked, went under, she grabbed at you and pulled you under too. You didn't mean to hit her, you were scared and pissing down your leg, and you hit her so she would let go. Then you pretended you didn't know what happened to her. Didn't you? Didn't you?"

He slipped his hand up my forehead, caught me by the hair and pulled my head around until I had to look at him out of the corners of my eyes. I was aware that tears were running down my cheeks, angry because Brassfield would think I was crying, but I was crying because my hair was being pulled.

"If there is a mark on that girl's body, I'll hold your head under the water until you have to breathe through your asshole."

"That's enough," Wink said. "I'm taking him home."

Brassfield didn't let go of my hair but he turned his attention on Wink. "Get out of my office, you old fool. Get back to Wanderer Springs where you belong."

Wink was old, scorned by those who refused to let him resign the job that had outgrown him. "If I leave I'm going to get his dad," Wink said.

Brassfield pulled my hair harder for a moment, then let go. "Get out of here and take this little shit with you," he said, then caught me by the arm when I stood up. "If that girl is pregnant, I will personally strap you in the electric chair."

Wink drove me home. It was less than fifteen miles, too long to be trapped in the car with Wink, too short to prepare myself to face Dad. "I don't know what happened and I don't want to know," Wink said, his eyelid punctuating his words. "I'm parking this car at The Corner and leaving my badge in it. If they can't find somebody else to do the job, they can do without."

We drove over the bridge of disappointment that spanned the Mobeetie River. "I know your daddy. I know he's going to be sitting up wondering what has happened to you. You tell him. He's your dad and he's a good man."

We rode in silence for a while, Wink tensing a little when he drove over the overpass that had made him not just the butt of jokes, but a joke himself. When he turned on the dirt lane that led to the farmhouse, he said, "Best forget about Brassfield. That didn't mean nothing. Best forget it."

Dad was standing on the porch when Wink drove up. I got out and Wink drove away. "What happened?" Dad asked when I went in the house.

"Roma Dean drowned," I started bravely enough. "A bunch of us went skinny dipping at Turtle Hole." Skinny dipping was harder to say than drowned and I wanted to get it out quickly.

"Did you try to save her?"

"We didn't know she was drowning."

"How could you not know?"

"I don't know."

The things that your children do make no sense, leaving you wondering whether it's your child in another world, or the same world but not your child; not the one you know, the one you sheltered, and fed and taught right and wrong, truth and falsehood, fable and fairy tale. Dad looked at me as though I were a stranger, wondering who I was. Wondering where I came from. Not his loins. Not Grandmother's stock or Grandfather's seed. Some wayward gene from Mother's side had invaded my body.

"Did you do something to be ashamed of?"

Dad was trying to believe, trying to organize it so he could believe, but the question was inappropriate. I was ashamed of everything. I was ashamed that I had been born. I was ashamed that I was the kind of person something like this could happen to. I was ashamed to have to stand before him like this. I thought I would never know anything but shame as long as I lived. "No," I said.

"Why did Wink bring you home?"

"Brassfield came. He took me to Center Point. He thinks I drowned her."

Dad sorted it out. Wink had called the sheriff. The sheriff had taken me to Center Point for questioning. "Did Brassfield shame you?"

That's when I cried. Big, tearing sobs like a child. Dad put his hand on my shoulder. When I stopped crying he said, "I'll take care of Brassfield." He seemed almost relieved. Here was something he could grasp, something he could do. "There's not much I can do about the others."

When Dad started dressing to go to Center Point, I understood what Wink Bailey meant. I thought he meant forget about Brassfield strapping me in the electric chair, but he meant, don't make your dad face Brassfield. In Wanderer Springs we were adamant about the right to bear arms, not just because we thought that the police couldn't protect us from criminals, or that the army couldn't guard us from Russians, but because without arms we were helpless before the law, no better than blacks. There was no respect under the law unless there was respect by the law.

I was so scared that Dad had to tell me to get in the car. We went to Center Point—it was day by now—and Dad accosted Brassfield on a public street in front of witnesses. He put his arm on my shoulder and said, "This is my son. If you ever lay a hand on him I'll kill you." Dad, already in his sixties, stood toe to toe with Brassfield who towered over him. I was scared, not of Brassfield, but because if Brassfield didn't back down, I knew Dad would go home for a gun.

They stared at each other to show that neither was backing down. "If he doesn't break the law I'll have no cause to lay a hand on him," Brassfield said. Then by mutual consent, they both turned and walked away. Now it seems stagy, but it placed me under Dad's protection. No matter what they said behind my back no one was openly disrespectful.

I was also unintentionally aided by the Center Point paper. A photographer had followed Brassfield's car to Turtle Hole and had arrived in time to photograph Jessie Tooley in that instant when she realized Roma Dean was not only dead but naked. Shock, grief, horror, rage were frozen forever on her face. "Nude body of Wanderer Springs girl found in Wanderer Creek. Mrs. Jessie Tooley, mother of the dead girl, watches as Wink Bailey recovers the naked body."

The photograph had been too good. The picture was picked up by the wire services and a stringer added a story about sin in small towns, describing a sex club in the high school, detailing the initiation rites, and relating how membership in the club had led to the death of a pretty teenager, Roma Dean Tooley, in "the dark glade where high school girls paid their dues."

It was a time when Communists had infiltrated the State Department, the Pentagon, the Supreme Court, the clergy, and Hollywood. In Wanderer Springs all teenagers, particularly those who had been at Turtle Hole, were viewed with suspicion that bordered on hysteria. In time, citizens realized that the sex club was a bit of press hyperbole, that teenagers were much the way they had always been—not corrupt but careless and willfully ignorant of consequence. Anger became directed at the Center Point paper that had turned a personal tragedy into a national scandal.

In time I came to be regarded not as a coward, which was unforgiveable, but as inept, which was almost as bad. Wanderer Springs had no use for a useless man, and a boy who let his girlfriend drown was useless. Especially if that same boy had dropped a pass that would have beaten Center Point. The judgment was retroactive. "Don't call him 'Will,' call him 'cain't,'" folks said. It was a Wanderer Springs joke.

I escaped, intending to escape forever, by joining the army. The army was in Korea so running away was honorable. But Korea was a big disappointment to me. I had intended to be a hero, maybe even ept. I was a clerk in Kansas. "Spent three years on K.P.," folks said.

After the army, I escaped to college, intending to escape forever, but Dad got sick, and I married Delores and came home. "He couldn't find a white girl to marry him," folks said, expressing less disapproval of Delores than of me. If I had married Miss Texas they would have said, "No local girl would have him."

Delores had no honeymoon. She went straight from school to taking care of Dad. Sometimes Dad got out the skillet, forgetting that Delores was preparing breakfast. Sometimes he took the bucket to milk, forgetting we had no cows. Sometimes he tried to grease or operate the equipment that Ira Ferguson's hands brought to the farm. Sometimes Dad realized he had said or done something stupid and was so embarrassed that Delores and I fled to our room. When crying became too painful, Delores and I laughed together, shaking our heads in repudiation that such acts belonged to the person we knew and loved.

We sat on the porch a lot that summer, the three of us. Dad spent the last summer of his life with folks from his boyhood. "Mother, I can't go any farther," he said once, and Delores and I sat in frozen silence. "You'll have to carry me the rest of the way."

"Emmett came to see me yesterday," he said. "He said we're going to have to get rid of the girl because he caught her wearing Mother's shawl. I told him I didn't care what she wore. Emmett's mad. He won't speak to me and he won't come in the house when she's here. I let her wear Mother's broach."

One night Dad spent in France, his voice tight, his face filled with horror. "November one, over top at 6 a.m., took Hill 243 in evening. November two, over top at 2 a.m., took Hill 321 and advanced to road beyond. One hundred twenty killed or wounded, in two days. Company A. The bear came over the mountain, hell fire and a fuzzy O. Swacenet—don't know. Nu for stay—don't understand."

Mostly he seemed content. One day I saw him walking across the field towards the railroad track. "Where are you going, Dad?" I asked.

"Borger." In his pocket was the pistol Uncle Emmett had carried to Borger. I led him back to the house and hid the pistol. After that he became cunning. He slipped out of the house while we were busy or asleep. Twice he slipped away from Delores when I was at school. Once, unable to stop him, she had followed him along the railroad tracks until she was able to get help. Once she did not see him leave and could not find him. Frantic, she walked the four miles to Wanderer Springs where I was teaching school. I called Brassfield, having to listen to his lecture about putting Dad in a state hospital before getting his promise to help.

I found Dad the next night. He was in the shinnery, a thirty-acre tangle of shin oaks, blackjacks, blackberry vines, and wild plums. Dad was hiding from me. It was dark and cold and he had been without food for no one knows how long, but he was hiding from me the way he had hidden from the Germans in the Bois-le-Petre. I was grateful for the dark because I was as embarrassed as he. "Don't take me back," he asked. "I want to die here."

Eventually Dad defeated his own wish to die at home and we had to put him in the hospital at Center Point. In the end he was removed from everything and everyone he loved, drugged beyond memory or feeling. With the doctor's fingers on his eyes, the nurse's hand on his wrist, death came slow and professionalized. Devoid of earth and sky and wind, bereft of family and friends, suspended between two white sheets in a room of white walls.

I think Dad would rather have died in the midst of the cotton field with the sun on his back and Grandmother at his side, in the mud of France with his comrades, in the street of a dirty oil town with Uncle Emmett, on the worn plank porch with Mother, in a weed-lined bridge abutment with Delores, or alone hiding in the shinnery. Just to die without being embarrassed by all that bother. To die with the things he loved. To die as a man instead of a body.

The house was never the same after Dad died. The gray old house that had once seemed inviting looked as shapeless and graceless as had Dad in the hospital. We always seemed to be waiting for him to come in and get out the skillet. His presence had tempered the loneliness and the wind. At least it seemed so for Delores. Sometimes at dusk when the stars were larger and brighter than they had been in San Antonio, Delores came almost to understand what I felt when I walked there.

When Delores was alive, I had not liked Rosa. She thought I was soft; I thought she was shallow. Whenever she went to the grocery store she sneaked a treat for herself. She called Mama every day from work. If her children did not contact her every day, she called around town until she found them. Whenever she wrote she chided Delores for thinking she was too good for her family. Every day she reminded Gilbert that he had not lived up to her expectations.

After I moved to San Antonio, Rosa and I became friends.

We sat on the porch waiting for Gilbert to come home, and she talked about her life in Alamo Heights. She liked being in the houses, being part of the pretty things. She was good at what she did and the women respected her. She took them pan dulces, empanadas, tortillas. They gave her presents.

She could not tell Gilbert about the women and the houses because he was embarrassed that she worked as a maid. She could not tell him she did not like the car Manuel had given her, that she preferred riding the bus to work—free to talk to other people, to look out the window at her beloved San Antonio. Manuel had given Gilbert a car, too, but Gilbert disliked the car and abused it. She could not talk to Gilbert about Delores because Gilbert walked away.

I listened to Rosa talk about Delores; it was painful, but in that pain Delores was alive. Delores was always different, Rosa said. She never wanted to be a cheerleader; she preferred gold stars from her teachers. She didn't sneak lipstick out of the house; she practiced her lessons in front of her dolls. In junior high she went to a birthday party in gold shoes and a purple dress and everyone laughed at her.

Delores and I went to Papa's house for Thanksgiving and Christmas. We were there for Papa's funeral. We went there every time Mama or one of Rosa's children was sick, knowing Rosa exaggerated, knowing Rosa was never happier than when all of us were crowded into the house. At such times Rosa rarely sat but cooked, washed the dishes, looked after the children, cleaned spills, wiped the table, and ate standing up, refusing all offers of assistance. When the dishes were done, the house straightened and the children put to bed, Rosa scolded Delores for living so far away, for never coming home, for not doing more for her family, for pretending she wasn't Mexican.

After Rosa and I became friends, Rosa showed me letters Delores had written her. Almost every day Delores had written to Mama, Rosa, or both. I didn't want to read the letters. They were the letters of an exile filled with longing for celebration as a part of life, the music of human voices, the sounds and smells of the street.

Delores wrote about who she was. She did not believe her marriage to an anglo made her any different. Her pride was not in the color of her skin. She believed Manuel made too much of skin, made it divisive, used it to set himself apart. She believed Rosa was a prisoner of the romance and prejudice of her color. No one in Wanderer Springs was mean to Delores. No one ignored her. Everyone was polite, friendly. But there was no one who confided in her; no one who had to see her every week, to call her every day.

She wrote about her religion. Delores went to church with me—there was no Catholic Church in Wanderer Springs County—but Delores was too mystical to be a Methodist, questioned authority too rigorously to be a Catholic. Delores believed that loving God meant you were kind to others and you were who you said you were.

She wrote about her dream of finishing college and teaching beside me. Delores was not dispirited by marriage, but like many women, she put aside personal for family ambitions. She was a woman of intense loyalty, and when she married me, I became the focus of that loyalty. I knew of her dream, of course, even applauded it, but she never complained, and while I never denied her hope, I did nothing to make it possible.

She wrote of her life on the farm. Like other women unaccustomed to the plains, it was the wind that most distressed her. There was always the wind. In the summer it withered the garden and parched the skin. In the winter it stung the eyes and penetrated the heaviest coats. Sometimes it blew sand, and sometimes it blew rain, sleet, or snow mixed with sand, but it always blew. The only good it did was to turn windmills. Sometimes it turned the windmills over.

Like other women of the county, Delores gave up full skirts and long hair, started wearing a scarf, and took clothes off the line quickly before the wind could whip out the starch. No matter how many times she wiped the table, the plates gritted when set upon it. No matter how many times she swept, there were tracks on the floor where we walked. Delores knew sand but she didn't know sandstorms.

I saw it when I started home from school—a red cloud on the horizon. Delores had seen it too. She was standing on the porch from which, on a clear day, she could see, across the plowed fields, a couple of windmills flashing in the sun. "What is it?" she asked.

"Sand," I said. I changed clothes and went outside to put away or tie down anything that would blow or roll. I came back inside and showed Delores how to hang blankets over the windows and doors, wrap a white bedspread in newspapers and put it in a box, and place sheets over the clothes hanging in the closet. Before we finished, our noses were choked with dust but the ground had not yet begun to boil. I got out the old coal oil lantern and put it and a box of matches on the table.

It got dark early, the sand blotting out the sun, the wind whistling around the windows, cans and tumbleweeds rattling against the walls. When the electricity went off I lighted the lamp so we could eat dinner.

Delores made a face like a child tasting unfamiliar food. "Don't chew so thoroughly," I said. "And wash it down with water." I laughed, the way one laughs at a friend mouthing his first oyster. Delores tried to smile but her mouth tightened when her teeth gritted.

The storm blew itself out during the night and the next day was bright and clear. Sand had blasted the paint off the house, stripped leaves from the trees and Delores's flowers, piled up against the side of the house, made tiny dunes in the grass, and covered the porch and sidewalk.

Before leaving for school, I helped Delores take down, shake out, and fold up the blankets off the doors and windows. When I returned Delores had dusted, swept the house, porch, and sidewalk, and was trying to sweep the sand dunes out of the grass. She had not stopped all day despite the hopelessness of her efforts because she knew no way to quit and no other way to fight back.

"Delores," I said, and stopped because Delores looked like she didn't want to be spoken to. She was angry, not at me but at nature that was heartless but impartial with men. With women who watered sickly pear trees, nurtured a few frail flowers, or treasured a clean house with white sheets and dust free dishes, it was cruel and spiteful. No woman who gave birth in a dugout or suffered menstrual cramps in a sandstorm believed that nature was impartial.

I put my arms around her to stop the sweeping. I held her close because I knew she was fighting tears. "Would you like to move to town?" I asked.

The sand had blown in town too. The streetlights had come on automatically in the sand-created dusk and burned until the power lines blew down. Sand, tumbleweeds, and trash had piled up at street corners and against every house. Those houses had been dusted and sandpapered too, but houses and stores had provided windbreaks for each other. Through the night, above the howl and rasp of the wind, women knew that neighbors were nearby. And in the morning when women went outside to inspect the damage and pick up the trash, they gathered to trade back garbage cans, flower pots, and toys, and to shake their heads over the futility of trying to moderate a hard land.

"There's nothing to hold us here," I said. "I wouldn't have to drive to town everyday. I could walk to school. I could come home for lunch." She cried. I knew then how Lowell Byars felt. His wife, Lulu, had endured a dugout without complaint until Lowell showed her the wonders of the Mollie Bailey Show. Having caught a glimpse of the glamour and excitement that life could offer, Lulu had never again known contentment. Delores was homesick, I think, not for the home and life she had left but for the one she dreamed of having, with neighbors and flowers, free of the dust and the distance.

"It's not being in the country," Delores said. "I never mind being alone until the wind starts howling and then it seems so desolate I feel lonely even when you're here."

We bought the house that Roy Dodson, the first citizen, had built to regain his place in the community. Delores remodeled the house, our children were born and reared there, and in that happy confusion we forgot our dreams. Delores spent her days with the children, P.T.A., and Scouts. She spent more time with other women, but she was no closer to having a college education, no closer to having friends.

I had received a better reception than I had expected when I returned to Wanderer Springs. Time had passed, folks thought it was right that I had come back to take care of Dad, and they were gratified when the young returned. It gave them confidence in the future. I wasn't forgiven but I was accepted, the way Center Point was accepted, as one of those wrongs that God would have to set right.

I still went to the farm. I checked on the crops, and how Ira Ferguson's crews were treating the land, and I poked around in the past. Maybe "dust thou art" was not as metaphorical as I had assumed. It seemed that I was formed as much by that earth as by genes or education, that I was bound as closely to it as to the memory of my mother. But standing on the porch where Mother died, or in the yard where Uncle Emmett had buried Grandmother's possessions, or walking through the shinnery where Dad had hidden from those who would deny him an artless death, I was as restless and forsaken as Mary McCarroll searching the night for her lost child.

That's why I took Branda to the farm. There was no knowing me without knowing that place. Branda thought I was perfect. "I'm going to call you P.M. for perfect man," said

Branda who saw in me things no one else had seen. That's how she referred to me in the code we used in the school, and also how she referred to the afternoons we spent in the farmhouse, and after it was burned, in the barn where Olin Tabor had died after shooting Mother.

I think Brassfield burned down the farmhouse. Drugs had appeared in the high school, and there was a fear that hippies would move into vacant farmhouses and corrupt the young. Brassfield said the farmhouse was accidentally set ablaze by crazed addicts during sex and drug orgies, but the only hippies anyone ever saw were those living in a school bus at Dead Man's Junction.

The house that Grandfather had built was gone. Maybe that's why I was so reluctant to get back in the car and drive down the weedy lane, used only by Ira Ferguson's crews, to the gate that shut out nothing, the sidewalk that led to nowhere. The scar that remained where the house had been did not seem big enough to contain my memory of it. Only ashes remained, and the stories. The trouble with stories is that ultimately they all end the same way—in the cemetery—unless you're a theologian or a poet. And even those stories pass through the graveyard. Like Uncle Emmett, I needed no remainders to feel the pain.

Not eager to step again into that time and that place, I got in the car and closed the door that shut out the sand and wind and Wink Bailey deserted by his God. I turned on the air conditioner to moderate the air. I turned on the radio to still the silence. I turned the car towards Wanderer Springs. Karl Marx was wrong. The automobile is the opiate of the people.

THE CORNER

a criminal, a saint,
a prisoner, a communist, a hero

IT'S true what they say about small towns, they never change. I hadn't been back to Wanderer Springs in ten years but it looked the same as ever. "The town is well arranged," Grandmother had written. The first photograph showed it to be a one-intersection, four-corner town with a few windwhipped cottonwood trees and barbed wire fences around the houses. It looked the same as it looked when I was a child, but it looked unchanged only from a distance. The four pillars of commerce still dominated the corners, Otis Hopkins's bank, Murdock's The Corner Drug, Shipman's Hardware and Farm Implement Store, and Whatley's Live and Let Live Grocery which was a little removed from the corner but because of its two stories—the bank was the only other two-story building in town—still imposed its presence.

Shipman's Hardware hadn't sold farm implements for years and most of the customers were looking for curiosities to decorate a ranch-style house or funky bar. The bank, imposing at a distance, was as defunct as Otis Hopkins. Dr. Heslar had acquired The Corner Drug, and now sold prescriptions at his nursing home, The Wanderer's Rest. He used the drug store for a mortuary. Biddy Whatley was able to keep the Live and Let Live open by living upstairs and selling sweets to convalescents able to walk the four blocks from The Wanderer's Rest. She also sold gift boxes of soaps, bath oils, and artificial corsages—all prettily packaged in plastic—to dutiful relatives who visited the penitents awaiting deliverance at The Wanderer's Rest.

The Help-Ur-Self Laundry, where Dad left me to do the wash while he went to the gin, the bank, the Live and Let Live, was not only vacant but shattered, the doors and windows gone, the roof collapsed. A mesquite limb reached through the window where Eli puzzled over a government that had asked him to kill his cattle to save the country. Once Roma Dean Tooley had helped me rinse clothes, while I feared she would catch her long hair in the wringer. "I'm never going to cut my hair," she used to say, giving her head a shake.

The N-D-Pendent Service Station looked solid but the covered drive-through between the pumps and the office was not big enough for modern cars. The hand-operated gas pumps had been vandalized and then stolen, although everyone, including Sheriff Brassfield, knew they were decorating the entrance to a Wichita Falls bar called "The Last Chance Filling Station." A rotting shell marked the barber shop where Oscar Spruill had been shaved and shot, where Melvin Perkins had puzzled over the circumstances that permitted his ex-wife to strut in Center Point on sturdy limbs, while his palsied hands pulled hair and nicked necks of those who believed patronizing his shop was a test of loyalty to Wanderer Springs.

The buildings had their stories, as did the families who built them—Roosevelt Hopkins would be pleased about that—but the books were intended for school children. Roo would expect some moral on the frontier virtues of independence, thrift, perseverance, hard work. I knew the stories. I didn't know the lessons.

Eli Spivey had left his ranch, out beyond Medicine Hill, to fight the Hun during World War I. Eli lost a leg at Belleau Wood but he came back a hero, wearing a pegleg that permitted him to walk, lurching from side to side. Eli went almost everywhere on horseback anyway, and he made himself a long-handled hoe so that he could weed his garden from his horse.

Eli rode his horse in Armistice Day parades and addressed the school assembly on Memorial Day. "I give one leg for my country," said Eli, standing with his pegleg cocked and holding to the podium for balance. Eli was a small man with deepset eyes, wiry hair that looked as if it had been cut with shears and left uncombed, and a face marked more by pain than laughter. "And I'd gladly give the other leg to keep this land free. The only thing that stops a man in this country is hisself. It don't matter if he's blind or deaf or only got one leg, if he's willing to work he can make something of hisself."

Eli made something of himself until the Dust Bowl. When the tanks and wells went dry, Eli hauled water from the Mobeetie River for the cattle, and his wife, Una Bea, saved the dishwater for the chickens to drink, the bath water for the hogs. There was no grass on the parched land and Eli had to buy feed for the cattle. When there was no money for feed, Eli and his son, Junior, went out every day to cut down mesquite trees so the starving cattle could eat the leaves, and sometimes the bark. Junior held back the bawling cattle while Eli braced his good leg and chopped down the tree. Still the weakened cattle went down, never to rise, and the survivors followed Eli and Junior to the house where they bawled all night.

"It makes you sick to see cotton burn up and blow away, but cotton don't hurt," Eli said. "It's hard to watch chickens and pigs die because they got feelings. But a horse or a cow expects a man to help him, and nothing hurts like watching them die."

Eli went to the bank and asked Otis Hopkins for a loan so he could feed his cattle, but Otis refused, offering instead to buy the mineral rights to Eli's land. One-Eyed Finch had smelled oil on Eli's land but had told no one but Otis. "Sell out," Una Bea had begged Eli. She had grown thin and worn with worry. "We'll start over someplace else." Junior's clothes were old and worn and Una Bea had to take them to the river to wash them. On his feet, Junior wore two of the right-footed boots that Eli had no use for, and at night Junior went to bed hungry, and too old to cry, he sulked. Una Bea lay in bed and wept. Eli sat on the porch and listened to the bawling of the dying animals.

When he could endure it no more, Eli sold the mineral rights of his ranch to Otis Hopkins. He bought feed for his cattle, and he bought the Help-Ur-Self Laundry for Una Bea and moved her and Junior into the room in the back of the laundry. Eli fed his cattle and watched heavy trucks bringing in derricks and pipes. Otis Hopkins struck oil. The rains came too late for Eli. His cattle died or were too poor to sell. Eli had to have money to rebuild his herd.

Eli went to Otis to ask for a loan, but Otis said he was a poor risk—a one-legged man who had already failed once. If Eli were to die, Otis would have nothing but the land, which was practically worthless without the mineral rights, which he already owned.

Una Bea went out to the ranch and begged Eli to give up the ranch and move to the laundry with her, but Eli hadn't quit in Belleau Wood and he wasn't going to quit now. Besides, it tore his heart to see all those tubs of water going down the drain. Eli went to his friends and explained that he had to have money to get back in business. He promised that he could take out an insurance policy in their name for the amount of the loan. If he died, the insurance would repay the loan.

Few of Eli's friends were much better off than Eli, but they loaned him what they could. Conditions were slow to improve and Eli had to borrow more. Eli saw his friends tip their hats to Otis Hopkins while they avoided him for fear he would ask them for money.

The drought returned, briefly this time, and Eli cut down trees to feed his cattle. He didn't have Junior to hold back the hungry cows while he chopped, and while Eli was chasing back the cows, a tree fell on him. A man checking Otis Hopkins's oil pumps found Eli pinned under the tree. Eli's one leg had to be amputated.

Una Bea was forced to sell the cattle, but Eli would not permit her to sell his land. He came home in a wheelchair, and unable to sit a horse, sold soap at the Help-Ur-Self and washed tubs. Women who were busy with volunteer war work paid him to dump their dirty clothes in the tub, poke them around in the soapy water, and push them through the wringer.

The country was at war and Junior had enlisted, but Eli was no longer a hero. He refused to take off his hat at a parade because the flag was carried by Otis Hopkins. At a rally where Otis asked citizens to buy bonds and rent deposit boxes to keep them in, Eli shouted that he and his comrades had given lives and limbs to end all wars, but their sacrifices had been betrayed by the draft-dodging, tax-cheating bankers. He said the only way to stop war was to take the profit out of it. "This war is the best thing that ever happened to American business," he said.

Sheriff Brassfield grabbed Eli's wheelchair and dragged him out of the crowd. He told Eli to keep his opinions to himself. Brassfield loved his country and while he himself wouldn't beat a legless man, there were patriots who would, and if Eli said one more thing against his country, Brassfield wouldn't be surprised if the laundry didn't catch fire.

Una Bea moved Eli out to the ranch. She had to keep the laundry open and with gas and tire rationing she couldn't get out to see him very often. Everyone else avoided Eli, some because they believed he was a traitor to his country; others, like Dad, because the money they had loaned Eli was an embarrassment between them. Eli sat in his wheelchair, looking across his useless land, listening to the pumps that every day made Otis Hopkins a more patriotic man. On V-J Day while church bells rang, the country went on a binge of joy, and Otis Hopkins closed his bank early to offer a prayer of thanks in church, Eli ate Rough on Rats to pay his debts.

Junior came home from the war, and, like everyone else in uniform, he was a hero until he looked for a job. Junior had spent the war as a mechanic at an air base in the Midwest and had married a beauty operator named Helen—she said it was Helene but everyone in Wanderer Springs knew better.

Junior rented the Dodson house, and Helen cut hair and gave permanents in the front parlor, but Junior couldn't find work. Una Bea had leased the ranch to a lawyer in Center Point who specialized in circumventing the law and delaying justice. He liked to wear boots and talk cowboy, and he needed a place where he could take his clients hunting, or his girlfriend to the bedroom where Eli died, and write it off as a business expense. Junior, having no background in law and tax accounting, wanted no part of the ranch.

Junior wanted security and Helen persuaded him to go to beautician school on the G.I. Bill. "A man goes to the barber shop like he buys underwear," Helen said. "When his wife tells him to. But it don't make no difference whether there's a war, a tornado, or what, a woman is going to get her hair fixed." Besides, Junior, short like his father and sturdy like his mother, had fair skin and blond hair so fine you could see his pink scalp. His face and hands were always red raw from the sun and wind and Junior wanted an indoor job.

Una Bea could not abide a beautician for a son. Not after her husband had disgraced the family by paying his debts. One-Eyed Finch, justice of the peace, had certified that Eli had died of a heart attack because the beneficiaries of Eli's will were citizens who voted for Finch, and because insurance companies were a bunch of crooks anyway—Yankees most of them. Nevertheless, everyone in Wanderer Springs knew that Eli had killed himself. Una Bea knew that if Junior started washing and cutting women's hair she might as well eat Rough on Rats herself.

Una Bea sold the ranch to the cowboy-lover-lawyer, gave the Help-Ur-Self Laundry to Junior on condition that he never put his hands in a woman's hair, and moved to Corpus Christi where she could look out the window any time she wanted and see water.

Helen moved her beauty shop to the back of the Help-Ur-Self. With the new, automatic washing machines, Junior found he had a lot of free time so he bought the N-D-Pendent Service Station across the street, sold gas, and repaired cars. His only competition was from Marshall Murdock who drove around in his pickup looking for people who needed help. Junior put a stop to that by pointing out to the Baptist pastor that he, Junior, was a veteran and believed in free enterprise.

Junior was elected chief of the volunteer fire department so that he would keep the old fire truck in running condition. For ten years Junior worked on the fire truck for free, and when he spoke of resigning, he was elected mayor on condition he remain fire chief as well.

Junior and Helen became prominent citizens although their businesses were failing. Most folks had their own washing machines, and improved roads made it easier to go to Center Point to buy tires, get gas, a tune-up, and go to one of the new beauty salons where young men styled, frosted, and bee-hived hair.

It was a time when parents learned the sex of their child and thought they knew what they were getting. Junior and Helen had two sons. Bubba Spivey, the older, was a popular student, a dedicated athlete, and was liked by everyone in town because he laughed with them, talked football and hunting, and blushed when they asked him about girls. Bubba was offered a scholarship when he graduated from high school, but instead enlisted in the Marines, like his grandfather Eli, and died in Vietnam of his country's vital interest.

Duane Spivey was slight, pimple-faced, had an arm that ended at the elbow, and refused the football uniform Vivian Whatley offered him. "They can't call you sissy then," Vivian said. Duane annoyed adults by not looking at them or speaking to them although they tried to treat him just like they did ole Bubba who was a pistol. He frustrated his teachers by showing flashes of brilliance but rarely turning in work, and he angered school and county authorities by his contempt for them and their values. Duane was sentenced to ten years for drug possession. Some believed the severity of his punishment was more a tribute to patriotism than to justice.

Duane was sent to Ferguson Unit Farm. Because of his deformed left arm, he was excused from the heavy field work. Instead he spent his days feeding and tending cattle. In one of his letters he wrote, "Are you sure my grandfather did this with one leg?"

Junior and Helen moved into Una Bea's home in Corpus Christi so they could take care of her and be closer to Duane. Helen cut and rolled hair in the living room and introduced herself as Helene. She wrote Duane every day, the way she had written Bubba when he was in Vietnam. Just as she had written Bubba's military service number she now wrote Duane's inmate number. "That's the hardest thing," she said. "Because sometimes my mind kind of pretends he's away at school or the army, and then I have to write down his inmate number."

Junior thought the hardest thing was visiting Duane. "He'd been beaten and raped," Junior said. "He didn't say anything but he was scared. I could see it in his eyes, that he could live down being a criminal, but he could never live down what they done to him there. I know Dad was scared in that Belleau Wood, and I know Bubba was scared in Vietnam, but they never . . . I know folks think we never amounted to anything. None of us." Junior puzzled over what had happened to his family. For a moment he looked like Eli addressing the school assembly on Memorial Day. "I give two boys to this country. That's all I got to say. I don't know what happened to either one of them."

Otis Hopkins was the most honored man in Wanderer Springs. Otis became a deacon when he struck oil, a pillar of the community when he opened the bank, and a saint when he died.

Otis did not look like a banker, he looked like a farmer who bought his suits at the Baptist rummage sale. He was a big man, round shouldered and hipless so that the back of his coat was always pulled tight across his shoulder blades while the seat of his trousers bagged, the crotch hanging halfway to his knees. His pocked nose was too large for his flat, florid face, and he grunted rather than spoke. "I'm proud to be a 'murcan," he said at the rallies where he sold Victory Bonds and rented safety deposit boxes.

Otis was not well-educated but he had a retentive mind and had gotten as far as "incomprehensibility" in the Blue Back Speller. His Aunt Velma, who reared him, promised him a shotgun if he memorized the New Testament. Otis memorized it in six months, Aunt Velma gave him the shotgun, and he blew her head off with it. Folks used to say, "She should have required him to memorize the whole Bible; that would have given her another year." It was a Wanderer Springs joke.

Otis inherited his aunt's farm, but Otis had no skills at farming and no inclination for hard work. One year he had the only cottonseed in the county because he never got around to replanting. He was rewarded when the price of cottonseed doubled. Otis doubled that price and turned honest farmers into thieves.

Otis was scorned until One-Eyed Finch smelled oil on Velma's place. With a farm and an oil lease, Otis had prospects, and he courted Selena Lance, Delmer's third child. Selena was eighteen, horse-faced, and already a byword, but she was a Lance, an heir to the Prod ranch, and a man could make something of that.

During the wedding at the Prod Store, Selena leapt through a window, jumped astride a Prod horse, and raced to

Center Point. The wedding guests consoled the disappointed groom by pointing out that even in her wedding dress, Selena did not ride sidesaddle.

Otis was further consoled when they struck oil on his farm. In a state of euphoria, Otis and One-Eyed Finch sat on the slippery derrick floor and considered the future. "You won't never have to work again," Finch said, "because you got the most powerful tool in the world. Money can go anywhere, do any job, fix anything. Love fails. Friendship fails. Money never fails." It was a lesson Otis's retentive mind never forgot.

Otis bought the two-story brick building at the corner. The upper story he leased to the Masonic Lodge at night and by day to what was called "the colored school." The Masons didn't like it, but they honored his fair-mindedness. Otis refused to serve his country during World War I because the French would not fly in a high wind. Draft officials honored his religious feelings.

When Dad, Eli Spivey, and the other doughboys returned from the trenches, they found that Otis had been elected mayor and had bought Shack Town, the colored section of Wanderer Springs. Shack Town remained without streets, sidewalks, gas, electricity, and water as long as Otis was mayor. The blacks paid their poll tax at the cost of three beatings, six burning crosses, and one burned house, and voted Otis out of office. They got electricity and water, and Otis raised their rent. Few blacks could pay the poll tax, and folks honored Otis's faith in the ballot by reelecting him mayor.

During the Dust Bowl, Otis refused a loan to Eli Spivey and bought the mineral rights to Eli's land. Folks thought it was hard that a war hero like Eli should be ruined, but they honored Otis's confidence in free enterprise.

During the Depression when the school board went broke and was forced to pay the teachers in scrip which some merchants honored, Otis bought the scrip at sixty cents on the dollar. Grateful citizens elected Otis to the school board, and as chairman, Otis bought the scrip back from the bank at full value. Some folks thought that wasn't ethical, but they honored Otis's skill in turning dross into gold.

When he was forty-five, Otis married an eighteen-year-old pregnant girl. Folks said Grace, the girl, was a virtuous widow and they admired Otis's generosity. After two years of marriage, Grace ran away with a piano salesman, leaving Otis with Rebel, the baby, and the piano. Folks said Grace was a tramp, and they honored Otis's courage in claiming the child as his own.

Otis became widely known for his good deeds. As mayor, he lowered property taxes in Shack Town. As chairman of the school board, he encouraged students to put their allowances in his bank. As chairman of the zoning committee, he moved the city dump to Shack Town. When Baylor University learned of his many contributions to civic life—Otis named the school in his will—they honored him with an honorary degree.

Despite his good deeds, some found it difficult to deal with Otis. The roads were so good they found it convenient to bank at the modern, efficient and courteous banks in Center Point. While in town they bought gas, tires, medicine, and groceries. It was Otis Hopkins who ended the economic boycott of Center Point. The whining of the town's merchants got no sympathy from him. If they lost business, it was because they were not true capitalists. He had advised them against layaways, time payment plans, and credit cards. Credit was the business of the bank.

Otis did not need their business or good will. Through his years of prosperity, Otis had the church for comfort and support. Otis smiled only in church. God was not Otis's judge; Otis had hired Him for defense attorney.

Every year the Baptist Church awarded Otis a gold pin for perfect Sunday School attendance. Every year they honored him for his charity—Otis gave Christmas turkeys to his prime customers, and to the poor he gave calendars imprinted with the Ten Commandments and the name of the bank. Every year at the Baptist revival meeting, Otis testified that accidentally shooting his Aunt Velma was the cross he had to bear. Folks used to say that was what "the cross of gold" meant. It was a Wanderer Springs joke.

Otis was in failing health his last years and his record for perfect Sunday School attendance was jeopardized when he had a stroke and Dr. Heslar had to fly him to Dallas in his private airplane. Knowing Otis's desire to preserve his attendance record, Dr. Heslar flew the Sunday School class to Dallas so they could meet in Otis's hospital room. His fiftieth gold star for perfect attendance was pinned to his pillow.

The hospital in Dallas reduced Otis's wealth by a third and prolonged his life but a few months, but it gave him enough time to change his will. Otis cut Rebel off with a thousand dollars because she was not his natural daughter. He gave the Baptist Church his religious library consisting of the Bible in which he had marked off the sixty-nine verses he required himself to memorize every day, and the collected sermons of Billy Sunday. He gave Baylor nothing, despite his honorary degree, because that school had turned Marshall Murdock into an atheist. The bulk of his estate he left to Dr. Heslar's Medical Clinic. Including the mineral rights to Eli Spivey's ranch, and most of the houses in Shack Town.

Otis's funeral was attended by state and local dignitaries, by politicians, ministers, and Baylor officials who had not yet read the will. Rebel and her husband, Vivian Whatley, sat on the front row, Rebel weeping bitterly over the loss of her father, Vivian patting his toupee into place. A few curious citizens listened from the back pews as the proud and pompous extolled the virtue of a humble man who never drank, smoked, or cursed, and never missed Sunday School. The Center Point paper printed an obituary calling Otis the "patron saint of Wanderer Springs."

Herschell Shipman managed to keep the hardware store open but the Shipman story was not a tale of perseverance but of entrapment. Guy Shipman, a consumptive on his way to Colorado to die, became ill on the train and had to stop at Wanderer Springs. He found the town so healthful that he bought a house, and to care for it he hired Genevieve Drieschner who had helped her father grease the rails at Paymore Hill. Soon Guy was robust enough to desire Genevieve, and within a month he married her. "Old Emil raised them girls right," folks said.

Guy Shipman had spent most of his life in bed, but Genevieve found that the unmade bed bothered her. "Don't you want to move out on the front porch where you can get some fresh air?" she said. Guy moved out on the porch but it bothered his wife to see him sitting idle so she started Guy repairing her wash tubs and cleaning the lamps—things that would not tire him.

Soon Guy was repairing other people's wash tubs and harness, and sharpening knives that Genevieve rounded up each morning and stacked on the porch. Without intending it, Guy had a business, and Genevieve said, "Wouldn't you rather have a place of your own to work so that I'm not in your way?" She rounded up some men and started them to work on what was to be the second brick building in town—Shipman's Hardware and Farm Implement Store.

Guy wasn't happy with his new store but Genevieve made out the orders, cleaned, and stocked the store. Guy sat in the rocking chair she provided him and nodded to customers who said, "If you was still in Mississippi, you'd be dead now."

The Shipmans had two sons. The first, Milton, drowned trying to swim Turtle Hole during a flood on a dare by Selena Lance who had slipped off her dress and crossed the creek without difficulty. Milton was too modest to take off his clothes; his trousers snagged on a washed-out barbed wire fence and he drowned.

The second son, Herschell, was born some years later, and Genevieve died of complications. People said she had waited so long to have Herschell she had forgotten how. "I'm right sorry, Guy," they said at her funeral. "I reckon Genevieve waited so long she forgot how."

With Genevieve gone, Guy seemed to lose ambition. He kept the store open, but he never cleaned or stocked the shelves, and unopened crates were stacked against the wall. Herschell crawled through the ropes and saddles, playing with stove bolts and sucker rods. The store was his playground and school, and as he got older, the unopened crates became his cellar, attic, and woods.

Herschell knew the store from the floor up. He was no better at organizing than Guy, but Herschell had a system— keep everything in view. After Guy died in the rocking chair— folks said it had been so long since the store had been cleaned that the dust finally got him—Herschell had rows of shelves built in the store with narrow aisles between them. Whatever he didn't have room for on the shelves—screen doors, plow discs, windmill blades—he hung from the ceiling. And all of it collected dust. The store was like a cavern with only bare, suspended, dust-covered bulbs to dispel the darkness.

Herschell married Maizell Ballard who couldn't stand dirt. Maizell claimed that she had been born in the Ballard dugout during a sandstorm and had taken her first steps on the hemp carpet laid on the earth floor and had seen all the dirt she could abide. Maizell complained all her married life about the dirty store, never entered it, and required Herschell to change his shoes and socks before he came in her house and to wear long underwear in her bed.

Despite such hardships Herschell fathered a daughter, Wanda. Wanda was pretty in a mean, square-headed way, and a troublesome child from her first colic. While in high school,

Wanda ran off with a sailor. Maizell said Wanda met and married him the same day. It was 1942 and folks were romantic about sailors. Wanda returned a few months later. Her sailor had been lost at sea, Maizell said.

Wanda ran off with an airman. Maizell said Wanda met and married him the same day. It was 1944 and folks were patriotic. In a few months Wanda returned home. The airman was lost in a training accident, Maizell said.

Wanda ran off with a veteran. She returned home a few months later. The veteran had been committed to a hospital because of battle fatigue, Maizell said. It was 1946 and folks were understanding.

Wanda ran off to Fort Worth with a truck driver. The next time she came home she brought with her a daughter, Dixie Davenport. No one ever met a Mr. Davenport, and Maizell could think of nothing to say. One day Wanda drove away in Herschell's car leaving Dixie behind.

Dixie was raised by Maizell, who every day until she died came to school at noon to brush Dixie's hair. Dixie ate breakfast standing up so as not to wrinkle her dress, and refused to go to the playground at recess for fear of getting dirty. Tall like her father, Dixie towered over the other children, neat, unhappy, and unpopular.

After Maizell died something happened to Dixie. She gave up soap, water, and ironed clothes. Dixie was Wanderer Springs's first hippie. Her blue jeans were torn and dirty, her long hair was tangled, her tongue was caustic and obscene. Herschell took Dixie to see Dr. Heslar who said she was pregnant and depressed. He prescribed pills for her. She still towered over her classmates, and she was untidy, but now she was happy and she was high. Dixie became a leader in the school and went everywhere with Duane Spivey. When Duane was arrested, Dixie disappeared. Her mother had sent for her, Herschell said.

Over the years Herschell's left nostril had become blocked

from the dust in the store so that his right nostril had become permanently flared in its search for breath. Herschell stood in the dust-coated window of the store, watching for Wanda and Dixie, his one good nostril pulling up the corner of his lip so that he seemed to be smiling at his loneliness.

Herschell developed a cough like the one that had troubled his father. "You ought to sell this store and go to Colorado," folks told him. But there was no one to buy the store, and Herschell kept it open, selling an occasional sucker rod to a rancher who still maintained windmills, or pieces of old but unused harness to decorators of rustic restaurants and bucolic bars. Trapped by the quiet authority of his mother, the patient acquiescence of his father, the desperate autonomy of his daughter and granddaughter, Herschell was hanging on to his dusty collection of useless goods, waiting for the turnkey, a small-town captive who thought his jail was a beacon calling the adventurers home.

Guy Shipman had never intended to be in Wanderer Springs, but Malcolm Murdock had come on direct orders from God. Malcolm, a Methodist circuit rider, had an enormous head, flowing locks, and a humorless disposition. Malcolm started a Methodist congregation in every community in the county, but if there was a lesson in the Murdock family, it was that the intentions of good men often do more harm than the inventions of bad men.

Reverend Murdock spared himself nothing in the service of the Lord. His only concession to the flesh was to take a wife, Trudy. Trudy was as dutiful to her husband as her husband was to God. In serving him, she had, at one time or another, lived in every settlement in the county, and every time she moved she left a clean house, a new gourd dipper and a fire laid in the cook stove.

Malcolm felt guilty for the comfort and pleasure his wife brought to his hard life, and when Trudy confessed she was pregnant, Malcolm could only assume it was a sign of the Lord's displeasure and his wife's perfidy. He and Trudy were of such an age and had been married for such a time that he had believed her beyond such treachery.

Their son, Wesley, was proof beyond doubt that God had never intended Malcolm to marry. From the beginning Wesley required of Trudy the time and attention that belonged to Malcolm and the service of the Lord. Wesley was a beautiful but spoiled child, and a handsome but reckless youth, and neither his mother's tears nor his father's preaching could turn him from his wicked ways.

One day, outside the church, while throwing firecrackers under horses to unseat the solemn churchgoers and amuse the young ladies, Wesley's celluloid collar caught fire. Trudy had always dressed Wesley like a little gentleman. Before he could get the collar off, his long wavy hair also caught fire. There was little that could be done for burns in those days, and for the rest of his life the left side of Wesley's face was red and slick, the eye puckered and the mouth drawn.

Malcolm's hopes that the accident would reform his son were premature. Wesley did not become a Methodist, he became a recluse and kept the scarred side of his face turned to the wall. He worked in the drug store because women asking for laxatives or medicines for the female trouble wouldn't look at him anyway. Wesley sought solace at Eva Wiley's door.

Eva Wiley had been a resident of Joe Whatley's boarding house when Joe was hanged. She moved to Center Point to a house of her own, and accommodated railroad work gangs until Sister Majors called upon her to repent. Eva repented and became a Baptist until lack of job skills and Sister Majors's trial caused a spiritual relapse.

Eva went back to the old life until, brought to contrition by age, she retired. Eva found it difficult to give up the sporting life as again and again she was called out of retirement. Eva was through with men and their demands when Wesley knocked on her door. She told him to go away. Wesley knocked harder, demanding to be let in. Eva fired a shot through the door.

It was not a serious wound, but Malcolm took it seriously. He ordered Wesley out of his house. Trudy, unable to leave her son, left her husband, and Malcolm went to his grave believing that while snatching other souls from the fires of hell, he had failed to save his wife and son from the burning.

Wesley was drafted during World War I and trained as a pharmacist. When he came home, he bought The Corner Drug and joined the Baptist Chruch to demonstrate his willingness to do business. Trudy went to church with him, sitting where she alone could see the bad side of his face. Faithful to the end, she never deserted the church of her husband, although the Methodists regarded her and her son as apostates.

No one liked Wesley, but they traded at the store because even the Methodists hated Wesley less than they did Center Point. Wesley sold notions and filled prescriptions but he scarcely spoke to his patrons and kept the bad side of his face to the wall. To avoid encountering people on the street, he slipped down to the Live and Let Live after closing time to buy his groceries. Sue, Benny Whatley's daughter, unlocked the door for him and added up his bill. Like all the Whatley women, Sue was fat, so fat that she could not get up the stairs but slept behind the counter of the store.

Wesley's trips to the Live and Let Live became frequent and then Wesley married Sue, granddaughter of Joe Whatley whom the Methodists had hanged. The Methodists believed Wesley married Sue to spite his father, but kinder folks—and some Baptists—found beauty in the union of two ugly people. "Two wrongs can make a right but they can't make a baby," folks said.

Sue, almost immobilized by fat, went to the drug store with Wesley every day, and sat at the cash register while he worked behind the prescription counter. One day Sue gasped for breath with what she thought was a gas pain, something with which she was overly familiar. Wesley thought she was having a heart attack and was trying to help her lie down when out popped Marshall. Sue was as surprised at the birth of their son as was Wesley. Wesley ran down the street to get Dr. Vestal. Encountering Lowell Byars, he said, "There's a baby in the drug store." "Whose is it?" Lowell asked. Wesley looked at him in bewilderment. "I think it's ours," he said.

The whole town shook its head in disbelief. "That's why Marshall always thought he was Jesus Christ," Marshall's cousin, Vivian Whatley, used to say.

Sue had to be taken home in the back of a truck, and she never recovered from the surprise. She was unable to return to the drugstore but every night she got dressed to go, and slept without turning because she was too large to sleep any other way. That's the way she was found one morning, smothered in her own fat. "Dressed for her funeral," folks used to say. Even Baptists said it.

After Sue's death Wesley ran the drug store and Trudy cared for Marshall until she died. Neither the Baptists nor the Methodists attended Trudy's funeral. The Methodists believed she had deserted her husband and church to idolize her child; the Baptists believed she had seen the light but was too vain to join the Baptist Church.

After the death of his mother, Wesley became more withdrawn, guarded in church, careful in the drug store, hiding the dark side of his face even from Marshall who worked in the drug store and went to church with him. Marshall seemed to be a throwback to Old Malcolm—religious, but in a quieter way.

Marshall was devoted to being helpful. In high school he dubbed his pickup "The Good Samaritan Truck" and towed cars, fixed flats, loaned tires and batteries, and offered a free can of gasoline to motorists in trouble, until the Baptist pastor asked him to stop. He was hurting business at the N-D-Pendent and Junior Spivey was a fellow Baptist. Besides, the Baptist pastor warned, people who didn't know him might think that

Marshall was a Communist. If Marshall was puzzled by God's inability to convert his followers to charity, he was careful to say nothing about it.

Marshall was handsome like his father, but careless of his good looks. His hair was clean but he never seemed to be able to find the part. His clothes were neat but not carefully assembled. Marshall was serious but not cheerless, and, in his quiet way, he was our leader. Those of us who were in high school with Marshall always thought things were different when he was with us. We were better, kinder, when he was there. When Marshall went off to Baylor to become a preacher, we all believed there was a touch of greatness about him, although perhaps not as the world saw greatness.

Wesley withdrew even more from an increasingly wicked world. He refused to sell items which were intended to lure men and women into sin. Hose, false eyelashes, cosmetics, and after-shave lotion disappeared from his shelves. He removed all magazines except religious ones from the store, and, convinced that comic books corrupted the young, he removed those also. He wrote anonymous letters to his niece, Biddy Whatley, demanding that she remove comic books from the Live and Let Live, and when she began selling magazines with pictures of naked women, he made anonymous threatening phone calls.

"Uncle Wesley, the only time I listen to you is when you talk dirty," said Biddy who was not fooled. "You cover up your face and I'll cover up my magazines." Although related by marriage, the Whatleys and Murdocks were not close.

When a black man came into The Corner Drug with a white woman and asked for condoms, Wesley knew that Armageddon was near. He talked of paying a nighttime visit to Shack Town the way they did when the blacks started paying their poll taxes so they could vote against Otis Hopkins.

Sheriff Brassfield said, "I won't stop you boys, you know that. I just want you to think about one thing before you go down there. The feds will be in here like nits on a nigger's ass. It's not like before. And when you get their attention, they'll stick like burrs in a nigger's nap. They'll escort niggers into your drug store, and into your school, and sit them right down beside you in church.

"Now hold on a minute, Wesley. I know you boys want to do the right thing. And I want to help you. But burning a cross in Shack Town ain't gonna help. That don't work no more. We're gonna have to get with the lawyers, and the judges, and the preachers, and the good people of this county, and we're gonna have to be smarter and dirtier than them nigger-loving, ass-kissing lawyers in Washington."

Wesley became increasingly disenchanted with the liberalism of the Baptist Church and the Communist and black infiltration into everything he held sacred. One day a young hitchhiker stopped in the drug store. Wesley, looking at her with the one eye he allowed the public, thought at first she was an Indian. She proved to be blue-eyed, blond-haired, wearing blue jeans, fringed leather boots, fringed leather jacket, with beads woven through her hair and tangled about her neck.

She had come to ask for a contribution to a religious group that lived a New Testament life in New Mexico, wearing natural clothes, eating wholesome foods, eschewing strong drink, and spending their lives praising God and sharing His love with one another. God's love had perfected their souls until they could no longer see—she had forced Wesley to show her his full face—physical imperfection. Also, no blacks or other minorities were allowed.

Wesley sold the drug store to Dr. Heslar, gave everything he had to the commune, and followed the girl to New Mexico. He gave Marshall nothing because Marshall had become a nigger-loving atheist.

Murdock was the "good" county name. At one time Malcolm Murdock had been the most powerful force in the county, but of all the churches he had started only the one in

Center Point remained, and no doubt he would have de-
nounced that comfortable congregation. Comfort was a sin of
the Baptists.

The only picture of Joe Whatley is of him hanging from
the Medicine Hill water tank. He appeared to be of medium
stature, with round shoulders, long neck, and droopy moustache, but that could be attributed to his posture. Joe was a
mean man but he was tolerated until he became a Methodist.
Once he claimed the name of Christ, he made himself liable to
Christian action. At least the Methodists seemed to think so.

Joe, who had seen the light while pouring whiskey, closed
his saloon and moved to Wanderer Springs where he opened a
boarding house. Still, the Methodists were not satisfied. Some
claimed the boarding house catered to railroad crews and
Jezebels, like Eva Wiley, that they attracted. The Methodists
expelled Joe from the church. In retaliation, Joe attempted to
expel Virgil Hight, a deacon, from a dugout that, maybe, was
on Joe's land. Mrs. Hight refused to move and when Joe attempted to assist her, he and Virgil got into a fight and Hight
was killed.

After Joe was hanged, his wife tried to keep the boarding
house open although Eva Wiley and the other women fled.
When Oscar Spruill set the livery barn on fire to destroy a
changed brand, the boarding house burned to the ground. The
livery barn and Whatley's boarding house was half the town.
No one made an effort to save the boarding house or Mrs.
Whatley. The Whatley children escaped by jumping out the
windows, and sought their future elsewhere, except for Benny.

Benny was an obsequious youth who, for a handout, did
whatever anyone wanted. Benny set up a tent over the ashes of
the boarding house and began selling a few items, whatever the
public desired. Benny's tent was handier than Dodson's store at
the springs, and Benny was more accommodating.

In time Benny built a two-story brick building with living
quarters upstairs and the grocery downstairs, and called it the

Live and Let Live Grocery. Benny intended to get along. Some suggested that the store was too heavily stocked with bay rum and vanilla extract, even for a county that forbade the sale of alcohol. Benny dropped his head, smiled his sad smile, and said he just gave folks what they wanted.

Benny married a fat but pretty woman, and she gave him a daughter, Fat Sue who married Wesley Murdock, and a son, Maurice who was a throwback to old Joe. When Maurice was still a baby, Benny's fat wife sat down in a chair in the store and began gasping for breath. Benny hurried about the store, assisting his customers, assuring them, "She's all right, folks, what can I get for you?" even after they told him his wife had died. Benny closed the store for half a day for her funeral when the Baptist pastor assured him folks wouldn't object.

Maurice was seldom seen in the store, but prowled the town, and when he was older, the countryside. Benny whipped Maurice when folks wanted him to, and after the whippings Maurice disappeared for a while to everyone's relief. Maurice's prowls took him farther from home for greater periods of time. One day he returned with a wife, Nadine, who was young, frightened, and pregnant. Maurice left when his daughter, Biddy, was born, returned when his son, Vivian, was born, then disappeared forever.

Nadine, a long-suffering, whiny woman, kept house for Benny and her two children and sometimes worked in the store. During the Depression there were complaints that Benny sold spoiled goods to the poor, and during the war there were complaints that he catered to hoarders, and that those who had enough money didn't have to have ration stamps. Some claimed that Otis Hopkins had meat and pie every day and gave sugar to those who rented a box to safely deposit their Victory Bonds. Benny dropped his head, smiled his sad smile, and said he tried to make everyone happy.

Benny died in the store, assuring everyone that he was all

right and that he would get them what they wanted. His desire to get along and to take offense at nothing had mollified feelings towards the Whatleys. Sue's marriage to a Murdock lent them a bit of respectability. But what made the Whatleys acceptable was Maurice's son, Vivian, who was the best athlete the town, some said the county, ever had.

Vivian wasn't as smart as Hooper Byars, as tough as Boots Bryant, as honest as his cousin Marshall Murdock, but Vivian won every athletic honor the school had to give, and it was accounted to him as greatness. It was a greatness those of us who played with him had to endure. Marshall Murdock called him "the acne of our success. Maybe I think I'm Jesus," Marshall said, "but Vivian thinks he's Doak Walker."

Vivian's sister, Biddy, was not admired, but she was a power to be reckoned with. Biddy had taken over the store when Benny died. She was a freshman in high school and already so fat she could hardly get down the aisles of the store, but she followed the policies of her grandfather. She sold comic books, male magazines, and condoms because boys asked for them. She sold junk food to the elderly at The Wanderer's Rest because it was easier than keeping fruit and vegetables. When a citizens committee asked her not to sell airplane glue to children because some of them were sniffing it, Biddy said, "Talk to them, don't talk to me. I just give people what they want."

Folks didn't like it but they had to agree it was a sacred American right to sell whatever anyone wanted to buy. Except for alcohol and sex, of course—that had gotten old Joe hanged. And drugs—that had put Duane Spivey behind bars.

Delores didn't feel that way about Biddy. When Delores asked Biddy for masa, anise, or cilantro, Biddy said, "Nobody eats that shit."

"I used to think the world would overcome the Whatleys," Marshall said after he had become an atheist and a Communist. "Now I think the world is the Whatleys. If nuclear war comes, the generals, and politicians, and scientists, and salesmen, and manufacturers, and workers are going to say, 'We just gave folks what they wanted.'"

The Corner was the commercial heart of the town and those were the stories, but where was the lesson? Only Otis Hopkins had lived without doubt or failure. Only Otis Hopkins was rewarded for his life. Only Otis Hopkins was certain he was destined for streets of gold.

I drove through Wanderer Springs and at The Corner, I turned on the road to Prod. I didn't stop at The Corner because I knew Jessie Tooley was lying in state in what was once The Corner Drug, and Herschell Shipman was looking out the dusty window of the hardware store, intent upon the strange car in town, his one good nostril flared with hope and necessity. And Biddy Whatley, a straight-haired mound of fat, sat behind the cash register surrounded by what millions of dollars of advertising claimed the public wanted.

HIDE CITY

the past, the future, the elephant

ONLY the rails remained to mark the spot where Dad had been born in a boxcar beside the tracks. No train had stopped in ten years. That link to the past and future was gone, that umbilical cord, that line dividing the land while drawing it together.

In Shack Town all that remained were weeds, litter, bare earth hard packed by the feet of children, wheel-less, shattered automobiles, abandoned buildings that leaned toward unconditional surrender—refuse of a battle that had moved to the suburbs of Center Point.

Off to the left, at the edge of Hide City, was the rusting, derelict Farmers Cooperative Gin. The gin had saved Lowell Byars from self-destruction and made him the most trusted man in town. As a young man Lowell had brought his wife, Lulu, to the county and they had lived in a dugout near Red Top, working as long as there was light to see. There was no time for visiting neighbors, or going to church, just day after day of chopping weeds and carrying water.

The roof of the dugout caved in during a rain storm, they were dispossessed for two days by a skunk, the crops blew away in a sandstorm, but Lulu stuck it out, and if she cried of loneliness or despair, it was when Lowell was away from the dugout. One morning Lowell got up early as usual and said, "Get dressed, we're going to Wanderer Springs to see the Mollie Bailey show."

Lowell milked the cow, fed the mules, hitched the wagon,

139

and when he got back to the dugout, he had to fix breakfast. Lulu was still brushing her hair. They drove to Wanderer Springs and watched the wagons come in, drawn by elephants. They looked in Shipman's Hardware and stared at the crowd of people in town. They bought sardines and crackers at Dodson's store, drank lemonade that a kid named Benny Whatley was selling at The Corner, saw the show, and it was over, time to get in the wagon and start for home.

It was a long way back to the dugout and Lowell knew it would be time to go to work before he got home, but he didn't care. The moon was bright, a thousand stars twinkled in the sky, and he had shown his wife a sight. Lowell was feeling pleased with himself.

"It ain't so terrible being married to me is it?" he asked Lulu who was sitting silent and sleepless beside him, her cheeks raw from pinching to make them rosy. Lulu began to cry. She cried all the way home. She cried all day. She stopped crying to fix his supper but she wouldn't speak to him for three days until he cut his hand heading red top maize and she had to ask how he was.

Lowell promised to take her to the Christmas dance and rather than disappoint her they rode fifteen miles in an open wagon in the face of a norther. Lulu, her cheeks glowing, danced every set of the all-night dance, went home with a fever, took pneumonia, and died of frivolity. That's what folks said. It was a Wanderer Springs joke.

Lowell wanted to get Dr. Vestal but Lulu begged him not to leave her alone. He held her and promised the things he had promised before—a real house, children, a school for the children, regular visits to Red Top, maybe even Wanderer Springs.

"Lowell, we didn't see the elephant," she wept.

"Yes we did. Remember? We went to the Mollie Bailey show."

"But we didn't see the elephant."

Those were her last words and they almost destroyed

Lowell. He was unable to endure the dugout without her and tried to drink himself to death. When he lost his farm not even Benny Whatley would talk to him. Only Hulda Codd took pity. Hulda Codd had not a frivolous stitch in her.

Hulda Codd was Wanderer Springs's first teacher in a one-room log house that was also used for the jail—prisoners were chained to the wall—and for the courthouse—notices were nailed to the door. Hulda told Lowell if he would sweep the dirt floors, wash the slates, burn out the wasp nests and red ant beds, cut wood, and start the fire each morning—all her jobs as teacher—she would let him sleep in the schoolhouse. If she never smelled liquor on his breath.

Hulda Codd was said to have looked like she just stepped out of a Sears, Roebuck Consumers Guide book in her tailored suits. She was always perfectly mannered, perfectly dressed, the epitome of dignity and respectability. When I knew her she was short and round-faced with a bald spot in the center of her head, a hard little mouth that was prim to the point of dourness, and blue eyes that glinted behind her rimless glasses. But she was still the town's ideal of dignity and respectability.

Hulda Codd's marriage to Lowell Byars was a shock, not only because of Lowell's situation, but because teachers were supposed to be above such things. They would have replaced her but, unable to find another teacher, they ignored the marriage, and she remained Miss Codd the rest of her life.

The marriage restored respectability to Lowell Byars. Folks spoke to him, but there were few jobs and those were seasonal—harvest or roundup. One day Lowell was in Shipman's Hardware and heard Grover Turrill tell Guy Shipman he wanted an ice cream machine. Guy, as usual, didn't care what Grover wanted. If Genevieve hadn't ordered it, it wasn't in the store, and if she had ordered it, it wasn't uncrated.

Lowell went home, asked Hulda Codd to invite the ladies of her Baptist Sunday School class to their house that evening, and took the train to Wichita Falls where he bought an ice cream machine and ice. He came home, made ice cream, presented a bowl of the cream to the ladies, and waited to take orders for the machines when their husbands came to retrieve them.

After Lowell sold several of the machines, he built an ice house close to the tracks and accepted delivery of ice every day. In saloon-less Wanderer Springs, ice cream became the center of social events. Folks reveled in the knowledge that while they were eating ice cream, Center Point still amused itself by baiting dogs and pulling taffy.

Despite the general disregard for Center Point, farmers had to haul their cotton and grain over muddy and rutted trails to Center Point for processing and shipping. Lowell told the farmers that if they would put up the money for a gin and grain elevator he would operate it for them. Such was Lowell's reputation for honesty that they did it. Hulda Codd kept the books after school. Such was her reputation for perfection that no one ever questioned the books. When a visiting evangelist pointed at The Farmers Cooperative Gin as the spawn of the devil Socialism, such was the reputation of Lowell and Hulda that not even the Center Point paper repeated the remark.

Nevertheless, when Hulda declared that the grandiose building, planned as a courthouse, was not efficient as a school, Hulda Codd lost favor with the town. There were other teachers in Wanderer Springs now, one of them a man. He assumed his natural position of authority as a man and assigned the women to the housekeeping chores—sweeping floors, tending fires, washing blackboards, supervising the washing, eating, playing, and learning of the children—while he sat in his office recording attendance, books lost or found, money received and spent. He also told the women how to do their job.

There was a new school in Bull Valley and to everyone's surprise, Hulda Codd took the job as schoolmistress—the only teacher the school ever had. It meant driving a horse and buggy along the railroad right of way, then cutting across fields and pastures. It meant going back to teaching all grades and doing the chores she had hired Lowell to do.

Hulda Codd taught through winters when farmers had to pull her buggy or Model T out of the mud, through the Depression when no one could afford to pay her, past retirement age. With no library, no visual aids, no counselors, no janitors, Miss Codd taught us to read, write, count, and spell.

For most of us school was the only respite from farm work, and Miss Codd felt no obligation to make education entertaining or painless. Nor did she accept excuses for failure although some of the children were undernourished, poorly dressed, shoeless, had to walk to school in inclement weather, and were often absent because of seasonal farm work. We had to measure up to her standards or face humiliation, whippings, and failure on our report cards.

Every year Miss Codd took the older girls from the school to spend the night with her—there were seldom more than five or six. She showed them her house that had a curtain on every window, a carpet on every floor, and a spread on every bed. She let them bathe, talk on the telephone, and file their nails while she set the table. During dinner she showed them the proper way to eat.

After dinner she took them into the parlor and talked about boys. She admonished them to save their kisses and told how Lowell Byars had promised that if she would marry him, he would make something of himself she could be proud of. "I said, 'Mr. Byars, being your wife would make me the proudest woman in the county.' He put his hand on my shoulder, leaned forward and kissed me. It was my first kiss but I would have waited even if I had known it would be my last."

Years later Emma Slocum Harkness said, "I think some of the girls cried but I wasn't really listening to the story. I was trying to count how many glasses she had." The Slocums drank out of the same dipper, and when they bathed, used the same water and dried with the same towel.

If Lulu Byars died of frivolity, Hulda Codd died of duty, teaching when she was old, tired, and ill because there was no one to take her place. Lulu had the circus and the dance, Hulda Codd had the school. I've never been certain whether Lulu was a silly woman unsuited for a rugged country, or a poet who knew that life was not measured by the years endured in twilight but by the moments spent in the candle's flame.

Hulda Codd wasn't sure either. As she swept out the school for the day, closed the door, and prepared herself for the drive back to Wanderer Springs to grade papers, Hulda must have thought about Lulu's feverish dance to death. Perhaps for all the years she had taught at the Bull Valley School she had held that fox to her breast. Because on her deathbed Hulda asked, "Lowell, did we see the elephant?"

Beside Lowell Byars's gin was the hangar for Dr. Heslar's airplane. Dr. Vestal, the county's first physician, had planned to retire among the people he had served so well, but he could get no one to take his practice and he could not idly watch their suffering. He moved to Galveston and never returned unless Hulda Codd saw him in front of Shipman's Hardware.

"He was standing in front of Shipman's with his stomach and jaw stuck out, cleaning his fingernails with his penknife the way he used to do," Hulda Codd told Lowell. Lowell set out to find him—like everyone else in Wanderer Springs, Lowell owed him money—but when he got to the depot, he found a telegram had just come announcing that Dr. Vestal had died that day at his home in Galveston.

After Dr. Vestal left, Wanderer Springs was without medical care except for Augusta Worley who nursed her father, Denver, a Confederate veteran, and after his death took the old, the infirm, and the alone into her home.

I, and some of my classmates—Hooper Byars, Boots Bryant, Vivian Whatley and his wife, Rebel—had come back to Wanderer Springs to teach in the school. We, and the town, saw our return as a renaissance. The town had been trapped in past wrongs and scandals; we were going to move it into the future, and that included better medical care. There were doctors and a hospital in Center Point, but we wanted our own.

We asked the mayor, Junior Spivey, to call for a bond issue that would allow us to hire a doctor and to buy two surplus barracks and convert them into a hospital. Junior convinced Otis Hopkins. No bond issue ever passed without the support of Otis Hopkins.

The doctor we hired, Dr. Heslar, was a tanned, handsome young man, prematurely gray at the temples, with the first trace of lines under his gray, emotionless eyes. Dr. Heslar was provided with a hospital, an office, and a salary to supplement the money he made from his patients. Wanderer Springs was not a competitive market, Dr. Heslar said. He was interested in providing us with the best medical practice money could buy. If we were interested in anything less, we were talking to the wrong man, he said.

The arrival of Dr. Heslar and the opening of the hospital offered us hope of more than good health. It seemed a guarantee of a bright future. A healer had come and everyone crowded around to touch the hem of his garment.

Dr. Heslar was friendly in his office, the hospital, the Baptist Church where he and his wife were faithful in attendance, but he was busy setting up his practice, seeing patients, and running his hospital. His wife, a small, stylish woman with perfect skin and teeth, was busy shopping in Center Point. "After Jerry has been God all day at the hospital it's hard for him to go somewhere and just be a person," she explained to Delores when declining our invitation. Dr. Heslar and his wife—"Children are not in our plans"—accepted invitations only from Otis Hopkins.

Shortly after Dr. Heslar's arrival, Lowell Byars fell from Augusta Worley's upstairs gallery and died of his injuries.

Lowell had been in a stupor since Hulda Codd's death. Augusta had taken him in, doted on him, spoon-fed him to keep him alive, but Lowell seemed to have forgotten he was at Augusta's. His home did not have an upstairs.

Dr. Heslar was furious at Lowell's death. Augusta's home did not meet health standards. She cleaned relentlessly, yet cobwebs hung, dust lay in places her dim eyes could not reach. She tried to tempt feeble appetites with special treats, but her meals were not always balanced. She sometimes forgot to remind her boarders to take their medicine, even got their medicines mixed up. And throughout her house, on the floors, the walls, the fixtures, the furniture, the food, was a fine covering of cat hair. Augusta also took in stray cats.

"I know what that woman has done," Dr. Heslar said, "but we are no longer a raw, frontier town. We have outgrown the day when individuals have to carry the burden because there is no institution to do it."

Augusta wept when her burden was taken from her. "Where will they go?" she cried. "Who will take care of them?"

Otis Hopkins, with Dr. Heslar as partner, opened a nursing home, The Wanderer's Rest, just down the street. It was a clean, antiseptic place with no upper floor for someone to fall from. In every room there were framed pictures of rural scenes—red-coated horsemen jumping their steeds over trimmed hedges, southern mansions beneath moss-draped oaks, steamboats on the river.

"A medically supervised retirement home." That was the way the advertisements described it in Dallas, Amarillo, and Oklahoma City newspapers. "A safe, quiet refuge for the elderly at country prices. Doctor in residence."

We were not happy that the town was becoming a place where people came to die rather than to live, but after all, they had to have some place to go. As Dr. Heslar pointed out, it was good for business. When relatives came to visit the elderly, they bought a treat at the Live and Let Live, filled their prescriptions at The Corner Drug, bought a souvenir at Shipman's Hardware, and got gas at the N-D-Pendent.

Dr. Heslar suggested to Junior that the town needed a flying ambulance service. Dr. Heslar was a pilot, and all he needed was for the town to provide an airplane, hangar, and landing strip. The finest care Dallas and Houston hospitals offered would be available to every citizen of Wanderer Springs.

That was farther into the future than we were prepared to advance, although Junior Spivey supported the idea; his station would supply fuel for the airplane. Otis Hopkins was also in favor. Otis gave a strip of land at Hide City and paid for an asphalt runway. Dr. Heslar offered to provide a hangar.

With much controversy the town passed a bond issue to buy the twin-engined Beechcraft that Dr. Heslar thought essential. Dr. Heslar could not afford a hangar, and after the city paid for damages to the airplane caused by high winds, the city bought a hangar as well. A few people were flown to hospitals but once they saw the bill—they had supposed that since they paid for the airplane and the hangar the ride would be free—most folks preferred to take a car.

Dr. Heslar flew Otis Hopkins to a Dallas hospital, and flew Otis's Sunday School class to a meeting in Otis's hospital room, and out of gratitude Otis left the bulk of his estate to Dr. Heslar. Actually, Otis left his estate to "Dr. Heslar's hospital." After paying taxes to build and equip the hospital, we thought we owned it. A judge, with the help of a team of lawyers paid for by Dr. Heslar, determined that all the town owned was the building and equipment. Dr. Heslar owned the name and the will stipulated Dr. Heslar's hospital. The court, in consideration of the personal service Dr. Heslar had rendered in flying Otis to the hospital and the Sunday School class to Otis, ruled that Otis intended his estate to go to Dr. Heslar.

Folks were not happy with Otis's will but they blamed Otis, or lawyers, or the courts that were the last refuge of the rich. They could not afford to be displeased with Dr. Heslar.

With the hospital and nursing home he was the biggest employer in the town with the biggest payroll. With Shack Town, Otis's farm, and the mineral rights to Eli Spivey's ranch, he was the biggest taxpayer.

No one was surprised that Otis left Rebel only a thousand dollars. She had brought shame to her father—first by being at Turtle Hole, and then by marrying a Whatley. Besides, he wasn't her father anyway. Most folks believed she got what was coming to her.

Justice may have been Rebel's lot, but mercy was tendered to Walter Slocum. Dr. Heslar discovered that Walter Slocum's health was important to Washington, and that the taxpayers would spare no expense to keep Walter healthy. Walter was one of three children born to Albert and Amanda Drieschner Slocum. Amanda was the younger sister, by twenty years, of Genevieve who married Guy Shipman. "Old Emil raised them girls right," folks said, but when they spoke of Amanda they meant unflagging loyalty. "Mandy, how we going to get some shoes and chewing tobacco for the boys?" Albert would ask. "We'll sell Mama's plates and the dining table Pa made," Amanda would say.

Albert dragged Amanda and her children to the kind of poverty that was devoid of poetry or pride. With never a thought of the children as his to care for, he spit out the seeds. Watering and weeding he left to Amanda, along with the unpleasant task of borrowing a milk cow to feed them.

Only Emma escaped the Slocum taint. When Amanda died of Albert's imaginary heart attack, Hulda Codd went to the rock bottom farm that only Albert would take and that not even Amanda could make a crop on, and took Emma home with her. Emma never went back.

Without Amanda or Emma to do the cooking, cleaning, mending, borrowing, and begging for credit, the Slocums were no longer a family, or even a pack. George got drunk on his father's moonshine that more nearly resembled ratsbane than

Jim Beam. George lay unconscious for two days in a cold rain and died of being a Slocum. That's what folks said.

Albert and his son Walter slept in empty houses, took what they weren't given—clothes from the line, food from gardens, orchards, hen houses. Earl Lance gave them a cow every year, even before Amanda died, because if he didn't they'd steal one, and this way he could give them his culls. Albert and Walter were arrested a few times but jail was too good for them and too expensive for the taxpayers. Brassfield or one of his deputies beat them and told them to get out of the county.

Dr. Heslar was the first to find any use for Walter Slocum. He removed Walter's appendix, gall bladder, tonsils, and the nails of both big toes. Walter had more trips on the flying ambulance than the rest of the citizens combined, and he was the first in the county to be diagnosed as having whatever virus was in vogue.

"Walter is a sick man and he's entitled to care just like everyone else," Dr. Heslar said to those who grumbled at the expense. "I can't refuse to treat him just because he doesn't have money."

"Those old operations just steal your soul," said Augusta Worley who was recovering from gall bladder surgery after she, too, had been moved to The Wanderer's Rest.

Everyone agreed that Dr. Heslar was a good doctor. A Dallas newspaper printed a feature story on Dr. Heslar and declared that his program of health care with the hospital, nursing home, and ambulance service should be the prototype of such care in small towns across the country. We had moved into the future but the future was out of control. The government was unrepentant, the military undisciplined, children ungrateful, their parents unfulfilled. God was dead and the telephone company was omnipotent, omniscient, and obnoxious. It was a time when entertainers preached and churches entertained. People turned to their horoscope to find good news, and everyone was on drugs.

After Dr. Heslar bought The Corner Drug, some of the residents of the nursing home took as many as eighteen different prescription drugs. Some of Dr. Heslar's outpatients were taking more. Many of the children in the elementary school were on medication, and in the high school, students traded drugs between classes. Duane Spivey, the mayor's son, was arrested for drug dealing. So was Manuel, Delores's brother.

Delores and I had bought the Dodson house, restored it, furnished it with things we bought at farm auctions, started our family. Those were the hard years, the happy ones. The girls started to school. I was away from home gathering material for my column on county history. Without either of us intending it, a space grew between us. Delores didn't know I had filled that space with someone else.

Delores became a fixture in my life, as useful as a well, and as little considered until the water failed. She spent hours making frilly dresses for the girls that they didn't like because the other children wore something else. She did volunteer work at the church, the school—cooking, cleaning, typing, running errands no one else wanted to run. She took care of my clothes, my meals, my house. Delores was not a complainer but she once compared her life to that of Rosa.

I had laughed. "It's your house," I said. "You're cleaning your own house."

In San Antonio, Delores's family knew they were in trouble. After Papa injured his back competing with younger men, the doctors said he was able to work but he should not lift. Papa had no other skill. He could not get compensation because he was able to work. He could not get a job because he could not lift. "There's nothing I can do for you," said a woman whose job was to humiliate anyone who needed help. She worked for the government. "You got one of those injuries that only a lawyer can see."

Mama had to take a job making tortillas for a restaurant.

Papa had hidden at home, leaving the house only at night, eating nothing, talking to no one. Rosa sat beside him and wept; she made special treats for him, but all her efforts to cheer him failed. One night Papa was hit by a train near the Commerce Street overpass.

Gilbert still had a job operating a steam press but wash and wear clothing, polyester fabrics, self-serve laundry and cleaners threatened his future. He spent more time at the ice houses. Rosa spent more time alone, cleaning empty houses for women she never saw, cooking and washing clothes for her children who came home only to eat and sleep, and who waited impatiently to escape forever.

Manuel had been expelled from high school in his senior year. He had taken part in a chicano boycott after a Mexican-American teacher had been fired. Manuel had gone to California to pick grapes and had been involved in a workers' strike. He had been beaten and arrested. He had returned to Texas to organize farm workers in south Texas. He had been beaten and shot at.

Manuel had returned to his mother's house. There was no violence in him but there was anger. "This country wasn't built by capital, it was built by slaves," Manuel said, reciting the history he had learned in the grape fields. "For capitalism to work you have to have workers without rights. They took the blacks out of chains and made them wage slaves. Women and children. They brought in Chinese, Italians, Irish because they were desperate. When they became citizens and demanded their rights, they closed the borders and brought in wetbacks who can be turned over to the law if they are injured, or get sick, or complain."

Manuel and Gilbert quarreled and there was violence in Gilbert. Gilbert knew that some of his countrymen exploited the helpless but he did not believe his government encouraged it. When Manuel said, "Land of the greed and the home of the slave," Gilbert argued the only way he knew, with his fists.

Delores and I had gone to San Antonio to take Manuel home with us.

Manuel had changed since I first met him as a slender, serious child. He wore a headband around his long hair, and hid his handsome face behind a short, unkempt beard. The excitement that had once lighted his eyes had been replaced by a cunning anger, a look that struck fear in anglo hearts.

Delores and I had hoped that Manuel would finish high school but he did not want to sit in the classroom with younger kids. He got a job working at Dr. Heslar's nursing home. After work he played with Maggie and Rebecca. They adored him. They followed him around the neighborhood and listened to his stories of La Llorona, Brother Coyote, and El Caballero Porfiado.

Manuel didn't talk to me much; he wasn't interested in history any more but in economics and politics. He talked to Delores about the grape fields of California and the vegetable farms of south Texas. His eyes blazed. "The children have been condemned to poverty by their government," he said.

"Manuel, if you want to be a teacher, Will and I will help you with college," Delores told him.

"Teaching is a vow of poverty," Manuel blazed. "If Will hadn't inherited a farm you couldn't live on what he makes. It's a vow of obedience, that you will always support the establishment, and you will teach only what they tell you to teach."

Manuel bought a car. He had no friends that we knew but he was gone a lot. Delores and I were worried about him when Brassfield showed up at the door with a state and federal narcotics agent and a Texas Ranger. It was my first sight of a Texas Ranger and it took me a moment to realize Brassfield was the imitation. "We're looking for Manuel," Brassfield said. Like everyone else in the county, he said "Manual."

"He isn't here," I said. I stepped aside so they could come in but they didn't.

"What is it?" Delores asked, pushing in front of me, confronting them.

Brassfield ignored her. "If you know where he is—" I shook my head. "We got some questions we want to ask him. If he's not in my office by dark I'll come back."

They left with Delores calling after them. "What is it? What kind of questions? What do you want?"

When I told her it was drugs, she didn't believe it. Such things did not happen in good families. They did not happen in small towns. Manuel didn't even drink, putting alcohol in a category with siesta and guitars, stereotypes of the easygoing, light-hearted Mexican.

"We must find him," she said, and when I told her I was going to the farm to look for him, she asked, "Why would he go there?"

I didn't explain that it was because Duane Spivey had used the farm for a cache. Duane had gone to the barn to get drugs he had hidden there and had discovered the car inside the barn with me and Branda in the back seat. We had just made love and were lying exhausted in each other's arms. As my senses slowly returned I realized that the barn doors were open. Frightened, thinking only that it might be Delores, I sat up and came face to face with an equally startled Duane. When Branda's head slowly appeared beside me, Duane understood. A half smile replaced the open mouth of astonishment. With studied insolence he walked to the corner and took bottles and packages of pills from an old stove.

From that day an uneasy truce had stood between us. I did not report his business, nor he mine. I can't be sure, I told myself. I can't prove anything. I don't want to misjudge him. It was a time when self-interest posed as tolerance.

Delores went with me to the farm but Manuel was not there. When we got home, we found him in the living room playing with the girls. Delores sent the children outside and turned on Manuel. She was angry, angry for her family that had tried so hard to prove itself good enough to gain acceptance if not equality. "How could you?" she raged at Manuel. "Don't you have any feelings for your family?"

"I got feelings for my family, all my family. There ain't no Mexican kid going to crawl out of a Crystal City spinach patch and become president."

"What am I going to tell Mama?"

"Tell her I'm going to make the kind of money that can buy my kids anything they want. Doctor's license. Law degree. Their kids can be governors and congressmen. Ask Will, he teaches history."

It was probably true that if Otis Hopkins hadn't shot his Aunt Velma, and if oil hadn't been found on his land, and if the government hadn't given special advantages to oil men and money lenders, Otis might be no better off than Walter Slocum. His only skill seemed to be collecting interest on money that had fallen into his hands with no more effort than pulling a trigger. However, it was a skill that was highly valued in his country, and highly rewarded.

"Where do you get such ideas?" Delores asked, unwilling to let me into the conversation. This was her family and she wanted to set it right. "What happened to plain old hard work like Papa believed in?"

"If hard work is a virtue, why isn't it possible for the best and hardest working grape picker to some day own his own vineyard, or even for his children or grandchildren to own their own vineyard? Do you think Will will ever be able to teach hard enough or good enough to send your kids to the best schools? Where they can meet the best people, make connections that will open the right doors for them? How are they going to compete with Dr. Heslar's kids?"

"I can't argue with you," Delores said, unwilling to hear more. "I just know that you've ruined any chance you ever had of getting ahead."

"Do you know what the new source of wealth is?" Manuel asked. "Bigger than gold or oil or insurance? Drugs. There's a lot of pressure to get people to use the stuff. Can you imagine what would happen if people stopped taking drugs? Pharmaceutical companies wiped out, people unemployed, doctors destitute, conglomerates damaged. The government would have to step in and make them loans, change laws to get more drugs on the market, maybe have a surplus drug program."

"Manuel, that's crazy." Delores believed he had destroyed his mind with drugs, but Manuel did not use drugs.

"They've arrested Duane," I warned him.

"Duane forged prescriptions," Manuel said. When Dr. Heslar had put Duane and Dixie Davenport on uppers, they sold some of the medicine to other kids. It was so profitable that they stole and forged other prescriptions. Manuel had not forged or stolen prescriptions; he had bought them from Dr. Heslar. "They can't do anything to me without busting him," Manuel boasted.

Delores was shocked. She had a belief in doctors known only to women who had delivered two healthy babies. "What are the children going to think?"

"You think they don't know?" Maggie was in second grade, Becky in fourth. "You think they don't see high school kids taking drugs? They see adults taking drugs. You take drugs yourself."

"I only take medicine the doctor—" In the medicine cabinet remained most of the pills Dr. Heslar had prescribed to help Delores lose weight and other pills to help her relax after the diet pills kept her awake.

"The best sellers in high school," Manuel said.

Delores and I looked at each other, unable to comprehend. Wanderer Springs was too ordinary, our lives too attuned to work, children, and planning next season's garden. The ground had opened and we looked into a world of which we had been only dimly and unwillingly aware. Delores's eyes were bleak when she turned to Manuel. "I have to know. Have you given drugs to the children?"

Manuel jumped from the couch where he was sitting. He was furious, almost in tears. "I don't go to people, they come to me. I don't use that stuff, my kids are not going to use it, I'll do anything I can to keep your kids from using it. But it's the only way I can give my children an equal chance and they have as much right to the future as anybody else." Manuel went outside and slammed the door behind him.

I ran after him, fearing he was going to flee. "Where are you going?" I asked.

"I'm going to see the sheriff. I got nothing to hide."

Dixie Davenport disappeared. Duane Spivey was found guilty of forging prescriptions and stealing and selling drugs. Manuel agreed to leave the county. Dr. Heslar agreed to move the drug store to the hospital where he would have better control over it, to reduce the number of prescriptions he gave to patients in the nursing home, and to discontinue the flying ambulance service.

There was talk but it wasn't the kind of scandal anyone enjoyed talking about. It was a time when the old were forgotten and parents did not want to talk about their children. After the horror wore off, people stopped thinking about it, except when Brassfield brought Herschell Shipman a photograph of some girl Dixie's age who had been found in a shallow grave or under refuse in a trash dump.

Such things did not happen in Wanderer Springs. We were the good people. If evil had come into our midst, it had been brought by someone else. All eyes turned on my brother-in-law Manuel. And on me for bringing him there.

The Spiveys moved away. Delores died. The school was closed, the children bussed to Center Point, leaving Biddy Whatley who sold hobby kits to the folks in The Wanderer's Rest and Herschell Shipman who waited inside his store for Wanda and Dixie to come home.

As I crossed over Wanderer Creek I looked back. The gin was rusting, the sheet metal sides rattling in the wind. Parked in the hangar at Hide City was a single-engine Beech Bonanza.

PROD

*chickens, sheep, mysterious children,
an Indian and a woman in black*

I drove down the old road to Prod. At one time as far as the eye could see from horseback everything belonged to the Lances, held together by Earl, a slight little man who walked in quick, short steps, his boot-heels resounding, his chin and eyes jerking. Earl who had shot Oscar Spruill, and maybe his own brother, was our example of how to get things done.

I told Gilbert about Earl Lance one night when Gilbert came home, his face and knuckles bloody. There was a lot of anger in Gilbert. When he walked out of the house in the morning he saw the cars that Manuel had given him and Rosa. Gilbert did not believe Manuel was a good American. He listened to the radio on the way to work and they never said anything good about his city, his country. The boss looked at him as though he was late and he had never been late. When he went to the courthouse to change the title to Manuel's car, they had treated him like he couldn't speak English.

After work Gilbert stopped at the ice house to have a few beers and relax with his friends. They talked loud, laughed, got mad together, and he felt better. Unless someone made a remark about his wife being a maid, or said that he was not an American, or said that he was not Mexican enough. Sometimes Gilbert did not find relief or a fight at the ice house. He came home drunk and morose and picked a fight with Rosa.

157

For some reason Gilbert never picked a fight with me. He sat on the porch and listened to my stories about Wanderer Springs. Gilbert was astonished that Earl Lance was our version of the gunfighter who rode into town and with nothing but courage and his skill with a six-gun, defeated the forces of evil. "What good did it do?" he asked. Like most students, Gilbert understood the lesson. Applying it was something else.

Wanderer Springs invoked the name of Earl Lance every time they lost control of events. "Old Earl would know what to do about them stealing the courthouse," folks said, although Earl did not involve himself in politics. "Old Earl would know what to do about them niggers trying to vote," folks said, although Earl did not involve himself in cross burnings or other religious matters. "Old Earl would know what to do if he caught Bud Tabor fooling with his daughter," folks said before Ed McElroy shot Bud through Box 287. Bud also trifled with Earl's niece, Selena Lance, but nobody thought Selena needed protecting.

Delmer, the youngest of the Lance boys, was always referred to as "Earl's brother?" It was not a question of Ma Lance's virtue, but Delmer's quality. Folks were always startled that the two boys were brothers.

When Ma Lance died Delmer decided he needed a wife so he went to Wichita Falls and got one—a short, broad-shouldered, cheerful girl named Cristobel. Although she bore him four children, stocked the store, held mules while they were being shod, chased Snuggles, hatched and dried chickens, and was decent enough to die soon after he did, folks thought there was something wrong with the marriage. It wasn't Cristobel they doubted; it was because Delmer never did anything right.

Delmer was a hulking, brooding, dark-faced man who decided the future was in commerce rather than ranching. His decision was better than his execution. The railroad was bringing farmers to the county and they were buying land, so

Delmer laid out a townsite on a corner of the ranch, built the Prod store, and secured a post office located in the store.

No one moved to the town of Prod, and the only thing that kept the store going was that Earl bought all his ranch supplies there. Delmer built a blacksmith shop but farmers preferred going to Wanderer Springs where they could lounge around Shipman's Hardware. Earl sent his horses and mules to Delmer, and Cristobel pumped the bellows and held the horses while Delmer nailed the shoes.

One year the grasshoppers were so bad that the only thing the farmers could raise was chickens. Delmer cleaned out the blacksmith shop and went into the chicken business. By the time he got the business going, the grasshoppers were gone and the county was in the grip of a drought. The ground broke open in huge cracks, the baby chicks fell into the cracks and died. Cristobel went about with a shovel, digging the chickens out of the ground.

The drought was broken by a violent thunderstorm that dropped six inches of rain in two hours. Wanderer Creek overflowed, Buster Bryant kept his horse saddled all night ready to ride with a warning if the dam at Earl's lake broke, and Delmer ran around in the rain with a bushel basket picking up his chickens and taking them to Cristobel who put them in the oven to dry. Some of the chickens died, the others—their feathers singed—sought safety under the stove, the bed, the furniture.

Delmer got out of the chicken business although it took him a time to get rid of the chickens. Earl fed them to his ranch hands until they stopped coming to the chuck wagon. When the cook asked Buck Fowler what piece of chicken he wanted, Buck said, "It don't matter, it all eats worms."

Chickens ran over the store, perched on the shelves, and pecked at the merchandise that no one but Earl ever bought. Folks used to drive to Prod at dusk to watch Cristobel with feathers in her hair and droppings on her shoulders chase the chickens off the roof. That was when automobiles were new and used more for entertainment than convenience. Folks didn't go for a drive unless there was something to see.

, Delmer saw a future in wool and had a flock of sheep shipped by rail. When the sheep were unloaded they developed an unnatural affection for an old yellow dog that had come to meet the train. The dog, embarrassed by the attention, ran through the town, the sheep racing behind it, Cristobel chasing the sheep, and Lowell Byars, Wesley Murdock, and Benny Whatley trying to head off the dog. Of the townspeople, only Guy Shipman did not join the chase, being prohibited by consumption.

Buster Bryant ran his horse through two clotheslines and a picket fence trying to turn the sheep. Old Earl was there but he didn't chase the sheep, he turned his horse and rode back to the ranch. Earl did not involve himself in town matters. Buster Bryant worked at almost every ranch in two counties but he never worked for the Prod. Earl said Buster ruined a twenty-dollar horse chasing a two-bit sheep.

Delmer sat on his horse at the depot, puzzling over what had gone wrong. When Cristobel returned empty-handed, Delmer told her he was quitting the sheep business. "Too un-certain," he said.

From time to time the dog and sheep showed up at some-one's tank or feed trough, the dog looking gaunt and haunt-eyed, the sheep looking unraveled. Elmer Spruill shot the dog. There was a story that the dog's appearance had become so altered by the rigor of leadership that Elmer mistook it for Josh Kincheloe's mysterious animal. Elmer said he shot it because he couldn't stand the puzzled look in the dog's eyes.

Without the dog the sheep seemed to have no reason to live but wandered off to die. "There's Delmer's sheep," folks said every time they found a bone. And when a man's dog was miss-ing, he said, "Delmer's sheep are after my dog." Delmer's sheep were talked about almost as much as his children.

Delmer and his wife had four daughters scattered over more than twenty years. "Delmer couldn't even have kids right," folks said. Mattie, the oldest girl, moved to the ranch headquarters when she was eight and took care of Earl. When she was twelve she found two stray children while picking blackberries near Turtle Hole. Children sometimes fell out of wagons, so Earl sent riders to look for parents, and newspapers as far away as Fort Worth reported the discovery, but no trace of their origin was ever found.

The boy, who was about four, said his name was Bobby Penn. However, he did not speak distinctly and those listening were not certain. The girl, perhaps two, could not or would not speak, and Bobby said he had never seen her before. To all questions as to where he came from and why he was in the woods, he said he was lost.

Mattie took the children to raise although most folks thought there was something wrong with them, especially the girl who was said to have "turtle eyes." Their suspicions were confirmed when Mattie sent Bobby to Grover Turrill's Mud College and the boy spoke what Dr. Vestal said was Latin. After that Bobby was not allowed to go to school or to play with other children. Everyone knew that Latin was a dead language.

Bobby was cured of Latin by Sister Druscilla Majors and Mattie sent him to boarding school. Although she showed pictures of Bobby in his school uniform, everyone believed he was in an insane asylum. The girl—Mattie called her Shirley—disturbed folks by looking at them with her "turtle eyes" and by taking walks along Wanderer Creek. Strange things happened around her. A hay stack caught fire, a dog was found dead although nothing seemed to be wrong with it, and a mule belonging to Grover Turrill went wild and had to be killed. Such things had happened before but folks believed the girl had something to do with it and they complained to Delmer although no one said anything to Earl.

One day Shirley went for a walk. On the same day, Bobby

was put on a train by school officials for a visit home. Neither was ever seen again. Mattie spent the rest of her short life try-ing to find them, chasing rumors, and following carnivals and freak shows. She came home confident the children would come to her because she was sick and she was their mother. Folks took that as a sign Mattie was deranged, and no one was surprised when she began taking long walks and died of what Dr. Vestal called "dew poisoning."

The children never returned unless one wishes to believe that the woman with the black cat was Shirley. During the De-pression a woman appeared in the county, prowling the roads, asking for food and permission to spend the night in the barn. Many believed she was Shirley because wherever she appeared barns burned, cows went dry, and dogs died without excuse. And because, when the woman disappeared, Mattie's grave was found opened and her body missing.

Once, after Mother died, I was sitting in the yard playing. Dad was plowing in a nearby field and told me not to leave the yard. A shadow fell across me and I looked up and saw a woman dressed all in black. A black cat, tail erect, eyes un-blinking, stood at her heels. That's all I remember except that her eyes, even beneath the folds of dry skin, were too big, too round, too green. I screamed for Dad. He couldn't hear me over the noise of the tractor but she left. I broke out with the measles.

I once asked Dad what happened to the woman and he said Brassfield put her in a hospital for the insane. "Did anything bad happen to him?" "No, nothing happened to Brassfield but every kid in the Bull Valley School got lice."

Delmer's second girl, Etta, ran off with an Indian, a scan-dal as Indians were on about the same social level as negros. Even Larissa Bell, so addled by reading she believed Indians could be Christianized, wanted them across the river.

Indian Joe, a cowboy for the Prod, went to the Fourth of July picnic at Turtle Hole and won every footrace. He even ran against the horses. It was a memorable occasion. Earl came to the picnic with Mattie and Shirley. When Lowell Byars was kicked by a mare known for its docility and two girls began sneezing and couldn't stop, only the presence of Earl prevented folks from turning on Mattie.

Folks grumbled and some of them moved to the other side of the creek, but no one approached Earl. Earl had found one of his cows dead beside the creek, and he sat down on the carcass to eat his dinner. Earl wasn't sociable. Roy Dodson sat down on the other end of the cow. "Howdy, Earl," said Dodson. "Find your own cow," said Earl.

Etta and Indian Joe slipped away from the picnic while Selena attracted attention to herself by tucking her skirts between her legs and climbing a greased pole after all the boys had failed. She was the only female who entered the contest and all the women and some of the Baptist men refused to watch. It was a terrible scandal until folks discovered that Etta had eloped with Indian Joe. In those days folks couldn't concentrate on but one scandal at a time.

Etta never came back, but Delmer and Earl kept track of her and when she died in childbirth, not long after Mattie died, they got her body and had it quickly buried in the Wanderer Springs cemetery, pausing only long enough to have their pictures taken with her coffin. The grave was never marked for fear the Indians would come and steal her back. Some folks believe the Indians did try to steal Etta and dug up Mattie instead. It was night, they reasoned, and besides Indians couldn't read.

Selena, the third child, was tall like her father, broadshouldered like her mother, and had a face like a plowshare with pointed chin and spreading cheeks. "She never even tries to look pretty," mothers said to their daughters. "Not that it would help."

Selena talked too loud, wore dresses as though she was trying to walk through and not in them, and when the opportunity presented itself, she lifted her long skirts to her knees and outran the boys. "Girls who attract attention never attract affection," mothers said.

At a Sunday School ice cream social, Hulda Codd asked Selena how she liked her ice cream. "There are two things I like hard," Selena said. "And one of them is ice cream."

Hulda Codd, the example of grace, dropped a bowl of ice cream in her lap. Benny Whatley's fat wife was so startled she farted. The affair was such a disaster the Baptists discontinued having ice cream socials, and Genevieve Shipman insisted that Selena be churched. "A woman who is entertaining is seldom entertained," mothers said.

When Bud Tabor tried to escape Selena by slipping into the barber shop where even Selena wouldn't follow, Selena threw a spreading adder into the barber shop, driving out Bud, Lowell Byars who ran into the street wearing lather and an apron, and Buck Fowler who was taking a bath in the back room and ran into the post office wearing nothing but soap bubbles. Sherry McElroy was in the post office and her father, Ed, fired two shots before he realized Buck meant no harm.

"A forward woman never gets a backward look," mothers said, and were beside themselves when Otis Hopkins asked Selena to marry him. The possibility that Selena could get married cast doubts on their argument that ladies put up their hair in curl papers every night, bathed their faces in buttermilk to make their complexions light, pinched their cheeks to make them rosy, and did not chew gum in public.

The wedding was to be in Delmer's house behind the Prod store, and Delmer and Cristobel had decorated the living room with a stand of tomato cans, each one displaying a bright red tomato on the label. Every cushion, chair, pillow, mattress, and sofa had been stuffed with chicken feathers—Cristobel's efforts to salvage one of Delmer's misadventures—and with all the moving around, feathers floated about the floor and clung to blue serge suits and the hems of dresses. Other feathers blossomed from vases or decorated picture frames. Both the bride and her mother carried a fan made of tail feathers.

Miss Codd played the piano that was hauled from the Wanderer Springs Baptist Church with much difficulty. The difficulty was that Selena had been churched for remarks made at an ice cream social at Miss Codd's house. The church got around their difficulty by loaning the piano to Otis Hopkins who loaned it to Delmer. Miss Codd handled her difficulty by agreeing to play the piano on condition she did not have to speak to Selena or wish her well.

Earl Lance attended the wedding but sat in the kitchen where he could see without having to speak to anyone. Earl was not sociable. Mattie was off looking for her strange children, Etta was living with the Indians, but little Lucy, Delmer's youngest, was flower girl. The flowers were made of dyed chicken feathers.

Just when folks thought they had enough to talk about, Selena hiked up her wedding dress, jumped through the window, climbed on a saddled horse, and rode off with her wedding veil streaming behind her. A lot of folks said Selena reared the horse and threw the bridal bouquet over her shoulder. More likely she dropped it. Selena was original but not theatrical.

The horse returned but Selena never did. She moved to Center Point and sold ads for Chris Arp's paper, wearing her wedding gown from store to store until the ruffle fell off. Mothers heaved a sigh of relief. "When a girl loses her blush she loses her chance," they said. When Selena was seen in the company of Chris Arp, they said, "A woman who laughs a lot can't be happy."

Lucy, born more than twenty years after Mattie, was everybody's favorite Lance. She wasn't as pretty as Etta, or as exciting as Selena, but she found a way to Clifford Huff's heart. Clifford was a khaki-clad, stiff-backed, long-faced veterinarian. Having been kicked, bitten, or butted by every animal in the county, Clifford knew a lot about human nature. "A horse is just like a man; you can reason with a horse. You grab him by the upper lip, twist as hard as you can, look him in the eye, and say, 'Stand, damn it,' and he'll stand. He may squat a little, but he'll stand.

"But God bless, a cow is like a woman. You got to chase her around and get mad before you can pen her, and then you got to gentle down and coax her before she'll give milk, and if you get in a hurry she'll step in the milk bucket ever time."

As Delmer never had much luck with animals, Clifford was out at Prod a lot, and Lucy had been attracted to him by the way he treated animals, kindly but firmly. "He had the strongest and gentlest hands I ever saw," Lucy said. Lucy had to hold the animals while Clifford treated them and they got used to yelling at each other. "Hold him tighter." "You're taking too long." So when Clifford said, "I could use someone like you," Lucy said, "All right, but I'll have to ask Pa."

The wedding was at Delmer's house and was a big disappointment. Earl didn't come. Mattie was missing from the cemetery. Etta was in an unmarked grave. Selena was maid of honor but her hair was combed, every button was buttoned, and her shoes and dress were the same color. Folks grumbled for weeks. "Well, I wouldn't a gone if I'd a known it was going to be like that."

Lucy was a talented musician and took Hulda Codd's place as pianist at the Baptist Church. When the Methodists bought a pipe organ to flaunt over the Baptists, they found Lucy was the only one who could play it. Clifford was already a Methodist, having been converted to that religion by a Baptist minister who ate his pet rooster, Doc. Although Lucy remained a Baptist, she attended the Methodist Church the rest of her life and played the organ for more than two hundred funerals, counting those who died in the nursing home. Even some Baptists had their funerals at the Methodist Church because they wanted to go in style.

"Lucy always thought better of folks than what they was," Clifford said. "She knew them by what the preacher said about them when they were dead. It gave her funny notions."

One of her notions was that people didn't know how to die any more. Lucy wanted to die at home. I had gone to see her at Delmer's house behind the ruin of the Prod store. "Folks are hot at me," Clifford said. "They want me to put Lucy in the hospital and let Dr. Heslar keep her alive with his machines. But what's the good of that? She's already starting to nod."

He went into the bedroom to check on Lucy, and after a moment returned. "When you get old and sick that way, you don't have nothing to look forward to. You just live in the familiar. To take her away from here would be to take her away from everything she knows."

Clifford stared at the hands that had once been the strongest and gentlest hands Lucy had ever seen. "Folks don't seem to believe in death any more. They just slip away a little bit at a time, slow as summer rain, until only a machine can tell if anything is left. Like they was afraid to go all at once."

Folks always expected to be astonished by the Lances, but the most startling thing about them was that they had slipped away a little bit at a time. The only thing left of the first family in the county was a handful of stories.

"You should write the stories," Delores had said to me when Clement Arp asked me to write a weekly column on county history for his paper.

"Why?" I had asked. I knew the stories, I understood the hows. No one except politicians and theologians understands the whys. Some want to ride, some have to ride.

"You have to save those people."

"Save them from what?"

"Hulda Codd loved Lowell, she saved him from ruin, she gave him respect, she worked all her life, and she lived in the shadow of a woman who wanted to dance."

"So which one was right?" I had lost certitude and for a historian that is a serious thing. What did Mrs. Crockett think of Davy going to the Alamo? "Victory or death," wrote Col. Travis from the besieged fortress. Did his children think he had other choices?

"They were both right. They were who they said they were."

I wrote the stories. I wrote about Clifford's pet rooster named "Doc." Doc was a dominecker that had a way of stretching its neck and cocking its head that reminded Clifford of Dr. Vestal when he said, "I know you can't pay me now, but—"

Clifford had trained Doc to come when he whistled, and he had made a little wagon that he trained Doc to pull. One day the Baptist preacher had dropped in at dinner time. Decency required that he be fed and there was nothing to feed him. "Go get Doc," Clifford's father said. Clifford was considering whistling for Doc and running away when his father said, "I know it's hard, son. I can't blame you if you run away. But one of us has got to give up something that's precious to him, and all I got left is pride."

I wrote the stories until they conflicted with what John Ballard and other merchants had decided was our legacy.

LOST LAKE FARMS

*a yearbook, a telephone call, a fight, a ride,
a look at the other side*

PAST the cemetery, beyond the broad wheatfields leased by Ira Ferguson, all the way to Red River on both sides of the road what once was the Prod ranch was now Lost Lake Farms, owned by a Dallas development company headed by Bitsey Bryant's father, Vernon Tabor. The barbed wire fence had been replaced by white metal that gleamed in the sun. Coastal bermuda and little bluestem covered pastures that once knew buffalo grass, switch grass, and sideoats gramma. Neat treelines of cottonwoods and hackberries had replaced the mesquite, sand sagebrush and saltcedar. The ragged, scrubby cattle that Earl Lance had known had been replaced by picturesque Arabian horses. Thirty years after Eli Spivey had eaten Rough on Rats to pay his debts, an omniscient government had decreed that the only people who could profit from ranching were those who could afford grand gestures.

Vernon Tabor, whose father had buried and plowed up Luster Cox, whose Uncle Bud had been shot through Box 287, and whose nephew had been shot by Dad, had owned a dry goods store in Quanah until he inherited a small farm near Dallas from his wife's family. He almost sold the farm but mortgaged it instead, bulldozed the trees, put in an artificial lake and a golf course and began building condominiums as fast as he could finance them. He had known nothing but prosperity since, although he kept the no-profit store open in Quanah to accommodate his old friends. He had bought the Prod ranch because Bitsey wanted it and because it was good business to lose a little money.

Bitsey was president of Lost Lake Farms, and Boots was general manager. They employed a staff of trainers, drivers to move the horses to shows and sales, and a woman to keep the house. Bitsey's duties as president left her no time for taking care of the old brick house.

The Lances had lived in a rock house in Palo Pinto County, but there was little rock in Wanderer Springs so the Prod headquarters was the first brick house in the county. That was enough to establish the Lances as different when most others were living in tents, dugouts, and tar paper shacks. But what folks talked about was the fact that the house had no porches, no steps, no stoop, no fence, no yard. One stepped out of the Lance house into the Prod pasture without transition. One tale had it that Wilbur, his back broken in a fall from a horse, had crawled from the pasture right into the house, but the truth was that railroad surveyors carried him home.

"Square as a jail," was the way folks described the house until Bitsey added a gallery all the way around it, with a gazebo in front, and a wishing well and flower garden in back, all of it surrounded by a fashionably rustic rail fence. A picture of the house had graced the front cover of some oil company's travel magazine.

Off to the right of the road I was traveling was what had once been the Prod community; on the left was a grand stone entryway with a sign shaped of horseshoes: Lost Lake Farms, Home of Champion Arabian Horses. A metal gate opened to an asphalt road leading between two gleaming white fences to the headquarters. I had never been inside the house. Until Bitsey's father bought it, neither had anyone else who was not a Lance—except for Larissa Bell. Earl was not sociable.

I had been outside the house lots of times. When I was in

high school most of our entertainment involved driving: (
ing to Turtle Hole for a picnic, driving to the river to shoot 1
driving through Center Point so that Boots could rope ho\
numbers. Center Point folks had metal house numbers that
they stuck in the yard and Boots stood in the back of the
pickup and roped them as we drove down the street. Driving
over Paymore Hill. The road over Paymore Hill was the only
one in the county with enough of a dip to make the girls
squeal.

Marshall was the only one of us who could ever think of
anything new. "Let's go out to the Prod and look for Ma Lance's
grave," he said. After Ma died, Larissa Bell rode back to Starvation Creek. Wilbur, Earl, and Delmer wrapped their mother in
a wagon sheet, carried her a few steps into the pasture and
buried her. Every time a Lance died there was talk about digging Ma up and moving her bones to the cemetery, but no one
would ask Earl where she was and Delmer couldn't remember.
Boots had called me in San Antonio to ask where she was before Bitsey dug her wishing well, but I didn't know.

Looking for Ma Lance's grave consisted of: A) Selecting a
mixed team—usually there were five or six of us in a car.
B) Talking about Mattie's body that wandered about looking for
its grave, Bobby and Shirley who lived in the attic and spoke
only in Latin, and the old woman with turtle eyes and a black
cat—sometimes she was Shirley and sometimes she wasn't.
C) Driving as close to the house as we dared.

There wasn't a gate in those days, just a cattle guard, and
no road. We rattled across the cattle guard and drove across
the pasture, weaving around the mesquite that threw ghostly
shadows in the headlights. Up on the knoll we could see the
square-as-a-jail headquarters, and everyone was silent until the
car lights reflected off the windows of the house or glittered in
the eyes of a possum or coon and someone yelled, "The black
cat." The girls screamed, the driver turned and raced back
across the pasture, dodging mesquites, as often as not being

unable to find the cattle guard and having to drive up and down the fence while our self-induced panic grew.

That was the most exciting thing we did until Vivian got so scared he drove through a fence, a violation of what we thought of as the rules of the game and what our elders considered acceptable wild behavior. Cutting a fence was serious and we all kept Vivian's secret but made no secret of our anger. We didn't dare go back to the Prod for fear of ambush by Texas Rangers.

I could see Boots and Bitsey, westerners down to the hospitality, waiting beside the rustic rail fence in the pose that had appeared on the cover of a magazine. I put on my going home face—not too happy lest I invite envy nor too sad lest I encourage pity. It was not wise to look like I had gotten far from Wanderer Springs.

I was surprised at how little Bitsey had changed except for some puffiness around the eyes and fullness of her cheeks. Bitsey had rosy cheeks but hands like a man. She was wearing designer jeans, western shirt, handmade boots, and her smile was friendly. Her whole family was friendly. When her father had a party in Dallas, his barber from Quanah was invited just like the governor of the state.

I first met Bitsey at a rodeo where Boots was a contestant. Bitsey rode in the grand entry as "Sweetheart of the Quanah Mounted Posse." She had been wearing a red cowgirl suit with silver boots, silver belt, and silver hat, and riding a palomino. She had given me the same friendly smile. "Quanah is the heart of the Greenbelt," she had said, "the dimple of the Panhandle. I'm supposed to say that." This time she gave me a hug as well.

"It's been too long, Will," she said, kissing me on the cheek.

Bitsey had a talent for being liked, and her father had trained her well. "Shoot, anybody can be a developer," he had been quoted in the *Wall Street Journal*. "Folks buy from me be-cause they like me." I had hoped Bitsey and Delores could be close the way Boots and I had once been close. They had tried.

"How can you not like someone who smiles at every-thing?" Delores said. "But you can't talk to someone who only talks to horses."

Bitsey's love affair with horses had left little time for making friends and little money for socializing. Until her father bought the Prod ranch and hired her and Boots to run it, they seldom had enough money to go to a movie in Center Point.

When Bitsey got through hugging me, Boots shook my hand firmly and nodded. Boots had been raised right. A cow-boy was polite, serious to the point of gravity, but once assured that he wasn't being taken lightly, he was a boy ready to play. Except for being a little fleshy, Boots looked the same. Stetson hat, western shirt, Levis that hung below the beginning of a belly, snakeskin boots. Snakeskin boots were not corral-and-cow-lot boots. They were designed for stables of Arabian studs.

Bitsey clung to my arm and Boots led the way up the sidewalk. He was taller than Buster had been, but like his fa-ther, without hips. On impulse I almost jerked on Boots's pants leg to see them fall but was intimidated by the gazebo and the gallery that ran all the way around the house. I wanted to ask Boots if he ever thought about the time he and I, with Roma Dean and Joann Emerson, had driven completely around the house one night in his pickup, something no one else had ever done. It had been our biggest high school triumph, and with proper arrogance we had assured our admirers that it was nothing, that we hadn't seen anything. Which was exactly the truth.

Before I could remind Boots of our triumph, Bitsey said, "I'll swan, we didn't get your bags. Boots, help Will with his bags, I'm going to check on supper."

Boots and I walked to the gate and stood by the car, he looking one way, I the other, trying to get reacquainted. Boots looked like a landowner, scratching his crotch, not viewing the land as much as appraising it. He offered me some Skoal which I declined; I hadn't tried that in years. "Bitsey doesn't like it in the house," he said, taking a pinch and settling it in his mouth. "I'm sorry I had to be the one to tell you about Jessie's death." Boots had a sharp face, blunted now with the extra flesh, but the gravity was still there.

I nodded acknowledgment and waited for time to indicate a change of subject. I wasn't ready to talk about Jessie. "Sorry about your dad," I said.

His father's death was like a stone between us. When Buster was fourteen he had ridden to Lubbock to warn his father that he was dealing with swindlers who were after his ranch. It was the greatest ride in county history, even, as far as I was able to discover, in Texas history. Buster had killed one horse, ruined another, rubbed the hide off his legs so that his trousers stuck to his skin, and he was so sore and weak that he was kept in bed for two days in the Pioneer Hotel and brought home in a buggy. But he had gotten there before his father had handed over the money.

Buster saved the ranch with an extraordinary ride and lost it with an ordinary life. He worked whenever someone needed a rider and whenever he got a little money he lost it leasing land and running cattle.

"There'll never be another ride like the one he made," I said, trying to move the stone a little.

Buster had waited all his life for another chance and had once stood all night in the rain beside his saddled horse, ready to ride if Earl's dam broke. But what most folks remembered was that his pants fell at the slightest tug and that he had once roped his own horse when some cows had escaped from a truck in Center Point, leading Brassfield and his deputies on a merry chase. Buster, who was working at the stockyards, chased the cattle past the courthouse, and just as he threw his rope one of the cows darted down a side street. Buster's horse, trying to cut, slipped on the brick street and slid through the loop. The horse, a gelding that Buster had raised and trained, broke a leg and had to be destroyed. The Center Point paper treated the incident as a comedy.

Buster's obituary in the Center Point paper hadn't even mentioned his gallant ride although I had written about it in one of my columns. True to his cowboy code, Buster wanted everyone to know about it but he didn't want to talk about it. Neither did Boots. It had been my job to come home and make Buster's funeral important.

"I just couldn't get away," I said. Boots nodded and spat to indicate he was thinking. "Becky was sick," I lied. I hadn't come back because it was too soon. Mary McCarroll and Mattie Lance weren't the real ghosts in Wanderer Springs. "I sure wanted to come." I looked at Boots. "Buster was the last of the real cowboys."

Boots turned and looked me in the eye. "I just want to know one thing. You don't think I'm a real cowboy?"

"I think you're a damn queer," I said.

Boots threw a punch at my stomach. I grabbed his arm. We wrestled, called each other son-of-a-bitch and asshole, and laughed until the uneasiness was gone.

I knew that Boots wanted to be a cowboy when I was fifteen and Buster hired me to help Boots chase down some Brahmas that had jumped a fence and run like hell. We chased those bulls for three days. The last morning I was tired, disgusted, and so sore I could hardly get in the saddle. "Boots," I said, "if you died and woke up on a horse would you think you had gone to heaven?" He said he would.

I swept an eye over Lost Lake Farms. "Well, you did it, Boots," I said, punching him on the shoulder. "You got what you wanted."

"Yeah," he said without satisfaction. The kind of cowboy Boots wanted to be was gone forever, leaving Boots and his father the trappings.

Boots had tried rodeoing for a while and had been successful until he was mauled by a bull. I went to see him in the
hospital. Bitsey was there, looking like she belonged. Boots
had been the toughest of all and not just on the football field
where he was fearless but without passion. In the hospital he
was wearing casts, bandages, and tubes, and looking thoughtful.
Bitsey held his unbandaged hand and smiled.

"Will you be able to compete again?" I asked. He shrugged.

Bitsey blamed the rodeo clown for Boots's injuries; he had
not gotten the bull off Boots quickly enough. Boots's code
brought him to the clown's defense. "He was the best there was
until a bull stepped his ear off," he said.

Bitsey wanted him to marry her and go to college. She
would get a job and help him. "I thought about teaching voca-
tional agriculture in high school," Boots said. "I don't want to
end up like Dad. He's always one friend away from the poor
house."

I applauded his decision, yet there was something in me
that tasted like regret. Something was gone.

Boots waved a hand at Lost Lake Farms. "Can you believe
this, Will? And it's all mine. Well, it'll be mine when Bitsey's
folks die."

"Too bad your dad couldn't see this."

"He'd ask what I'd done to deserve it." Boots still lived
under his father's scrutiny, and by his father's measure, and although he had done more than Buster had dreamed of, he did
not measure up. Boots looked over the land that would someday be his, the pleasure of ownership tempered. "There wasn't
no way I could earn this. If I'd been world champion cowboy
ever year of my life, I couldn't pay for this. Does that mean I'm
not supposed to enjoy it?" He spat out his tobacco. "Come on
and let me show you what Bitsey has done to the house."

The gallery was appropriate, the sliding glass doors permitted natural light into the house and made it less jail-like.
The ceiling fans and chandeliers were an effective use of the

high ceilings. Bitsey had chosen the designer well, the same one who had helped her dad win an award for his condos that "effected an aesthetic compromise between modern comfort and fashionable authenticity, being totally engaging while maintaining that tranquil detachment of a gentler time." The designer had also selected the handsome oils of horses among bluebonnets, longhorns with cactus in bloom, and windmills in the sunset, by one of the most expensive painters in the Southwest.

Boots was proudest of the alarm system that covered the barns and stables as well as the house and placed telephone calls to his neighbor and the Center Point sheriff and fire department. "This was old Earl's burglar alarm," Boots said, patting a handmade gunrack. Boots's rifles, shotguns, and handguns filled the rack and a gunsafe in the corner. He had several times more guns than the three Lance boys and their cowhands. "Do you know there wasn't a lock on any door? They had just been nailed closed."

The Lances didn't lock the house because there wasn't anything in it anyone would want. The only person ever shot on the ranch was Wilbur Lance. After the surveyors brought him to the house, Earl rode to Wichita Falls and got Dr. Vestal who liked the county so well he moved to Wanderer Springs and set up practice. But there was nothing a doctor could do for Wilbur. He was paralyzed. Wilbur, who had endured agony crawling over the prairie with a broken back, could not endure being a cripple. He shot himself. Most folks figured Earl gave him the pistol, maybe even shot him as a favor. Such were the tragic heroes of Wanderer Springs rather than the adventurer dying on some romantic quest. Boots preferred the Revised Standard Version. It was unbelievable but expected.

"You wouldn't believe the condition we found the house in," Bitsey said. "I had to tear out the floors, the walls—about the only thing that hasn't changed is that staircase, and I wish now I had taken it out. I like a broad sweeping staircase.

"There's not a closet in the whole house. The decorator wanted to leave it that way, so we put wardrobes in the bedrooms, and china safes in the kitchen. It would have been easier to have designed our own house but Boots wanted this one. I thought he was crazy, but then I thought Delores was crazy for trying to restore the Dodson house. It's not like they were historic. What did the Lances ever do?"

"One of them crawled down the stairs with a broken back, got a six-shooter, crawled back upstairs, got into bed and shot himself."

Bitsey smiled at me the way you smile at a bullsnake in your hen house—smiling because it's not a rattlesnake but not really amused. "What do you think of it?"

It was clear who the conquerors were, but Bitsey accepted her victory with charm and good grace. "I don't see a trace of the Lances," I said, earning a smile.

"It's just amazing to me that people like that tried to ranch when they did not know numero uno about breeding, showing or marketing," Bitsey said, shaking her head in merriment. "We just totally tore down the barns and corrals. We found all kinds of stuff—bottles, saddles, calf blabs. The designer wanted it, so we let him have it; it'll all show up in Dad's condos.

"Dad got this place for a song minus the chorus. He had to deal with Clifford Huff and Clifford didn't even want to talk about money, he just wanted to talk about what we were going to do with this place." Clifford sold the ranch to Boots because he didn't want the ranch broken up by developers. He never understood that Boots was the front man for an investment group headed by Boots's father-in-law.

"When I said we were going to raise Arabs, he just shook his head. If he'd studied the market like we did, he'd know there's no money in cattle; people don't want meat, they want glamor. Shoot, if our stud shows the way we think the next two years, his colts will be worth a million dollars when they hit the ground. And Clifford talks to me about cows? I don't think he knew any more about animals than he did about real estate."

I looked at Boots, but Boots looked away. I had been with Boots when The One Roan, Boots's first horse, went down. "You like this old horse, don't you?" Clifford said, bending over The One Roan, his wire-frame glasses hanging precariously from one ear. His lips were stiff from the sun and wind, his face guarded against the hostile environment. "I know what it's like to lose a friend, but he can't get well. He's already starting to nod." Boots was kneeling beside his horse, one hand on the horse's neck. "You boys go on to the house. I'll see that he don't hurt none."

Boots and I had walked back to the house. It was the only time I saw him cry, but we both knew Clifford was the kind of man we wanted to grow up to be.

Bitsey's judgment of Clifford had created a stiff silence. Bitsey, who believed it was her job to make everyone happy, tried to set things in motion. "Boots, show Will to his room so he can put his things away. We need to go to the stables."

Boots picked up my bag. I took the garment bag with my suit and followed him up the narrow stairs. I thought Boots should have come to Clifford's defense, but Boots probably thought I should have come back for Clifford's funeral. Neither effort would have been much help to Clifford, but Clifford never expected help. When Lucy was dying, he rejected the efforts of Dr. Heslar to put her in the hospital and the offers of others to sit with her. Lucy, the last of the Lances, died without a woman present.

Boots led me down the hall and into a bedroom dominated by a huge portrait of a young horse. Boots explained that each of the bedrooms had been dedicated to one of Bitsey's studs that were going to bring glamor to people's lives. Maybe the Lances didn't know much about ranching, but they didn't bring their horses in the house. I opened the heavy drapes and looked over the countryside that had been tamed by Bitsey's father. On the horizon was a line of green that marked Red River.

"I wanted balconies up here," Boots said, "but Bitsey said there wasn't anything to see."

I nodded. Boots took a silver-framed photograph from the dresser and handed it to me. Despite their haste to get Etta from the Indians and into the ground, Earl and Delmer had paused long enough to stand Etta's coffin against a wall and have a picture made with them standing beside it. Earl and Delmer are neatly attired in suits and hold hats in their hands. Etta looks young and thin in a ruffled dress with gathered skirt, full length apron, bonnet, and moccasins. Her unsewn eyes are slitted, her mouth ajar. In death she looks rueful.

"I found it with Clifford's things," Boots said. "I've been saving it for you."

"Thanks, Boots." I was touched although I no better knew what I was going to do with the picture than why Earl and Delmer had it taken.

He clapped me on the shoulder. "Make yourself at home, Will. I've got to go help Bitsey."

I sat down on the expensive brass bed. It was a handsome room, engaging my eyes while leaving my feelings detached. Nothing of Ma Lance's loneliness, Wilbur's desperation, Bobby and Shirley's scribbling remained. The walls of most houses were records—smoke from fires, stains from fights and accidents, scars from the furniture of years, lines that measured a child's growth, marks that measured his reach. All trace of the Lances' mystery and misfortune had been covered with tasteful wallpaper and thick carpet.

If it had been my house would I have left the walls bare? "I've finally got it figured out," Delores had said after we bought the Dodson house. "I'm going to leave it the ugly way it is." But she had painted the walls where Roy Dodson had toted his customers' bills.

"Why are all the houses men's houses?" she had asked.

Houses in Wanderer Springs were built to accommodate a man at those times when he was in the house—to sleep and eat. In the house Grandfather had built the biggest room was the kitchen, designed so that Grandfather, Dad, and Uncle Emmett could come in from chores, hang their hats and coats on nails beside the door, eat by the light of the window, read at the table by lamp light, and invite company directly to the table when they visited.

Grandmother, and after her Mother and Delores, had been required to cook, wash dishes, sew, iron, can, and do their other chores with men, children, and guests under foot, and not a single window placed where it would light their day or relieve their boredom.

"Fine for men and dogs," they used to say about Texas, "but hell on women and horses." Things had improved for horses, and women had gotten the vote. Despite their inequality there was nothing weak about the women who settled the county. And despite their separation by miles and chores and the infrequency of their meetings, they seemed to forge friendships and alliances that supported them through loneliness, grief, and dying. I wondered if women still did as well.

Delores had no close friends to talk to about our first child, Papa's death, Manuel's expulsion from school, restoring the Dodson house, my need for some interest outside of school and family, her need to be more than wife and mother. Bitsey was too preoccupied with horses and money. Branda was too occupied with herself. Rebel loved the children and I thought she would be Delores's friend, but Rebel, who in high school had been the only girl who cursed in front of boys, had become dull, shrill, and fault finding. She spent too much time talking football and pep squad, and besides, I didn't want to spend that much time with Vivian.

Despite the difference in their ages, Emma Harkness was the woman Delores felt closest to, the one she could discuss ideas with, or politics, or her feelings for Wanderer Springs.

But I had failed to come to Emma's defense when she was retired by the school, and while their relationship remained friendly, it became guarded.

At parties and school functions, Delores sat with Rebel, Branda and Bitsey and pretended to be interested in talk about school, recipes, fashion, and horses. When she tried to change the subject they listened, nodded, and went back to their specialties.

Sometimes, hearing the men in heated argument, Delores would join us, eager for any kind of passionate discussion. The conversation would become polite, or Vivian would say, "Delores is listening. We better not talk about politics." Or whatever the subject was. Everyone admired Delores for her honesty and directness. No one wanted to talk to her.

I left the upstairs bedroom, walked down the narrow stairs and outside. I didn't see Boots or Bitsey, but I felt more comfortable outside. The earth, springtime and harvest, was something I understood. I sat in a wicker chair on the well-appointed gallery.

"Mister Will, would you like something to drink?"

It was Madeline. Seeing her was a surprise. I stood. "Madeline, how are you?"

"Ise fine. Miss Bitsey say I should ask if you want something to drink," she said, so stiffly I thought she hadn't recognized me.

Living in San Antonio, working under the direction of a black man, I had forgotten that in Wanderer Springs Madeline was an inappropriate color. In Wanderer Springs blacks and whites lived parallel lives, like railroad tracks that never touched and seemed close only at a distance. Friendship between the races was as relative as a child's good behavior—dependent upon who was looking.

Madeline waited my pleasure, looking beyond me, filling her role in a way that diminished not her but me. "Thank you, a cup of coffee," I said.

Madeline was as alien to Wanderer Springs as Bobby and Shirley, and incredibly, as devoid of a past. I discovered that when I wrote a column on her grandmother, Zollie Cox Turkett, the first black born in the county. Her father, Luster Cox, had been a blacksmith and cowboy for the Prod.

It hadn't been easy writing that column because few records were kept at the time and those were white records. I had dated her birth from a story Chris Arp had written in the Center Point paper. "Two buggy loads of citizens traveled to the Prod ranch last weekend for an outing and to see the infant darkie born to the wife of Luster Cox. They reported that the infant equalled in health and spirit any white child they had seen, and that the mother was pleased to show it to interested visitors. They made camp at Turtle Hole and report a picnic at St. Joe's Crossing."

I wrote the story but I didn't mention that during a fever epidemic Luster Cox had ridden to get help for his sick family. There was only one doctor in the county, Dr. Vestal, who treated whites, blacks, and animals in that order. Luster was sick himself and had fallen off his horse behind the Tabor house. The Tabors watched him die, not because they were cruel, but because they feared the fever and were determined to shoot Luster if he approached the door. Luster crawled toward the house but died before he was shot. Folks figured he was delirious. He knew the rules.

There was no black cemetery so they buried Luster where he was, behind the Tabor house. The Tabor house had been gone for years and Luster had been plowed up so many times no one knew where he was. I didn't mention the incident because it was considered impolite to write about black and white relationships—unless of course it was a labor relationship.

I wrote instead that at a Juneteenth picnic at Turtle Hole, Zollie met Tomoliver Turkett, a stringy, peanut-headed man with a pencil-thin moustache, who won her heart with his easy smile. She married him and bore him ten children in a succession of frame houses without electricity or running water. Zollie, who had been taught to read and write by Mattie Lance, taught her children after the work was done. None of them were ever arrested, ever on relief, ever divorced. Two of her sons died for their country in France and her grandson, Tom, died in Korea.

In addition to her children she had raised the children of her daughter, Haiti, who had married Jafus White. Jafus, a Baptist preacher, encouraged the blacks to pay their poll tax and vote. He was dragged out of his house by white-sheeted men led by a Baptist brother, Wesley Murdock, beaten as a lesson in humility, and left on a county road to learn patience. A cross was burned in his front yard. The cross toppled over, catching his house on fire. There was no running water in Shack Town, and the volunteer fire department refused to respond to the call. I didn't write about that incident either.

Jafus was still staggering back to town; Haiti was severely burned trying to rescue her babies, Tom and Madeline. There was no doctor in the county who would get up in the middle of the night to treat a black woman. When Haiti died, Zollie took her two grandchildren to raise herself. Tom and Madeline came to the farm when Dad hired Zollie and Tomoliver to replace Mother's family who had moved to California.

Harley Arp had not printed my story on Zollie. It was not bigotry. Harley was less prejudiced than either Chris or Clement, but the business of the paper was advertising and there were no blacks who advertised in the paper.

Except for the military records, Zollie and her family had no place in history—the part that was recorded and studied. No one thought of blacks as actually belonging to the county. No one referred to Luster Cox as a pioneer, or Zollie as a Gold Star Mother. No one ever spoke of Madeline's heritage. She might as well have been discovered wandering in the woods like Bobby and Shirley.

Madeline returned bringing me a cup of coffee on a silver tray with silver bowl and pitcher. Madeline was pretty. Why had I never noticed that?

Outside of school Tom and Madeline had been my only playmates. We had worked together in the field under the watchful eye of Tomoliver. We tried to play together when work was done. Tom and Madeline had no toys and didn't go to school. There was a school for blacks above Otis Hopkins's bank but Tom and Madeline had no way to get there. They didn't know any school games and I got tired of explaining "hit me a fly, hit me a skinner, hike the ball, go for a pass."

They refused to play hide and seek although for a long time I did not know why. Our house had a fence around it, and once I had run inside the fence and hidden. Tom and Madeline could not come inside the fence without asking. I don't know if that was something they were taught or something they knew, the way I knew I could wrestle with Tom but not with Madeline.

I didn't understand about the fence until the night Tomoliver died. Zollie knew he was dying and she wanted Dad to drive him to Center Point and persuade a doctor to see him, but she did not come to the door. She stood at the gate plaintively but softly calling, "Mr. Will, please Mr. Will."

Dad took Tomoliver to Center Point and got a doctor to see him. I lay in my dark house, and Tom and Madeline lay in their dark house, all of us praying for Tomoliver. That night I knew there was something between us, something invisible and largely not understood, that not even the love of Tomoliver could bridge.

After Tomoliver's death, Zollie moved in with one of her children in Center Point so that Tom and Madeline could go to school. I saw them from time to time and we eyed each other as curious and wary as deer. I didn't know when Madeline got married. Whites were told such things only when they were employers. I read in the paper that Tom had died in Korea. The story said that he had been awarded the Silver Star. No one spoke of him as a patriot.

When Madeline served me coffee on a silver tray, I wanted to laugh with her, to laugh all the way back to those innocent days before I recognized fences. I knew she could not leave me until dismissed, but I wanted her to stay because she wanted to talk to me. "How's Demp?" I asked.

"He died," she said.

Demp Turkett, one of Zollie's sons, had been assistant janitor at the school. The school had hired Walter Slocum as janitor because he came to school everyday, stood outside the classroom and begged Emma Harkness, his sister, for money. To save themselves and Emma embarrassment, the school had given Walter a job. Walter spent his time hiding in the mop closet, so they hired Demp as an assistant because no one but a black would work with Walter Slocum.

Demp did all the work at the school so Walter was fired. It was unthinkable to fire a white man, even Walter Slocum, and give a black man his job, so they kept Demp as assistant janitor. That was when I was a student. When I taught there Demp, the only janitor in the school, was still assistant janitor.

"How's Leroy doing?"

"Leroy drives trucks for Mr. Boots. He gone most of the time now," she said, holding the silver tray stiffly by her side.

Madeline's husband should have been a Wanderer Springs success story having risen from Shack Town to propertied middle class. When Junior Spivey had been elected mayor, he hired Leroy to pump gas at the N-D-Pendent. It didn't look right for the mayor to take orders from folks. When, as mayor, Junior learned the Interstate would bypass the town taking the motor trade with it, Junior sold the station to Leroy.

Neither of them ever mentioned it. Junior didn't want the taxpayers to know that in his several jobs he was making enough to live on, and Leroy didn't say he owned the station because it was easier to deal with customers and brokers as the surrogate of Junior Spivey. "Junior say you can't have no more credit."

When they started surveying for the Interstate, Leroy saw he was going to lose a lot of business, but he still had his regular customers, and he supplied gas for the school buses. When his son, Tommy, quit the football team, word got around that Leroy owned the N-D-Pendent. When they closed the school, Leroy had a business but no customers and no one who would buy the station.

"What do you hear from Tommy?"

"Been 'bout a year since I heard anything," Madeline said, her head down, the tray tapping softly against her leg.

"We didn't do much for your boy, did we, Madeline?"

"You taught him them games you tried to teach me and Tom. You didn't teach him to be nothing."

I tried to meet her eyes but she wasn't looking at me, she was looking at the stables, expecting the return of Boots and Bitsey. "Can I go now?" she asked. I nodded and she walked away.

We had believed in education as deliverance from limitations of any kind—poverty, handicap, the past. We believed this was especially true for blacks, although for them we didn't mean educaton so much as school. Tommy—"Running Waters" the Center Point paper had called him—had almost single-handedly integrated the school. Blacks had been permitted in the school out of fear of federal bayonets, a love of federal money, and because it was the right thing to do. They were there but not there, like Demp, who after twenty years as assistant janitor could walk through the building and not be seen unless someone needed him to do something.

Tommy Waters was noticed right away. Everyone liked him with his confidence and his ready smile, and he could play football. The students elected him to class offices because he could play football. The teachers gave him special consideration because he could play football. Citizens showered him with attention. At one time Tommy had three watches because he could play football.

Madeline had come to the school to see me. "Mr. Will, my boy is confused."

Madeline too was confused. Madeline recognized fences, invisible though they might be, but Tommy had been sucked through the fence, into a yard that was neither white nor black but representational, and he could remain only so long as he was colorless.

Tommy was angry with his father because Leroy was not black enough, because he honored with his shuffle the same men who honored Tommy for his stride. "Sho good to see you, Mr. Will. Would you want that windshield warshed?"

Tommy was angry with his mother because she was not white enough to cut him loose, to let him seek his own level, to believe the future was free of the past.

"Mr. Will, Coach Vivian tell my boy he got to have pride, he got to be aggressive. Them ain't virtues in no black boy," she said.

I had assured her that the world had changed, that Tommy had opportunities she had not dreamed of, that the future was wide open and it was without color.

"When he can't play football what will he do?" she asked.

Neither of us had realized how imminent the time was. Doll McFrazier was injured. Dr. Heslar said that whether Doll should play or not was an ethical question and that was outside his specialty. Doll thought getting a college scholarship was more important than beating Center Point. Vivian thought the good of the team—winning one for Vivian—was more important than the future of any team member. Vivian told Doll to play or quit the team.

Tommy went to see Vivian. He was captain of the football team, its star, Vivian's favorite, and he was liked by everybody. Vivian was incapable of backing down; admitting error was admitting weakness. He impugned Doll's courage and manhood. One of the remarks had racial overtones.

Tommy and the other blacks declared they would not play unless Doll was kept on the team. Like a lot of people committed to success, when success became impossible, Vivian became committed to excess. He kicked them all off the team. Wanderer Springs suffered the defeat they had so arduously avoided over the years.

The students who had cheered Tommy avoided him. Citizens who had congratulated him muttered insults behind his back. Once he had been required to run a lap around the football field for every minute he was late for practice but he missed four days of school before anyone noticed he was not attending class. Tommy came to see me.

"Tell Coach Whatley you're sorry," I advised him. "He needs you." Tommy was also the star of the basketball, baseball, and track teams.

"I'm not sorry," he said. Tommy was angry and his eyes glittered.

"Tell him you're sorry." Pretense had always been the secret of good race relations. Why didn't he know that? "Tell him you'll do anything to get back on the team. The more you seem willing to do, the less you'll have to do." I hadn't taught school for nothing.

"What about Doll and the others?"

"You'll have to cut your own deal." Why hadn't his mother told him these things? "You have a great future but you can't take anyone with you."

Tommy slumped a little, his head hanging and turning from side to side either in denial or disbelief. "Coach said if I wanted to be a success I had to be proud, I had to be confident and aggressive. I had to put the team first. Now you tell me to be a success I have to be dishonest and I have to forget about my friends."

Coaches, and politicians, had taught us that we could be

proud, aggressive when we represented them, that we could believe in teamwork when we worked for their good. "Tommy, when you are wearing the uniform of the school you can be proud and confident and aggressive because you are representing the school. When you go see Coach Whatley you are not representing the school. He represents the school and he will be proud and aggressive. You have to convince him that you are what he wants you to be, and that does not include putting your friends before the good of the school."

Tommy looked at me as though he had just discovered the key to the jail. "If I represent the school I can be a success, but if I represent myself and my friends, I can't be a success."

Why did he think I made the rules or that they applied less to me than to him? I represented the school just as he did. The school was more than the students, more than the teachers, it was an entity unto itself. Not to represent the school, or something, was to be useless, and nothing was worse than being useless.

"I don't want no white man's success," he said. "And I don't want to represent this school. I don't want to represent nothing." He left my office, the school, and Wanderer Springs.

That had been hard to take, that the young like Tommy didn't want to represent Wanderer Springs. I could understand Tommy wanting to leave. Hadn't I wanted to escape? Not to another place but to another and acceptable me. To a time when I was free of the humiliations of youth, free to do what I wanted. But I had always represented Wanderer Springs, even as town clown at the Texas Institute for Cultural Research. Tommy and Duane Spivey and Dixie Davenport were pursuing a life of abuse and indulgence, trying to escape any identification with us.

We had promised them Camelot and delivered Babel. The school was our tower, success our god. To reach the heights, sacrifices must be made. Excess baggage must be thrown overboard. We began with the most devout. Emma Harkness.

Hulda Codd had saved Emma from the Slocums when Amanda had died of Albert's imaginary heart attack. Albert had fattened his cow in Ira Ferguson's corn field until Ira threatened to shoot it. Albert and Amanda chased the cow for a while and then Albert lay down in the shade and told Amanda he was having a heart attack. Amanda, worn to scarcely a hundred pounds by the years of looking after Albert and feeding her sons the biggest portions, ran to the house, got a straight chair, tugged Albert into it, and dragged him across the sandy field to the Bull Valley road where she flagged down One-Eyed Finch.

Finch took Albert to the hospital in Center Point. When he took Albert home—the doctor said Albert had indigestion—they found Amanda dead in the rocking chair. Finch took off her soiled socks and put house shoes on her feet because he knew Amanda would be embarrassed for neighbors to find her in dirty socks.

When Hulda Codd heard of Amanda's death, she got Emma, a teenager, and took her into her own home. She and Lowell helped Emma attend Texas Tech. Emma graduated, married Bill Harkness, and returned to Wanderer Springs to teach the same kind of hope that Hulda Codd had given her. Her loyalty to the school was such that when Bill was drafted she told him she could not leave her students to follow him to the training camps. After Bill died in Sicily, Emma seemed content to invest her life in the school. Such dedication earned her the duties, schedules, and classrooms no one else wanted.

When Hooper Byars, Hulda Codd's grandson, returned to the school as superintendent, he insisted that his wife, Branda, be hired as homemaking teacher, although Emma had held that position for years. Emma was hopelessly out of date, Hooper explained to the board. She was still teaching home canning and how to make lard. Branda could teach nutrition, meal and wardrobe planning, interior design, cosmetology, and family relations.

It sounded modern and convincing and no one said any-thing when Emma was told it was time for her to step aside and let someone younger take over. Emma was permitted to teach first grade, until Emma, like Hulda Codd a stern disci-plinarian, punished Hooper's son, Rudy. Rudy collapsed in an asthmatic attack. Emma made no concessions to weakness or privilege. There was a scene in the school with Hooper, Branda, and Emma yelling at each other.

Hooper could not take Rudy out of her class because Emma was the only first grade teacher. He could not move Emma because all the positions were filled. He could not fire her without cause. He asked her to resign. Emma came to me.

Hulda Codd had given Emma hope but nothing of grace. Emma's plain face was coarse, her make-up uneven, her hair neglected, and her clothes seemed neither to fit nor match. Every day she wore the same chalk-smeared and ink-stained gray suit, a yellowing white blouse with lace cuffs that accentu-ated her large, mannish hands, and heavy shoes appropriate for the farm. She looked at me through the thick glasses that made her eyes owlish. "Hooper said he was concerned about the way I was acting. He said Dr. Heslar had noticed it too."

Hooper had given Emma a choice. She could resign or she could prove her mental competency. "He said I would have to go to court and stand up in front of all those people I've taught and prove I'm sane. Like Mary McCarroll." She began to cry, awkwardly, the way a child cries. "How can I be crazy when I act the same way I've always acted?"

I patted her square shoulder and assured her that every teacher in the school would come to her defense. "I'll talk to Hooper," I said.

Hooper hadn't changed since high school. He was thicker through the body which made him seem not so tall. He wore glasses that made his frank brown eyes seem big and staring.

Once we had thought him neat because we wore the same blue jeans three days in a row and he wore a shirt, tie, and trousers, but now that I was wearing ties to school, he dressed in sport shirts and denim suits. But the Byars confidence, the quick smile and deep, easy laugh were still there. And the air of brilliance and success. Hooper had the reputation of being a winner but he picked his opponents with care.

Hooper had gone to Princeton and taught at an eastern prep school but agreed to return to Wanderer Springs as school superintendent. It reassured folks when their children measured up in far-off places, like Princeton or Korea, and it reaffirmed their faith in the future when Hooper returned. The school was the center of the community, the only entertainment, and the only institution with which the entire community could identify. As long as there was a school there would be a Wanderer Springs.

When I went to talk to Hooper about Emma, Hooper had greeted me like the longtime friend I was, but before I could mention Emma, he began to recite his problems. Both the elementary and high school were in the old inadequate building that had been designed for a courthouse. What little equipment we had was broken and out of date. The library contained no source materials and few books of any kind. Every year it was harder to get good teachers. Every year the school buses went farther down country roads for fewer students. The state education agency recommended that the school be closed and the students bussed to Center Point.

Those were the problems Hooper had been hired to solve and for which he was being paid a salary far above that of the rest of us. He had asked sacrifices of everyone to save the school and we had been willing. I was sympathetic but not credulous. "You told us you had a plan. You even had a strategy for building a new school."

"I'm working on it, Will, but right now we're overtaxed trying to pay for the hospital and Dr. Heslar's salary. When the hospital is equipped and the doctor has adequate compensation he has promised he and Otis Hopkins will support a bond drive. It's going to take dedication on the part of everyone."

"A lot of us were dedicated to the school before you came, Hooper." Only in front of students did I call him Dr. Byars. "There is no one more dedicated to the school than Emma Harkness."

"I'm glad you mentioned her, Will. My grandmother practically raised Emma. That's why this is so hard for me to deal with. But there have been too many complaints for me to ignore."

Emma had grabbed the flowers out of the vase on her desk and drunk the water. She had felt a lump in the sleeve of her dress and pulled out a pair of panties that had lodged there in the dryer. She had, while marching her students out of the cafeteria, absent-mindedly put her slice of pecan pie in the pocket of her jacket. Everyone who had ever been in her class had an Emma Harkness story. "She's always been like that," I said.

"There is a difference between eccentric and inappropriate behavior, and in the first grade this is inappropriate. What if a pupil went home and drank out of a vase? I went to Dr. Heslar because of my concern for Emma and, of course, for her students. Dr. Heslar said he saw symptoms of what might be mild stroke, incipient senescense, arteriosclerotic damage, perhaps even Alzheimer's disease. And confidentially, Will, there are complaints that Emma has physically and psychologically abused some children."

"What children?"

Hooper sighed heavily, looked unhappy, and stared at his hands. "One of those children is my own. I don't want to put Branda in the position of testifying against Emma, and Branda doesn't want to. But I can't ask other mothers to speak against a woman they like and excuse Branda from the same duty."

The first time I saw her she was pink; even her dress and

shoes were pink. But what I noticed was the graceful way she turned her head; the movement of a woman who knew that she was beautiful and that I was watching. How can I explain what fascinated me about her when I have never understood it? I saw her as one of those frail, beautiful children too lovely to climb trees or make mud pies. Someone who needed my protection.

"The only other choice is to put Emma back in the high school and ask Branda to resign. Branda isn't certified to teach first grade."

"Emma isn't certified to teach first grade either."

"That was a mistake, but I did it for Emma. I know it was wrong but I probably would do it again. For Emma, but not for Branda. No, if I decide to handle it that way, I will ask Branda to resign. As superintendent I can't ask that of her, but as her husband I can."

Maybe it was curiosity; if so there was an animal intensity to know her, to be near her, to hear her voice. She was so different from Delores, so different from anyone I had ever known. She was different and she was dangerous. My senses, dulled by years in the school, salivated as we stood beside our doors between classes, exchanging smiles, glances, sometimes words. "I could stand outside your room and listen to you talk about history all day," she said. "You are so sensitive. You have such feelings for the people of this place. You could be a great writer."

"Will, we have to think of what's best for Emma," Hooper said. "No one wants to see her hurt, but if this becomes a public fight she will be hurt. And we have to consider what is best for the school. Emma isn't useful any more. She does not represent us well. I want you to persuade her to retire."

"No." I couldn't do it, but I could watch her be forced out of a vocation. For the good of the school. And because no one wanted her to be hurt.

No one came to her aid. We avoided her the way our parents had avoided Eli Spivey. Some avoided knowledge as well, preferring the crime of willful innocence. We were the school and the school must survive, no matter how painful it was to abandon her. It was a sacrifice we volunteered to make.

When Boots and Bitsey returned from the barns, Boots sat down on the gallery with me; Bitsey went into the house to see about dinner. "Send us out a beer," Boots yelled after her. Madeline brought two beers on a silver tray.

"You know Bitsey's dad is hardnosed Baptist. If we didn't have to entertain his business associates, he probably wouldn't let us keep alcohol out here," Boots said, taking a deep draft. "It just kills his soul to have to furnish girls in order to get a loan or a permit or whatever. And it's not even their money they're loaning." Boots took another long drink and set down his empty glass. "Having to bribe people to do the job they're paid to do. Just like teaching school. Every time I wanted equipment, or a field trip, or something for my classes, I had to do Hooper a favor. Every decision was made on the basis of what he got out of it." He shook his head. "Ever miss teaching, Will?"

"I sometimes miss the kids." I had believed there was something grand, even heroic about teaching young people. Hooper and Vivian believed the classroom was for failures. The successful moved into administrative positions in charge of buses, janitors, finances. The longer one stayed in the classroom the more inept they believed him to be. No matter how good I was in my chosen profession, unless I left it I was a failure in the eyes of those who controlled it.

I had thought that in my classroom I could provoke thought, incite ideas, but I was a salesman whose duty it was to tell the customers how to use the system to get from here to there—say from sophomore to junior standing. Any suggestions as to how to improve the system, or God forbid the customer, were met with hostility and suspicion.

A request to move a student from one class to another struck terror in the hearts of administrators and required days to study the ramifications and consequences. I had requested permission to take a Texas history class on a field trip to visit Zollie Cox, to apprise the students of the fact that blacks had a part in county history. Hooper took the request under consideration where it remained until Zollie died.

"I should have quit when it stopped being fun," I said. "When I stopped believing." Like Emma Harkness I had held on to the familiar until the only familiar was the abasement.

"More beer," Boots yelled.

Madeline was followed by Bitsey who carried a glass of white wine. "I just talked to Rebel," she said. "She and Vivian are coming after dinner."

"Great," I said, with more enthusiasm than I felt.

We sat and stared across the prairie at the sunset. "Best time of the day," I said, feeling nostalgia overcoming me.

"Yeah, but ain't it purty," Boots said. It was a Wanderer Springs joke.

"It's like something you'd see in a movie," Bitsey said. Bitsey was from the country but not of it. She succumbed too easily to money, or if not to money, to its attendant, assumption. Boots and I lounged in our chairs; she perched on hers. "Don't you miss all this, Will?" she asked, waving a wine glass at Lost Lakes Farm. Bitsey had not lived an authentic life.

"You know what I miss?" I said. "I miss knowing how to look at the land. How to see a tree, a stand of corn, a pasture. Reading it, understanding it the way our folks did."

"Hey," Boots said, "just because I can't find it doesn't mean I lost it."

"Thank goodness," Bitsey said when Madeline announced dinner was ready.

Madeline served us thick, sizzling steaks. As we ate, we talked about the syndication of Sultana Halim, Bitsey's breeding stallion. The syndicate consisted of twenty-five shares at fifty thousand a share. "Everyone who has a share can nominate two mares a year for breeding. And they contribute five hundred dollars a year to promote the syndicate. In five years we could be as big as Bentwood Farms." Delicately she licked her lips.

"What's their value?" I asked, and she looked at me in astonishment. "I mean, as a breed what are they used for?"

"They are treasures, Will." She smiled but it was a tone I had heard, even used before—exasperation at willful ignorance. "What's a painting good for?"

"Or a child?" I asked.

Bitsey smiled graciously. "Here we've gone on about our children," she patted Boots's knee, "and we haven't even talked about yours. How are Margaret and Rebecca?"

I replied that the girls were fine, but Bitsey, a practiced hostess, was determined to give me equal time. "Remember the time one of them broke something and you asked who did it and whichever one it was said, 'It wasn't me, and besides it was an accident.'"

"Rebecca," I said. It's not as easy to talk about children as it is to talk about horses. To list their accomplishments seemed immodest, to discuss their dreams, improper. Yes, it would be hard for her to recognize them now, although under my constant eye the change had not been dramatic. Rebecca, who always asked Bitsey for her fastest horse and who had told Boots she was going to be the first woman bronc rider, had changed her goal but not her ambition.

There was still something tentative about Maggie, as curious and wary as a colt at a loading gate. Maggie had loved Bitsey's horses. She had cried when Bitsey traded them for better bloodlines; Bitsey was not sentimental about horses. She didn't like a horse as much as she liked what she could do with it. Maggie preferred washing and brushing and feeding horses to riding them. Becky rode life, Maggie tried to envelop it.

"How do they like college?" Bitsey asked.

"They like it," I said. What else did I know about them as students? "Their grades are good."

"They are so pretty you must have to beat boys away from your doorstep."

An unpleasant image, that, of dogs sniffing after heat. It was not a subject I liked talking about. I was glad I had nothing to do with the choices they would make. "I don't think either is planning to settle down right away."

"And you still like living in San Antone? You don't feel small in such a big place?"

"I don't feel any smaller than I did here." In Wanderer Springs the weather dominated our moods, our conversations, our fortunes, our lives. In San Antonio it was the politicians.

"Well, I guess things worked out for you then." Bitsey flashed her dimple of the Panhandle smile. "Daddy wanted us to move to Dallas so Boots could be his partner, but I said no. I'd die in a big city."

"San Antonio is not a big city, it's a collection of small towns." Life in Wanderer Springs was dull but there was contentment. When I went home after school I knew everyone else was going home too. When the girls came in from play, they knew everyone else had been called home also. And when we turned out the lights at night, lights went out all over town. In San Antonio there was always the promise of something more exciting in the next neighborhood, the hazard that life might be happening where one was not.

"I have to have a lot of land around me," Bitsey said.

No one wanted a house by the side of the road, or a balcony overlooking the town square. They wanted castles on cul-de-sacs with privacy fences and twenty-four-inch living-color windows on the world.

"I never understood what it is you do, Will. You're not still teaching are you?"

Luckily I had been snatched from the jaws of shame. "I write supplementary materials for the schools. I couldn't teach and send the girls to college." Yeah, Manuel, I thought, your kids will go to Harvard and become lawyers and politicians and determine the laws and ethics of the future. My children will support you in the style to which you have become accustomed.

I told Bitsey about the booklets I had written and Roo's request that I write about small-town life. Bitsey burst into laughter. "I'm not laughing at you, Will. Roosevelt Hopkins sounds like a nigger name."

I watched her enjoying her simple pleasures. Sometimes what passes for tolerance of bigotry is really frustration. "Roosevelt Hopkins is the best man I ever worked for," I said.

Bitsey slipped on her mask of graciousness. "Living in San Antonio you must know a lot of coloreds and Mexicans." They were something she associated with cities—like roaches.

Boots shifted in his chair. "Bitsey," he said softly.

"Oh, Will, I forgot about Delores." Her remorse was genuine. Bitsey was not intentionally cruel; she just could not permit those who did not look like her or live like her to have feelings similar to her own. "I never think of her as being Mexican. She was so smart. And pretty. Whatever happened to—uh—her brother?"

"Manuel is fine."

"Manuel, of course. He—" Suddenly she remembered his arrest and was caught up short again. "Oh, that's good. It must be very hard for him, I mean, to get a job."

"Manuel is doing very well. He and your father probably know the same people."

Bitsey studied my face, trying to decide whether I was making fun of her. "And that other unfortunate boy?"

"Duane Spivey. He is not doing so well. He reformed." It wasn't a home run but sometimes you win on balls.

Until Vivian and Rebel arrived, Bitsey smiled, chattered, bustled, served coffee, and watched for their car. When Boots opened the door, Vivian pushed in ahead of Rebel as usual. He clapped Boots on the back, spoke to Bitsey, then stood too close to me, squeezing my hand too tightly, speaking into my face. Vivian was our apostle of competition as the meaning of life, our high priest of the will to win. I knew better than to relax my grip until he did or to step back. Vivian was not sensitive enough to know he was not liked.

"Hey, Will, you been writing any books lately?" he said, thrusting his face into mine and laughing, rising on his toes because he was a couple of inches shorter. Vivian would have traded Rebel for four more inches of height; he would have sold his sister for an inch and a half. "Will is a writer now," he said, chuckling at his own joke, feeling it necessary to explain to the others. "Aren't you, Will? Don't you write textbooks or something that nobody wants to read? Way down there in San Antone?" He chuckled again, looking at the others for their approval.

In high school when Vivian laughed we all laughed with him. He still followed his half-witticisms with a laugh that was more signal than mirth. These days he called signals only for Rebel.

Vivian was handsome at a distance, the way his father, Maurice, had been, but his face was lined from hours in the sun, his eyes were too close together, his thin, often broken nose was crooked, and his teeth were too small for his mouth so that when he smiled his face seemed out of place. Above it all floated a cheap hairpiece that hung precariously above his forehead. Vivian claimed his premature baldness was caused by wearing a football helmet. Marshall said it was because the blood never reached his head.

Rebel waited patiently until Vivian relinquished the stage. "You're looking good, Will," she said, extending a hand. I gave her a hug and she turned to stone. Rebel was thin and cheerless but she seemed to be doing better. Her clothes fit.

Bitsey got us settled again and offered drinks. "Nothing for me," Rebel said quickly. She did not drink and she did not like others to drink in her presence.

"A Coke, but I'll get it," Vivian said, showing inclinations of normality. He was going to put bourbon in his drink. Rebel would accept the pretense as long as he did not openly drink in front of her.

Drinks in hand we discussed those personal things it was their right to know. "You still have the farm, don't you?" Boots asked. I said yes to reassure them I hadn't slipped my traces, and they relaxed a little. I still paid taxes in the county; I still owned land. I might be AWOL but I was not a deserter. I could go home.

"Do you ever consider getting married again?" Rebel asked, meaning, are you seeing women?

"I still think about it," I said. That satisfied them that I had not forgotten Delores nor been emasculated by grief. "The worst thing about being alone is that when you ask, 'what do you want to do?' there's no one to answer."

"I guess the girls have forgotten all about us," Bitsey said.

With a sense of wonder, the girls questioned me about Wanderer Springs as though it might have been a dream. Yes, there was a woman who traded her horses in on newer models like they were used cars. Yes, there was a man who wore a toupee to school and all the students made fun of it. Yes, their mother saved egg shells and made cascaronnes for them to take to Rudy Byars's birthday party and they were sent home because his mother had never heard of such a thing and because there was confetti on her floor. Yes, that was where a man waited for his children to come home, where the sheriff had charged hippies with impersonating a school bus.

"They wanted to come with me but they couldn't because of school," I said.

"How are the girls?" Rebel asked. Rebel loved children and because she had none of her own, she was close to the girls. She wasn't satisfied to hear that they had grown, she wanted to know what they were like.

It's hard to describe your own children, easier to tell stories about them. I told how Maggie had stopped for a red light one night and a man got in the car. Her little dog, Angel, started barking. Angel looked more like a hairbrush than a dog, but she barked so the man got out of the car and ran away. Angel pursued him.

Maggie called but the dog didn't come back. She followed the dog up the alley, jumping at every sound. Angel was barking at cans of garbage near a broken door. Maggie called but that encouraged Angel to acts of bravery. She ran to the garbage cans, then ran back again. Maggie grabbed the dog and began backing out of the alley. The man followed. He held out his hand as though trying to give her something.

Maggie backed up to the car but still he held out his hand. He handed her a piece of paper. On it was an address. Maggie took the dog and got in the car. The man got in beside her. She drove to the address. There was a crowd of people in front of a huge ramshackle, two-story house. When the man got out of the car, they ran up and hugged him; some of the women cried. Maggie left.

Halfway through the story I realized I had made a mistake. They knew Maggie as a child who took in every sick animal. I wanted to show them that she was the same caring person. Maybe I wanted to show them the vulnerability of a caring person in the modern world. Perhaps I wanted them to know some of the fears of being the father of a daughter who all her life would have to consider my gender as a threat, whether it was a stranger, friend, father, brother, or lover.

They saw none of that, envisioning instead dark-skinned

Mexicans with rape on their mind. They forgot that except for myself, the only relatives Maggie had were Hispanic. She felt at home in the barrio.

"He was retarded," I added lamely. "Maggie took him home."

"Aren't you afraid living in San Antonio?" Rebel asked, shuddering.

As long as I avoided the criminal and civil courts and remained neither rich enough nor poor enough to attract the attention of officials whose purposes I might serve, I had nothing to fear. "What would I be afraid of?"

"Isn't there a lot of violence in San Antonio?"

There were bars where Earl Lance wouldn't know what to do. There were shootouts that made the O.K. Corral look like a French duel, young killers who made Billy the Kid look middle-aged. Shootings and stabbings were spice to add credulity to the pages of advertisements, to allow newscasts to compete realistically with entertainment.

"Tell me the truth," Vivian said. "Do you feel safer in Wanderer Springs or San Antone?"

In Wanderer Springs the violence was personal, almost intimate. If Bud Tabor had seen the pistol when he looked into Box 287, he knew whose hand pulled the trigger. Joe Whatley knew his lynchers by first name. Violence in Wanderer Springs was a bigger tear in the fabric of the community and could not be repaired without a scar.

There would always be a seam between Zollie's children and the children of those who watched her daughter's house burn. Lances and Spruills had spent lifetimes avoiding each other. Although Joe Whatley's granddaughter had married Reverend Murdock's son, the families remained at odds, and Marshall and Vivian, though cousins, were never close.

In San Antonio there was the fear of being caught in accidental violence or random mayhem. "The chances of dying of an unaimed bullet by an unknown assailant are greater in San Antonio," I said.

"Do you have a gun, Will?" Boots asked.

"Yes." I had Grandfather's old pistol that was rusted to uselessness, but if I had been without a gun I would have lied about it. Every man in the county had a gun, but except for the hunters, few kept the guns in working order. They had been passed down from father to son to grandson, packed away and largely forgotten, yet fiercely kept for That Day. That Day was when all true Texans would be called to take up their God-given arms and stop Them. Them were sometimes rapists, but more often Communists, dopers, or immigrant hordes, usually from the south. It was perhaps the most cherished of all Texas myths.

"I got out my guns the other day and gave them a good cleaning," Vivian said. Vivian was the kind of man who thought a fart required a response.

Vivian's guns consisted of a .22, like every boy in high school owned and used to shoot jackrabbits, turtles, tin cans, mailboxes, road signs, and street lights, and a double-barreled shotgun that Joe Whatley had kept in his Sand saloon. The first time the shotgun was fired was when Vivian, Boots, and I had gone duck hunting when we were thirteen. Vivian wasted two boxes of shells shooting at the ducks before they got into range. He wounded one that he chased down and killed and crowed over for months.

"The day I give up my guns is the day I stop calling myself a man," Vivian said. "I'd give up my Bible before I'd give up my guns."

"That's sacrilegious," Rebel said.

"If we didn't have guns there wouldn't be a Bible in this country. They'd have taken them away years ago."

"Who?" I asked.

"The same people who took prayer out of the schools and put dirty books in the library."

The only library in town was in the school, and the only books were outdated encyclopedias and whatever had been donated. Marshall Murdock had loaned his extensive library to the school so that his English students could write research papers.

Marshall was a dangerous teacher who created enthusiasm in his classes. Students were taking books home just to read. If parents or students were offended by the books, they were silent until Rebel overheard one of the Pep Squad girls make an obscene remark. Rebel tried to persuade the girl that such words were the mark of an ignorant and degenerate person.

"Then how come Mr. Murdock says this is a good book?" the girl asked.

Rebel confiscated the book in which Marshall had found beauty and truth and she saw nothing but obscenity. She showed the book to Vivian. When he was a senior in college, Vivian had discovered a nuance; he hadn't seen one since. Vivian, as principal, ordered Marshall's books removed from the school.

The only time I like obscenity is when I use it, but I went to Vivian and explained that the books were known and regularly used in high schools and colleges.

"Don't shit me, Will. I went through one of those books and counted the dirty words," said Vivian who had never read a book that was not required or finished one that was.

Marshall and I went to Hooper asking him, as superintendent, to overrule Vivian. As superintendent he was as approachable as God and as quick to answer. Hooper had read most of the books and knew of the others, but Hooper did not like problems. Hooper was an intense, uncertain man who hid his fear beneath a mask of genial rationality. "If the parents or the school board want the books back in the school and make an official request to me, I will order Vivian to put the books back," he said.

Rebel's complaint could take the books out of the school but it would take a concerted effort by the school board to put the books back in the school. This is the law of educational equality: a complaint is worth a thousand compliments.

"What about a request from the students or teachers?" Marshall asked.

Hooper put on his face of calm reasonableness. "The schools do not belong to the students, they belong to the public. That is why they are called public schools," he said with infinite patience. "Public schools are not operated for the benefit of the teachers, and if that's why you're here, perhaps you'd be happier in another career." The language was obscene and Hooper had not used a single vulgarity.

"When I think what those books did to Duane Spivey and Dixie Davenport—" Rebel said. "Marshall might as well have brought poison into the school."

It was an old fight. Duane lived in the shadow of his brother, Bubba, who was Mr. Everything. Everyone forgave Bubba for impregnating Dixie Davenport because Bubba could have gone with any girl in the school and fifteen-year-old Dixie was plain, unpopular, taller than any boy in her class, and should have known what he was after. "The books didn't bring drugs into the school," I said. "They didn't get Dixie pregnant."

"If it hadn't been for those books the kids wouldn't have been thinking about sex all the time," Rebel said.

"Bubba died for his country when a lot of people were running to Canada," Vivian said. "I'll bet you're glad now we made Bubba valedictorian."

Bubba was a good student but he had been challenged by a black girl, Melinda Schuman. Bubba had won the valedictory and the scholarship that went with it because both Vivian and Rebel gave extra credit for school spirit, which could mean anything from selling spirit ribbons to wearing school colors on the days of athletic contests. Bubba was captain of the football team. Melinda was a cheerleader but refused to lay a wreath at the statue of the Confederate soldier. Bubba had a

104.5 average in Vivian's class. Most of us thought it was unfair but no one said anything because Melinda didn't expect fairness, and because we represented the school. Bubba eschewed the scholarship and went to Vietnam. Melinda, unable to afford college, sold shoes in Center Point.

"Will, did Bubba come to see you when he came home that last time?" Boots asked. I nodded.

"It was like he knew he might never see Wanderer Springs again," Rebel said.

Bubba had come to tell me he was going to Vietnam. Perhaps unwisely I asked him why he had enlisted when he could have gone to college instead. Perhaps deliberately he told me. All his life he had been taught there were good people and bad people and it was the duty of the good people to protect the weak from the bad.

"I remember how many times you used to say, 'Ask what you can do for your country,'" Bubba said. "I remember you telling how Charles Martel stopped the Muslims at Tours and saved Christianity. I remember you telling us how our country had let the Nazis murder six million Jews. Well, this is what my country has asked me to do. The Communists have to be stopped somewhere, and I don't want somebody to tell my kids that we let them kill fourteen million Vietnamese."

Bubba had more personal reasons. He had been a high school hero. There was the lure of danger, the rites of manhood. With a grandfather like Eli Spivey, what else could a boy like Bubba do? Nevertheless, Bubba Spivey had been as much a victim of Camelot as Ngo Dinh Diem.

"You can deny responsibility if you want to, Will," Rebel said. "That's one thing people get out of books: nobody is to blame for anything, do whatever you want and blame it on your parents or society. But you and Marshall took away their heroes. He let kids read all those anti-hero books, and you told them things about Washington and Jefferson and Lincoln that they didn't need to know. You made them smaller than they were at a time when there were no heroes."

It had been a time when everyone was tolerated and no one was respected.

"There were lots of heroes," I said. "Every event produced them." They were camera fodder, their actions devoured, their lives left as curios. A brazen deed, an impassioned word had the attention of the world, an heroic life went unnoticed.

"Old Earl Lance was a hero," Vivian said. "He knew how to get things done."

Bitsey smiled at him. "Boots has done more for this place than the whole Lance family."

"I think it's marvelous what you have done with this place," Rebel said. "I think preserving the past is just one of the noblest things a person can do. Don't you, Will?"

"Sure." We who reinvented the past were as heroic as those who invented it. And we did it with both physical and moral comfort in mind.

"You too, Bitsey," Rebel said. "I know that you deserve just as much praise as Boots."

Rebel and Bitsey had to work at getting along, partly because of their reversed positions. Rebel had been raised in Otis's big house and had the best clothes and biggest car in high school while the Tabors ran a family grocery in Quanah. Rebel had been the rowdiest girl in high school; Bitsey had been Sweetheart of the Quanah Mounted Posse. Then Rebel had dedicated her life to the Lord and Bitsey had devoted her life to horses. Now Rebel lived like the wife of a school teacher, and Bitsey lived like the daughter of a land developer. Rebel tithed her pennies and wept for the homeless and oppressed; Bitsey enjoyed being rich as though she deserved it. Rebel had a hard time justifying the mysterious ways of the Lord.

"Preserving the past and being noble is Boots's area," Bitsey said. Bitsey disapproved of Rebel's determined dullness.

"My job is to take care of my horses, and when I come in the house I want my life to be as good as theirs."

Rebel clenched her teeth to prevent herself from screaming scriptures about fools and riches. "Wouldn't Buster be surprised to see those horses," she said.

"Wouldn't he be surprised to see me," said Boots.

"You know who would really be surprised? At all of us? Roma Dean," Rebel said.

I cringed. I knew that moment would come, had to come, but I was not yet ready for it.

"Wonder what she would be today?" Vivian asked. For a referee, Vivian was slow to catch on to the rules of the game. Roma Dean was the ball and Rebel had possession.

"She would be Will's wife," Rebel said.

"Wonder if she would have gone deaf, too," Vivian said.

Girls have a trick of not hearing what they don't want to hear so I was never certain whether I had said something gauche, or whether Roma Dean was suffering the Spruill disease. Nevertheless, everyone looked at Vivian as though he had said something stupid, so I did the same.

Like an old dog, Vivian regarded wherever he stood as his territory to be guarded. "She was hard of hearing sometimes," Vivian said. "Remember when Potts said he was going to give us a little quizzie, and Joann Emerson said, 'If that's a little quizzie I'd hate to see one of your little testes,' and we laughed so hard the principal came to see what was going on? And Roma Dean didn't even know what we were laughing about."

"She pretended she didn't hear it," said Rebel who had been the first to laugh. "She couldn't stand it when people were cruel to each other."

We all partook of Roma Dean's goodness, her tragedy and shame, but Rebel was high priest. "She was the kindest person I've ever known."

"She always looked so sad," Boots said. "Maybe it was because she was so thin it made her eyes look big."

"She was not sad," Rebel said. "Was she, Will?"

I tried to remember the Roma Dean I had known. The real one who smelled like gingerbread and ocean spray; who made most of her clothes and had won an F.H.A. award for them; who wrote notes to Rebel and Joann in class although they were together all day; who didn't like spending the night with Rebel because Otis's house was too big and gloomy with his presence; who wore with pride the little silver football I had been given by the school, along with everyone else who had attended practice. Roma Dean seldom laughed but she smiled when she saw me. Her dark eyes were close set and seemed masked with some inner pain. "I thought she was sad," I said.

"Boots, where are your yearbooks?" Rebel asked.

I went to the kitchen to fix myself a drink. Whenever we got together, someone always pulled out the yearbooks. I kept mine—historians never throw away anything—but I didn't look at them. The pictures were not records so much as editorials. By a mysterious process some were chosen to be pretty, some smart, some leaders, some popular, chosen to receive whatever attention, honors, or rewards the school had to give.

I already knew what the books were going to show and what the others were going to say. Hooper Byars standing beside his bicycle with his pants leg rolled up. Hooper was the first we'd seen do that. The girls didn't wear pants, Boots and I didn't have bicycles, and Vivian and Marshall who did, tucked their pants legs into their cowboy boots. "He never was one of us," Boots would say.

There was a picture of me with the track team, looking like the survivor of a shipwreck. "God, Will, you were skinny," Bitsey would say.

"His muscles were shy and didn't want to expose themselves." Hooper was the first to say it, but Vivian had taken it as his own joke, still expecting people to laugh.

There was a picture of Emma Harkness's house with blossoms of toilet paper stuck on the pear tree. Vivian had learned that in the cities students were papering their teachers' houses. Not knowing the procedures, Vivian had stolen the paper from the N-D-Pendent, where they had a dispenser of single sheets, and had spent half the night trying to stick the sheets on twigs, and then borrowed a camera to record his triumph.

"No one but Vivian," Boots would say, and Vivian would reply, "Whose house did you ever paper?" Vivian still considered it one of his accomplishments, along with painting the water tower. As with Elmer Spruill, folks might deplore his methods, but they had to admit his success.

"Who is that?" Rebel would ask, pointing at the picture of a boy called Splatter. He had one of those throw-up diseases and vomited every day after lunch. Strange as it may seem, in our small class there were some who went unnoticed. Except for Vivian we did not lord it over them. They were part of the school, too, part of the class, part of the team, therefore we loved them. We smiled upon them, gave them pet names, and told them jokes. We just never got to know them.

When I went back into the living room, Rebel held a year-book in her lap. She was animated, more like the old Rebel than I had seen in years.

"Does that look sad?" she asked, pointing at a page called Who's Whose? We were paired off, Roma Dean and I, Boots and Joann, Rebel and Marshall, giving permanence to passions that were as yet general rather than specific.

"No, look at this one, this one's clearer. Look at how short her hair is. She cut her hair just because Will liked it that way. She would have done anything for Will. Look, Will," Rebel said, thrusting the picture in my face.

I knew the picture. Roma Dean as school sweetheart. There was something wistful about her, a bruised, frightened look. Or maybe you can read that into the picture of anyone who dies young. Until she died, Roma Dean was the nice one, not the pretty one.

"She looks sad in this picture," Boots said. "Doesn't she, Will?"

She looked defenseless. That's how I remembered her. The girl I dreamed of rescuing. I wanted to be her hero. I wanted to earn her admiration. That she gave it unconditionally made no difference; it was not hers to give, it was mine to earn.

"That's the last picture taken of her," Rebel said. "I think she knew. I think somehow she knew something terrible was going to happen to her. She was the prettiest girl in the school. Even with her hair cut like that. Will, you should be ashamed of yourself."

When I saw my sticky gum nesting in the hair above her ear, I had left quickly without apology or explanation. It was the last time I saw her with long hair. Roma Dean cut her own hair so her mother couldn't stop her, and pretended she liked it that way. Rebel believed she cut her hair because I was getting bored with her.

Bitsey, who was left out of the conversation, shook her head to indicate that Roma Dean would not have been considered pretty in her yearbook. "This girl is pretty," she said, pointing at a picture of Joann Emerson, but we ignored her. Years ago some judgment had decided that Roma Dean was pretty, Joann was "fun."

"Look, Will," Rebel said. "Here's a picture of Roma Dean and her old dog. She loved Red more than anything but Will."

Boots looked at me, remembering that I had killed Red, but I avoided his eyes. I looked at the rows of faces like faded flowers, devoid of color or distinction. There was a full page picture of Rebel as Miss Personality, Marshall as Mr. Wonderful, Vivian as Mr. Everything. I was undistinguished, special only because I was Roma Dean's boyfriend.

Roma Dean seemed to understand the fire burning in me to be somebody. "You're special, Will. They can't see it, but they will," she said. Roma Dean made me feel worthy of the love she had for me. Time had proved how fallible those yearbook opinions had been, but like a referee's call, the judgment remained.

I looked at the pictures of the faculty, looking younger and plainer than I remembered them, commonplace now and even shabby. Emma was standing at the blackboard with her flat, inexpressive back facing the camera. She looked over her shoulder through glasses filmed with chalk dust. Her slip showed at one corner.

There was a picture of Vivian's old '38 Ford. The car didn't have a radio but it had an antenna, and Vivian had attached a pair of panties to it for a flag until the school made him remove them.

"Were those your panties, Rebel?" Boots asked.

We had teased all the girls by asking them that. Rebel had been the only one who hadn't blushed. "You ought to know my ass better than that," she had responded. "You spend enough time looking at it." But Rebel had changed. She stared at Boots to indicate her opinion of such humor.

"Listen to this," Bitsey said with a laugh, ". . . the unique, undying spirit that will keep Wanderer Springs High School alive forever in the ripening harvest of the years to come."

"That's from Hooper's valedictory address," Rebel said. "Doesn't that sound just like him."

"Do you ever wonder how Hooper felt about being valedictorian?" Boots asked. "His big triumph wasn't real."

"But it was," I said. "That's how he got the scholarship, how he got into Princeton, and became headmaster, and superintendent, and everything else. It wasn't true but it was just as real as if it was true."

"Wait," Bitsey said. "I don't understand."

Boots explained how Marshall was actually valedictorian, but when school officials read his valedictory address, they refigured the grades, and announced Hooper the winner.

"But they couldn't do that," Bitsey said.

No one answered her. It was their school; they could do whatever they wanted. Baptist or Methodist, there was some Presbyterian in all of us. Having to stay the planting for the rain, and the harvest for the sun, to wait upon the favor of Otis Hopkins to tide us over when rain was late or sun was cool, we knew our lives were in the hands of fate. Most of us called it The Will Of God. Our power came from being The Good. God was on our side; He would avenge.

"Marshall was never the same after he wrote that thing," Rebel said.

"What did it say?" Bitsey asked.

"No one knows," Boots answered, exasperated with his wife's lack of understanding. "Emma Harkness was supposed to help Marshall with it, and she showed it to the superintendent, and he told her to burn it."

"It had awful things in it," Rebel said. "About all of us. We all had such expectations for him. I've never been so disappointed in anyone as I was in Marshall." Rebel jumped up and left the room. Bitsey excused herself and followed. We three men sat and stared after them.

"Rebel's still mad at Marshall for making students read them dirty books," Vivian said. "I told him he should make them read the Bible. You know what he said? He said it was unAmerican and unChristian. Can you believe that? He got to where he didn't believe in anything."

Like Otis Hopkins, most folks believed that Baylor's liberalism had undermined Marshall's Christian faith. Marshall said otherwise. "Baylor is about as liberal as the Center Point jail," he said. "Hell, you have to cross Fifth Street to fart."

Marshall had written to me while he was in college and I was in the army. He rejoiced at what the Lord was doing at Baylor, he confessed his worldly temptations, he urged me not to give in to the weakness of the flesh.

While I was in college studying history, trying to find the

meaning of events that were like smoke—a guide, a sign, a portent, an obfuscation—Marshall was in the seminary. Everyday he dissected the Bible looking for its soul.

We all ran into Marshall from time to time when he came home to visit his father. Marshall held a week-long revival at the Baptist Church. When I saw him on those occasions, it was for but a few minutes and he was a minister, his greetings full of religious words, his face full of the sorrow of the world and the hope of Christ. At his side was a small woman afraid to be pretty. Her eyes snapped open as though in constant astonishment. Apparently she did not like what she saw in men's eyes. She tried to hide under the thin protective layer of skin, to shrink deep inside where rough hands could not touch her.

Marshall had been a pastor until his church asked him to resign because he had insulted a man who had given a million dollars to Baylor. Marshall had gone back to college to take education courses that only the dull or the devoted could endure to gain certification in a profession headed by a bureaucracy that could not tell the difference.

Marshall was hired by the Wanderer Springs school because they couldn't get anybody else, but they were suspicious. Marshall raised a serious theological question. Can a man be different and love Jesus? Divorces weren't rare, nor were ex-ministers, but there was something perverse about a man who lost his church, his idealism, and his wife in the same month.

Apprehensions about Marshall proved correct. He was a real teacher and therefore a real problem. His students couldn't always understand what he was saying. A cardinal rule taught by education professors and demanded by principals and superintendents was that every statement made in a classroom had to be simple enough to be understood by the dullest mind present and bland enough to be forgotten by the end of the class period.

Marshall said things like, "Maybe God creates babies, but He doesn't create teenagers." Some believed that Marshall had denied God and affirmed evolution. "Question everything. You must always ask questions. But sometimes you must listen to the answers." Some heard him say there were no answers.

"Why can't God be more responsible? Why does he leave everything up to me?" Some complained that he was teaching religion in the school. "Sin is the only thing in life that lives up to its advertising." Some complained that he was teaching sex education. "In this country neither a beggar nor a millionaire pays income tax. That's what we mean by equality." Some said he was a Communist. "If greed and arrogance are Christian virtues, then this is a Christian nation." Some students thought he said America was a Christian nation, others said he did not.

"Atheism has little to do with morality just as Christianity has little to do with morality," Marshall said. Everyone believed Marshall had declared himself an atheist and perhaps a homosexual. It was a time when truth was always new, improved, and repeated three times for easy recall.

Marshall's enthusiasm and provocative teaching struck at the heart of the system. Next to a good teacher, the most feared thing in education was a disquieted student. Above all else the system required order. Comfort them with athletics, appease them with passing grades, delight them with audio-visual spectacles, but don't disturb their apathy. We had reached nirvana—docile teachers of apathetic students. Order, or at least routine, was maintained, and if no one, including the parents, teachers, or students, held the school in esteem, decorum was observed.

From the beginning there was tension between Marshall and Hooper and Vivian. It exploded when Marshall gave a failing grade to a football player making him ineligible for a game. Hooper called a faculty meeting, and to punish Marshall, berated all of us for a failure of spirit. He declared that only a beginning teacher thought that failing a student was a sign of success. We had been through such scoldings before and whether we believed them earned or not, afterwards we tried to regain Hooper's favor by assuring him that we would do better.

Marshall stood up and said, "I didn't fail him. He failed himself by not reading the assignments and not turning in papers. But worse than that, this school failed him by letting him believe that playing football for the school is more important to us than doing his lessons."

There was a moment of stunned silence. Then Hooper said that if Marshall's ideas and values were in conflict with those of the school, he might be happier some place else. There was no room in our school for unauthorized ideas—or false doctrine.

Football, that was supposed to be a diversion, had become our natural religion with its own prophets, priests, myths, and creeds. It was not an entertainment but a ritual of salvation and damnation, the source of past glories and future hopes.

When the team was victorious no one doubted that Wanderer Springs was the greatest place on earth, with the most courageous boys and virtuous girls. The town received favorable attention in the Center Point newspaper, and no one complained of the school budget. However, to lose a game suggested a softness, a lack of resolve, and brought a shudder of fear to the whole community that foreign ideas and strange gods had sapped the vigor of our youth, contaminated our hearts, and undermined our will.

Our garden had its serpent asking why with our natural and moral superiority and our unflinching courage and undying resolve, our Davids had never been able to defeat Center Point's Goliaths. There had to be treachery in the camp. A blasphemer, an unbeliever.

Marshall had never been a true believer. He had played the game, had even been captain of the team. But Marshall, who as fullback paved the way for Vivian's triumphs, harbored an independent spirit.

Once we had traveled to Seymour for a game that would decide the district championship. Before the kickoff we huddled together and recited our creed. "When the going gets tough, the tough get going; a quitter never wins, a winner never quits; a team that won't be beat, can't be beat." We didn't quit. Vivian scored three touchdowns, all of them called back. I recovered a fumble that was ruled not a fumble. We lost by one point.

The Seymour coach had gotten on our bus after the game. Coaches know nothing of shame, but we thought he would be embarrassed to win the championship with a victory he did not deserve. He did not apologize for the victory or the championship, but for the officiating. "I'm afraid the officials got carried away," he said. "If it hadn't been for the officiating, you'd have won. You earned it."

"Why don't you forfeit the game?" Marshall asked. It seemed reasonable to us. After all, that's what we were expected to learn from sports, that it wasn't whether you won or lost, but how you played.

Doughbelly, our coach, berated Marshall for being a whiner and for embarrassing him in front of another coach. "Forget this game, we've got another game next week," he said.

We went back home and waited for the newspaper account, expecting some measure of vindication. The paper said that Seymour, in spite of being outplayed, had won the contest. The paper treated the partiality of the officials as though it were irrelevant to the victory.

The next week Doughbelly worked us harder than ever. We could no longer win district, but we could work together to make Vivian All State. That was the only way the school could win recognition. The coach paid Vivian the highest compliment he could pay a man. "He'll do what he's told to do."

"To win this game we got to stop Scott," Doughbelly said. "He's a little guy so when he goes down I want to see a pile of bodies on top of him. I want to see you cut his britches off. Put some hurt on him. I want somebody to hit him on every play.

I want to see him limping back to the huddle. I want to see fear in his eyes."

In the third quarter, Marshall blindsided Scott, who lay on the ground for several minutes before regaining consciousness. They took him to Center Point fearing his back was broken. Scott recovered. Marshall quit the team on the eve of the Center Point game.

Even the Baptist minister was appalled. "They'll call you coward," he said.

"What's brave about running over someone smaller than I am?" Marshall asked.

"You are part of the team," his pastor said. "You represent the school. You can't let those people down."

Marshall played against Center Point, but he had raised a serious moral question. Could a boy be different and represent his school?

"Hey Will, look at this," Vivian said. He and Boots were looking at the football pictures. How serious we looked posing for the yearbook in our football uniforms—untested soldiers. Upon our young shoulders rested the good name of our town. Our friends, families, neighbors eyed us warily. They had no one better than us to defend them.

Vivian turned the page and I saw the picture of a football bouncing from the hands of a player wearing my number. "Victory eludes grasp," the caption said.

I remembered the glittering, dew-dampened ball spinning in the floodlights, my legs springless as lead, my hands formless as water. Wanderer Springs remembered it as "the year we lost because Will Callaghan dropped a pass."

"The pass was high," I said. We didn't have game films and the camera angle of the yearbook picture was tricky. It was Vivian's reputation as an athlete and his insistence that he hit me "right on the fingertips" that settled the blame on me. Vivian never had doubts.

Vivian had already flipped to the picture that showed him being awarded a letter jacket his senior year. For four years Vivian had been a starter on every team the school fielded and his senior year he had been All State in football and All District in basketball and baseball. The jacket had stripes for all the years he had lettered, stars for the years he had been captain, and All District and All State patches on the sleeves. It was a magnificent coat and for a time it was displayed in the trophy case of the school.

I was a member of the same team. That's what it was all about, working together for the good of the team, the good of the school. Vivian's triumph was for all of us. But it wasn't the team who strutted on the stage that afternoon. It wasn't the team who got a college scholarship. It wasn't the team who was coach of the year and given a job at a bigger high school.

"Remember this?" Boots said, pointing at a picture of the water tower with ARAB painted on it.

After the Center Point game, Roma Dean and I, and Marshall and Rebel had gotten a malt at the Susie Q in Center Point. The girls were in their cheerleading outfits and were still excited about the game, and the cheering, and how brave we had been, how close we had come. It was one of those magical moments when talking to girls seemed easy, even natural. It was our last game in our last year of high school. We had shared four years of something that was over. It was a feeling akin to triumph.

When we drove into Wanderer Springs we saw that Vivian, frustrated in his last chance to beat Center Point, had painted CRAP on the water tower. Except for Rebel, that was about as daring as we publicly got. While I stayed with Rebel and Roma Dean, Marshall climbed the tower and by painting the C into a bowlegged A, and the P into a B he had changed CRAP into ARAB. The word puzzled strangers and our parents for years, but in our minds we had demonstrated that we were defeated but not debased. In our minds, Robert E. Lee would have doffed his hat.

When Rebel and Bitsey came back, Vivian was talking about the game where a tornado had struck nearby, scaring away the fans and dumping several inches of rain that washed out the sidelines, stopped the game clock, and covered the field with ankle-deep water. "Let's call it off," the Center Point coach said.

"We came to play and we're not quitting until the gun sounds," the Wanderer Springs coach said. Characteristically, he didn't say, "until we win." In disgust, the referees walked off the field and the Center Point team followed. Wanderer Springs quit the field too, but not before the coach got the game ball that had washed past the goal posts. The ball was displayed in the trophy case, along with Vivian's letter jacket, until the school was closed.

When he was coach, Vivian recited that story before every game, and he repeated, "We came to play and we're not quitting until the game is over," at every pep rally.

"And we never did quit either," he said to Bitsey. "Until that game when the niggers wouldn't play. I'll never get over them boys quitting the way they did."

Vivian had been forgiven for being a Whatley because he was our best athlete, but he had not quite made it into Wanderer Springs myth because neither as a player nor coach had he ever beaten Center Point.

Rebel and Bitsey remained standing until he stopped talking and gave them the floor. Rebel was beaming. "We've decided to call Hooper and Branda," she said. "It's still early in California."

I didn't look at anyone, thinking only of how I was going to escape.

"Let me see if I can find their new number," Bitsey said, leaving the room.

"Have you talked to them since they moved?" Rebel asked me.

"No," I said, my voice sounding funny in my own ears.

I hadn't talked to them since I left Wanderer Springs.

"Branda had an affair with a man in Hooper's school. That's why they had to move."

It didn't hurt. What was curious was that I wasn't curious. I was glad they weren't coming for Jessie's funeral and I hoped Bitsey couldn't find their number. What was left was not anger or remorse, least of all, love. It was dead pain, ashes, and I didn't want them stirred up.

"I don't know why he puts up with that," Vivian said. "I knew she was trouble when he brought her here."

Branda was not a small-town girl. I had hoped she and Delores might be friends. "Did you look at her watch?" Delores said. It was a thin, elegant watch useless for keeping time. Delores had the kind of watch nurses wear. "And she did not make that dress she was wearing." Delores was rarely uncertain in her opinions. I didn't think Branda made the dress. I also didn't think Delores could know whether she did or not.

"She said she liked your dress," I reminded her, appealing to Delores's generous nature. It was a peasant dress, a background dress that blended pleasantly without attracting attention. "She bragged on your cooking."

"She didn't eat anything."

"She said she was on a diet."

"She said she wished she could eat like I did," Delores corrected me with her smile that was not a smile. "Will, I try to like your friends."

"She is not my friend. Hooper is my friend." I was wrong. Hooper was not my friend; he was my superintendent. I was the only friend Branda had.

"Her fingernails are all the same length," Rebel said. It was the mark of a woman who did not wash dishes or scrub floors, who spent more time manicuring her nails than digging in her garden.

"She fills the tub to the top," Emma Harkness said. "And she lets the water run all the time she's washing dishes." In a country where people hauled water for cattle, saved dish water for chickens, and emptied the bathtub on the garden, those were signs of an extravagant woman.

"How far is it to Seymour?" Vivian asked, seeing Branda's eye-catching dress. "Sometimes it ain't very far." It was a Wanderer Springs joke and was revived every time some woman tried to make too much of herself by hiding too little. It had been used with varying degrees of success on Selena Lance, Sherry McElroy, and Wanda Shipman.

Branda still practiced her skills of meeting men, catching their attention, inviting their interest. That was the fear in Hooper's heart, the mote in Delores's eye. The first time Marshall saw her, he said, "Uh oh, trouble."

It was a time when it was not enough to declare one's beliefs; they must be declaimed—not enough to avow one's sexuality; it must be asserted. All across the country girls bared their knees and half their thighs to demonstrate their contempt for uniformity. Boys bared their armpits and frayed the crotches of their jeans in praise of naturalness. Across the country dress codes were under attack, but in Wanderer Springs, it was blamed on Branda. Branda had caused Emma Harkness to lose her job. Branda had subverted traditional values, like sewing and canning, and was teaching fashion, make-up, and social behavior.

I knew what it was like to be the target of the town's anger and frustration. I was amazed that my friends did not see in Branda what I saw in her. I came to her aid. As every historian knows, in times of crisis you turn to the circus. It was time for the school to put on a show.

I went to Hooper with a plan for Operation Glitterbug: Clean Up, Paint Up, Fix Up. Wanderer Springs was a windswept little town beside a weedy railroad track and a trash-littered highway—a bit of an eyesore. Deserted houses loomed over rusting automobiles, vacant stores gaped windowless and doorless on Main Street, roofs collapsing, floors rotting. The town should fix itself up. To gain favor with the taxpayers and to instill civic pride and responsibility in the young, the school should lead the way.

Hooper bought the plan, or to be more exact, expropriated it. Elementary teachers would lead their students in picking up litter. Rebel's Pep Squad, in uniform, would go door to door asking people to clean up their yards and paint their houses. Boots's F.F.A. students would mow vacant lots, tear down decaying buildings, and haul off junk cars. Vivian's football team would paint the houses and fences of the elderly. Branda and I were named as co-chairmen.

Branda and I stayed after school to plan and coordinate the activities. I walked around town to be certain that none of the buildings were of historical value. I dug through garbage dumps and poked around weedy lots looking for old foundations. Branda went with me.

I told her about Hooper's grandfather's first wife, Lulu Byars who died of frivolity. I told her about Mary McCarroll who lost her child on the prairie, and her grandson, Ira Ferguson, who seemed afraid of attracting his grandmother's illness—becoming attached to something he was unable to let go.

"I always read your column in the paper," Branda said. "I love the way you write."

I told her how I was trying to justify the lives we lived in Wanderer Springs, why we came there, and why we stayed, and how the common people of that place had altered history and given shape and meaning to progress.

"You should write a book," she said.

I had often thought the same thing, but I had never been able to find anyone whose life had made the slightest impact outside the county. We had lived as obscurely and died as inanely as people anywhere, and I had no wish to write the town's epitaph. Born at the end of the railroad track, died beside the Interstate.

"Maybe you should go someplace else, Will. Someplace where you would be valued, where you could write about important people."

I'm not sure when I began to feel cheated by life, when I wanted a sports car instead of a pickup, a West Coast haircut and New York clothes, appreciation for my teaching and recognition for my writing. I was angry at the unalterable past that limited me. I had been deprived of some right. Nothing Delores said could convince me that I was not the only victim of injustice. They were querulous times, a time when "freedom" was on everyone's tongue and "for me" was in their hearts.

Delores had tried to be what I wanted. She read the textbooks I taught, read the student papers, went to school games, parties, plays, P.T.A. She learned the latest educational jargon so she could talk about curricular development and maximizing the application of instructional programs. I loved her for it. I laughed at her. "You don't have to do that," I said.

She had gone with me to poke around Elma Dell, Red Top, or Lank, talking to people and learning the stories. Then we bought the Dodson house; the children were born. We busied ourselves making a home, family, career. We didn't talk about our dreams any more, either of us. We had abandoned them in the joys of home, children, career. We had abandoned all but the disappointment. When we talked, it was of chores, not possibilities, and the words were the language of business.

Delores loved me but she had no illusions about me. Maybe that is the purest kind of love, the way a child loves. Maybe love isn't blind after all, and it is something less than love that needs moonlight, moonshine, and music. Delores's eyes never lied and I was in love with the Will Callaghan I saw in Branda's eyes.

One weekend Delores and the girls were in San Antonio, Hooper was at a conference in Dallas. I drove Branda to the farm to show her the house where I was born. I led her through the gate that shut out the world, up the sidewalk that led to a secret place. Inside the house I kissed her. Only the young underestimate the power of a kiss. That kiss had answers to questions I had not asked, had not thought of. "Since the first time I saw you, I wondered what I would do if you kissed me," she said. She slipped her arms around my neck, her fingers through my hair, and told me what she would do. "I don't care if you mark me," she said.

Branda was quick, compliant, greedy. Branda was a carnival—danger, excitement, thrills, sideshows, games, lights, illusion—and it had just come to town. The roller coaster left me breathless and dizzy with a memory of shrieks and lights and gut-wrenching plunges.

"Will, I'm scared. I've never been in love before," Branda said, clinging to me, her nails like knives in my flesh. "What are we going to do?"

How could I have planned the whole thing without thinking of that? I had thought about the greenness of her eyes, the softness of her lips, the fineness of her skin. I had dreamed of kissing her toes, defending her with my life, chasing her across the alfalfa field, seducing her mind, bending her body to my will. I had never thought what I was going to do with her afterwards. Nothing had prepared me to share the emotions and words we had just shared and to deal with them by myself.

I told her we had to think, we had to talk, we had to plan. We kissed and nuzzled instead. We took solemn vows that Delores, Hooper and the children would not be hurt. If there was pain we swore it would be ours. Impassioned by our goodness, we made love again. I fled back to Delores. I think she was surprised by my relief at her return from San Antonio. For a while I was safe. But Branda was at school, across the hall, and every day after school we met.

Glitterbug was a success, and the anger towards Branda was forgotten in the uproar over what right children had to tell taxpayers to clean up, who tore down Uncle John's house, and who hauled off the automobile that someone was planning to restore.

Branda and I continued to meet whenever we could get away. Hooper was frequently at meetings. Delores was accustomed to me going to the farm, checking the house, looking at the crops.

I hungered for her flesh like a leech, a mosquito—not for pleasure but for life. "What do you like best about me?" Branda liked to ask when we lay side by side, temporarily sated. What I felt had nothing to do with like. I was surprised by her, disappointed, bewildered, amazed. "If you could change something about me what would it be?" Does a knight wish to change his dragon? A saint his demon? A snake its charmer?

We made love. We made plans. We were going to flee Wanderer Springs. I was going to write and she was going to inspire me. We were going to live in a small apartment in New York or Paris. She would go to the market every day and buy fresh vegetables and flowers, and every afternoon we would drink wine and make love. Then Duane Spivey discovered us in the barn.

Bitsey returned to the room waving a scrap of paper in triumph. "Now, how are we going to do this? Rebel, you take the phone in the kitchen. Boots, you can use the one upstairs. Will can use this one as soon as I get off."

"That's okay," I said.

"You have to say hello," Rebel said. Bitsey picked up the telephone and began dialing. "Wait," Rebel said. "What are you going to say?" We looked at each other. "Vivian, you can tell him about refereeing. I'll tell him about my school and our new house. Will, you can tell them about Marshall. Or . . . Boots?"

"No," Boots said. "Will can tell them."

"Is there anything else they need to know? Bitsey, you and Boots can tell them about your horses. Don't say anything about Hooper quitting his job."

"And don't say anything about the company he's working for," Vivian said. "They're in trouble for selling classified items to the Russians."

Bitsey looked around. Everyone seemed to be set. She picked up the telephone and Rebel and Boots headed for their assignments. I tried not to listen to Bitsey's greeting, her talk about her horses. I tried not to imagine the other end of the conversation. Apparently, Hooper pretended he wanted to buy into the syndicate. When Bitsey relinquished the phone, I insisted that Vivian take it, hoping at least for the semi-private phone in the kitchen.

"I'm refereeing now," Vivian said. "Eighth graders, mostly. You should come and see a game. I make them play by the rules." At last Vivian was in control of the game, and nothing was left to chance. "Will's here, he's got something important to tell you." He handed me the telephone.

I listened to Rebel talking about Jessie's funeral, and who was going to be there and who wasn't, and who had called or sent telegrams.

"It sounds like an exciting party," Hooper said.

"Will, are you on the phone?" Boots said. "I'm going to hang up now."

"Hello," I said.

"Let me tell you about my new job," Hooper said expansively. All his life Hooper had been waiting to be saved by a better job. Although he talked in terms of perquisites and salary it appeared that he headed a training program at a high tech company. He told of plans for a better job at a bigger company. "You gotta keep moving." He had adopted, at least for the conversation, a California style.

"Don't you get tired of all that moving around?" Rebel asked.

"If you're not on your way up you're on your way out." He had also adopted a California philosophy. "Are you still writing those school booklets, Will?" Hooper had reached the point in his career where his only triumphs were the failures of his friends.

"Yes."

"You should come out here. Anyone who can write at all can make three times what you're making." With great power comes great responsibility; with little power comes great ego.

"Hooper, is Branda home?" Rebel asked. "I'd like to say hello."

"Oh sure. Our other phones haven't been installed yet. Let me get her."

I waited. Boots and Bitsey, feeling part of the conversation, watched me.

"Hello." Branda's voice was low and sweet. Had Hooper told her who was on the telephone? Was he watching? I listened while Rebel asked about Rudy. How old was he? How did he like Berkeley?

I had broken my life to pieces on her. Willfully. Stupidly. Doing something stupid doesn't mean you're stupid. Not knowing it's stupid, even in retrospect, means you're stupid. I knew; all along I knew it was stupid. Therefore, I wasn't stupid. I was insane.

"Well, I'd better get off the phone and give someone else a chance," Rebel said, hanging up, leaving me and Branda connected, with only one power over each other, the power to remind of old hurts and humiliations. We spoke with the cruelest words we knew, cruel not because they were intentional but because they were dead. Hate would have been kinder.

"How are you, Branda," I said. It was not a question.

"I'm fine." It was not an answer.

"How do you like California?"

"Fine. How is the writing going?"

It might as well have been "How is the garden going?" "The golf game?" "Do you still work crossword puzzles?" "Just fine."

For a moment neither of us could think of anything to say.

The distance between us hummed in my ears. Once we had been so close I could feel her bones shift under my weight, hear her heart beat, smell her hair, taste the salt of her body. All the words that had passed between us left us nothing to say. "Branda, I want the best for you," I said and heard the hollow ring.

"Thank you," she said politely.

"Well, Boots is paying for this so I'd better get off the phone."

"Goodbye," she said.

I heard the phone click and then slowly put down the receiver. I listened in numbed silence while the others dissected the conversation. They were agreed that Hooper was not doing well. "You can always tell," Rebel said. "He's always so cheerful and optimistic when he's down. What did you think, Will?"

"It's hard to tell."

"Wasn't it strange that Branda didn't come to the phone," Bitsey said. "Do you think she knows that we know about her affair?"

"Will and I talked to her, but I had to ask Hooper to call her," Rebel said. "She didn't sound very happy to me. How did she sound to you, Will?"

"I thought she sounded okay."

"Remember how she used to bounce around, smiling at everyone, like she was Mrs. Superintendent?" Rebel said.

"Yeah, like if she was happy, everyone was supposed to be happy," Vivian said.

Branda did radiate happiness. "I have found what I want," she said, holding me. Hooper said, "Glitterbug has made a world of difference in Branda." It was his way of thanking me for the idea. "I can always tell when she's happy, she doesn't complain about her period."

"Branda couldn't be very happy or she wouldn't be having affairs," Bitsey said.

"Do you think Hooper is queer?" Vivian asked.

We ignored him. Hooper was not homosexual, but I always thought with him women were an acquired taste.

"Obviously there is something wrong," Bitsey said.

"Obviously there is something right or they wouldn't still be together," Boots said.

He was a man trained in rationalization. She was a woman trained in suasion. They were Americans trained in acquisition. They were a married couple trained in semblance. They were parents trained in submission.

"I know what's missing from their lives. It's Jesus Christ," Rebel said. We shifted uncomfortably in our chairs. The love of God, like the love of a woman, was best discussed when drunk and tearful. "I didn't know peace until I gave my life to Jesus." Once Rebel had been blessed with the curse of want, now she was cursed with the gift of contentment. "Can't you see that's why they're so unhappy? Why their lives are so empty?" Rebel was all screwed up and thought that made her the prototype for woman.

In Wanderer Springs we were religious; our vices those vices that were acceptable in church—avarice, envy, spite, prejudice. We had a church attitude that we put on like Sunday clothes. We raised our children to go to church, bless their food, quote the golden rule, and think of themselves as Christian Americans. To be Christian without being American filled us with suspicion.

"I know you're going to say they went to church," Rebel said with that disappointed anger that Christians love. In Wanderer Springs we liked to maintain a religious balance of power. There was concern when Hooper was hired as superintendent of the school because the Byarses had been Baptist and Otis Hopkins was chairman of the school board. However, Hooper and Branda attended the Presbyterian Church in Center Point, which made them politically correct but religiously suspect. "But it was just for show," Rebel said. "They never gave their lives to Jesus."

Rebel was Bible-scarred. Her religion had robbed her of charity, yet that was accounted to her as faith. Marshall's religion had made him intolerant of pretension, particularly religious pretension, and that was accounted to him as unbelief.

"Vivian and I may not have much," Rebel said. "But we have the Lord."

Boots and Bitsey hastily confessed that they subscribed to the Malcolm Murdock Memorial Chapel. Both the Baptist and Methodist congregations had become too small to keep up the drafty old churches and to support pastors. Dr. Heslar, who needed a church for the consolation of those who lived in The Wanderer's Rest and for the funerals of those who died there, achieved a compromise between the two congregations to support one pastor, one church. The combined church was renamed the Malcolm Murdock Memorial Chapel. It was the final indignity to the old circuit rider, and he probably would have gotten a sermon out of it. "Vanity of vanities, saith the preacher—"

Membership in the Murdock Memorial Chapel entitled Boots and Bitsey to Dr. Heslar's attendance at horse shows and Brother Bob's prayers at auctions, dinners, and business meetings.

Rebel gave us a verbal tour of her church in Wichita Falls that was a full-service church with a minister trained in theology, a minister trained in psychology, and a minister trained in recreation. There was a Sunday School building that was better equipped than the public school where Rebel taught. There was a gymnasium with a six-lane bowling alley, an indoor skating rink, indoor swimming pool, a game room, and two racquet ball courts, where everybody was somebody, and Vivian coached the church softball and basketball teams and benched players for smoking, swearing or missing Sunday

School. There were camping trips, sight-seeing trips, hiking trips, skiing trips. Rebel dreamed of having enough money to make the church the social center of their life.

"God is just so real there," she said. "You never have to worry about people getting rowdy or not bathing. They're just our kind of people. And every year we have God's Family Reunion, and people come for miles just to spend the day together."

"Are any of them Methodist?" I asked.

"Visitors are always welcome," Rebel said without a smile. Wit in a Baptist is like subtlety in a snake; it's been heard of.

"Will, do you belong to a church?" Boots asked.

"Yes," I said, although I don't think people belong to a church any more. The church belongs to them. I took the girls to church as long as they permitted. It was a pleasant church, even genial. In Wanderer Springs folks went to church to get mad, if not at the minister or the choir, then at the government, or the Communists, or the humanists, and we left church feeling better for having given expression to our feelings. Our church in San Antonio discouraged that emotion, and we left church with an unhappy tolerance of everyone.

The church did not attempt to prove to the girls that they were evil. The deadly sins seemed to be prejudice, poverty, and nuclear armament. The church was less interested in confession than in apology, concerned less with forgiving mistakes than in drawing moral lessons from them, dedicated less to redemption than to improvement.

The girls learned about Moses the reformer instituting the law and fighting the oppression of his people, and Jesus the radical throwing the rascals out of the temple and demanding justice for the poor. But they didn't have much feeling for Cain killing Abel, Jacob having a dream, David making up songs while watching sheep, Jesus walking on the water. In San Antonio they had the same cast of characters, the same setting, the same plot, yet the movie was different.

It wasn't that I wanted my children to know the church I had known. Far from it. From the beginning I knew that God loved me. Sometimes it was so simple I couldn't believe it; sometimes it was so complex I couldn't believe it, but I knew. How could I not know? A boy on the Texas plains with the sky above, the grass below, the glory of the day, the wonder of the night, the beauty and mystery of girls. But that was later, and with girls came faith and doubt.

Dad always took me to church although he did not attend with me but waited at the fire station with other men waiting for their families. The church was the one place a man could not forbid his wife to go; consequently, the congregation was composed largely of women and I was patted and squeezed and kissed by them. I inhaled the perfume of their powdered bodies and listened to their soft words and laughter. The church had been mother to me. I had been cradled in the lap of her songs and prayers. I had not been prepared for Turtle Hole.

The town was staggered. It was a horror beyond dimension, unaccountable in history or myth. We were the only good people we knew. How could such evil exist in our midst? Folks turned to the church for an answer. Both the Baptist and Methodist ministers condemned the whole of American society, and particularly our parents and teachers. They magnanimously included themselves. They had gotten soft on sin. It was time to get back to our beginnings, to the frontier virtues that had driven the saloons and bawdy houses out of the county.

Joann Emerson's parents moved immediately, not even waiting for graduation. Hooper left town because of a family emergency, but was able to keep up his school work and return in time to be valedictorian. Vivian was a Whatley and not even the Baptists expected anything of a Whatley. Rebel and I, too old to escape our debt, too young to pay it, were left to face the wrath of the town.

Rebel avoided me. There was no one else who knew what

it was like except Vivian and Vivian was already telling everyone how hard he had tried to save Roma Dean. I was scared.
And I was angry. How could such a thing happen to me? I was
the only normal person I knew.

In the Baptist Church, Rebel publicly asked forgiveness of
her fellow Baptists, Biddy Whatley, Wesley Murdock, and her
father, Otis Hopkins.

I had hoped I would be sick that first Sunday after Turtle
Hole. I had contemplated suicide. It was easier to think about
killing myself than to think about walking into church. "Get
up, son," Dad said. "Get ready for church." I did my chores
hoping the barn would catch on fire, the milk cow would die.
Anything. I went back to the house to wash and saw that Dad
had put on his suit. I did not have to walk into the church
alone.

In church there was an altar call for those who needed to
rededicate their lives. I needed no preacher to tell me that I
was unacceptable. I was an alien in the only place where I belonged. I knew I needed forgiveness. I would have let them
lash me with whips. I would have let them nail me to a cross.
Instead, aware that all eyes were upon me, lonelier and more
afraid than I had ever been, I went to the altar to ask for forgiveness. What I received was accommodation.

We were returned, Rebel and I, but not restored. Since
there was no prescribed punishment everyone assumed that
we had escaped justice except for whatever retribution they
were personally able to extract. Blessed is he whose crime has a
penalty prescribed by law.

"I guess I never showed it much," Vivian said, feeling left
out of the conversation, "but I was religious from the time my
grandpa told me about Earl Lance seeing heaven on his deathbed. Old Earl saw his mother standing with Bobby and Shirley,
and Wilbur was talking to Davy Crockett and Jim Bowie. Ain't
that right, Will?"

There were two versions of that story. The authentic one

seemed to be about Fred Dodson, only son of Roy Dodson who ran a trading post at the springs when the railroad came through a quarter mile to the north. Dodson realized he was going to have to relocate closer to the depot. He sent Fred, a dreamy seventeen-year-old, to Dead Man's Junction to cut timber for the store. Fred disappeared.

For several years no one heard from Fred until one day he walked into the tent Roy was using for a store, threw some gold on the table, said, "There's your damn wood, build your own store," and left to hunt diamonds in South America.

Roy built the Dodson house with a store downstairs and his living quarters upstairs, and a porch on both levels. Roy was unable to truckle to those he did not like, and Roy liked no one. He would not greet customers as friends, carry a sack of flour to the wagon when the flour no longer belonged to him, or let mothers weigh their babies on his meat scale.

Folks traded with Benny Whatley and Roy was left alone in his store, eating whatever groceries remained. Dr. Vestal, who found him dead, said Roy died of a torpid liver caused by eating candles.

Fred came back and lived like his father, sitting on the upstairs gallery and looking over the town. Folks did not approve of Fred living without drudgery or wife. Such a life could not be Christian and they began hounding Fred for the benefit of his soul. When Fred became ill, a band of faithful Methodists gathered around his bed, singing, and praying, and striving for his soul.

Before he died, Fred uttered a single word. "Gold." Those keeping vigil believed that Fred had seen the pearly gates and streets of gold. The story of Earl Lance seeing Wilbur with Davy Crockett I have always regarded as a pious borrowing by the Baptists.

For a historian it was disappointing that after all those years people did not know the true story. It was enough to make a historian throw away his index cards. However, as a

Christian I did not correct Vivian. In Wanderer Springs an up-
lifting falsehood was preferred to a depressing truth.

Vivian said they had to be going as Rebel was spending
the night with Biddy, and Biddy went to bed when the television news came on. Biddy got her information from television game shows because there were more facts on the game
shows and they were at least as relevant. Vivian was driving
back to Wichita Falls because he had to be at school.

Rebel asked if she could ride to the funeral with me. "It's
going to be a sad day for all of us, but I know it's going to be
harder for you than anyone," she said. "We're all going to
be thinking about Roma Dean. We have to pray."

For a moment I thought Rebel was going to insist that we
all pray together, but Bitsey got busy picking up the empty
glasses and the moment passed. We said our goodnights, they
left, and Bitsey said she was going to bed. Boots and I got a
fresh drink and settled in our chairs.

"Damn if Rebel can't stop fun quicker than anyone I
know," Boots said. "Vivian's got to where he's just as bad. When
was he ever religious?"

"He prayed before every game."

"He prayed we'd win. Hell, I can see him being devout if
we'd ever beat Center Point but we never did."

Boots raised his glass to me in a salute. "I appreciate you
coming back, Will. I know it isn't easy with Rebel talking about
Roma Dean all the time."

"Yeah."

"I never blamed you for old Red, Will. I'd a done the
same as you."

"Thanks, Boots."

After Roma Dean's death, folks worried about Jessie because both she and Roma Dean's dog were deaf. Those who felt
responsible for Jessie met at her house. Dad and I were there,
of course. I had been Roma Dean's sweetheart and was the closest thing to a relative Jessie had. She was sitting on the porch

swing when we assembled. The women tried to talk to her but she didn't seem to recognize them. "Off came her hair," she said, her voice creaky from disuse. "She got on the bus, went down to the creek, and off came her hair."

It was decided that she should be taken to Augusta Worley. The women packed her clothes, and Dad, Buster and Boots covered the furniture, packed the dishes, and boarded up the house. I didn't want to go in the house so Dad sent me to put away the tools in the barn and to take care of old Red. I knew what that meant. Red was deaf, almost blind, and so old he tottered. He had to be disposed of as quickly and painlessly as possible. I would have refused the job if going into the house and packing away Jessie's and Roma Dean's things hadn't been even more unpleasant.

I moved the tools into the smoke house, except for the shovel to bury Red with. Red remembered me from all the times I had come to see Roma Dean. He had gotten so old he was orange, even bald in spots, and smelled of death. Large knots appeared along his back and tail, he had lost control of his bladder, and almost lost his bark.

I didn't want to touch him, so I coaxed him into the barn and closed the double doors. Red tried to wag his tail. Even with the doors closed enough light came through holes in the roof and walls so that I could see, and stepping behind Red, I lifted the shovel and swung. Old as he was, the dog shied so that instead of killing him, the shovel destroyed his eye. He tottered, and too old to run or right, he lay down in the dust, rolled over on his back and tried to whimper.

I had already put away the axe and as the shovel was too dull to cut off his head, I had to push him on his stomach with my foot and hit him on the head to kill him. The dog kept showing me his throat while the dust clotted his missing eye, coated his silent but eloquent mouth, and sifted into my nostrils.

I hacked at him, trying to dispatch him with a merciful

blow, while he looked at me with his single teary eye. He died while I was throwing up in the corner.

I had planned to bury Red outside under the cottonwood tree but not wanting to carry the mangled body into the light of day, I had hidden it in a corner of the barn. When I threw open the barn door, eager to escape the close and breathless dark, I found Jessie standing before me. "I come for my little girl's dog," she said.

I was frozen to the spot. She looked past me into the darkness of the barn. "What have you done with Roma Dean?" she wailed or shrieked, unable to judge the tone and intensity of her voice. She swept past me into the barn and stood over Red's shallow grave. "What have you done to my little girl?" She wailed her accusations until the women came and led her away.

Yes, Boots would have done the same. Maybe he wouldn't have done it any better, but it would have been remembered differently. I knew that I would be forever identified with old Red, the way Elmer Spruill was remembered for killing the last buffalo. Acknowledged but not admired.

"Drink up because I'm going to ask you a heavy question," Boots said. I finished the drink and Boots took our glasses into the kitchen and added ice and bourbon. "A&M made a study of water last year. The most useless thing you can do with it is ruin good whiskey."

"Damn right. Useless as a stop watch at a beauty contest."

He handed me my glass and sat down. "Was my dad a hero?"

"He was to me."

"I saw Dad stand in the bank, his hat in his hand, waiting for Otis Hopkins to let him sit down." He shook his head to clear it of the memory. "Dad made the greatest ride this county has ever seen. Why wasn't he treated like a hero?"

"Endurance went out with polar expeditions and flights

around the world. Today endurance means the Guinness record for the longest kiss or rocking in a rocking chair. I don't know what you'd have to do to be a hero any more."

"You have to be a bastard if you want to be somebody," Boots said.

"It has to be something that can be repeated at regular intervals. It has to be something that is unrelated to the hero's personal life. That's why our only heroes are athletes and entertainers. They can do the same heroics over and over, and it doesn't matter if they're mean, or vain, or stupid. They just represent the heroic for a while and then they have to die or at least disappear from the screen before they become boring."

"God, Will, I had forgotten what a cheerful character you are."

"What do you expect of a historian? Everybody I know is dead."

"Then you come to the right place. Everybody in Wanderer Springs is dead or dying. Hell, the center of the community is the nursing home. That's where everybody goes, that's what everybody talks about—who's there, how expensive it is, how understaffed, the food, the color of the walls. Not ten percent of those people have ever seen Wanderer Springs before. They think they're in Grand Prairie or Shreveport or someplace."

Boots went into the kitchen and returned with tobacco in his mouth and a paper cup in his hand. "The people who stayed are an insult to those of us who came back. At least we tried to make a community. I told Herschell if he'd stock blankets, stall decorations, show halters, jackets and windbreakers and trophies, I'd buy from him rather than going to Center Point. Not interested."

He spat into the cup. "Same thing with Biddy Whatley. When I have a show, I have balloons, banners, buttons, tee shirts, gimme caps. Not interested. They like living in a ghost town. Hell, they're a couple of ghosts themselves." Boots went into the kitchen, brought back the bottle and filled our glasses. "What happened to Wanderer Springs, Will?"

After years of fearing it would be supplanted by Center Point, Wanderer Springs wasn't replaced by a town at all but by an interstate highway to get people faster from some place they didn't like to some place they didn't know. "The town died because it wasn't needed any more."

"What happened to us? I heard this guy on television say we lost our virtue in Vietnam."

I could imagine Manuel's laughter. How could we be disappointed in government when it was so perfect a representation of us? Virtuous men had owned and traded slaves because it was good business. They had worked children for twelve and fourteen hours a day without thought for their health or safety because it was good business. They had exterminated the Indians because it was good business. They had armed our enemies in Germany and Japan because it was good business.

We fired Emma Harkness for the good of the school. We made Bubba Spivey valedictorian for the good of the school. We removed books from the library for the good of the school.

"The school" was narrowly defined as Hooper, and occasionally, Vivian. My evaluation as a teacher had nothing to do with my classroom but what I did for "the school." For a good evaluation I wrote letters and reports for Vivian who could not write. For classroom materials I supported Hooper. If you had no soul you had no problem.

Three times I had ordered a set of maps for the history classes. After the first time I reordered the maps. The second time I went to Vivian. The third time I went to Hooper. "It was my mistake," he said. "I'm sorry."

"What can be done about it?"

"Nothing can be done about it, the money has been allocated. I said I was sorry, what more do you want?"

"I want the maps."

"How many times do you have to be told? It was a mistake."

"Do you think it could happen again?"

"It depends on whether your attitude changes."

"What's wrong with my attitude?"

"I don't like it."

"What does that have to do with maps?"

"When you prove to me that you're serious about the maps, you'll get the maps."

"What do I have to do to prove I'm serious?"

"Change your attitude."

"Hooper, just tell me what it is you want me to do."

"Marshall is telling people that I'm trying to censor books. I am not a censor. That kind of talk is not good for the school."

"What do you want me to do?"

"Think of the good of the school."

Marshall told me he was going to the school board. He didn't ask me to go with him—we had reached the point where one did not ask friends to take moral stands—but the invitation was implied. I did not consider the maps and the good of my students. I did, briefly, consider the morality of standing on principle before a man when I was having an affair with his wife. The deciding factor was the certain knowledge that it would do no good.

I advised Marshall not to go. He was not dissuaded. "I can't do what I think is right only when I think it's going to work," he said.

"Be careful," I warned. "You are not dealing with honorable men." Individually they were respectable, but as "the school" their only obligation was to "the school."

The school board was polite. Nobody believed in censoring books; this was, after all, America. The policy was that school books could not be removed from the school without the express consent of the board, but they weren't school books. Marshall asked that they consider a petition signed by more than half of the student body. The board could not concern itself with people, but only with policy. However, they did reprimand Marshall for bringing books into the school without the approval of the board.

Marshall's reward was that the administration became openly disrespectful to him before parents, teachers, and students, hoping to undermine his authority. They interrupted his classes to call him to the office for inconsequential matters. They punished him by punishing his students. They canceled the student newspaper that he sponsored, the senior play that he directed, and the senior picnic because he was class sponsor.

No one did anything. What the school did to Marshall might be wrong, it might be immoral, but it was policy. We were not responsible for school policy. Policy was the province of those who represented us.

Boots spat in his cup. "So you think we sold out the school?"

"We waited for a cause worth fighting for. We didn't have enough information. It was someone else's decision. We gave up responsibility for the school."

"I just don't see it, Will."

"Boots, we were willing to sacrifice everything, values, beliefs, individuality to be part of the team."

"I don't see what's wrong with being part of the team."

"We weren't part of the team." I may have spoken a bit loudly here. "We were pawns, serfs. We were fodder."

Russia was producing some individuals who were willing to face prison, exile, even death for their beliefs. We were producing teams who were willing to sacrifice all for a title. Usually the title was owner, boss, president.

"Are you saying it was Hooper's fault?"

I wanted to blame Hooper. It was Hooper who said, "Will, I'm going to resign, and I'm going to recommend that the school be closed and the children bussed to Center Point where they have better facilities and better teachers." Hooper resisted to the end any temptation to applaud the teachers who had supported him, to say that even though the team had lost, we had played well, or at least tried.

I had, most of the teachers had, talked of leaving Wanderer Springs and leaving teaching. Why did I feel such loss? It wasn't just that something was ending, the curious way you can grieve the end of pain and fear, cherish moth-eaten uniforms and baby shoes set in bronze. Something important to me was dying.

"I never wanted to come back here." Hooper was not looking at me but staring at his desk, his glasses making his eyes look enormous as though he were in shock. "I loved the prep school, but Branda got involved with one of the faculty." Branda hadn't told me that. Hooper paused, staring at his desk with that fixed look he had, waiting for the pain to set before going on. "Branda has a way of seeing people as special. She thought he was an artist. She thought he was going to be famous and make a lot of money. He painted red barns in the snow. He had an art show and sold one painting. Thirty-five dollars.

"The big mistake. With Branda you always make one sooner or later, and then you are no longer perfect. I've been a big disappointment to her, I know that," he said in the solemn tones of a former prep school headmaster. "We've both been disappointed. I promised her no more than five years. If I could do something with this place, that would guarantee me a better job, and if I couldn't, there wouldn't be any reason to stay anyway."

I was outraged. Hooper had spent our meager funds on junkets to vacation resorts to learn the latest educational jargon and the newest theory, and the real purpose had been to look for a job. "You mean all the time you were preaching loyalty to the community, and dedication to the school, you had already made plans to leave? And all the sacrifices you asked us to make were to help you get a better job?"

"Don't get righteous with me, Will. I know about you and Branda." I stared at him, unable to look away, unable to lie. I didn't know how long he had been suspicious or how certain he was. "I know something else. Branda is never going to leave me until she finds something better and you're not it. I'm not going to tell the students or faculty about closing the school at this time for reasons of morale. I told you because I wanted you to know there's nothing you can do to stop me."

I got up, wanting to escape before I said or did something stupid. "Oh by the way, Will, Branda thinks you should give up sex. She says you're not very good at it." I looked at him in disbelief. "She said all men are poets in public toilets. In the bedroom they're all plumbers. That's all." He waved a hand in dismissal.

I wanted to blame Hooper for the closing of the school. Over-edited son-of-a-bitch. But I couldn't.

"I don't blame Hooper any more than I blame myself," I told Boots.

"I blame Vivian," Boots said. "I really believe we could have beaten Center Point that last year. There wasn't any reason to kick the blacks off the team. If Vivian had talked to Doll—"

"Why didn't you talk to Doll?"

"I couldn't interfere with the coach's authority. But if Vivian had talked to Doll about playing for the team and playing for the school, I think Doll would have played, even if it cost him a college scholarship."

"Boots, Hooper had already decided to close the school. He had already accepted a better job some place else. The blacks were loyal to the school until they discovered the school was not loyal to them. I don't know why they didn't quit when we refused to let Melinda Schuman be valedictorian."

"Laying a wreath on the Confederate statue had nothing to do with slavery and she knew it. I don't know what happened to those kids, Will. And it wasn't just the blacks. Hell, it wasn't the black kids who were selling and taking drugs. What happened to kids from good families like Dixie Davenport and Duane Spivey?"

After Duane stumbled upon me and Branda in the barn he was not insolent or disrespectful; we were after all partners in deception. It was an uneasy truce but it held until some of the students balked at an assigned paper on either Dick Dowling and the Battle of the Sabine Pass or Rip Ford and the Battle of Palmito Hill. After years of sitting apathetically in class, the students were beginning to question assignments. "Why do we have to learn that?"

"Because it's part of this class, because I'm the teacher, and because I say so," I said.

Students had never questioned the assignment before and neither had I. It had begun as a fun assignment. Dick Dowling with forty-one men had driven off an invasion force of three Union gunboats and five thousand Yankee troops. In the last battle of the Civil War, Rip Ford had defeated Union troops at Palmito Hill a month after Lee had surrendered. The Confederacy had lost the war but the assignment gave students a chance to reinflate the myth of Texan invincibility. Many of the students, including Bubba Spivey, had told me it was their favorite assignment.

"It's not relevant," the students grumbled.

We had argued that all year in every history class. What happened yesterday was irrelevant. I had gone through "past is prelude," "escape the errors of the past," etcetera, and they hadn't listened, so this time I said, "Do it anyway."

"All we ever study is killing," Dixie said. "Why do all our heroes have to be killers?"

It was an awkward question to answer because Bubba Spivey's death in Vietnam was fresh on everyone's mind, and

Duane was in the classroom. It was awkward because except for Moses and Stephen Austin, Texas heroes were associated with violence.

"When you're older you can choose the heroes for your children, but this year we're studying these."

"Did either of these battles have any effect on the outcome of the Civil War?" Duane asked.

I don't think Duane wanted a confrontation. He must have felt compelled by Dixie and his other followers to take a stand. So did I. Unfortunately, he was right. They were not significant battles. Heroic deeds had been done, men had died, but the result was insignificant except for the purpose for which I had been using it.

I should have required the students to write a paper on how the rights granted to the negros by the Civil War—to vote, to sit on juries, to hold property—had been subverted, but that was not mentioned in the textbook or any book in the library, so they could not research it. The textbook had an apology for the Ku Klux Klan and stated that due to better understanding between the races the need for such a society no longer existed. It was a section of the textbook that I never assigned. I was lucky the students read only the assigned materials if they read the textbook at all.

Recognizing my mistake was one thing, but I did not dare back down to Duane. "Without history every generation would have to begin again without experience, or traditions, or accepted standards. Maybe Dick Dowling didn't affect the course of the war but he is part of the tradition—"

The intercom buzzed. "This is your principal with a few reminders." Vivian was the athletic leader who could bring glory to the school and he could not understand why the students ridiculed him behind his back and made fun of his toupee. He tried desperately to win their favor. He made speeches on school spirit, and told jokes over the intercom.

"Here's the thought for the day," Vivian said. "A poor rider and his horse are soon parted." The students groaned. "Think that over for a minute, Mr. Bryant." The intercom buzzed while Vivian gave us a moment to think about that bit of canned humor. Then he reread it.

I hated those moments. Not only did they destroy whatever continuity or rapport I had painstakingly established, the students were openly disrespectful, and I had to face them down while masking my own disgust. Everyone, including Rebel, had complained about the interruptions but Vivian insisted it was his way of maintaining contact with the school.

"All F.H.A. girls who have not turned in their candy money to Mrs. Byars please do so immediately. There will be a meeting of the F.F.A. club in the F.F.A. room tomorrow during club schedule. You must attend this meeting if you plan to attend the barbecue. Rebel Raiders who have not turned in their flags must do so tomorrow."

The intercom snapped off. I began again. "Without a sense of history you have no perspective, no frame of reference for interpreting and understanding—"

The intercom crackled again. "This is your coach reminding you that tomorrow will be a spirit day so wear your school colors. Teachers are reminded that students displaying school spirit may be considered for special credit. Let's all wear our red and black and show folks what our true colors are."

It was too late to retrieve attention, useless to shout over the noise of the students picking up their books and suddenly coming to life. "You can work on the assignment in class tomorrow," I said.

There had been other bad days, other mistakes, other failures, but I had lost these students and I didn't know if I could regain their confidence or respect. I had lost confidence and respect for myself.

I walked Maggie and Becky home, ignoring their moods, stuck in my own.

"I don't want to go to scouts," Maggie said. I didn't say

anything. We never pushed Maggie, but I knew she would go
as she always did. Maggie moved to times and tides that were
her own and it made her uneasy when others tried to organize
her. It also made some adults think her sullen and even slow,
but she was not. I knew she would put on her uniform, and at
the meeting, once she had gotten accustomed to the rhythm
and flow, she would laugh and play with the others.

"I do," Becky said. "I'm going to make a bow and arrows."
The other girls were stringing beads or weaving baskets but
Becky insisted on making a bow and arrows. I had taken her to
collect branches and feathers and flint. I knew she couldn't
chip arrowheads but she had insisted.

While the girls were changing into their uniforms and
Becky got her materials together, I told Delores I was going for
a drive. "School was that bad?" she said. I nodded without
looking at her. I knew she wanted to go, to help, to be told
what was wrong. Once we had talked about such things, but I
could not tell her about Duane Spivey.

I dropped the girls at Rebel's house and drove to the
springs. The springs had always had utilitarian rather than
scenic value, a hole where the water bubbled up through the
sand and began its course along Wanderer Creek until it emptied into Red River at Dead Man's Junction.

Construction work for the new Interstate had closed the
springs and a concrete pipe carried the water under the road
bed to the creek. It wasn't the same, but I sat down beside the
pipe to think. I was not a hero to my family. I was not a leader
to my students.

What was I doing in a doomed town, teaching the virtues
of independence, self-reliance, and public spirit to boys and
girls whose lives were controlled by forces of which they were
scarcely aware, industrial and financial and communication
empires that transcended governments, subverted customs,
determined the price of their homes, the value of their work,
the worth of their children, the place they would live, and

whether or not they would die on foreign soil protecting the private interests of acquisitive men?

What did I want for my students? What myths, what heroes to sustain them? To give them courage in the unequal struggle where only organizations had power, where only excess gained attention, where only money was given dignity and respect?

Dick Dowling and Rip Ford were not suited for such a world. Who could imagine Crockett or Bowie being law-abiding in such a place, or even Travis? Who could imagine Houston succeeding, or even Lincoln?

The students were going to leave Wanderer Springs, all of them. Was there anything I wanted them to take with them? To preserve? Or was it not mine to give but theirs to find?

I held my hands under the pipe and let the water from Wanderer Springs flow over them. I made a cup with my fingers and took a drink. The only non-failing source of water between the Mobeetie and Red River was brackish.

The next day the students filed sullenly into class, determined to give as little as possible and to accept even less. "Since you weren't excited about reporting on Rip Ford or Dick Dowling, I'll give you another choice," I said. "You can use any hero from this county."

They looked at me as though I were insane. "What hero?" Dixie asked.

"Your hero. Maybe you'd like to use your grandfather Herschell."

"Who'd he ever kill?" She was serious.

"The only requirement is that the report be relevant to you."

They looked suspiciously at each other and then back at me. "There ain't any heroes in this county," Dixie said.

Like other teachers I had retreated on "ain't" to fight a last ditch battle against profanity and obscenity in the classroom.

Students who had once complained, "Why can't I say ain't? My daddy says ain't," now complained, "Why can't I say shit? My mama says shit."

"Think of hero in the sense of model or ideal," I said. "Ask your parents who their heroes were, ask your grandparents, then pick your own, one who has meaning for you. Would you like a victim of injustice? Pick Babe English who was arrested for cattle rustling and shot during his trial. No attempt has ever been made to prove his innocence or guilt. Read the records and reach your own conclusion.

"What about a person who has overcome in spite of prejudice and oppression? Report on Zollie Cox Turkett, the first black woman in this county. Her father died unattended during a fever epidemic, her daughter died of a fire accidentally started by some of your relatives. Zollie raised ten children of her own and her daughter's two children and taught them to read and write. Maybe there are no medals for that kind of life but it was heroic.

"Do you feel like you're mistreated, misunderstood? Here's a hero for you." I held up a brittle, yellowed newspaper clipping. "This is an editorial from another town. Three young people took their own lives within a few hours of each other. They would have graduated from college the next day. They were not friends and there seems to be no connection between their deaths. One of them left a note stating that he did not choose to live in such an ugly and confused world."

I read the editorial. "That three young persons acting independently could decide to take their own lives seems too incredible to believe. But such seems to have been the case. The death of these young people must leave us with some questions. Have we adults created a world of such confusion and trouble that three fine young people who should have been the hope of the future could have feared to accept its burden? Are the pressures of contemporary life too great for these sensitive, idealistic children? Young people are losing their faith in the world, faith in their parents' ability to control events and decide the future. We as adults must do something to restore the faith of the young in mankind."

The students were wary but I had their attention. "The dateline on this editorial is 1921." They were stunned that before their birth, before Hiroshima, and Watts, and Vietnam, someone could have found life meaningless. "One of those young people attended this school, sat in this very classroom." I looked at Duane. The note had been written by his great-uncle. Eli Spivey's brother, who had been spared the horror of Belleau Wood and amputation, had refused to live in an ugly and confused world. Eli had refused to live in a country where profit was counted as patriotism. I wanted Duane to think about his grandfather and great uncle. It wasn't too late for him to choose.

"History is the story of man's mistakes and failures and maybe we can learn something from them. Maybe knowing that Elmer Spruill killed the last buffalo will prevent us from destroying the whooping crane. Maybe knowing that in 1921 some people thought the world was a bad place to live might help us in the search for values to live by. History is a story that hasn't been finished and I'm giving you a chance to discover part of the history of this county, or of your family. I'm giving you a chance to find a hero closer to your needs than Dick Dowling or Davy Crockett."

I told them how the county was formed and what had brought their families there—not oil and usually not cattle but the railroad, the windmill, cheap land, and a dream of freedom and independence. I talked about what motivated them to stay through droughts and depression and prosperity. I told them the story of Grover and Edna Turrill.

Grover and Edna married, when Grover was sixteen, at the request of both families. Crowded out by younger children they set out for a life of their own. Grover's father gave them a milk cow and Edna's father gave them a steer. It was the best

their families could do. Grover yoked the cow and steer together and they started to California in a wagon. It was his
promise to Edna.

They crossed Red River and stopped near Preston where
Edna had a baby boy with no one to help her but Grover. They
named him Grover, too. They started moving again as soon as
Edna was able to travel, Edna and the baby in the wagon, and
Grover walking beside the wagon, prodding the ox and milk
cow, and picking up firewood. After Preston there was little
wood and Grover picked up whatever sticks he saw for the
evening fire.

One day, tired of sitting, Edna placed the sleeping baby in
the back of the wagon and got out to walk beside the cow.
Grover found a tree stump and, not knowing the baby was in
the back of the wagon, he threw in the stump, killing his child.
Some cowboys found them, two teenagers traveling across the
prairie with a dead baby wrapped in a quilt and carried in
Edna's lap.

The cowboys dug a grave and buried the child, still
wrapped in the quilt Edna's mother had given them. After the
cowboys had gone, Grover and Edna made a cross of two
pieces of firewood. For a long time they sat by the grave, trying
to decide whether to abandon the grave of their firstborn.

"California is purty," Grover said, renewing his plight.
Grover had been stunted and hardened by a life of misfortune,
but Edna's steel had been warmed by motherhood. "It'll be
easier to forget."

Grover and Edna were still on their way to California
when the milk cow died near Wanderer Springs. They lived in
the wagon while Grover broke the land, with the steer and
Edna pulling the plow, and planted a crop. The corn was to
buy oxen to take them to California. Grover had a good harvest and Edna had a baby girl named Polly. The wagon was no
place for a mother and baby. Grover built a lean-to for the
winter.

In the spring Grover and the steer pulled, and Edna plowed, leaving the baby at the end of the row. By fall there was enough corn for an ox, but Edna had another son, this one called Billo. Grover traded the corn for a milk cow. He enclosed the lean-to and put in a door.

The land Grover had chosen was not good enough to make him forget his dreams, not rich enough to provide the means to accomplish it. There was always enough but more than enough was soon required by boils, fevers, broken bones. Drought alternated with flood. Hail alternated with grasshoppers. There was high wind, early frost, unseasonal rain. Grover and Edna still talked of California but they built a regular house for the children. Grover traded the harvest for mules to pull the plow.

Others came to settle the land, break the soil, to share the joys and trials. While the children played, the adults talked about the friends and family they had left never to see again and the freedom they hoped to find in the hard land. They sat or squatted near the earth, looking out across the prairie that was as silent and empty as a dream. They waited for the sun to fade and the wind to rise. "Best time of the day," they said. Edna told of the gentle life Grover had promised her in California. "It's purty," Grover said.

Billo was small and tough like his father, and like his father, he was always in a hurry. When he was eight, Billo went coon hunting with some older boys. They ran a coon up a dead tree on the creek, and Billo climbed the tree to shake the coon down. A pile of brush had been washed up under the tree and the older boys set it afire so that Billo could see. The dead tree caught fire and Billo was burned so that he couldn't lie down and Edna and Grover took turns holding him the four days it took him to die.

The neighbors came to tend the fields and livestock, to look after Polly, and to feed Edna and Grover, who sat like double images, their faces set to bear all, do all, to spare Billo pain. They scarcely moved except to shift Billo from one lap to another.

When Billo died, the neighbors dug his grave, and Grover took him from Edna and laid him in it. The neighbors buried him and sat for a while with Edna, and Grover, and Polly. They stared at the unforgiving earth and talked of the land where Billo had gone, a land without memory, without tears. Edna and Grover held Polly close and told her of California and the sweetness of life there. "It's purty," Grover said.

When Polly was thirteen, she complained of a stomach ache. Polly was not fat, but like Edna she was slope-shouldered, solid, and a good eater. Polly was no whiner, but she tossed all night on her bed and was unable to eat breakfast. Grover hitched the team to the wagon, made a pallet on the back, and with Edna to comfort Polly they started for the doctor at Wanderer Springs several miles away. The wagon had no springs, the road was just a set of ruts across the prairie. Polly whimpered the whole way although Grover drove as slowly as he dared.

When they got to Wanderer Springs they found that Dr. Vestal had been called out of town. Over near Medicine Hill folks thought, expected to be gone all day. Polly was too sick to wait for his return, so they started for Medicine Hill, sending word ahead by twelve-year-old Buster Bryant who volunteered to ride with the message.

It was August and the sun was hot and Polly cried out at every bump, so Edna stood and held a quilt to shade her, and Grover drove the mules as fast as he dared for Medicine Hill. They met Buster coming back. He had missed Dr. Vestal who was on his way to Bull Valley. Grover turned the mules towards Bull Valley with Buster racing ahead. Somewhere along that road Grover stopped to kill a rattlesnake that was so big when it coiled it reached the hub of the wagon wheel. Polly was dying, but Grover was a father and there were other children to think of.

Dr. Vestal had left Bull Valley for Red Top. Buster rode to

head off the wagon, telling Grover to go home. He would find Dr. Vestal and meet them there. The mules had played out and Grover was walking beside them to lighten the load. Edna was standing with her feet spread, holding the stout little girl in her arms, trying to absorb the bumps and shocks of the wagon with her body.

It was almost dark when the wagon got back home and Buster and the doctor were waiting. Edna was sitting beside Grover holding the child so that she lay across both their laps. The mules stopped of their own accord and neither Grover nor Edna made a move to get down. Dr. Vestal started to the wagon but Grover said, "I don't want you to touch her. We've been praying for you all day and listening to her die. I know it ain't your fault, but I don't want to see you now."

Grover got down, lifted Polly, and followed by Edna he started towards the house. "Are you sure, Grover?" Dr. Vestal asked.

"She's not screaming any more, is she?" Grover said. "I'd rather have her dead than have to listen to that."

Dr. Vestal left but Buster stayed with the Turrills, although he didn't dare go in the house. He unhitched the mules and fed them and sat on the graceless porch. After a while Grover came out to water the single tree in the yard, a stunted, ugly pear tree that Edna had planted and watered until it had finally dropped a few sun-baked pears as warty as horseapples.

Grover sat on the porch and stared out at the empty, treeless miles over which he had ridden that day, listening to the shriek of the wagon wheels and the dying cries of his last child.

After a while Edna came out also and leaned against the porch post, hugging the porch post as though it were a child, her head hanging down a little as though permanently bent from ironing clothes and chopping cotton. She waited while the last light of day faded and one by one the stars came out, watching the prairie that under moonlight had a sheen like a silent sea.

"If that cow hadn't died we'd be in California," Grover said.

"Old Boss," Edna said, remembering the name over all the years, recalling the dreams they had as they traveled across the prairie in the wagon.

"Damn country. Washes away ever time it rains. Blows away ever time there's a wind. Hail or grasshoppers ever damn year. I've sweated over it. I've broken my back. It has taken every thing I have and given me nothing."

"Yeah," Edna said, looking over the miles and years they had traveled together. "But ain't it purty."

Grover and Edna had left no heirs but they had left a legacy of endurance, of hope, of finding beauty and meaning in meager lives. I looked at Duane and Dixie. They were not looking at me but I believed they had heard. I dared believe they had seen the truth that Edna and Grover had found. The country was mean as hell, but sometimes in the spring after the rains and the wildflowers came, or early in the morning when the wind was soft and the land lay peaceful and silent as a dream, or coming home at dusk through a wheatfield swept clean by harvest, there was a kind of beauty that brought contentment and love so intense that those who had seen it endured the droughts and floods and sandstorms.

That revelation was more wondrous than Dr. Vestal's appearance in Wanderer Springs the day he died, more mysterious than Mattie Lance's disappearance from her grave. For that moment I wouldn't have traded places with anyone, not for all the glories of introducing students to Keats or giving them their first glimpse through a microscope at a hidden world.

I told how civilizations that did not preserve their history lost more than their history, and families who did not keep a history in traditions and Bibles and picture albums became rootless and even nameless. I was ready to encourage them to find a hero in the county, perhaps a parent or grandparent, to take with them when they left Wanderer Springs, when Vivian came in.

"I got what you been waiting for," he said, handing me my paycheck. "Maybe I ought to give this to you behind your back," he said, putting his arm around my shoulder and looking at the students. He laughed to amuse them but they did not respond. "Naw, I think you've been doing a pretty good job and when a man does a job like that I like to see him rewarded. Now you can go to Center Point and see the picture show, get your kids a play pretty."

Vivian patted at his toupee to be sure it was in place and then clapped me affectionately on the back. "You students listen to this man, now. This here is a good man. If he says it happened on a certain date you can believe that's when it happened."

I looked at my students. The dull, guarded look had returned. I put my arm around Vivian's shoulder and walked him out of the room, closing the door behind us. "Vivian, if you ever do that to me again, so help me, I'll throw you out of my classroom."

Vivian was surprised. "I think it's good for students to see their teachers get paid. That way they know we're professionals."

"I mean it. Don't ever interrupt my class again."

I paused at the door a moment trying to regain my poise, then walked briskly back into the classroom. "Now, what I'd like you to do is find your own hero—yes, Duane?"

"What is the purpose of this assignment?"

Probably students had a good reason for asking that question. I had given assignments where the only purpose was that I had always given the assignment. But I did not want to limit this assignment by specificity. I did not want it to sound like a goal to be attained. I wanted them to discover something that would tie them to this place after they had left it.

"The purpose of the assignment is to find a personal hero, someone whose values and ideas are similar to your own."

"What if we don't believe in heroes?" Dixie asked.

"I said they could be models or ideals. Surely you have those."

"What if my ideal is Walter Slocum?" Dixie asked, determined to be obstinate. Walter Slocum, who had hidden in the broom closet, had been fired by the school, just like his sister, Emma Harkness, who had given the students everything she had.

I knew if I didn't head that off some of the students, in order to ridicule the assignment, would choose Walter, or his father Albert, who had never worshipped the gods success, soap, or security. "Before you begin your research, you'd better check your hero with me."

"What about Bud Tabor?" Duane said.

That was a challenge but thankfully the other students did not understand it, and I thought it better to ignore it. "By Monday I want the name of the person you're going to write about."

Most of the students chose to report on Rip Ford or Dick Dowling because the essential information was provided by the textbook and a handbook in the library. One girl wrote, "My father is my hero because he bought me a pony for my sixteenth birthday." Dixie wrote, "I can't write this paper because I don't believe in heroes."

Duane, whose brother and grandfather had been decorated war heroes, chose Bud Tabor with the dark wavy hair and hungry eyes, all teeth and gonads—"who made history rather than taught it." God made too great a variety of women and Bud was fascinated by all of them. Was his heart too big or too little? Bud had an appeal to the young. He had lived fast and women had fought over his corpse. But Bud had brought pain to everyone who loved him, and everyone who loved someone who loved him, ripple after ripple of hurt that went on long after his death.

Goaded by what Earl Lance would do, Ed McElroy had

set Bud Tabor straight—after God failed to attend to it—and folks accepted the necessity of it. Except for his daughter, Sherry, who never forgave her father but publicly called him a murderer. Ed left the county.

Bud's wife also left, taking her children with her, hoping to escape that dark stain in the post office. Pregnant Sherry had married J. C. McKinney who had lost an arm in the saws ginning for Lowell Byars. It seemed to have been a loveless marriage. Sherry needed a father for her baby; J. C. needed someone to cook his meals and pack his lunch. They lived like mutual tenants sharing nothing but properties until Bud's daughter, Darlene, chose to be called "Buddy" and unveiled hungry eyes.

Sherry and J. C. divided a starfish of fear between them, a fear that multiplied by division. They moved to Quitaque, Sweetwater, Levelland, Tahoka, Idalou, looking for the right environs, trying to escape Bud's death grip. No one who had been touched by Bud escaped his grip entirely. And Duane thought I had been teaching the virtues of Grover and Edna Turrill and living like Bud Tabor.

I wanted Duane's respect but I never got it. After his arrest, I went to jail to see him. I tried to apologize. Duane gave me a mirthless smile. Duane didn't take adults seriously. They weren't sincere.

I could understand why he didn't have much respect for me, but I wanted him to respect his parents, his teachers, the school. "Most adults try to do what's right," I told him.

Duane dropped his head and laughed to himself. Vivian had promised him that if he played football, they would put a cast on his partial arm so that he could hit people with it and make them respect him. Rebel had given Bubba extra points so he could be valedictorian. Hooper told Dixie a pregnant girl could not attend high school but a girl who had had an abortion could. Junior had paid Dr. Heslar for Dixie's abortion.

I was not comforted that I did not stand alone in Duane's

disregard. "But the drugs, Duane. That doesn't justify selling drugs."

Again Duane laughed his mirthless laugh. His father took pills for tension. His mother took pills for weight control, restlessness, and after Bubba's death, depression. Dr. Heslar had prescribed drugs to Duane to give him confidence. After Dixie's abortion, he prescribed drugs for her to avoid depression. He sold them all the drugs they could pay for although he knew they were selling them to classmates.

"Duane, is there anything I can do to convince you that we are not the evil people you think we are?"

"Yeah, admit you're just like me and let me out of here."

Boots wanted to blame Vivian for the failure of the school. It was true that the best football team in years came apart because Vivian was the team and his pride was more important than a player's health, more important than winning. For the first time no one said they stole the game just like they stole the courthouse. I wanted to blame Vivian but I couldn't.

"They lost respect, Boots. They lost respect for the school, they lost respect for the teachers. Not just the students, the whole town. We let it happen, Boots. When we didn't respect Emma Harkness, neither did anybody else. The value we put on her was the value we put on all of us."

"Hell, Will, Emma was old, and you know how she dressed. She didn't make us look very good. It's like Bitsey's dad says, if you can't show, you gotta go," Boots said.

Boots and I said goodnight in the upstairs hall, and I went into my room and went to bed. I was tired, drunk, and sleepy, but I did not go to sleep. I had never learned to let go of a day, instead hanging on until it was far into tomorrow. In the old Prod headquarters, ghosts drifted through my thoughts.

I don't know when Branda slipped into my future as well as my present, at what point I began to include Branda in "we" instead of Delores, when my family was no longer ballast to my life but a millstone to my ambition, when I came to believe I had been deprived of some entitlement.

When Duane saw what Branda and I were doing, I saw it clearly for the first time. "I can't live like this, Branda," I said. We agonized over what we were going to do. That agony became part of the glue that held us together. If we suffered so, we had to be selfless, loving people. It was the others, thinking only of their own comfort, who made our lives so hard.

The hardest thing to give up was not Branda but the idea that I was special. Branda had a way of making me feel special. I didn't know I wasn't the first she had made feel that way. The touch that erased tomorrow, the sigh that said she was mine, I didn't know that perfection had come through practice. I wanted to be the man Branda thought I was. It was my last dream of escape and I wasn't sure I could give it up.

Branda wanted me to sell the farm, for us to run away to happiness. Branda believed in movie endings. "I'll go anywhere with you," she said. "I don't care as long as I have you."

"I can't sell the farm," I said. Land represented a place where one belonged, the Callaghan place. Apartments had numbers. "What about our children?"

"I love you so all I can think of is us. We have each other," Branda said.

My world had shrunk until it was no bigger than Wanderer Springs. No bigger than my family. Finally, until it was no bigger than me. I didn't learn that lesson until Duane Spivey wrote about Bud Tabor "who made history rather than taught it."

I tried to tell Branda about that class. The lives of Grover and Edna Turrill meant something. My life had diminished their story. I never wanted to stand that naked again.

"I offered you the chance," she said. "I could have helped you. But you don't want anything better than the little wife and the kids, and telling your silly stories. Let me enlighten you, Will. They don't mean anything. They're dead. Nobody cares.

Something else you might want to know. You really should give up sex, you're not very good at it."

"You said I should write a book telling other men how to love."

"What you know you could write on a restroom wall."

There was pain and anger at the end but also relief. It was over, and I had escaped disaster. Duane knew but would say nothing; Hooper knew but could say nothing. All I had to do was endure contempt at the school and keep the secret that Hooper had made plans to close it. Then Duane was arrested for selling drugs and Brassfield came looking for Manuel. I drove Manuel to Center Point to turn himself in while Delores stayed with the girls and tried to prepare them for the coming scandal.

When I came home, Delores insisted on going to see Brassfield although I advised against it. To Brassfield there were four kinds of people—niggers, blacks, whites, and trash. Mexicans were trash, along with Irish, Italians, gypsies, and women. Even his wife, the finest person he knew, was trash.

Trash had nothing to do with money or morals. It had to do with standing before the law, or more precisely, standing before the badge. Before the badge, women were something to be kept out of the way. Brassfield was polite, even courtly. He removed his hat, he said "ma'am" even to black women.

Brassfield did not look at women. He did not listen to them. No need to—he knew their eyes were puffy with tears, their mouths square with fear. He knew they were going to say, "Is he all right? Is he hurt? Is he scared?" They wanted their man, and they'd do anything to get him back. Better not to look, better not to listen. They could turn a man's head, worse than money that way. The law was supposed to be blind. Maybe he looked at a vote now and then, but he never looked at a piece of ass.

"They wouldn't let me see Manuel," Delores said. She went into the bedroom, and I followed.

"Did you talk to Brassfield?"

"He wouldn't tell me anything," Delores said. She sat down in a chair and looked at me. I could see the hurt in her eyes. That bastard Brassfield. "The sheriff said I should spend more time at home worrying about my husband. He said if I spent more time in the bedroom maybe you wouldn't go looking in other people's bedrooms."

Without taking my eyes from her face, I groped for the bed and sat down. How could I have worried about this moment for months and never planned what I would do?

"What did he mean, Will?"

I knew the words but my tongue recoiled.

"Have you been seeing someone?"

I didn't want to say it. The word was torn from somewhere inside. I was sick of the lies, sick of pretending, even espousing, virtues I did not possess. I felt guilt. "Yes." Fear. "Yes." But mostly I felt relief. The pretending was over; being the future with Branda, being the past with Delores; being Grover Turrill in the classroom and Bud Tabor out of it. I might not be whole, but I was myself.

Delores turned away from me. She was pale, shaken. "I can't believe it. Our marriage has been so good." She was appealing to me to help her understand the unreasonable. "How could it happen?"

How? I wanted her to explain to me. I wanted her to take me in her arms and make it all right.

"Why, Will?"

Why? Because Delores couldn't save me from who I was and Branda promised she would. Because Branda would run away with me and Delores wouldn't run. It was a crazy dream but it was the only dream I had left. Is that what Bud Tabor had sought in all those other women? Affirmation that he was someone other than himself?

"What do you want to do, Will?"

I wanted to run. Around my shoulders was the wreckage

of our marriage. Nothing in my life suggested that I could put it back. Nothing I had done seemed worth the doing, nothing I had left to do seemed worth living for.

"Do you love her?"

What were all those words we had said to each other, Branda and I? Those brave words, full of self-love and pity. What did they mean now? Delores was a treasure, Branda was a prize.

"Do you want her, Will? If she's what you want, I won't stand in your way."

I thought about life without Delores. Starting over in another place. The freedom to be anyone I wanted to be. I watched as Delores packed her bags. Sexual attraction was not enough to hold people together. Love didn't seem to be enough either. What Delores and I had was a history, made palpable by our children. We had a commitment to the common good for the four of us. We had a small community of friends who recognized and supported our union. We were not alone.

I did not want Delores to go but how could I ask her to stay? I had never been what she wanted me to be. Now I had betrayed her. How could I ask her to accept the failure that I was?

"Help me," I said.

Delores sat beside me on the bed and put her arms around me. Branda was a night on the town. Delores was coming home, not to that green and mystical Ireland Dad had dreamed of but to that peace that Edna Turrill had found in twilight.

Like the peace that Edna found, it was not without its price. Delores could not understand. When she understood, she could not accept. When she accepted, she could not forgive. When she forgave, she could not forget. We were like two wounded lions in the same cage. Roaring. Sometimes biting our own wounds, sometimes biting each other. Only the cage of marriage, children, history kept us together.

I knew no better how to please Delores than when I first dated her. I pretended passion I didn't feel. I encouraged her to spend more time in San Antonio. I made plans for her to finish her degree.

"Why can't you act the way you are?"

"What way is that?" I cried.

"You are a good person, Will, better than you give yourself credit for being. If you could only believe in yourself the way I believe in you."

I believed in nothing except that I had destroyed everything I cared for.

"I've never seen anyone change like Delores has," Rebel said. "It's like the life has gone out of her." Like everyone else, Rebel thought Delores's unhappiness was caused by Manuel's arrest. Manuel's arrest and the discovery of my infidelity had been a double shock. Manuel had been released from jail but Delores had not been released from fear.

"I'm going to put this behind me," Delores pledged. "I'm going to forget this and get on with my life."

And she tried. We both tried. One evening we took the children to a movie in Center Point and then to the Susie Q to eat. We laughed together, without caution, for the first time since Delores had talked to Sheriff Brassfield. Delores put her hand on mine. "Do you know why I married you, Will? Because you cared. I thought I could live with you because you cared, and you still care."

She handed me a little box wrapped as a present, and she smiled. The girls were masking their smiles; they had already seen it. I opened the box and took out a tiny carved bird. "It's a frigate bird," she said. "Some people call it a booby, but if anyone ever says booby to you, you tell them 'frigate.'"

Delores sat close beside me on the way home, too close to wear a seat belt. I saw the glare of the car lights weaving towards us as we approached the Mobeetie River bridge. I swerved to miss the on-coming car and instantly realized I was going to hit the bridge. For a moment there was no thinking—

just sound and shock and then a sudden ticking silence and the growing awareness of pain.

I did nothing, not breathing or daring to move, tightly controlling my mind against sensation, afraid to discover how hurt I was. Then I heard the children whimpering and Delores saying, "It's all right, Becky. It's all right, Maggie."

"Don't move," I said. "I'll get help." Carefully I moved. The door had popped open, the front and rear seats had come loose and there was a loud, insistent noise. Despite my seat belt I was jammed against the dash and the door post, the steering wheel tight against my chest.

At first I couldn't get free until I remembered the seat belt and unhooked it. I fell to the ground. The horn stopped blowing. I tried my legs. I could stand although my left knee wobbled loosely so that I could not trust it. A car had stopped and the driver was coming towards me. "Anybody hurt?" he asked. I was embarrassed that my family's need was so help-lessly exposed. "Get an ambulance," I said, and turned back to the car. There were car lights and faces in the darkness. Curi-ous, shocked faces, wanting to help but not knowing what to do. Someone helped me to the side of the car. All I could see was the tangled mass of the interior and the darkness of De-lores's hair against the whiteness of the children's faces as they clung to her and whimpered. "Mama, mama." She responded calmly, "It's all right, dear, it's all right."

Delores and the girls were put in the back of the am-bulance and I was helped in front with the driver. We were taken to Wanderer Springs. I walked into the hospital on my wobbly knee, patiently waited my turn while Dr. Heslar exam-ined my wife and children. I felt it necessary to explain how the accident happened, how I had hit the bridge rather than the other car, how the other driver must have been asleep. I amused a nurse by demonstrating how my knee moved freely in new directions. I was on the verge of hysteria when Dr. Heslar ordered me on the table to look at my knee.

"Your children are all right," he said. "Superficial cuts and bruises. They'll be sore for a few days. You're going to have to have some support for this knee for a while but it'll be all right. I'm sorry, there was nothing I could do for your wife."

I didn't understand and was afraid to ask. "She was all right," I said.

"Her skull was crushed. She probably never regained consciousness. It's remarkable she lived as long as she did."

"She was talking to the children. I heard her. The ambulance driver heard her. She said it was all right."

"On some level of consciousness she could hear the children and answered them. That happens sometimes. Maternal instinct I guess."

I sat on Hulda Codd's carved mahogany sofa that Delores had rescued and restored after Branda had thrown it away to make room for a sectional couch. With Rebecca on one side of me and Margaret on the other, I told them their mother had died. It was hard to overcome the feeling that when Delores died I had died too, that the family had perished with her. We sat crying, trying to hold the fragments between us, holding us together. I told them how to conduct themselves before grieving friends and relatives and death's officials. When there is nothing to say, I tend to give orders.

I sat on the couch with Gilbert on one side and Mama on the other. The rawness of life in Wanderer Springs where there was not even a Catholic Church had always horrified Mama. Now she encompassed everything in her grief—Papa's death; Rosa's future with two children and a husband who could find voice only in drunken rages; the fear that Manuel was not who the family thought he was, that they had placed their future in a changeling.

Mama cried uncontrollably. "I don't know how she could be so different from me." Sometimes Rosa, sometimes the children, tried to comfort her. "You sent her soul to hell," Mama wailed. None of them went to church except for weddings and funerals. Yet they lived within view of the church, its spires and crosses their boundary, its calendar their seasons, its prayers their tongue. To die without a priest was to die without a name.

"I look at this house," Mama wailed. "I look at these things. Where is Delores? Where are her things?" Mama cried on the verge of hysteria.

"Mama, Mama," Rosa cried, kneeling on the floor beside Mama, trying to take Mama into her lap while the children sobbed, Gilbert helpless and I stricken.

"God don't blame Delores," Gilbert said, struggling with unfamiliar feelings, trying to find the words to say something that was hard to say. "Don't God know Will loved Delores?"

"You tell all those stories, Will," Manuel said. Manuel sat with the family, yet apart. His way was strange to them, his thoughts foreign. They watched him cautiously, trying to discover who he was. "What's Delores's story? When I was little Delores took me to the Majestic Theater. I got lost and when an usher asked me Delores's name so he could page her, I knew I didn't belong there, and I knew when they said 'Delores Hinojosa' over the speaker everyone there would know that Delores didn't belong there. I told the usher I didn't remember her name. Did you remember her name, Will? Did you tell them she belonged here? Did you tell them her story?"

I sat on the couch with Gilbert on one side of me and Marshall on the other and wept for Delores. Too close for glasses, we had passed a bottle back and forth and talked of Delores. "Hell of a woman," Gilbert said. "Damn shame." Marshall and I were not so eloquent as Marshall tried to explain Delores's death and I tried to explain her life.

"You told me about a woman that died alone," Gilbert said. "Larissa Bell."

"Delores didn't die alone."

But I had been in the front seat with the driver, explaining the accident. In death Delores comforted the children.

I remember nothing of the funeral service except the rustle of clothing, the rattle and snap of purses being opened and pawed through, the smell of lipstick, shaving lotion, shoe polish. It was a raw, windy day and at the cemetery I shared Mama's horror at the thought of leaving Delores in the ugly treeless earth. "Is that all?" Mama cried. "Is that all they're going to do?" There was no "enough."

As soon as school was out the girls and I moved to San Antonio. I didn't escape Wanderer Springs but I moved far enough away that in time Josh Kincheloe's mysterious animal and Mattie Lance's strange children became whimsy. I turned the death of Bud Tabor into low humor.

I opened my eyes upon the portrait of a horse that was going to bring glamor to people's lives. I dressed and went downstairs. Bitsey was at the barn talking to the trainer. Boots wanted to go for a ride. "Nothing like a ride for a hangover."

"That's not the way I remember it," I said.

"I got to clear my head. I been on the phone all morning with an equine-law specialist in Dallas."

I laughed. "Are his clients horse thieves?"

"It's that damn syndication. You got to have a specialist. Sometimes I feel like a farrier in a one-horse town. What I have to keep in mind is marketing, merchandising, and product development—the future growth potential," Boots said, the words sounding foreign in his mouth. "This is a developing industry as opposed to a more mature type industry and has a lot more growth potential."

"Wow."

Boots smiled self-consciously. "Bitsey's dad didn't even finish high school and he taught me more about business in five minutes than I learned in four years of high school and five years of college. I still don't have the hang of it, but Dad Tabor helped me do a business plan and I have to live with that business plan until it's no longer viable.

"That's the kind of guy he is. He says business is the mortar that holds a family together. That and prayer. That's certainly true for me and Bitsey. Hell, we couldn't afford to get a divorce. He is one smart man."

As we talked, Boots showed me the horses. "All these stalls are twelve by twelve, except for the foaling stalls that are twelve by sixteen. This is the mare barn. The stallion barn is just like it, concrete floor with a twelve-inch drain topped with rubber matting and six inches of shavings. We have two electric walkers and a pool in the work area. The show arena is over there. All the paddocks have pipe and cable fencing. Each building has its own temperature gauge and they are all connected to the burglar and fire alarm."

In the stallion barn was the trainer's office with files of feeding and breeding records, bloodlines, leases and contracts. On the walls were ribbons, trophies, and pictures of satisfied customers. Boots handed a picture to me. It was one of those pretty but nondistinctive faces that seem to glow from attention. I recognized the picture as that of a beneficiary of media attention. "She bought one of our horses. She said, 'I just flashed on one of your horses. How much is it?'"

"What does 'flashed' mean?"

"It meant forty-three thousand bucks. Dad Tabor says if you deal in superior quality stallions you associate with superior quality people."

"Come on," he said, leading me out of the stable. "Those are Bitsey's horses. The trainer would quit if he saw me get on one of those."

We walked out to a small trap and caught two old knee-sprung cow ponies. "I had to go to Spur to get these," he said. We led the horses to a shed and got two old saddles that must have belonged to Buster.

I couldn't get my horse to stand still while I got on. He was an ugly off-black brute with a head like a sheep and his eyes rolled looking for phantom cattle. Getting on the horse didn't transform him but it did me. Magically I felt better. Better than I was, better than anyone on the ground. The automobile had interrupted the evolution of man and horse into man/horse.

It was easy to understand Bitsey's love affair with horses, although her love was different from that of Boots. Bitsey loved horses like a choir director loved children who did her will and proved her worth. Boots loved horses like a farmer loved his children who with varying effectiveness helped him with his chores.

We rode over to the work arena where Bitsey was working a horse, all attention and determination. Her riding lessons showed. She sat her horse expertly, stylishly, an elegant addition. She looked good on a horse. Boots looked like part of the horse. "We're going for a ride," Boots yelled at Bitsey, who seemed not to hear. "Come on, I got something to show you."

Living in San Antonio with cedars and live oaks, I had forgotten that Wanderer Springs was long glimpses of autumn brown beneath clear blue skies. But the grass didn't rustle the way I remembered it, a miracle of money and irrigation. And the wildflowers were gone—a miracle of fertilizer and herbicides.

There used to be a story about Earl Lance walking across the pasture with Shirley, who picked wildflowers and charmed birds out of the sky where they were eaten by one of the black cats that always followed her. But no one believed it. Earl didn't walk anywhere, and he for sure didn't pick flowers.

Ace, the horse I was riding, was a thinking horse. I was trying to follow Boots but Ace was thinking, "There aren't any cows up there. We better go off to the right here," and I'd have to turn him back. "There's a road right over there, I'll walk down the road," and I'd have to turn him back.

"Look here, Will," Boots said, pointing at a gnarled mesquite. "I wanted you to see this, the ugliest tree in the county."

The thick tree had been stunted by the blazing sun and

lack of rain, twisted by the wind, knobby from being browsed by hungry cattle, scarred by animals that had burrowed in the slight shade at the base of it, but it was tenacious, with roots older than the Lances. It wasn't stately like an oak, or elegant like an elm, or sweet-smelling like a cedar. It was ugly, but not evil, and root plows and herbicides had not been able to break its will.

"But that's not what I want to show you," Boots said, and we loped over to the ghost town of Prod. Delmer's store was still standing and looked unchanged. We tied up at what was probably a corner post of the corral, walked across the bare ground where Cristobel had dug up chickens and up on the porch.

The notice board still hung on the outside wall. Folks used to tack up notices of cattle auctions, horse sales, stray animals, church meetings, and personal messages. Only strangers had passed the store without stopping to read the news and have a Dr. Pepper and peanut pattie with Delmer, or later, Clifford Huff.

Like Dr. Vestal, Clifford could get no one to take his practice and folks would not let him retire. He put on an apron and said he had to help Lucy in the store. The farmers and ranchers loaded up their stock and brought them to Prod for Clifford to look at. Still nailed to the board was Clifford's announcement of retirement. "I am no longer able to look after sick animals. Take them to that dog doctor in Center Point."

"I put this lock on here myself," Boots said, fumbling with his keys. "Collectors were coming out here taking anything that wasn't nailed down. Hell, barbed wire collectors had cut up the whole fence."

Inside, the store looked less familiar. The potbellied stove remained, and the counter that had glass bins with windows for displaying dried peas and beans, and in the back the copper tank for coal oil and the walk-in wooden chest for ice, milk, and watermelons. But the groceries were gone from the shelves, and the stands of Levis, kegs of nails, rolls of barbed wire. Only Clifford's collection was left.

Clifford knew the county better than anyone, having driven, ridden, or walked over most of it while tending sick animals. He had decorated the Prod store with things he had found—buffalo skulls, rusted pistols, spurs, branding irons, glass insulators, old bottles. He was most famous for his collection of arrowheads, but he took no pride in them. "I wish to crops I had never picked them up. I wish I had left them for someone else to find. Sometimes I think I ought to take these arrowheads and things and scatter them back along the creeks and trails so kids could find them the way I did. There's nothing left to discover. When I was a kid it was all new."

"Look at this, Will," Boots said. It was Eli Spivey's helmet. "Here's that long-handled hoe he used." Like Earl Lance, Eli looked tall only on a horse. "What should I do with all this stuff?" Boots asked. "People are driving me crazy trying to buy it to hang on the walls of restaurants and bars."

Was that the end of the story, that family treasures, souvenirs of private joys should decorate the halls of frivolity?

"Billo's spurs are in there. And the wheels off the wagon they carried Polly in. And a hand-carved bread pan that belonged to Ida Ballard."

The history, the relics of Wanderer Springs were in the Prod Store. "Boots, let's burn it. I hate to see Eli's helmet decorating a bar."

"It don't really belong to me," Boots said. "It belongs to Dad Tabor. He's thinking of using it for theme party houses in the condos he builds."

Boots closed the door on the Prod store and we rode to Wanderer Creek. Snake doctors hung over the water and if we had looked closely we could have found traces of Indian campsites and buffalo wallows. Somewhere on the other side of the creek was the rutted trail where Polly Turrill had been bumped to death in her mother's arms.

"Did you ever wonder what Grover and Edna thought seeing Dad coming, knowing that meant he hadn't found Dr. Vestal?" Boots asked. "They must have seen him for miles."

"Did your dad ever talk about it?"

"He said they were singing songs."

"Hymns?"

"No, they were singing songs for Polly. 'When you wake we will patty-patty cake and ride the pretty little pony.' This is Earl's Lake. Best grass we have."

We were riding through a low pasture of thick grass. Earl's Lake had filled with silt. "Remember all the dove and quail we shot here," I said.

"Not any more. No water for the dove, and the quail don't like coastal. I wanted to leave it natural grass but Bitsey won't hear of anything but coastal."

Earl's Lake had never been more than a red-rimmed stock tank, but at one time it had been the biggest body of water in the county. Buster Bryant had waited all night with a saddled horse to carry the alarm if the dam broke. All around him were alarms: portents of wars, economic mirages, progress with its offerings of communications and transportation wonders that would isolate the county. Such things were beyond his ken. The rest of his life Buster waited, a messenger without a message.

"Mud College must have been right over there."

Frustrated in his attempts to leave the county, Grover Turrill had built a one-room school for his children and employed a teacher. Lucy Lance and Mattie's strange children had also attended the school called Mud College because every time it rained Earl's Lake had backed up to the school door. The school only lasted a couple of years and closed when a cowboy came from the Prod on a stallion that no one else could ride and asked the teacher, Miss Gladys Tidmore, if she'd like to go for a ride. She said yes and neither was seen again although rumor was that they homesteaded in Oklahoma Territory.

"Ain't it purty," Boots said. "God, I love this country. The only thing better than living in Texas would be dying in the Alamo."

I didn't laugh because I felt the same way although I knew better. It was not reasonable that a man should love such harsh and unforgiving country. Such love must be ranked with patriotism and mother love for sheer willfulness to refuse to believe what one knows.

We were the real Texans and were jealous of the distinction because we had earned it. In spite of all the Texas brags about bigness, the smaller and more sequestered the town, the more of a real Texan you were. That's what we thought. We knew Texas because we got down in the dirt with it.

We knew the salt of Texas better than those city boys in Center Point. Fort Worth was acceptable because it was still Cowtown and because every year the F.F.A. traveled to the Fat Stock Show, and San Antonio was the home of the Alamo. But Dallas and Houston were closer to California than to Wanderer Springs, and California was somewhere east of Texarkana and north of Texline.

We may not have known our geography, but we could pinpoint artificial squints and counterfeit swaggers long before they were discovered by Hollywood and other fashion designers.

"I have never understood how you could leave this place," Boots said.

To an outsider this scene would have been a comedy, even an absurd comedy. We were riding along a nearly dry creek, across a treeless prairie. To the south I could barely make out the grain elevator that marked Wanderer Springs and the bump of Medicine Hill. To the west I could see the glitter from the lifetime metal roof of the Prod store. North, beyond the smudge of salt cedars that marked Red River, was Oklahoma, and that was all. Only someone from Odessa could think it attractive. Yet, Boots was talking like this was the fairest spot since Eden, and I didn't laugh.

"You could have gotten a job teaching in Center Point," Boots said.

Teaching was a profession in which most of the rewards came as favors from those I did not admire and could not respect. Delores had been aware of my dissatisfaction and had encouraged me to try something else, but I wasn't teaching for the rewards. I had taken that vow of moral and intellectual poverty because I had seen other towns die—Prod, Elma Dell, Bull Valley, Medicine Hill, and with them went the stories of the faithful who had staked their lives and built their dreams on the mirage of peace, rain, and hard work. I believed Wanderer Springs was worth saving, and that by saving the school I could save the town. But I hadn't saved the school; I had been one of the destroyers.

"The Turrills stopped here because their cow died," I said. "The Lances were running from a cattle feud. There is no magic to this place, Boots."

Boots bowed his head a little, not in submission but in stubbornness. He couldn't argue history with me, but neither would he accept my version of it.

"Do you think I could teach at Center Point after they stole the courthouse and beat us in football?" I asked. To Boots the answer was accceptable. In Texas, football, like oil, is not a subject for humor.

"I sometimes go to the Center Point games," Boots said apologetically.

Sometimes with the clear vision that comes from fifty years, from sitting in a book-lined office in San Antonio trying to give significance to Three-Legged Willie and the Baron de Bastrop, I can laugh at the importance we gave to that game. But I didn't laugh at Boots. Not even when he said, "I believe we could beat them now."

He meant that if we could go back to our youth, taking nothing with us but what we had since learned of courage and the rightness of things, that we could beat the present oversized, over-equipped, semi-professional Center Point team.

Dreams are never surrendered. They bleed away from the cuts of disappointment. Or maybe it was truth that cut like a razor. If so, Boots's veins were deep and safe from the blade. We had sat in the picture show and applauded cowboys in fringed britches, with silver tipped buckles and pearl handled six-shooters while Eli Spivey chopped down trees to feed his cattle, Earl Lance went to a pauper's grave with title to a half-million dollars worth of land, and Buster Bryant prodded milk cows at the auction barn.

Boots rode a range unknown to Buster, Earl, and Eli. He rode the river with straight-shooters who didn't count Mexicans and Indians, who hanged horse thieves and niggers, and who wanted commies and welfare leeches out of town by sundown.

"You know what this is?" Boots asked, reining up at a grass-and-weed-filled depression. Two stunted hackberries grew nearby. "This is Turtle Hole. The creek changed its course."

"It can't be," I said. The dark glade where high school girls paid their dues? "It's not right." I understood that physical things seemed to shrink with time, even things of the spirit. Who would have dreamed that Shakespeare's England was a little island? I was prepared for Turtle Hole to seem small; I was not prepared for the earth to have swallowed it.

I got off the horse and Boots did the same. In Wanderer Springs the earth was given identification and import by people and events. There were no Grand Canyons important unto themselves. Paymore Hill. Hide City. The land across the creek would always be the Turrill Place no matter who owned it. And this spot would always be Turtle Hole. How could it have ever been big enough for all the pain? "It's not right."

"Hard to believe someone could drown here," Boots said.

"Two people. Three if you count Aubie Thrasher who drowned farther upstream." Aubie rode for the Prod, and he drowned trying to swim his horse across the flooded creek so that his sixteen-year-old wife would not have to spend the night alone. "Milton Shipman drowned here," I said.

I was skirting Roma Dean and we both knew it. That was the way things were done in Wanderer Springs. It was no accident Boots had led me to Turtle Hole, and having made his intention known, he would allow me to digress until I was ready to talk about what he wanted.

"Selena Lance swam Turtle Hole and pikered all the boys. Milton was the only one to take the dare, and he drowned. The Shipmans never forgave the Lances."

"I thought it was because Delmer opened that hardware store at Prod."

"Guy Shipman was not competitive," I said. Both the Lances and the Shipmans went to the Baptist Church, and the Shipmans nodded at the Lances but they watched Selena with eyes like stone tablets. Even the men had stopped saying she would gentle out when Selena threw the snake in the barber shop. "It was Genevieve who got Selena thrown out of the Baptist Church."

The Baptists expected young ladies to faint at the sight of snakes or men with lather on their faces until they had a proper church wedding and moved to a dugout where visitations of scorpions, rattlesnakes, and lathered husbands were a nightly occurrence. Nevertheless, Selena remained a Baptist until she told Hulda Codd ice cream was only one of the things she liked hard.

Whatever our private opinions, there was the public and collective "folks say" judgment of the town that overrode all other judgments. Selena owned a home in Center Point, had visited every state in the union driving her own car, was national president of two women's clubs, was a delegate at two Democratic conventions, but the "folks say" judgment of the town was "A woman who travels alone can't be happy."

Boots hooked his thumbs in the pockets of his jeans and spat to let me know he was going to begin. "I always stood up for you when others talked you down. It didn't matter who they were." Boots was establishing that he was not prying, but was a true friend and he had a right to certain answers.

"Thank you, Boots. I know you did."

"I got to know. Did you and Hooper screw Joann?"

"No. Neither of us."

"You promise? I don't mean promise that you're telling the truth, I mean promise that you know for sure."

"I promise. It wasn't a date. It was just something to do." Except for Marshall we were not inventive about things to do. Mostly we drove around looking for the girls who were driving around looking for us.

"She never let me. You know how girls were back then," he said. "I figured something must have happened out here."

"Nothing happened," I said. We were as horny as teen-age boys at any time but the girls were different. At least we thought they were different, and movies and popular books reinforced our opinion. That was before best-selling self-help books were written to assist people in overcoming their modesty. Until their wedding nights girls did not think about sex. And some of them didn't think much of it then. "What difference does it make? That was thirty years ago."

"Maybe you've forgotten, Will, but we used to think that virginity was the one thing a girl had to give you."

"No, we used to think that was the one thing a girl had to give."

Boots sighed. "The love you never forget is the one you lose," he said.

"And you lose them all."

"Have you loved many women, Will?"

"One too many." He looked at me sharply. "Isn't that the usual number? No one loves two too many do they? Or five?"

"I never loved anyone but Bitsey," he said. "I've thought about Joann. I carry her on my mind. But it's not daydreams, I just want to talk to her. I was hoping she would come to the funeral. I don't care if I'm disappointed, or if I can't think of anything to say. I just want to see her. I want to put a conclusion to all my thoughts about her. Do you understand that, Will?"

"Sure. You want to say you were young and stupid and didn't know any better and you'd like for her not to remember you that way."

"I was going to talk to Joann, but her family left."

"You had a few days."

"Dammit, I know I had a few days. I figured what happened was that you guys were screwing around, maybe taking turns, and you forgot about Roma Dean and that's how she drowned."

"It wasn't like that, Boots."

"If it was as innocent as you say, how come it got so big?"

Big? Roma Dean died. The rest of us, some who weren't even there, dated our lives before and after Turtle Hole. It was the most attention Wanderer Springs had ever gotten. The whole nation gaped at a personal tragedy promoted to national amusement.

"That moonlight tryst crap was all started by the paper," I said. "It was dark as hell. There wasn't any moon. And didn't there use to be a lot more trees?"

The truth was recorded in the almanac, but no matter. The paper said "moonlight" and in Wanderer Springs it would always be "that moonlight swim." That story became the reality of Turtle Hole. The autopsy verified that Roma Dean had died a virgin, but the information came too late, the distorted story had already become valid in most minds. Only her classmates remembered that Roma Dean was the best one of us.

Roma Dean's nakedness eclipsed the tragedy of her death. In time her nakedness eclipsed her life. Those of us who knew her had to re-invent her life. And ours as well.

Nothing about Turtle Hole was real. Boots and I were standing in the dusty weeds in the spot where Roma Dean's body was found. How could I calculate the dimension of an event that had been distorted the moment it occurred, in a place that seemed never to have existed?

The incident had been exaggerated by all of us. Yet, the exaggeration was actually an understatement. Something had died at Turtle Hole, some dream of grace, of special favor, of being incapable of harm or failing someone in need. On the once limitless horizon loomed the cloud of retribution.

"I figured you didn't tell anybody what happened because of the girls' reputations." Boots was trying. He had his face screwed up and he was squinting like thinking made his head hurt. "I admired you, even though I thought you probably screwed my girl, because you took all that crap to protect the girls. I thought Hooper and Vivian should have taken more of the heat. But if nobody screwed anybody—it doesn't make sense, Will."

Boots and I hadn't been butt-slapping close since Turtle Hole, but we were friends, and now our friendship was on the line.

"You loved her, didn't you, Will?"

You have to admire a man who remembers a high school romance with anything but embarrassment. What did I know of love? It wasn't even a word teenagers used. I loved Roma Dean with a body that was just discovering itself and wanted to leap mountains, swim oceans, and spill seed over the earth, that hungered for a body she did not know. She loved me with a heart that had just discovered itself and wanted to be broken and healed, that yearned for glances, for caresses, for music and words, for a heart that I did not know. It was a teenage romance, rich in frustration and misunderstanding. Only her death made it a tragedy rather than the comedy most teenage romances were.

"Boots, I was seventeen years old." Roma Dean thought the best of me. She was my friend, the one to whom I could admit folly and fear without scorn. "For God's sake, Boots. Seventeen. You were still fucking sheep."

Boots and I stood shoulder to shoulder, kicking at the weeds, looking off toward Medicine Hill where Roma Dean had lived. Boots's signs were up. Slowly he turned to face me and look me in the eye. "She was your girl, Will."

It troubled Boots that Delores had taken Roma Dean's

place. Roma Dean and I were the stuff of tragedy, not Greek tragedy or "Romeo and Juliet" but the real James Dean-Natalie Wood thing—misunderstood teenagers in a world that never grew up. Roma Dean, the eternal virgin, loved but not embraced, and I, doomed to suffer but not to learn, left to walk the earth forever alone, my grief her monument. Boots felt cheated.

Being identified with another person, even in high school, was not a pure pleasure. A man was supposed to protect what was his. Taking what another was too weak to hold or too ineffectual to use was not considered wrong—it was thought good for the country. I had failed to save Roma Dean's life. I had failed to save her reputation. Thirty years after her death I was going to have to prove that I was worthy to be her boyfriend.

"She was your responsibility."

"Frigate," I said.

My first punch missed Boots's jaw and hit him on the ear but it was the best punch either of us landed. The others bounced off arms, shoulders, wrapped around necks. I tore my knuckles on Boots's rodeo belt buckle and accidentally bit him on the neck when my fist missed him, and our momentum and exhaustion carried us both to the ground. We rolled apart and sat up, panting for breath.

I was weak with laughter. At least I hope it was laughter. A man does a lot of foolish things to prove the one thing that should be unnecessary and I felt foolish. Nevertheless, it seemed to have worked.

"Dammit, Will, I knew you loved her. I don't know why it's so hard to get you to say it," Boots said.

I put my arm over Boots's shoulder. I felt closer to Boots than I had felt to anyone in a long time. I thought of how close we had been before Turtle Hole. Joann, Rebel, and Roma Dean could be apart for thirty minutes and when they got together again they hugged and jumped up and down and squealed like they had been separated for years. Boots and I exchanged handshakes, punches, and insults, but in our way we were just as affectionate. And all the years since Turtle Hole Boots had defended me.

"Boots, Roma Dean is not the girl we remember."

"Dammit, Will, don't start that again." He got up, stared at the ground for a moment. "I'll race you to Dead Man's Junction," he said and ran for his horse.

Ace was dancing by the time I got to him and running before I was fully in the saddle. I had been off the horse long enough to have gotten stiff, my jeans pinched my thighs, the saddle pounded my testicles, my head throbbed, and I felt great. "Ya hoo," I yelled.

Boots outraced me the way he always did. We reined up on a low bluff overlooking the salt cedars that almost hid the slow, muddy river in the mile-wide riverbed. To the left was a stand of post oak trees where Roy Dodson had found the team and wagon that his son, Fred, had left when Roy sent him to cut timber for his new store.

Fred decided he had rather look for gold in Alaska than cut timber. Since he had left no message, it was feared that Fred had drowned or been kidnapped by the Indians. Prod cowboys rode both banks of the river looking for his body, and Earl Lance and Roy Dodson rode to Fort Sill to search the Indian reservation. It probably would have amused Fred to know that his father was searching for him while he was searching for gold. Fred was a cynic.

To the right of us was the junction of Wanderer Creek and Red River, called Dead Man's Junction after Joe Whatley had killed Virgil Hight because Virgil was a deacon. The Hights had been headed for some western promise when one morning Minnie Hight refused to repack the wagon or get back in it. "I'm not going another step," she said, and she didn't. Virgil built a dugout into the high bank of the river between the old creek bed and the new one. Ownership of the land was not clear because the creek had shifted its course and both Earl Lance and Joe Whatley claimed it. Earl had sent a couple of cowboys to tell the Hights to move but Minnie refused. When she stopped, she stopped.

Joe Whatley wanted the Hights out because Virgil had signed the billet dismissing the Whatleys from the Methodist Church. Joe was more resourceful; when Minnie refused to move, he picked her up to remove her. He and Virgil got in a fight and Virgil was killed. The lynching of Joe Whatley had made Ferguson the Fiddler useless, it restored the purity of the Methodist Church, and it gave the Baptists a foothold in the county. Joining the Baptist Church were the Whatleys, Joe's friends, and some who were glad that Joe was dead, but believed that the manner of this death violated the wall of separation between church and state.

The lynching seemed to have done nothing for the Hights. Minnie, a stringy, gotch-eyed woman with bad teeth and a good memory, never went to church again, or to town either, but hid in the dugout when anyone approached as though she thought they would try to evict her. Her sons, Homer and Buford, grew up wild and reclusive. They never went to school but fished and trapped, trading hides for salt and flour at the Prod store. Later they gathered bottles along the river and roads to claim the deposit, made stink bait which they sold to fishermen, killed coyotes for the bounty, and picked up freshly killed birds and animals along the highway for their table.

"Did you ever know the Hight boys?" I asked Boots.

"Bought stink bait is all."

"My grandmother used to come see them. Dad said Mrs. Hight hid in the dugout and Grandmother went in and talked to her. He used to come and see about the boys. Sometimes he had to eat with them. He said undamaged quail was the best."

When Mrs. Hight died, her sons received a flurry of attention from those who wanted to help them. The country had a New Deal and Homer and Buford were among the nation's unemployed, perhaps drifting into Communism. They were given their first shaves, haircuts, and jobs. The reclusive Hights were to mow the courthouse lawn under the curious eyes of the citizens of Center Point. The politicians and photographers had scarcely turned their backs before the Hights were gone, slipping down the street where Buster Bryant had roped his own horse.

Buford was the first of the boys to die. Homer lived on in solitude, fishing, trapping, and picking up freshly killed animals, until he was joined by five hippies, three men and two women, who lived in an old school bus parked in the vee between the old and new creek channels. They fished and trapped and ate road-killed animals with Homer, and at night he sat with them beside their fire. Then Dr. Heslar reported that someone had broken into his office and stolen prescription forms. When the farmhouse burned down Brassfield blamed it on hippies although Branda and I were the only ones who used it. Brassfield went to Dead Man's Junction and ordered the hippies to leave.

"What law are we violating?" they asked.

"Impersonating a school bus," Brassfield said.

The hippies laughed. They said, "Aw shit." Brassfield handled them the way he handled uppity niggers. He broke a bus window with his night stick. "You'd be happier some place else," he said. He broke another window. "After I break windows, I break heads," he said.

After he had persuaded the hippies to leave, Brassfield took Homer Hight to The Wanderer's Rest where he was scrubbed, shaved, dressed in pajamas and gown, and put on the porch with ten other people to watch television, the volume tuned to dull ears. Twice Brassfield had to go to Dead Man's Junction and return Homer to the Great Society before Homer died strapped to his bed. "I be dog," Clifford Huff used to say. "The best thing you can hope for is to die by surprise."

Boots was sitting easy, looking across the river. "If you'd been born over there you'd be an Okie," he said. "I come out here sometimes and look across the river and say, 'thank God I wasn't born over there.'"

"How do you think you'd feel if you'd been born over there?"

"I'd hate myself."

"No you wouldn't. You'd look over here and thank God you weren't one of us."

"Bullshit. Being a Texan is better than being anybody. Even if you're a Hight."

"Even if you're a Hinojosa?" I asked.

Boots turned in his saddle and looked at me. "I respected Delores as much as I respected anyone in Wanderer Springs. But her brother—I just never could understand how someone who was born in this country and had the advantages we have could turn against everything we stand for."

"What about Dr. Heslar?"

"Dammit, Will, he did wrong and he is sorry for it. I'm on the hospital board, and I assure you it is a straight business operation. There are very few pills prescribed. That airplane is to fly tests to Lubbock or Amarillo, sometimes Dallas or Houston. He has to run tests to prevent us from being sued. Granted, it is as expensive as hell, but Dr. Heslar is the only one besides me who brings any income into the town."

Money has rights. That's what Otis Hopkins used to say when as chairman of the school board he addressed school assemblies. For Otis that meant the right to build and rent eyesores without regard for health, safety, or aesthetics. For Boots it meant the right to recreate the West in his own image. For Manuel it meant the right to be equal. "Rights don't come from the constitution," Manuel said, echoing Otis Hopkins. "They come from the bank."

"Wonder if Vivian ever comes out here," I said.

"It's not his. Vivian said he was going to take it to court

but he doesn't have the money." Vivian had joined the ranks of those too poor to buy justice, too old to expect it.

We started back to the house without conversation. Boots had that lord-of-the-range look. Boots believed he could stop crime with a bullet, hunger with hard work, and social and environmental ills with an independent spirit. It was something that only an elected official could believe. Or someone who had married wealth.

A private jet flew over us and circled the strip at the headquarters before landing. "Oh, shit," Boots said. "That's Odeen Sitz."

Odeen Sitz was a born-again entrepreneur of such magnitude that the state was required to give him political appointments and honorary degrees as a tribute to his religious faith.

"Odeen owns part of Shalimar and that means I'm going to have to spend the day with him praying and playing cowboy. Don't say anything about drinking or parimutuel betting in front of him."

"I've got to pick up Rebel," I said. "I thought I'd take her to lunch."

Boots screwed up his mouth trying to decide between sentiment and commerce. "I'll just have to tell him there's a funeral I have to attend. I can't not go after insisting you come all this way." He paused, waiting for me to suggest that he might miss the funeral but I didn't. "I'll have Madeline take the chuckwagon to the river and grill steaks, and we'll ride over for lunch." Boots had a chuckwagon built onto a pickup bed. "That ought to hold him for a while. He can talk to the trainer while I'm at the funeral. Bitsey will be mad as hell, but I just have to do it."

We galloped back to the headquarters, and I unsaddled the horses and turned them loose while Boots telephoned the house and gave Madeline instructions for lunch on the river. I said goodbye to Boots, who had his mind on playing millionaire rancher, and went by the breeding barn to tell Bitsey I was leaving but would see her at the funeral.

"He went beautiful," she was saying. "I've never seen such presence. When he came into the arena and saw the judges he just went beautiful."

"Ain't that horse the prettiest thing God ever made," Odeen said. "I don't see how a man could look at that horse and not believe in Jesus. 'Course I felt the same way when the Cowboys won the Superbowl. There's always them diehard atheists who believe in luck and Lombardi. I don't believe I caught your name," Odeen said, mistaking me for a stablehand.

Odeen, who had been Phi Beta Kappa at Duke, a jet ace in Korea, and a flag waver during Vietnam, was leaner and stronger than I had imagined. I was prepared to dislike him, but his greeting was open, his handshake firm, his desire to be liked overwhelming.

"We're just admiring this piece of horse flesh and praising God," Odeen said, fixing me with his clear blue eyes. "There ain't no man on earth can convince me that that horse is the product of luck, or evolution, or natural selection, or whatever they're calling it this year," he said, gripping my arm. "But that's what children are learning in the public schools. The governor says he's a Christian, and maybe he is, but I'm afraid those Jew York publishers have wrapped their pockets around his fingers."

He apologized when I said goodbye to Bitsey. "I don't want to stop nobody from doing what they need to be doing. I don't want to get in nobody's way. It's just that sometimes I have to get away from Dallas and telephones, and I get in my little old airplane and fly out here where life is real." He took a deep breath. "I like to walk on real grass, and feel the sun, and look at the stars. I just feel closer to God out here." He opened his arms to include the barns, the paddocks, the arenas.

"Sometimes I wish God hadn't given me the responsibility He did." God and Odeen's father had given him a major insurance company and a large slice of an oil corporation. "I'd move out here and sweep stables, just to be with horses, and to lie on the grass under the stars, and enjoy the simple things of life."

The only simple thing about Odeen was his theology. When I left, he and Bitsey were talking futurities and genetics.

I bathed and dressed for the funeral and drove the empty highway back to town, out of habit looking both ways before crossing the railroad tracks. Once eight trains a day had disgorged farmers hungry for land and drummers hungry for coins. Once folks had set their clocks by the trains. Now the trains didn't stop at all and passed so infrequently that cattle once more grazed the right of way and no one greased the tracks at Paymore Hill.

TURTLE HOLE

where high school girls paid their dues

I PARKED in front of the Live and Let Live. I could have parked anywhere I wanted, but once farm wives had competed for places in front of the store so they could judge other women by the size of their grocery lists. Bought bread meant a woman too slack to bake biscuits. Eggs, milk, and bacon meant a woman too house-spoiled to feed chickens, milk cows, and slop hogs. Candy meant a mother who didn't care enough about her children to make cookies, and fruit out of season meant a woman too lazy to raise a garden and can the produce.

Benny Whatley had built the two-story, brick Live and Let Live with glass windows in front, and it had not changed. On either side of it stood doorless, windowless buildings with floors rotted out, roofs fallen in, and sickly weeds growing through the debris. It was hard to tell the ruin of vandals from the wreck of time but time had been kinder. The only other occupied building in the block was Shipman's Hardware across the street, and I could see Herschell watching out his window.

I stepped up on the high curb, suitable for mounting horses, and looked through the dirty window. Biddy was sitting at the back of the store behind the cash register, reading a romance novel and sucking on a gumdrop. The only books sold in Wanderer Springs were romance novels, and it was safe to say that Biddy had read every title before the book was sold.

The store seemed not to have changed since Benny built it—same naked light bulbs, same wooden posts holding up the shelves or ceiling or both, same plank floor, same fat woman behind the cash register. No, it wasn't the same fat woman.

"You better come in here and say hello," Biddy called, having looked up from her romance. Biddy was short, triple-chinned and double-breasted. Starting below her hair that she kept in short curls, her flesh descended in a series of folds that almost obscured her eyes, obliterated the distinction between chin and neck, and hung over her knees and ankles. She wasn't as fat as Marshall's mother but when she sat down behind the cash register, she seemed to settle, first her shoulders, then her bosom, then her stomach and hips spilling over the chair.

"How's business, Biddy?"

"Come and see, come and sigh," she said. "Slow as a cow with sore teats. Them niggers that works for Boots comes in and asks me to stock balloons and crap like that but I ain't going to be at their bacon call."

Biddy's grandfather, Benny, had taken trade from Roy Dodson by being accommodating. He called customers by name and thought they liked him. Biddy thought her customers were deaf and senile. "Back wall, same place as last week," she yelled. She thought they were bores. "I got bowel trouble of my own," she yelled.

"It's a doggy dog world," Biddy said. "I swear to God if I wasn't eating my own groceries I'd starve to death."

Except for her fat, Biddy hardly seemed a Whatley. She was more the reflection of Roy Dodson, living off capital intended for others, the dead end of rugged individualism.

"Rebel. Hey, Rebel," Biddy yelled without getting out of her chair, but aiming her voice at the ceiling. "Will's here."

A few minutes later Rebel came down the stairs at the back. "I thought I'd take you to lunch," I said.

"I wish you would get her to eat something," Biddy said. "If you was to render her down you wouldn't get enough fat to fry an egg."

"Give me five minutes," Rebel said, running back up the stairs.

"Set down, Will, you're giving me the heebie-jeebies." I sat down on a squat stepstool that allowed Biddy to reach the top shelves. "Your kids must be growed by now."

"Yes, they're both in college." Biddy didn't like children. They moved too much and they stared at her bulk too openly.

"I remember one time the oldest one was in here to get a sody pop and she was carrying a purse as big as she was. I said, 'What you got in that purse?' And she said, 'I got everything a real woman's got. Comb, brush, compact, gun.' And she pulled out this toy six-shooter. Lord God, what kids think of."

"I guess you won't be able to go to the funeral."

"I don't owe Jessie nothing, but I can see how you might, bare-ass naked out there at Turtle Hole. I told Rebel last night, you kids will never know how much you hurt Jessie. I just never could understand how a little loving was worth all that."

It was hard to know what drove the Whatleys but it didn't seem to be sex. If, as some believed, Joe kept women for pleasure and profit, the only pleasure he took from them was profit.

Benny did get two children, Maurice and Fat Sue, from his fat wife, but his greatest desire seemed to be getting everyone's approval. He ran about the store assuring everyone his dying wife was all right, afraid they might disapprove of her dying in the store.

Vivian never made a fool of himself for a pretty face, never forgot who he was because of a sidelong look, never forgot the lure of success in the flash of a shapely leg.

Vivian had always been attracted to Rebel and jealous of Marshall who was the boy Rebel had preferred, but the stirring in his blood seemed to have been competition. He did not lie awake at night trying to recall her smell. He did not know that sweet ache for her, sweet because she inspired it. He did not treasure the pain she brought him—the pain of goodbye—knowing that the inevitable end of togetherness was disengagement.

Biddy's only passion, besides food, was for tender feelings on the misty moors where lovers touched but never held, sighed but never moaned, longed but never ached, knew bliss but never guilt or joy or ruin.

Biddy's passion was understandable because there was precious little romance on the plains. Women no doubt dreamed of romance but they clucked their tongues at romantics. Like Lulu Byars who wanted to dance; Mary McCarroll who lost her mind, her daughter, and the cows the same night; Sherry McElroy who left mash notes in Box 287; Selena Lance who escaped her own wedding just because Otis Hopkins was a bore and a fool—a lot of women had made something of that.

The women saved their admiration for the level-headed wives who looked after their husbands and children whether they liked their lot or not. Women like Ida Ballard who had to cross sixteen fences to get back to an idling husband and a passel of sore-eyed kids; Amanda Slocum who gave her life to save a worthless man from an imaginary heart attack because no matter how sorry he was, he was after all the only husband she would ever have; Grandmother who held on to her land without a husband, educated her children without a school, and convicted Joe Whatley without a jury.

Rebel came down the stairs carrying her bag. "Vivian is going to try to make it to the funeral. If not I'll catch the bus," she said to Biddy who nodded. That was their only gesture of farewell.

"Thank you for coming early," Rebel said when we were outside. "I couldn't wait to get out of there. You know what we had for breakfast? Stale cereal and less than fresh milk. Her milk is always blinky but this was bad. Let's drive to Medicine Hill, we have time."

"Why do you want to go to Medicine Hill?"

"I just want to see it, I don't want to climb it."

I drove to the corner where Herschell kept watch and took the old road to Medicine Hill. Although there was nothing left at Medicine Hill but the cemetery and the hill itself, the road had been blacktopped to reduce unemployment among engineers and heavy equipment operators.

We rode in silence for a while. Rebel and I had been friends for a long time, but she hadn't always been the same woman. In high school she had greeted each day as a challenge and lived it with abandon. Rebel had been fascinating to me in a way that Roma Dean could not. She had arm wrestled me, run footraces, played tug of war while I dreamed of her seducing me. Roma Dean had never joined in, but she became so quiet she couldn't be ignored.

Once Rebel and I had been riding around in her car looking for the others. When Rebel saw Vivian's car, she turned off the car lights and we played ditch 'em. She pulled up in the shrubs at the base of the water tower. We both pretended to be excited by the chase; we kept looking out the back window until we were shoulder to shoulder and then face to face. We were kissing when Vivian pulled in behind us and turned on his headlights.

Marshall and Roma Dean were riding with Vivian. Marshall never said anything. Roma Dean didn't either, exactly. One cold day Rebel couldn't find a scarf and came to school with a towel around her head. It started a fad that seemed not to have caught on in the larger world.

"I'm not like that," Roma Dean said with asperity. "Rebel is vain, and a show-off, and when she takes pictures I'm always out of focus. And I'll never wear a towel to school I don't care how cold and poor I am."

Roma Dean tried to be more like Rebel, and I tried to pretend I didn't notice, because I didn't dare express approval or disapproval. She said damn a few times, she tickled Hooper, she told Marshall an off-color joke. It didn't work because she cared what they thought. There was a weight in Roma Dean, a gravity that she could not change.

Medicine Hill was visible from the time we left Wanderer Springs, and I drove along the old road past the land that Buster Bryant had saved by a magnificent ride and lost through an ordinary life while he waited for doom to come to his rescue. In the distance we could see the sheepshead pumps that nodded over the land Eli Spivey had tried to hold on to for too long, waiting for rains that never came.

"Did I tell you I got a letter from your girls?" Rebel asked.

"No." They called me but seldom wrote.

"Becky wrote two or three months ago to tell me that she was going to be a lawyer and to thank me for encouraging her in scouts. Becky was always so serious. I'll never forget the time she said, 'You know what I like best? God and dogs.'"

We laughed. Rebel laughed at a happy memory. My memories were tinged with sadness, with loss, because the wonderful people the girls had been at two, and five, and eight were gone, and no matter how wonderful they were now, and how much I admired them, they would never be those children again. I missed the people they had been, their cheer, and their wit, and their magical insights into life.

Maggie's letter hadn't said much about what she planned to do except that she wanted to help people, and she had thanked Rebel for teaching her how important people were. "I had forgotten it. The girls were making little play houses and Maggie made this round thing that I didn't know what was. 'It's for those people who live in those round things,' Maggie said. Eskimos? 'No.' Indians? 'No.' Martians? 'Yeah, Martians.' I guess I said it was better or more fun to play with real people than with Martians. You did a good job with the children, Will."

I was proud of the compliment, perhaps because I worried about the children in an uncertain world, and I needed to believe that I had given them some certainties. I was moved that they maintained ties with Wanderer Springs.

Weeds grew along the unused railroad spur to Medicine Hill and the depot where Joe Whatley had been chained to the stove. The water tank from which he had been hanged had long ago rotted into the earth.

"You and Delores, of course. I really admired her, Will. I wish I had been closer to her. I know she went to church with you, but there was something Catholic about her. I don't know if I can even explain this," Rebel said, "but I've been to Catholic churches, and they're so bizarre—candles, and incense, and those awful statues. They're so dark and—foreign."

The Baptist Church was so light as to be bright, the only decorations were a Christian and a U.S. flag, and it reeked of being American from the democratic polity and assembly line organization to the Tin Pan Alley tunes.

A few trees surrounded by a field plowed by Ira Ferguson's crews marked the place where the Tooley house had once stood, where Pat Tooley had bled to death calling for help, where old Red had seen death descending like a shovel. I drove across the field and parked under a mulberry tree that I remembered as being in the front yard.

"Talk. We used to sit up half the night talking," Rebel said. Jessie rarely let Roma Dean have the car so Rebel drove to Medicine Hill to get her. She often spent the night. They walked to the store or sat on the porch. "I wonder that we found so much to talk about. Mostly Roma Dean talked about you. What you said. What you did. How cute you were. She always defended you, Will. Even when you hurt her. She wouldn't let me say one word against you. 'I know he loves me,' she'd say."

Being a Tooley, it was important to Roma Dean that everyone love her.

"She used to look in the mirror and cry about her hair. When I said something, she'd say, 'If Will wants it this way I'll wear it like this the rest of my life.' The plans we made. Our weddings. Sometimes we were going to have a double wedding. Our honeymoons. Our houses that were going to be side by side. How many children—" Rebel pursed her lips, unable to continue. "Do you remember when the worst thing that had ever happened to you was algebra?" She began to cry.

"I used to be so angry with you, Will," Rebel said. "I wanted children more than anything in the world and you had children; I thought you had gotten off free."

It was Marshall who first suggested a midnight swim in Turtle Hole, but when Rebel went home to get her swimsuit, Otis wouldn't let her leave again and the plan collapsed. The next time Marshall wasn't with us. Vivian suggested a swim, and the girls were unwilling to go home for their swimsuits, afraid their parents would make them come in. "We can swim in our panties," Rebel said.

"God didn't make you barren as punishment," I said. Rebel's God didn't like people very much. "You don't even know that you were infertile." Vivian and Rebel had both said that Rebel could not conceive, but she had never taken tests because Vivian could not bear the humiliation of being sterile.

"The boys have to go first," Rebel said.

"And you have to turn your backs until we get in the water," Joann said.

"I can't," Roma Dean said.

"The Bible says you reap what you sow," Rebel said, her face hard as she looked across the Tooley farm.

The water was red, the banks were red, and Roma Dean refused to swim because she couldn't explain her mud-stained panties to her mother. I was angry because Roma Dean was always holding back. Nothing ever happened, nothing was ever going to happen. She wanted to live the same dull life in the same dull town—and Hooper and Vivian were going to blame me because she spoiled everything. "I don't care," I said.

"Rebel, don't you think that's more of an observation of life than a threat of God?" I asked. Rebel was not appeased.

I slipped out of my pants, shoes, and shirt, and gritting my teeth, slid down the slippery bank and into the water. Vivian did a cannonball into the water and came up splashing, trying to find someone to dunk. I slid away from him; it was so dark he could not see me. I heard Rebel gasp and moan as she slipped into the water.

"Let's be honest, Will. We deserved to lose the thing we wanted most." I thought of Delores, but she meant Roma Dean.

I felt an arm slide around my neck and pull me under. I thought it was Vivian and I fought back, catching him around the waist, but the flesh was smooth and slippery beneath my fingers. It was Rebel. We broke the surface of the water, gasping for breath, her breath in my face, and I could feel the length of her body like fire against my skin.

"I've always felt a child gives birth to a marriage," Rebel said. "Like the birth of the child is the birth of the family. Is that silly?"

Her mouth was against mine. Rebel was strong, athletic, and we wrestled in the water, not a contest of will but of want, her body panting against mine.

"It's not silly." It was inaccurate. A child gave birth to a different family, a different marriage. "If you wanted children so much, why didn't you adopt?"

I pinned Rebel against the bank, pressing her against the earth. Her fingers were in my hair, around my neck, down my back, pulling me to her panting body.

"If God didn't want me to have children, then I shouldn't have children, and I couldn't bear it if I had adopted children and He had taken them away."

My hands rose from her waist, caressed her breasts, slipped under her arms, and lifted her up, up

"Oh, Will." She was crying.

out of the water, up the slippery bank

"We were animals."

onto the damp grass and

"No. No."

I lunged after her panting body.

"That was the worst thing that ever happened to me."

With a shock I realized that she was not talking about Roma Dean's death but our panting in the grass, struggling to subdue each other.

"I wish I had died."

Joann screamed. Rebel and I rolled apart, certain we had been discovered. Vivian and Hooper were wrestling and splashing in the water. Joann screamed again. "Roma Dean's in the water."

"We might as well have been two dogs. I have never felt such disgust. That I could do such a thing."

From that moment I dared not think of what it meant. I plunged into the water looking for Roma Dean. Hooper went to get Wink Bailey and to take Rebel and Joann home. Vivian and I covered Turtle Hole looking for her.

"Everything bad that has ever happened to me was because of Turtle Hole. And it's never going to be over."

Rebel's God was a mean, vindictive God who had made Otis Hopkins in his own image. In high school Rebel had a high level of sexual energy that made her restless, headstrong, head cheerleader, and captain of the volleyball team. All that had died at Turtle Hole.

"Life is so deceptive, isn't it?" Rebel said. "In high school I seemed to have everything. Everybody envied me. You know who I wanted to be like? Roma Dean. She was so good. Wasn't she good, Will?"

She wasn't good; she was innocent. "You weren't Roma Dean and you shouldn't try to be her now. Why can't you be the Rebel everyone loved?"

"Because I hate her, Will. Everyone hates her."

"I don't hate her."

"You lost respect for me, Will."

How could I tell her it wasn't respect I lost, it was desire. She was something wild and free that I wanted to hold for a moment—like a bird, a butterfly—to know and understand and marvel at. And then to let go. To see free and wild again and yet to know that for a moment I had held it close, had felt its beating heart and looked into its wondrous eye.

Rebel did not fly again. She could not preen the mud of Turtle Hole from her wings. "That's the past," I said. "We can't change it, but we can learn from it. We can put it behind us."

"I'm trying to be obedient, trying to follow Jesus, to be as harmless as I can. Why was I given this awful name? Why couldn't I be Grace or Hope or Faith? I did everything I could to rebel against my father and then I broke the ultimate law."

"Rebel, the ultimate law is to love one another."

"Then why didn't you stay with Roma Dean? Why were you with me? She loved you, Will. More than anything."

"It was a mistake, Rebel. It wasn't a crime. It's taken me a long time to realize that, but it wasn't."

"It was a sin."

"Okay, a sin. It wasn't murder. It wasn't malice. Rebel, maybe my glands were fooling my heart, but I loved you, and I've loved you since. It's not a romantic love. It doesn't require any response on your part. It's the kind of love you're always talking about that seeks nothing for itself. You've always been more important to me than I've been able to say or show. I care what happens to you. I wish the best for you. I wish your life were fuller."

"If I had been more like Roma Dean none of this would have happened. Marshall would be pastor of the Baptist Church, I would be his wife, you'd be principal of the high school and married to Roma Dean and our children would have played together. And we'd all go to see Boots and Bitsey. Or maybe he would have married Joann—"

Maybe Rebel and Marshall would have married. She acted tough, but it seemed a way to get the attention of Marshall who tried to gentle her. Marshall was the only one who could get away with reproving her, and in high school that had passed as love. Since high school Rebel didn't seem to like Marshall, yet she clung to him as a lost love.

"I don't know about you and Marshall but Roma Dean and I were drifting apart. It was a high school romance and it was over."

"Will Callaghan! I'm going to forget you said that. If I believed you meant that I'd hate you. Roma Dean loved you more than anything in this world."

More than anything in this world—except a punitive God—Rebel believed young love was forever. That dogma robbed me of the memory of a real flesh and blood girl who blushed all over like a fireplug but got mad like a flag with a white stripe across her mouth and another across her eyes, who scratched her teeth with her nails because they itched, who looked puzzled because it made me laugh.

"Something is over, Rebel, can be if we will let it. This is the first time we've been able to talk about it. We can forgive each other. We can forgive ourselves." Blessed are they whose sentence is not for life.

Rebel was struggling. "I knew then that if I could do that to my best friend I was capable of anything. I knew that if I was pregnant I would kill myself and go straight to hell. I prayed that I was barren, Will." She began to cry, openly, her hands twisted in her lap. "I said, God, I will do anything you ask me, only don't let me do anything like that again, and don't let me be pregnant. I didn't know what I was doing to Vivian, praying away the child we could have had."

"Vivian never cared that much for children."

"You only know Vivian the way he is in public when he's trying so hard to be confident and proud. You've never seen him when he's down, when he cried over games."

When we were in high school, Vivian was the most aggressive—meaning he cared the least about the feelings of others. Great things were expected of him in business or politics—in our minds the two were close enough to be, if not synonymous, at least inseparable. Instead, Vivian chose coaching where victory was God's reward for being good, and Vivian was not a success.

"Those boys were his children, and no one wants him to coach any more."

A lot of folks wondered why Rebel married Vivian. Delores said it was because Rebel had rather be married than be smart, and when I asked if Rebel couldn't be married and smart, she said, "Not to Vivian you can't. He wouldn't allow it."

"Vivian and I have a good marriage. Sometimes I think I would like—" She waved a hand. "I never want to feel that way again—that I was just a body, just an animal. That's why I loved Marshall. He brought out the best in me. I could never have done anything like that with him. After that I knew I could never marry Marshall. I could never tell him what I was like, and he could never forgive it. I thought I had to marry someone from Wanderer Springs. I couldn't marry you, Will, I couldn't even look you in the eye knowing what you knew about me. That left Vivian."

I nodded as though I understood. Maybe adversity doesn't build character but it makes you thoughtful. "If we're going to eat lunch, we'd better get a move on," I said. For old times sake I took the back road through what was once Bull Valley and over Paymore Hill.

"Vivian had always been sweet on me," she said. "One time in high school he gave me a perfect Eskimo Pie—not cracked or melted or anything. You know what that meant to him? He and Biddy ate anything that was damaged but he had to pay for that with his own money."

Her only reaction to Paymore Hill was to sigh, lean back and look at the roof of the car. "I'm too hard on Vivian. He always liked me just the way I am; I didn't have to act some way like I did with Marshall or my father. We get tired of each other

sometimes. Bored more than anything else. If we had children—We went to a marriage counselor, and he had us make
up lists of what we needed from each other. Number one on
his list was that he needed me to watch football games with
him. I go if he's refereeing, but I can't watch every game on T.V."

"What did you want?"

"I needed more hugs. I just wanted our life to be a little
more exciting. I can't blame Vivian for that. Being a Christian is
the most exciting thing in the world, and if I just give myself to
Jesus he will take care of my needs. We're supposed to go back
to the counselor next week, but I don't know. Vivian wants to
have it worked out by next week."

I offered to take Rebel to the Susie Q but she preferred
the Sonic Drive-In so we could sit in the car and talk.

"Will, do you think that Roma Dean saw us?"

"It was so dark you couldn't see the trees, remember? No
one saw us."

"Sometimes I think she saw us and ran and fell in and
that's why she drowned. Sometimes I think she was trying to
call to us for help. The two people she loved most—that she
would have done anything for. She cut her hair for you, Will.
She was naked because of you."

"I know, dammit."

"Do you think she died hating us?"

Dared I believe that unlike old Red, Roma Dean had not
seen the hand that wielded the shovel? "Roma Dean never
hated anyone," I said, surrendering the girl who tripped Vivian
in the cafeteria because he said I was the clumsiest player on
the team, who wouldn't let Hooper copy her homework because Hooper ran against me for class president—taking part
in that apotheosis that would make the Roma Dean we remembered someone we never knew.

MEDICINE HILL

some goodbyes, some understandings

W E drove back to Wanderer Springs, quickly this time by the Interstate, to go by the funeral parlor and view Jessie's body before the service. Not to have done so would have been like going to a wedding without a present.

Dr. Heslar had turned The Corner Drug into a funeral parlor under the direction of Brother Bob Schlutter, pastor of the Malcolm Murdock Memorial Chapel. The ill and infirm saw a lot of Brother Bob and Dr. Heslar. One grieving relative said, "I knew the end was near for mother by the look in their eyes. They were measuring her for a coffin."

A sheet of green plastic covered the window that had once displayed ads for bunion plasters and pile ointment. The plastic cast a green shade on everything inside so that I thought I had entered a subterranean cavern. Prolific, artificially-scented plastic flowers hung from the ceiling, clung to the walls, and sprang from the floor. The dignified fake oak paneling and subtle recorded organ music could have convinced me that I was in San Antonio had it not been for the greenish cast to the room.

The main room of the drug store had become a reception room and a replica of a Louis XIV table with a plastic vase of plastic flowers, a plaster of Paris lamb, and a gilt-edged guest register stood where Fat Sue had given birth to Marshall. The flowers were the color of Monday-morning Easter eggs.

The prescription room where Wesley had hidden the scarred side of his face now hid the form of Jessie Tooley inside a glow-metal coffin that was being overrun by plastic ferns.

Waiting attendance on Jessie was Emma Harkness. "I dropped by to see Jessie, and I thought I'd wait and see who else showed up," Emma said, her smile showing too much gum. Emma seemed scarcely to have changed since she was my teacher, as though she had always been old and her years were only now catching up to her. Her dark suit did not fit or hang straight, her thick glasses had a film of dust.

Rebel went to the table to sniff through the guest register and leave her mark. Emma patted the chair beside me. "Sit down, Will," she said. She always spoke to me as though I were still one of her students, and I was as obedient as ever. "Tell me about your books," had the same tone as tell me about your summer vacation.

I told her about the work I was doing with the Institute, trying to put children in touch with their heritage that had been lost in the scramble for survival, sold for social pottage, or abandoned to avoid prejudice and other special attention.

Emma patted me on the knee. The lesson was over but I was not dismissed. "I always felt something special for you, Will, above the others. Maybe because we both went to Bull Valley and had Hulda Codd as a teacher. You were a good teacher. I sometimes listened outside your class and thought, 'That's one of my boys.'"

Emma grabbed a handful of skirt, slip, girdle and whatever else she had on and gave it a tug to set it right. "School was the only chance I had to escape being a Slocum, and I did, Will. They took my job but I knew no one but me could make me a Slocum."

"I'm sorry, Emma." When Emma needed her colleagues to speak on her behalf, she was met with silence. We had surrendered our voices to gain certification; it was the condition of employment.

"I was puzzled at first," Emma said. Her smile was tight, the hurt still there. "Then I was angry. At everyone. Then at myself. I had been silent too. I loved teaching and in order to do it, I was willing to be silent."

Emma had allowed herself to be mocked for the amusement of secretaries and new teachers. She had allowed her class time to be invaded by announcements, pep rallies, speeches by Otis Hopkins, who had replaced Eli Spivey as patriot. "Hope is as close as the bank," Otis said. She had allowed the egotistical and the close-minded to dictate the textbooks she used.

"I don't want you to feel bad about me, Will. You only did what I had done earlier. I should have fought them. I should have said, 'This is my classroom and you will not intrude with your ego, your ambition, your theories and jargon. This is my classroom and I will challenge my students and I will dare.'"

Emma patted me on the knee again. I was dismissed. I stood up.

"Will, I haven't asked about your children."

"They're fine, both in college."

"I don't think I ever told you about the time I saw Maggie going to scouts, and she was so distressed I asked her what was wrong. You had taken her to the farm and she had seen a calf being born. 'I went through all that,' she said, 'and now Mrs. Whatley isn't going to believe a word of it.' I told her, 'Don't you worry. Mrs. Whatley is a lot smarter than she imagines.'"

I nodded to Rebel who was waiting to take my place and went in to view Jessie's body. No doubt at one time in man's development families kept the bodies of the dead until they could no longer endure the decay to satisfy themselves that the person was indeed dead. As insurance.

The bodies of national heroes and patrons were laid out so they could be inspected by the curious, most of whom had never been so close to nobility. As education.

The bodies of criminals or rebels were displayed so that

citizens knew the consequences of deviant behavior. As warning.

The present practice of dressing and decorating bodies, placing them on cushiony satin sheets inside polished metal containers, seemed to serve no purpose save advertising.

I didn't want to go into the room with Jessie. I didn't want to see her, but if I hadn't folks would have said that I, who had faced her at Turtle Hole, who had faced her at Roma Dean's funeral, who had faced her at old Red's grave, could not face her. I not only had to go, I had to go alone, and I had to stay awhile. All of it would be duly reported. Maybe I wasn't a good sport but I played by the rules.

Jessie looked like the winner of a Mary Kay facial. She had a small mouth that she made smaller by pursing in anger and deafness so that at times her lips seemed to disappear into the wrinkles and folds of her mouth. She had always been unhappy about her thin drab hair and her high, lined forehead. She had kept a rain barrel for rinsing her hair to make it shine. She had dried her hair in the sunlight to give it body and rolled it into a bun. She protected her hair from the dust and wind with a scarf or bonnet.

Roma Dean had brushed and knotted her mother's hair. She cut Jessie's hair and put rats in it to make it fuller. Jessie wasn't happy with it but she kept her silence.

After Jessie was moved to Augusta Worley's, Augusta washed and brushed her hair and gave her home permanents. "Now don't you look pretty?" Augusta said. Jessie didn't hear and her thin lips disappeared into the folds of her mouth.

In The Wanderer's Rest, the aides washed her hair twice a week and sometimes a visitor brushed it. When she died a cosmetologist came from Center Point to make her face, and a hair dresser came to cut, style, dye, and blow dry her hair. In her coffin Jessie was reposed, her brow smoothed, her lips filled, her full-bodied hair colored and brushed forward over her high forehead. Jessie kept silent but there was the suggestion of a smile for her creator.

I shifted my feet carefully so as not to appear ill at ease to curious eyes. I was standing not two feet from the spot where Sue Whatley Murdock had bumped against a steel cabinet and burst her fat. It wasn't a hard blow but her skin was so tight it split and gobs of yellow fat burst through the skin and had to be cut away before the wound could be stitched. After that Fat Sue sat on a swivel stool in the front of the store until Marshall was born. After that she went to bed every night dressed for her funeral.

The recorder was playing lachrymose music to elicit tears for poor Jessie but silence would have been more appropriate. The Spruill women chose to live in silence. Ruby went deaf because of her husband's constant yelling. Jessie went deaf because her husband would not talk to her. Horace talked but he talked about the weather, the crops, and how many eggs the hens laid this week compared to last week and the same week last year. Jessie was a want-to-know-everything woman and Horace was a wolf-to-the-bosom man.

After the first blush of love had fled, Horace left the table without eating; he left the house for two days without saying where he was going; he lay in bed for two days and she had to ask if he was sick; he didn't come to the house at the end of the day and she had to go to the field and ask if he was angry. Horace rarely answered such personal questions, and when he did it was with a yes or no.

Jessie went deaf. When Horace shook her at night and told her the baby was crying, she could hear neither him nor Roma Dean. When he needed her to back the truck so he could hitch the trailer to it, she could not hear his instructions although he yelled in her ear, and when he got between the truck and trailer she almost ran over him.

When Horace tried to fill out the income tax form, she couldn't hear his questions although he beat her. When he had to amputate his arm, caught in the hay baler, she couldn't hear his cries for help although he bled to death in the front yard.

The Tooleys all blamed Jessie for her husband's death but she couldn't hear them. Neither could she hear the gossip of curious or unsympathetic neighbors. She hired hands to run the farm and scolded them when they were careless or slow, but she could not hear the names they called her. The only person she could hear was Roma Dean, and she could not always hear her.

Over the years the community's attitude towards Jessie softened, and her hearing improved. When I dated Roma Dean I always spoke to Jessie but I never knew whether she heard, and I don't remember her speaking to me.

What I remember is Brassfield's flashlight on murky Turtle Hole. I remember the limpness of Roma Dean's naked body as Wink Bailey lifted her out of the water. Her cropped hair was plastered to her head, and in the glare of the light, her scalp looked bare—that nakedness most obscene of all.

I remember flashbulbs popping like corks, so that Wink's straining body and Roma Dean's lifeless, swinging limbs jerked in and out of vision like crazed dancers under strobe lights.

I remember Jessie, her small mouth made enormous by grief, by rage, by words ripped from deep inside her, drawn crosswise up her throat, and torn from her mouth. "What have you done with my little girl?" But Jessie could not hear me. My mouth opened, my lips moved, but I had no words, and my groans, like Horace's, fell to earth short of her ears.

We had shared a bond, Jessie and I. She could not hear; I could not speak. I prayed that I too might be deaf. I stopped my ears to whispers, but my mind recorded forever those shrieking eyes, that torn mouth. Her words were lodged forever in my heart just as Horace's cries for help must have been lodged in her own.

"I didn't kill your little girl, Jessie. I forgot her. The way you must have forgotten that Horace was working with the baler. She never made a sound. She must have slipped, choked, couldn't get her breath, couldn't call for help. She never cried out, Jessie, I swear. I forgot her for one moment, and I've never been able to forget her since. The way you couldn't hear Horace for a moment and lived with his cries ringing in your ears. You have known silence, Jessie. May you now know peace."

Rebel stood beside me. "Were you praying?"

"Yes." Goodbye, Jessie, I said. Goodbye, Roma Dean.

"She looks good, doesn't she? So peaceful. Do you think death is the only peace there is?"

"It's the only peace that lasts, but how much peace can you stand?"

"I guess it depends on how much you need."

"Like everything else in my life, all I need is just a little more," I said.

We stood shoulder to shoulder staring at Jessie, who as her last act had become a commercial. "Do you think we can go now?" Rebel asked.

"In a minute. What did Emma say to you?"

"She's happy that I'm still teaching. I'm not to surrender my classroom and I'm to dare to live or something like that. Emma's never going to let me graduate. What did she say to you?"

"About the same."

"Will, you're not going to write about Wanderer Springs, are you?"

"I don't think so."

"It wouldn't help anybody. You know all the stories and it didn't help you."

That was a bit of the old Rebel, hitting below the belt, and like most fouls it was effective. I passed history; it was current events I failed.

When we were in the car I told Rebel I wanted to drive by the Dodson house. As I backed from the curb, I caught a glimpse of Herschell Shipman, watching the funeral parlor, hoping that Wanda or Dixie might come home.

I parked under the persimmon trees that Roy Dodson had planted to attract customers away from the Live and Let Live. Delores had been surprised when I took her to see the Dodson house. It was as plain as the country, as sturdy as the people, as immutable as the Dodsons. It was styleless, graceless, discordant. Raw no matter how often it was painted, large but not grand, airy but not open. For all its size and windows and upstairs gallery the house did not appear to rise into the air but to cling to the earth. I couldn't tell whether Delores was surprised that I was willing to move to town or surprised that I would think of buying such a house. "Do you really want to?" she asked, meaning both.

Delores was not captivated by the house, but she accepted it as a challenge. Every morning I dropped her at the house on the way to school and she spent the day studying it and making plans. "I'm going to leave it the ugly way it is," she said. "All I'm going to do is repair it, paint it, and fix it inside so a woman can stand it."

Delores attacked the house the way she attacked everything. Study the problem, make a plan, throw away anything that doesn't fit the plan, execute the plan. Rebecca got her lawyer's mind from Delores. "I haven't changed it; sometimes I think I haven't made a mark on it," Delores said once. We were sitting on the upstairs gallery eating ham and mustard sandwiches while Demp hauled off what we had torn out of the house. "What do you see in the house?"

"You," I said, and Delores made a face because she thought I was avoiding her question. "No, there's something about this place that reminds me of you. It's durable."

"Blue denim, right?" It was not easy for Delores to accept a compliment.

"You are the strongest person I know. You don't bend to be liked, and if they don't accept you, you're willing to spend the rest of your life sitting up here on the gallery not talking to anyone."

"Only if you sit with me," she said, giving me a kiss that tasted like mustard.

I leaned back against the house in contentment, imagining that we would sit forever on the gallery, looking over the town, and watching our children grow into our image.

After the heavy work was done, we spent our weekends at farm auctions buying furnishings. We turned the auctions into shopping, picnicking, field trips. Families were leaving the farm, looking for kinder places to spend their last years, or the children were returning to put mom or dad in Augusta Worley's home and to sell whatever had become extraneous to their lives—the land, the house, champagne glasses that had been a wedding gift and never used, luggage bought for some trip never taken, a radio stored in the attic until electricity came to the farm, a cedar hope chest filled with hand-embroidered dreams by some woman who waited forever for the right man.

We looked through a museum's treasure of useless things—medical implements sold by Dr. Vestal who needed the money to escape the people he had served, a hand gristmill that had belonged to Ida Ballard, family albums, picture postcards, souvenir ashtrays, a poster of the county's first air show decorated with a bullet hole courtesy of Buck Fowler.

While Delores shopped for things we needed, I collected the stories. A hand-cranked Victrola with which Vernell Finch, One-Eyed's unmarried sister, had tried to charm Buck Fowler into a proposal; a dresser trunk that Sister Druscilla Majors had given—along with a matched pair of horses, a buggy, and a toilet and manicure case—to her lawyer; a Seth Thomas adamantine-finished mantle clock on which Grover and Edna Turrill had watched the hours pass while Billo died of burns; a bookcase with etched glass doors that had belonged to Earl Lance, and then Mattie, and finally to Selena. Behind the glass doors was an almanac, a dictionary, a Blue-Back Speller and the family Bible in which someone had dutifully noted the death of Ma Lance and Wilbur, the marriage of Delmer and the birth of his children. But no one—not Earl, Mattie or Selena—had recorded the discovery of two strange children. They had been objects of curiosity in the county; in the family Bible they were without allusion.

Delores had made the house comfortable without making it look decorated, but she never came to love it. When I came home she always seemed to be waiting for me. It wasn't until I read the letters she had written to Mama and Rosa that I realized she was waiting for me to take her to the kind of life she knew—people and talk, school and books. Or even a walk across the farm, a drive through the country. Something besides working in the house or sitting on the gallery looking over the town and waiting for our children to make us proud.

When I brought Delores home from the hospital after Rebecca was born, she said, "I don't like this house, but I like being home."

Delores was gone and nothing could change the fact. Not hard work, or sacrifice, or conscientious prayer. How hard it had been for me to accept. How long I had looked for evidence to the contrary, in her closets, in our children, in my dreams. My grasp of her was no stronger than my comprehension of Mattie Lance's strange children. Yet something of her did remain, some gift that was more than children, more than memory.

Rebel patted my hand. "You loved her, didn't you, Will."

I loved the way she smiled when she saw me. I loved the way she welcomed me home. I loved the way she played with the children, and read to them, and explained away their hurts and fears. I loved the comfort, the tenderness she brought to my life. Did I love her? I never knew her. How could I think I knew the town?

"Yes, I loved her," I said. Delores's love was every day. Like blue denim.

"I love Vivian," Rebel said. "He'll never be a great lover or a big success, but he thinks he's lucky to have me. It's not what I expected love to be, but it never is, is it?"

"No, it never is." What I had expected was that Delores would be all that I would ever want and that she would always be there. "I am in love with a wonderful person," Delores said. "And you don't even know him." While trying to be the Will Callaghan that never was, I lost the Delores Hinojosa who had no illusions about either of us but believed our imperfect love could cover our imperfections.

Once when I visited Delores in the hospital after Maggie was born, Delores had cried because she had put on makeup and the nurse made her take a shower, and now her face was smudged. "I wanted to be pretty for you," she said.

I had laughed. "You don't have to be pretty for me."

"You don't have to be perfect for me," she said, and I never was. I wasn't even Will Callaghan.

Rebel looked at her watch. "Maybe we'd better go," she said. "We don't want to be late."

Rebel wanted to get there early to see who was coming to Jessie's funeral. In Wanderer Springs going to funerals was as much a social duty as going to church, and for some, more frequent.

The men were waiting outside the Murdock Chapel to see who drove up, the women were inside, waiting to see who came in. Marshall and Boots were standing side by side, talking to each other but watching the arrivals. Rebel waved at them and hurried inside. I walked over to see them, trying not to stare at Boots's swollen ear and the mark on his neck. Marshall was delighted to see me, and he squeezed my arm as well as shaking my hand. I winced a little as both my hand and arm were sore but immediately I felt better. Marshall had that effect on me. Vivian had been our star, Rebel our spirit, Roma Dean our sweetheart, but Marshall had been our leader.

Marshall looked the same as ever. He still hadn't learned to comb his hair, and the suit he had worn to the funeral looked foreign to him.

We talked, the three of us, reminding each other where we were geographically and financially. Dr. Heslar arrived, looking the Christian in a gray silk suit, black Italian shoes, his handsome face tanned by hours on the tennis courts and golf links, his trim athletic body pampered with natural foods, vitamin supplements, laboratory tests, immunizations, and other indulgences to secure him eternal life.

Dr. Heslar warmly greeted Boots, a member of the hospital board of directors, cautiously greeted Marshall, a suspected atheist and perhaps socialist as well, and welcomed me to Wanderer Springs as though it were his town. "I'm glad you came," he said, fixing me with his grave gray eyes. "Jessie would be pleased." He nodded gravely, claiming Jessie as his own, then turned to greet Brother Bob.

Reverend Schlutter—Brother Bob he preferred to be called—had been a real estate salesman, a radio evangelist, a marriage counselor, and a funeral director. These gifts had uniquely equipped him to serve souls in Wanderer Springs, Dr. Heslar said. Brother Bob was small, slight, and middle-aged, but with an energy that belied those facts, he smacked his thin lips over his bright teeth and sprang forth each day to serve. "God's errand boy" he called himself, believing it was a token of humility.

Dr. Heslar put an arm over Brother Bob's shoulder to walk him into the church, laying claim to all around him. Maybe it wasn't his church, but since he paid his salary, Brother Bob was his minister.

Boots, Marshall and I nodded our way into the church past curious eyes and sat with Rebel and Bitsey under a stained glass window of Christ the Good Shepherd who left ninety-nine secure sheep to find a lost lamb. The window was dedicated to Otis Hopkins.

I had known when I left San Antonio that this was going to be one of the worst moments, sitting in church, essentially alone with Jessie and my thoughts, listening to a plaintive melody played on the piano. The pianist was Bobbi, Brother Bob's wife, who was taller and broader than he and irrepressibly cheerful. Bobbi played the piano and performed a song at each funeral.

Lucy Huff, who had played the organ at the funeral of almost everyone buried in Wanderer Springs, because even the Baptists preferred organ music for a funeral, was dead. There was no one to play the organ at her funeral, and the minister had said that Lucy was a dutiful daughter, an uncomplaining wife, and a lifelong Methodist. Clifford was furious. "If Lucy heard that, she'll know they been lying to her all these years, and she didn't really know anybody."

Unlike Lucy, most folks didn't pay much attention to eulogies. Like flowers, music, and prayers, they were used to mask that gaping maw in the earth, giving folks time to accommodate to reality. At the funeral of Milton Shipman, who had drowned on a dare by Selena Lance, the cemetery was flooded by the waters that had flooded the creek. Water ran into the grave. On wet ropes they lowered the little coffin into the muddy water. "No, no, no," screamed Genevieve. The coffin bobbed on the water as grim faced men shoveled mud to sink it. "No, no, no," Genevieve screamed. In church the next Sunday she said she knew her boy was in heaven. It was his new suit she had been worried about.

Funerals are cumulative. That's why the older you get, the harder they are. It isn't just the present pain that must be endured, but the residue of old griefs, old goodbyes, old stories. When Fat Sue died, four extra pall bearers were required to carry her coffin. At Mother's funeral I was puzzled by all the attention I received. At Hulda Codd's funeral I was surprised that the church was banked with flowers and crowded with

and they had sent a message of love, for a moment uniting us all again. They were Delores's gift to me, even from the grave.

How often had I been frightened, disappointed, puzzled by them, all to be vanquished by a single act of love. I would not mention the flowers to them, just as Dad would not have mentioned such a thing to me. "I stopped by your mother's grave," I'd say, and they would know.

There was a double headstone marking Delores's grave, with my name on one half waiting the final date to be inscribed. I had reached the age where I was sentimental about gravestones, enjoying the sorrow of my own death.

Sometimes I regretted having Delores buried in Wanderer Springs. Not that I wanted to sit beside her grave every day, but without the girls there was no way to locate her, no central place. It was like trying to worship God in the great outdoors; sooner or later man always designated a spot. Except for the girls, almost nothing of Delores remained. Her pictures brought nostalgia with its mixture of pleasure-pain, but they were not Delores. Unless they provoked dreams they rarely made me feel closer to her; they sharpened the pain.

Mama had forgiven me for burying Delores in that forsaken place and then leaving her, and there was something appealing about having Delores buried with Grandmother on one side, Mother and Dad on the other, with room beside Delores for me. I was wallowing in melancholy but I indulged myself.

Someone came up behind me and I assumed it was Marshall. "I saw you standing here by your wife's grave. I knew you was thinking about her. I bet you miss her, don't you?" It was Vivian, smelling of experienced sweat. He patted at his head to straighten his toupee. It's hard to lie about being bald.

To escape Vivian I walked back to Roma Dean's grave. Vivian followed. We all stood awkwardly around her grave thinking of ways to escape.

"Old Will was over at Delores's grave," Vivian said. He had a rare talent for stating the obvious. "What were you thinking, Will?"

Rebel caught his arm to distract him. "Look, Will, Hooper and Branda sent flowers."

It was an expensive wreath with a plain card bearing Hooper's name. No Regret. No Farewell. No Remembrance. Hooper had escaped Jessie's death just as he had escaped Turtle Hole.

"Sure are a lot of important people here aren't there, Will?" Vivian said, surveying the gravestones. I couldn't think of any but I knew Vivian's heroes—Denver Worley, a Confederate veteran and a mean, selfish man who appropriated his daughter Augusta's life, and Earl Lance who had shot an unarmed man and maybe his paralyzed brother.

Vivian clapped a hand on my shoulder. "You could have been a hero, Will," he said. "If you'd caught that pass and beat Center Point."

I looked at Vivian, not knowing what to say. It was too trivial to comment on, too insignificant to make important by saying nothing. "What would happen if we had beaten Center Point?" I asked.

"They would have had to admit we were better all along."

"We've got to be getting back," Bitsey said. "We've got a bunch of horses that have to be taken care of, and Boots has a guest he has forgotten all about." She was smiling but she was tugging at his sleeve.

"I've got to be getting Rebel home," Vivian said, putting his arm around her. She was Otis Hopkins's daughter and his pride in her was touching. She was his perfect Eskimo pie who showed him what women were supposed to be like. For the first time I saw how Rebel could live with a man who sometimes annoyed, sometimes embarrassed her. It's easy to scoff at others' scars.

There was a lot of handshaking and vowing to get together soon and not waiting until someone was sick or dead. I smiled and waved through the door slamming and car starting, and they were gone, leaving me and Marshall in the cemetery.

Marshall walked over to the Murdock plot to his father's grave. "I'm sorry about your father," I said, following him.

"Did I tell you about the time I went to see him in that commune? They believed that if you can see how beautiful and wonderful God and life are and how inconsequential your problems are, you'll laugh. What difference does it make if your face is scarred if God loves you and your friends don't care what you look like? I don't think I'd ever heard Dad laugh before. It was worth whatever it cost him."

"How come you didn't stay?"

"I almost did. I told them that people come to me—a woman with three children who has been deserted by her husband and I tell her the law says you can have this much money. And she says, I can't live on that. If I don't sell my body, my kids will starve. I tell her, it's against the law to sell your body and it's against the law to give you more money. It's not against the law for your children to starve. Now how could Otis Hopkins say I was a Communist when I uphold the law like that? The commune thought I was the funniest thing they'd ever seen. I started laughing myself."

"Is the commune still going?"

"The last I heard they were running out of money. Every time the leaders said they had bills to pay, everyone laughed."

We both laughed at that. "The moral," I said, "is that it's all right to laugh as long as you haven't given up all your concerns—moderation in all things."

"If moderation is such a virtue why doesn't God practice it?" Marshall asked.

"Damn Baptists never can get it straight," I said. "We don't judge God, God judges us."

"I was going to save the world and then I discovered that all I was saving was the idea that the world was perfectable. I tried something specific, like stopping the war, but what we were stopping were the cameras. When the cameras came home nobody cared that the war went on."

"In war truth is the first casualty."

"In the Garden of Eden truth was the first casualty. I thought I'd try something elemental, like seeing that no one is treated like a disease to be eradicated, that no one has to scratch their name on walls to be more than a number, because if the Statue of Liberty doesn't mean that it doesn't mean anything. So I got a job with a poverty agency. I'm not trying to end poverty. I'm not trying to feed the hungry. I'm just trying to fill out the proper form so that a qualified person gets inadequate assistance."

"You're laughing but you still have some concerns."

Marshall shivered. "Let's get out of the wind, it's getting cold."

"Let's climb Medicine Hill," I said.

"Why?"

"Just for the hell of it. How long has it been since you did something unreasonable?"

"Too long, but I wasn't wearing a suit."

"Life is unreasonable. One plus one is more than one times one. Is that reasonable? K comes before L and M comes before N; is that reasonable? Simple to complex, right? And what is T doing way over there with U and V? Is it reasonable that you and I came back for Jessie Tooley's funeral? Or that Vivian and Rebel and Boots and Bitsey and I sat up half the night last night looking at high school yearbooks? Or that Malcolm Murdock's grandson—"

"Let's go watch the sunset from high atop Medicine Hill," Marshall said.

Marshall got in the car and I drove back through town and then along the road I had driven with Rebel, only this time I didn't have to be on guard against ghosts.

"High school yearbooks, huh?" Marshall said. "Too bad I had to miss it."

"Yeah. There was a picture of me dropping a pass that would have beaten Center Point. Vivian would have been immortalized, and we would have been special."

"Thank God it was you," Marshall said. "I thought it was me."

"How could it be you?"

"Doughbelly said I wasn't playing with enough intensity. I wasn't hitting hard enough. I wasn't hurting anybody."

I drove past the Tooley place, the ghost town of Medicine Hill, and stopped at the side of the road. We climbed over a barbed wire fence and walked across a field that had been plowed by one of Ira Ferguson's crews. Ira's triumph wasn't his prosperity but his anonymity. While the rest of us struggled with our names—in Wanderer Springs you were who your family was—Ira had escaped his family, at least his family identity.

How readily I had accepted the town's values as my own. How difficult I found it to discard them. "Shit. I wasn't even specially bad."

"You were different, Will. That's what I admired about you."

We paused at the edge of the plowed field. Medicine Hill looked more bleak and rugged than I had remembered, but it was no time to be reasonable. "You admired me?"

"Well, not a whole lot," Marshall said, beginning to huff a little from the climb. "You weren't always trying to look better than everybody else."

We paused to take a breath. I was getting stiff and sore from the morning ride, my knees creaked, my knuckles stung, I had tripped over rocks and stumbled into cactus, ruining my shoes and trousers. But I didn't care. "What were you going to say in your valedictory address?"

"I said that they owed it to us to let us make our mistakes, to take our chances, and to give us their confidence and approval. I said we owed it to them to take what they had given us and to do our best with it, that we were bound to Wanderer Springs in that sense."

"You had to say more than that."

"Emma Harkness said it wasn't positive enough."

"You didn't say we were better than other people. We had to be better. How else could we expect to beat Center Point?"

"When did you catch on that they had lied to us?" Marshall asked.

"I'm a late bloomer. I thought I was going to be a hero until I became the villain."

"We were all villains, Will, all disappointments. There are no heroes any more."

"We don't need them. We have successes. Otis Hopkins, Dr. Heslar, Hooper. You don't have to die for success, or suffer. You don't even have to work. You just have to be fortunate. Heroes are messy. They die for lost causes, like Bubba Spivey. Or their lives don't measure up to their deeds, like Denver Worley, or Buster Bryant, or Eli Spivey."

"Wait a minute. Eli Spivey was one of my heroes," Marshall said of a man who had once been a suicide. "He saw that people like Otis Hopkins had the laws written to benefit themselves and then preached that the way to be religious and patriotic was to obey those laws. When Eli resisted that kind of oppression he was treated like an outcast, but he lived his whole life the same way, he didn't look for loopholes, and he paid his debts."

We had reached the top of the hill. I looked over the flatly rolling countryside. In the west the sun was disappearing, turning the sky to red. To the south a dark line marked the winding of the Mobeetie River on its way to Center Point. To the north lights were beginning to appear in a stream of cars and trucks moving along the Interstate, bypassing Wanderer Springs on their way to somewhere. The wind was stronger at the top and now that the sun was going down, cold. I huddled inside my suit coat.

Probably everyone who had ever lived in the county had climbed Medicine Hill at one time or another. Stern old Malcolm Murdock to question his uncompromising God, Grandmother to escape the profane, wicked crowd at the railhead, Buster Bryant to look for some sign of Dr. Vestal, teenagers seeking a glimpse of something beyond the narrow boundaries of their lives. I looked for the green of Dad's Ireland, the beauty Edna Turrill had found beyond her pear tree. "I guess Edna and Grover Turrill were my heroes," I said. Their life was hard, their government was unfeeling at best, but they endured because they believed.

"Did they ever get to California?"

Marshall had never heard the rest of the story so I told him. The day following their futile search for Dr. Vestal, they brought Polly to the cemetery. Buster Bryant rode ahead to notify folks and get the grave dug. Grover and Edna held Polly in their laps and Edna bathed Polly's face with soda and water to keep it from turning dark. Those who saw them pass saddled a horse or hitched a team and followed behind the wagon. Grandmother, Dad, and Uncle Emmett were helping dig the grave when the procession arrived.

Grover and Edna seemed embarrassed by all the attention, but Edna asked for a hymn. "There ain't nothing a song can't make a little better," she said. Uncle Emmett, who was supposed to be a fine Irish tenor, sang "Will There Be Any Stars In My Crown." Reverend Murdock was on his circuit so Grandmother read from the Bible, then they wrapped Polly in a quilt and laid her in the grave. Dad and the other boys picked wildflowers and Edna took the ribbon off her hat, wrapped it around the flowers and dropped them in the grave.

Grandmother passed Uncle Emmett's hat through the crowd and folks gave or pledged what they could, money if they had it. "This is to help you get to California," she said.

"I thank you," Grover said, not taking the profferred hat. "Right now we got a crop in the field. Next year we'll think about California."

"It's going to be nice in California," Edna said. "Peaceful. Lord, we ain't never had no peace."

"For whenever you wish to go to California," Grandmother said.

"There ain't but three things life has taught me," Grover said. "Don't look too far ahead. Don't quit too early. And turn loose when the sun goes down." He helped Edna into the wagon and then climbed up himself. "California is for dreaming," he said. "Texas is for living and dying."

"And they left nothing," Marshall said. "No children, no heirs."

I had collected the stories as curiosities, like the gas pumps from the N-D-Pendent. I had saved them as treasures like Bitsey's Arabian studs. I looked at the superhighway that carried streams of cars from ocean to ocean, safely bypassing time-locked towns like Wanderer Springs, in their race to the future. I was a historian doomed to record a society's love for the false and inane but also its strength to hope and to endure.

The last of the light glowed on the metal roofs at the Prod. The name of the ranch had changed, the look of the land had changed, the house had changed. The stories remained. Myths, like the wheel, are subject to re-invention. "Ain't it purty," I said.

"Let's go," Marshall said. "I'm freezing."

"There's Billo's spurs, and at least one wheel off Grover's Peter Shutter wagon, and the rattles he cut off the snake he stopped to kill, and Polly's cradle—"

"Where?"

"Clifford Huff's collection. Still in the Prod store. And arrowheads, and Eli Spivey's helmet—"

"Let's go to Center Point and get some coffee."

"Let's break into the Prod store."

"Let's get some coffee and talk about it."

"Break into the Prod store and liberate the Turrills from the clutches of Vernon Tabor and his investment group."

"Okay, if we tell Boots," Marshall said.

"Okay, but only if we break in."

We stumbled down the hill. Marshall fell and tore his trousers and scraped his knee. I walked blindly into a prickly pear, and after we had crossed the plowed field and climbed the fence, I had to stand in the headlights of the car and pick cactus from my pants and person.

We drove to the Prod where Bitsey was less than happy to see us. "Boots is with someone," she said cheerfully. "From out of town."

"We're from out of town," I said.

Bitsey looked at Marshall, imploring reasonableness.

"We're going to break into the Prod store," Marshall said.

Bitsey left the room. In a few minutes, Boots came in, looking apprehensive but acting friendly. He shook hands and smiled and asked what he could do for us.

"We're going to break into the Prod store," I said. "We're going to liberate the Turrills and the Spiveys and the Indians from the clutches of collectors and investors."

Boots looked at Marshall and then at me. He started to protest, then thought better of it. "I'll get you the key."

"No," I said. "That would mean you owned those things, and you don't. They belong to all of us. Everyone who lived here and everyone who will ever live here."

Boots looked from me to Marshall and back again. He shrugged. "Okay, break into the damn store, steal whatever you want."

"You have to go with us," I said.

Boots raised his hands and eyes to heaven, calling on God to witness the foolishness he had to endure. He whispered dramatically, "I can't. There's this guy in there who means a lot of money to us. A lot of money." His mouth was big with money.

"We're not talking about money," I said. "We're talking about saving Wanderer Springs from the decorators. We're talking about saving it for the people who find it. Are you a rancher or a huckster?"

Boots glowered at me. "You can't call me that," he said.

I was tired, my muscles sore from our earlier fight, my knuckles raw, and I no longer had the element of surprise. "Wanderer Springs rebel or Center Point slick?" I asked, ready to fight him again.

"Wait for me in my truck," Boots said.

"Bring a bottle," Marshall said. "Maybe two."

We went outside and got into Boots's truck. Boots came out in a few minutes. Bitsey came out on the gallery and glared after him. "I got to be crazy listening to you guys," he said. "Odeen is annoyed. Bitsey is mad. Dad Tabor is going to be pissed."

"When was the last time you did something crazy?" I asked.

"Not long enough," he said, uncapping one of the bottles.

We drove to the store, broke in by taking turns kicking the door, fumbled in the darkness with boxes and buckets of arrowheads, rusty pistols, spurs, button hooks, horns, saddles, sewing machines, Polly's cradle, Grover's wagon wheel, and loaded them in the truck.

"Where to first?"

"Dead Man's Junction," I said.

Boots drove across the pasture, approximating the route we had ridden that morning. "Stop," I said somewhere near Earl's Lake. I lifted the bottle. "Here's to Buster Bryant and whoever finds this saddle," I said, taking a drink and passing the bottle. I dropped the saddle beside the truck.

We left Billo's spurs, Polly's cradle, and Grover's wagon wheel near Mud College, a rusty six-shooter and arrowheads at Dead Man's Junction, a sewing machine close to one of the places Limp and Ida Ballard had farmed, Eli Spivey's helmet and hoe at his ranch. We scattered arrowheads around Medicine Hill and left a washboard at Paymore Hill because we could think of nothing else. And we drank a toast to each one.

It was near dawn when we finished distributing the county's mementoes and we were at St. Joe's crossing, opposite what had once been Sand. "I'm going to go over there and drink a toast to Joe Whatley and leave the bottle in his honor," I said.

"How are you going to get across the river?" Marshall asked.

"Walk."

"That water is cold as hell," Boots said.

"No one in this county ever said a good word for Joe Whatley and I'm going to say one," I said. Joe and I had something in common. I got out of the truck and was instantly sorry. It was cold. I would have backed out had not Boots joined me. We took off our shoes and with Marshall following, waded across the wide, shallow river, walking on dry sand in most places, but plunging knee deep in water near the other bank. We stood huddled together, our teeth chattering.

"Hurry up," Boots said, "I'm freezing."

"I can't think of anything good to say."

"Hurry up," Boots reiterated.

"To Joe Whatley," Marshall said, "who found religion on this spot and tied the first knot in his noose."

"The saloon was the first knot," I said. "Religion was third or fourth."

"Hurry up or I'm leaving," Boots said. "Bitsey is going to be pissed."

I took the bottle from Marshall and held it to the pale sky. "To Joe Whatley who was as much a part of this community as those who considered themselves his better. On behalf of Grandmother and the good souls who hanged you, I pronounce you forgiven. And may whoever finds this bottle be as forgiving of us."

I took a drink and passed the bottle to Boots and Marshall who were less ceremonious. Then we ran back across the river, put on our shoes, and got back in the truck.

It didn't take long to change out of my ruined suit, get my bag, and say goodbye to Boots and Bitsey. Especially to Bitsey, who was asleep and found it hard to smile when we stumbled in. I drove Marshall to his car and agreed to meet him at the Susie Q for breakfast.

I stopped at the farm on my way to Center Point. I drove down the weed-lined lane between the fields farmed by Ira Ferguson's crews and stopped beneath the cottonwoods. I walked through the gate that shut out nothing, up the side-walk that led to nowhere, through the yard where Delores had tried to sweep sand out of the grass, and stood in the ashes of the house that Grandfather had built. I brought no gift. Only myself. Others had their achievements to comfort them, their horoscopes and holy books to guide them. I had my grand-mother, and Dad, and Grover Turrill. I was their child and I took that understanding with me.

SAN ANTONIO

where the river runs like history

IT took longer to say goodbye
to Marshall. It's hard to know what does and what does not go
without saying. I probably wouldn't see Marshall again for
years but the most important part of a person is the part of
them that you have when they're not around. I wanted to tell
Marshall I carried a big part of him with me. Instead we talked
about how we were going to get together more often and not
wait for someone to die and how next time we were going to
The Wanderer's Rest and set the residents free, maybe even
scatter them around the county.

"And we have to break in," Marshall said, "because they
don't belong to Dr. Heslar."

Impatient as I was to be home, I also wanted to see the
girls, not just to see them but to encompass them the way I
once had. Not too long ago Delores and I had been their whole
life, Delores more than I. All the world their eyes and ears
knew, their hands and mouths encompassed. My need for my
children grew in inverse proportion to their need for me.

Once grown, their eyes flitted past me, not really seeing.
Only when their ears registered tension or anger did their eyes
look at me, concerned for a moment with who I was and what
I thought. Otherwise my face was to them the most easily
identified face in the world and the least examined. In trying to
spare them worry and pain, I had made myself something

335

comfortable and neglected, an old shirt that one keeps to wear when a new shirt chafes.

The Chevrolet Manuel had given the girls was parked in front of their apartment. I had forbidden the girls to accept it so Manuel gave them the keys and left it in the street.

I didn't see much of Manuel in San Antonio. He was too busy with his investments in oil, insurance, and recordings to spend much time with Mama. "It's my capital that makes the country work," he told me and Gilbert. "What have you invested in your country?"

The same as Eli Spivey. And Bubba. And Duane. But neither Gilbert nor I had said that at the time.

The girls were happy to see me and wanted to hear about the trip. "Did you see Mrs. Whatley?" Maggie asked.

"Yes. I didn't know you had been writing her."

"There's a lot of things about us you don't know," Maggie said impishly. They laughed, comfortable with themselves, comfortable with me.

"That's what worries me," I said, playing the assigned role. It doesn't hurt to be typical sometimes. They seemed different, animated. Was Maggie letting her hair grow long? "Don't you have a date?" I asked Rebecca.

"I think we're having a fight," she said. "I'm not sure because I don't want to call and find out."

"Don't you have things you need to do?" I asked Maggie.

"I need to get a battery for the car, I lost my biology notes, my face is broken out, my membership expired at the zoo—a whirlwind life."

"We want you to stay," Becky said.

I told them about the funeral, the people I had seen, reminding them who some of those people were. I told them I had gone by their mother's grave. They nodded. A moment of silence, one of those unplanned moments, passed for Delores.

"Thanks for sending the flowers," I said and they both hugged me. Sometimes it doesn't hurt to be obvious.

I told them about breaking into the Prod store.

"Hey neat," Maggie said. She was so excited that I reminded her that Boots was along and that all those things legally belonged to him. I needed not to have bothered. Maggie was a reformer, not a revolutionary.

"I still think it's neat," she said. "I remember when you took us to see those things and told us about them."

"I thought you were bored."

"It was kind of boring," Becky said.

"Yeah, and they were so sad," Maggie said. "Why is history so sad?"

I laughed because she looked and sounded so much like her mother when she said that. "History is the story of man's rise and fall from the ocean to the moon," I said. "It's not a sad story as long as there is another generation to tell it to."

"You know the story I like best?" Rebecca asked. "When you were a kid and you were plowing one night and the plow hit a root or something that made this scream and you thought it was the ghost of that woman who went crazy."

"Mary McCarroll." I was thirteen or fourteen and half-asleep and it sounded like a deranged woman calling, "Beth."

"And you were afraid to go to the house and tell your dad so you started yelling something."

"Beth. Mary's daughter's name was Beth, so I started calling her too. If that was Mary McCarroll out there, I wanted her to know I was helping look for her daughter."

"Didn't you wake up your dad?" Maggie asked.

"Your grandfather," I reminded her. "When Dad was a little boy he sometimes had to follow Mary around at night, and call her daughter. When he heard me calling, it probably gave him a nightmare. He must have thought I was crazy. The next thing I knew he was on the tractor with me, standing on the drawbar. I don't know how he got there so fast. He didn't say anything; just rode with me for a while. I didn't even know when he jumped off but I wasn't scared any more. I knew he was there somewhere."

"I remember Mama telling us about when she was a little girl and she had to walk home from the market and it was after dark and when she walked under the expressway some anglo boys started following her, and she shouted, 'My papa is Jose Hinojosa and he is the strongest man in San Antonio,' and they left her alone," Maggie said.

My children were free to be Callaghan or Hinojosa, free to be neither, free to be whomever they wished, free to be nobody. But they took those stories with them.

"I like the story where you break into the Prod store and scatter all those things over the county," Maggie said.

"That's not really a story."

"It is too. It's one I'm going to tell my children," Maggie said.

One can only admire man's genius for making bricks without straw.

"What's the matter with your arm?" Becky asked.

My arm was blue where Boots had hit me and I was so stiff I could hardly move. "I had to fight for my honor," I said. They shook their heads in genial reproof.

Becky's telephone rang and she went into her room to answer it. Through the closed door I could hear her muffled voice. She and her boyfriend were having a fight, and sometimes I could hear "father" and "can't come over now." To avoid overhearing, I went to the bathroom. When I returned, Maggie was reading a textbook and taking notes.

Becky came out of her room and Maggie put aside her notes. I told them I had decided to drive on home as I had to be up early the next morning. The girls protested, but seemed relieved. We were a family; we didn't have to be under the same roof.

"Dad, stop worrying," Becky said as I started out the door. "We believe in the same things you do. We just do them differently."

"I know," I said, a half-lie. Sometimes I knew and sometimes I didn't.

Roosevelt Hopkins was waiting to see me when I got back to the office and took me to lunch. We sat outside at a table beside the river and threw tostados to the pigeons and fish. "Did you get everything taken care of, Will?"

"Yes," I said. "Everything."

Roo looked at me, wanting more but not knowing how to ask. "Any conclusions?" he asked.

Wanderer Springs was all conclusion, and progress comes not from conclusions but from revelations. "I'm turning loose," I said. "I'm letting go."

Roo smiled. "Writing the book is a way of letting go." The unrewritten life is not worth living.

"I don't have to write it," I said. "I don't have to look back. All I have to do is remember. That country is mean as hell. It tears the heart out of some men. It shrivels the soul of some women. From some it takes everything they have. But sometimes, if the rains come, and the wind is moderate—"

"But ain't it purty," Roo said.

I was startled. Roo laughed. "You told me that story, Will."

"Yeah, but—"

"You think I never said, 'If my granddaddy had gone to Liberia, or if my daddy hadn't thought Chicago was the way out of the cottonfield, or if I hadn't gone to college——.' Then I'd look out the window—hell, Chicago ain't no paradise—and I'd think, but ain't it purty."

"Chicago is for living and dying," I said. "Texas is for dreaming."

"What?"

I vowed to tell him that story sometime, but right then I was eating tacos, drinking Lone Star beer, and watching the river that was as straight and clear as history.

Typesetting by *G&S, Austin*
Printing and binding by *Edwards Brothers, Ann Arbor*
Design and illustration by *Whitehead & Whitehead, Austin*